Suddenly he was standing before me, very close, and I felt myself drawn hypnotically into his arms.

His lips seared mine in a brutal, passionate kiss that was wicked and wonderful all at the same time. I tried to push him away, but his arms tightened around me. Our bodies fused together as one, and I could feel his heart pounding against mine.

I felt myself sinking deeper and deeper into an intoxicating state of complete submission, and with a gigantic effort I brought myself back to sanity. "Please, Sir Gavan," I gasped, pushing against him with all my might.

He released me then, and I sagged back against the wall, overcome by weakness and the strange feeling that my body was no longer my own.

The mask slipped back over his face, and he was again calm and completely in control. "I'm sorry," he said, "I meant no dishonor. You're a very beautiful woman, and I am human in spite of what you may have heard."

I avoided his eyes and tried to summon what little dignity I had left. "I think we should join the others," I said.

GOTHICS A LA MOOR—FROM ZEBRA

ISLAND OF LOST RUBIES
by Patricia Werner
(2603, $3.95)

Heartbroken by her father's death and the loss of her great love, Eileen returns to her island home to claim her inheritance. But eerie things begin happening the minute she steps off the boat, and it isn't long before Eileen realizes that there's no escape from *THE ISLAND OF LOST RUBIES*.

DARK CRIES OF GRAY OAKS
by Lee Karr
(2736, $3.95)

When orphaned Brianna Anderson was offered a job as companion to the mentally ill seventeen-year-old girl, Cassie, she was grateful for the non-troublesome employment. Soon she began to wonder why the girl's family insisted that Cassie be given hydro-electrical therapy and increased doses of laudanum. What was the shocking secret that Cassie held in her dark tormented mind? And was she herself in danger?

CRYSTAL SHADOWS
by Michele Y. Thomas
(2819, $3.95)

When Teresa Hawthorne accepted a post as tutor to the wealthy Curtis family, she didn't believe the scandal surrounding them would be any concern of hers. However, it soon began to seem as if someone was trying to ruin the Curtises and Theresa was becoming the unwitting target of a deadly conspiracy . . .

CASTLE OF CRUSHED SHAMROCKS
by Lee Karr
(2843, $3.95)

Penniless and alone, eighteen-year-old Aileen O'Conner traveled to the coast of Ireland to be recognized as daughter and heir to Lord Edwin Lynhurst. Upon her arrival, she was horrified to find her long lost father had been murdered. And slowly, the extent of the danger dawned upon her: her father's killer was still at large. And her name was next on the list.

BRIDE OF HATFIELD CASTLE
by Beverly G. Warren
(2517, $3.95)

Left a widow on her wedding night and the sole inheritor of Hatfield's fortune, Eden Lane was convinced that someone wanted her out of the castle, preferably dead. Her failing health, the whispering voices of death, and the phantoms who roamed the keep were driving her mad. And although she came to the castle as a bride, she needed to discover who was trying to kill her, or leave as a corpse!

Available wherever paperbacks are sold, or order direct from the Publisher. Send cover price plus 50¢ per copy for mailing and handling to Zebra Books, Dept. 3125, 475 Park Avenue South, New York, N.Y. 10016. Residents of New York, New Jersey and Pennsylvania must include sales tax. DO NOT SEND CASH.

THE STOLEN BRIDE OF GLENGARRA CASTLE

ANNE KNOLL

ZEBRA BOOKS
KENSINGTON PUBLISHING CORP.

ZEBRA BOOKS

are published by

Kensington Publishing Corp.
475 Park Avenue South
New York, NY 10016

First printing: September, 1990

Printed in the United States of America

For Renée, with love

*My thanks to Juggy, for total love and support, and
to my fellow writers, especially Rosemary, for help
and encouragement*

Chapter One

County Down, Ireland

I looked out the carriage window at rolling hills and lush fields, dotted here and there with foxglove and goldenrod. The countryside was beautiful, but unfamiliar to me, for I had not seen this land, or the man who sat across from me for eight long years.

My brother dozed, and I took advantage of the opportunity to study his face. He was four years older than I, which would make him twenty-two, and yet in sleep he appeared boyish despite his elegant gray top hat and fashionable morning suit. Like all the Kincaid men, he was short, a fact I recalled that had given him much concern as a lad.

He was lean, though his body was muscular, but I rather fancied that in years to come he would acquire our father's rotund figure. His complexion was ruddy, his hair, curly and dark, but his eyes, like my own, were blue. It was the only resemblance we shared, for I favored my mother's family with my blond hair and fair skin. My brother, I thought; and yet he is a stranger, as is this land I call home.

The carriage lurched, and he awoke with a start. "What? Oh, sorry, Elly. I'm not usually such a clod." He smiled sheepishly. "Too many tankards last night after you'd gone to bed, I'm afraid."

We had docked in Belfast and spent the night at a roadside inn before continuing on this morning. The inn had served as a reminder to me that I was no longer in England, for none of the amenities that I had grown accustomed to were present. Hugh, however, accepted it with good grace and laughingly confided, "Irish inns are noted only for their ale, Elly."

He interrupted my thoughts then in a hearty voice. "Does anything look familiar to you?"

"Not yet," I answered. "But I can hardly wait to see Glengarra."

"It won't be long now," he promised, and glancing out the window, sighed. "I wanted you to see it in the sun. Ah, well, this is what we Irish call a soft morning."

His words stung me a little, and I said, "I'm Irish too, Hugh."

He gave me a smile of satisfaction. "You bet you are, Elly. And it's glad I am to hear you say it." He took off the elegant top hat and brushed back his hair. "We may be a little coarse and countrified, but you'll get used to us again." I smiled back at him, and an anxious look suddenly crossed his face. "You are here to stay? I mean—you haven't left a suitor behind, have you, Elly?"

"One or two," I said lightly. "But none I want to claim."

He reached forward eagerly and patted my hand. "Good, because I want you to marry an Irishman."

He looked so serious that I couldn't resist teasing him. "You act like you have a gentleman in mind."

To my surprise, he smiled slyly and answered, "Perhaps."

I was a little annoyed by his presumptuousness, but in the same light vein I replied, "Ah-ha! And who might it be?"

He gave me a petulant look. "I'll not be telling you his name. If you're half as stubborn as you used to be, you'd turn him down for spite."

"He may not even make me an offer," I said.

His expression changed, and his eyes appraised me.

"That I doubt, little sister. You're a very beautiful woman, and a lady of gentility, too. I wager you'll not lack for suitors in Ireland."

I didn't like the calculating look he gave me, but suddenly his voice softened. "You favor Mother, Elly. Do you remember her?"

"Not the way you do. You remember Mama when she was well." I thought a moment. "I couldn't have been more than seven or eight when she took sick, and after that I really didn't see much of her, except to say good-night before I went to bed. And yet," I said, "I'll never forget the day she died."

He nodded. "Aye. That was a dark day, especially for me. She was my buffer against Fa." He looked out the window then and said, "I know you don't understand, Elly. He always had a smile for you. Saved his frowns for me, he did." I didn't answer him and he gave me an obstinate look and added, "It's true. We never could see eye to eye, and still don't."

I didn't want to hear this. I hadn't seen either of them for eight years, and I wanted nothing to mar my homecoming. I made no comment, but he wouldn't let the subject drop.

"He's getting old, and I'm willing and able to take over, but he won't hear of it. He's afraid I might change things." A look of determination—or was it triumph?—crossed his face and he said, "But someday I will be master of Glengarra, and then I'll put my own ideas to work about the land and how to get the most out of it."

Despite my resolution to remain neutral, I found myself rallying to Papa's defense. "Glengarra has always prospered, Hugh. Perhaps Papa is wiser than you think."

His eyes turned dark in anger. "Wise? Is it wise to let ignorant tenants hold land that could be put to better use? England wants beef, Elly, and we need land for pasture. Some of these tenants have been on Glengarra for generations, tying up the land and paying a pittance in rent. No wonder they stay, and when they do leave, he replaces them, renting even to Catholics!"

I knew he meant the James family, but I ignored it. So, he still resents Avery, I thought—and after all these years.

I closed my eyes and let my mind drift back to childhood days and to the very first time I set eyes on Avery James.

I sat again in my starched pinafore beside Hugh while the open carriage bounced along a road just like this one. Our mother sat opposite us, and I remember that she was wearing something in lavender, or was it blue?

Suddenly Hugh stood up and pointed. "Look," he shouted. "There's a lad following us. See him, trying to hide behind that bush?"

The child stepped out then, mocking us with a bow. He had the reddest hair I'd ever seen, and though his feet were bare and his clothes were patched, there was an air of freedom about him that I envied.

He sprinted along, trying to keep pace with the carriage like an agile little monkey and Hugh called ahead to our driver. "Go faster, Brendan."

Later we learned that the lad was Avery James, the son of new tenants on Glengarra. His family had recently arrived from a small village to the south. They were Catholics and when Hugh discovered this, he became indignant. "Father shouldn't rent to them," he told me. "They're the spawns of the devil. The vicar said so."

I smiled to myself, remembering how I had called the lad that very thing when I came upon him later in the woods. "Get out of my woods, you spawn of the devil," I had screamed, and then been afraid he might strike me.

He had laughed, though, and answered me back in

a quaint brogue. "Your woods, is it? Why, 'tis God's woods, ye silly lass, and this clearin' yere standin' in is a magic place. Ye'd best go home afore the fairies spirit ye away."

He could have passed for a leprechaun himself, and my confidence slowly evaporated. "How is it they haven't spirited you away?" I asked.

"Because God's on me side, but a cheeky lass like yereself had best take care."

So clearly had I remembered it, I half expected to see a barefoot Avery run across the field and follow our carriage again. What does he look like now, I wondered, and does he still remember me?

Hugh shattered my daydream with a shout. "We're almost there, and look—here comes the sun!"

Like a good omen, it broke through the clouds just as I sighted the house over the crest of the hill.

Glengarra's spires rose against the blue sky, and more than ever it appeared to me like a castle out of a fairy tale. Seeing it now, after all these years, a wonderful feeling of pride and love overwhelmed me and my eyes filled with tears.

I looked at Hugh. His face wore an impatient frown. "There he is," he said. "Waiting with open arms. He'll be having the fatted calf ready."

I followed his gaze and saw a frail-looking white-haired man standing at the entrance to Glengarra. As the carriage drew up closer, he hurried down and I was shocked to see that my father was but a shadow of his former self. His cheeks, always so rosy, were pale, and the ample girth that had disguised his short stature was gone, making him appear small and a little pathetic. I flung open the carriage door and rushed into his arms.

It was an emotional reunion, and I rather think we embarrassed Hugh, for he turned his head and busied himself with instructing the servants about my trunks.

After we had both dried our tears, Papa stood back and looked at me. "Ah, but you are your mother all over again, Elly. You look the way she did when first I saw her, sitting in her father's garden among his prize roses, and she the most beautiful prize of all." He shook his head sadly. "I've missed you both, and it's happy I am to have you home, Elly."

"I'm happy to be home, Papa," I told him. "And I'm going to make it up to you for all those lost years."

"We'll not be calling them lost," he said. "When I look at the fine young woman you've become, it's grateful I am to your Aunt Celia and Uncle Roger for all their love and care."

My heart spilled over with love for Papa, and I put my arms around him and laid my cheek against his. "I'm grateful, too, but I'm home now, where I belong, with you and Hugh."

Looking over Papa's shoulder, I reached out with a glance to draw my sullen brother into the warmth of our little family circle. But he turned abruptly away, like an outsider caught looking in.

There are fences to be mended here, I thought, and with my usual optimism assumed that I should be the one to mend them. How naive I was! And in my innocence I whispered a silent prayer to my mother in heaven. "Help me to bring peace and harmony to Glengarra again."

I often spoke to her this way. It was a little bit of comfort I'd picked up from Avery. "You can pray to her now," he'd told me. "She's a saint in heaven, same as the others." It had proven to be quite a consolation to me that first year in England when I was lonely and far from home.

I awoke to see sunlight filtering through the delicate lace curtains and spilling across my room. I lay in the comfortable feather bed and let my eyes roam from corner to corner. Nothing had changed. The shelf that covered one whole wall still contained my dolls. They stared back at me, and their china-blue eyes seemed to question my right to be there. After all, they had waited eight years for their little mistress to return.

And so has Papa, I mused, and the thought made me feel guilty. I recalled how quickly as a child I had adapted to my new surroundings, and I remembered that sometimes my aunt had to remind me to answer Papa's letters. But I'll make it up to him now, I told myself. I'll make Glengarra a happy home and a gracious one, too, like Aunt Celia's in London.

I got up and looked out the window—to the woods that separated Glengarra from the tenant farms. Avery had discovered a secret glen there, and we had named it The Paradise. I longed to see it again, and Avery, too. His pixie, little-boy face flashed before my eyes, and I tried to picture him grown-up, but couldn't.

A rosy-cheeked maid brought hot water and offered to help me dress. I declined her offer, graciously I hoped, and dismissed her. I didn't want to be fussed over this morning. I was eager to get downstairs and begin my campaign to restore beauty and tranquility to Glengarra.

I would start with the flowers, I decided. At Aunt Celia's, fresh flowers were picked daily and placed in all the rooms. I would follow that same custom at Glengarra, and I would begin this very morning.

I ate a solitary breakfast and then I went to the greenhouse to pick my bouquet. The air was heavy with the fragrance of gardenias, and I closed my eyes and drank in the perfume that always reminded me of my mother.

Later, when I was arranging the cut flowers on a table in the foyer, I heard angry voices coming from Papa's study.

"I'll not be having a Mitchell in me house!"

"You don't even know Gavan Mitchell, Fa."

"That's right, Hugh, but I've heard enough about him."

"Heard what?"

"That he's a Mitchell through and through—wild, a heavy drinker, and a land grabber!"

"So that's it. You don't like it that he's buying up land for pasture."

"That, and other things about the family, Hugh."

"Old wives' tales!"

"No, son. 'Tis common knowledge the Mitchells are violent, maybe even mad. Did you know your friend's grandfather ordered an eviction, and when the family didn't leave quick enough for him, he burned them alive in their cottage?"

"Rumors, but even if it's true, that's all in the past, Fa. I'm not interested in what his grandfather did."

"Then there's the lad's late, unlamented father, another harsh landlord, and a mean-spirited, brutal man he was, too. Married a foreigner and mistreated the poor woman so badly she ran away. Blood tells, Hugh, and there's bad blood there. No respectable house in Ulster has ever received a Mitchell, and I'm not going to be the one to start."

"Ah, why don't you admit it, Fa. It's not his family, it's Gavan himself. He's part of a new age and you don't like that. You want everything to stay the same, but it won't, I tell you. Change is coming and you can't stop it!"

A door slammed and suddenly Hugh appeared. When he saw me, he scowled and spoke sharply. "You shouldn't be listening to private conversations, Elly."

"Then you should be careful to keep your private conversations private," I answered.

He smiled weakly and apologized. "I'm sorry. I'm

14

out of sorts. He's just impossible. There's no reasoning with him."

I had a curious nature, and I couldn't help asking, "Is it true, what Papa said about those Mitchells?"

"I don't know the truth, Elly. The old Mitchells, I'm sure, were eccentric, and the villagers are full of superstitions about the castle, but Gavan can't be held responsible for his ancestors, can he?"

I said I didn't think so, and he suddenly brightened. "Good. I knew you'd feel that way. You always were fair-minded, and adventurous too. I'll bet you can hardly wait to see that dark and evil old castle."

I said, "Hugh, I've no interest in Gavan Mitchell or his castle."

He looked disappointed. "I never thought you'd be afraid of anything, Elly."

His eyes challenged me, and I protested. "I'm not afraid, Hugh."

"Then you won't mind accompanying me to Bonnie Brae sometime, will you?"

"I haven't been invited."

"But you will be," he answered, and left the room with a satisfied smile on his face.

I jammed the remaining flowers into the bowl. I knew I'd been manipulated, and it annoyed me. The mysterious Gavan Mitchell had piqued my interest, though I would never admit it to Hugh.

I spent the rest of the morning unpacking my trunks and arranging my clothes in the large armoire that had belonged to my mother and had been moved into my room before my arrival.

Megan, the little maid who'd been assigned to me, was ecstatic. "Oh, Mistress, never have I seen such handsome gowns. You'll be the envy of every lady in Ulster, you will. Look at this! Fit for a queen it is," she exclaimed, gazing in wonder at a peach satin ball gown with flounces of cream-colored lace. It had come

15

from Paris, a gift from my generous aunt and uncle. And I had worn it only once—to the farewell ball they had given in my honor.

I felt a little homesick for them and for England, but I was determined to reclaim my homeland. I glanced out the window at the vast stretch of land that belonged to Glengarra, and on an impulse I snatched up my blue riding habit and started to unbutton my gown. "Megan," I said. "Find my boots, please. I'm going riding."

She looked confused. "But what about the unpacking, Mum?"

"You do it," I said. "You'll do a better job without me."

I felt exhilarated as I made my way to the stables. There was nothing like a brisk ride to raise my spirits.

The young groom greeted me warmly. "Master Hugh told me to be expecting you, Mistress. I'll have the gray mare saddled up in no time a'tall."

My eye, though, was on a chestnut stallion, and when I voiced my preference, the lad hesitated and said, "Ah, but Master Hugh said I was to give you the mare. Warwick's a little hard for a lady to handle."

A pox on Master Hugh, I thought. "I'll be riding the stallion," I said simply, and the lad hastened to do my bidding.

As he helped me mount, he added in an undertone, "Master Hugh will be right upset with me about this."

I dug in my heels, and left him with the clatter of hooves ringing in his ears. Maybe Hugh can intimidate the stableboy, I thought, but he's not intimidating me!

When I was out of sight, I slowed Warwick to a trot and breathed deeply. An early morning shower had bathed the fields, and the air smelled fresh and sweet. I feasted my eyes on hills of incredible green against an azure sky. Hugh was right about one thing. There is no fairer land than this.

Looking down from the rise, I saw the woods, and it beckoned to me with the same Gypsy call I had heard as a child. Although it had been eight years since I had visited our secret glen, I recalled it vividly, coloring it perhaps with a child's imagination.

A huge rock formation overhung with ferns dominated the clearing, and one could almost picture a Gaelic chieftain addressing his tribe from its lofty height. Clusters of heather shading to deep purple covered the ground, and an unusual grasslike weed grew in abundance around the perimeter.

As I moved deeper into the wood, the air grew dank, and I shivered. The forest had taken on an eerie quality, and I almost regretted coming. Several times I heard rustling sounds, and I nervously imagined someone, or something, walking through the underbrush behind me.

I came to a small stream and guided the stallion across it. The foliage was thicker on this side, and I dismounted and led the horse. After several yards I found myself in a clearing, and there stood the pedestal rock! It was just as I had remembered. I tied Warwick to a tree and it was then that I noticed the carving on the trunk. "Elly and A.J.," I read haltingly, for it was barely decipherable.

A twig snapped behind me, and instantly alert, I spun around and faced a man. Big, he was and powerfully built, and I knew a cold fear, for my instincts told me he had followed me. He wore rough clothes, and his cap was pulled down to shield his face.

Hiding my panic, I spoke calmly and with authority. "This is private land."

"I beg to differ with you, Mistress," he answered. " 'Tis God's land." Then he bowed low and swept off his cap.

My sharp retort was cut off in my throat as my eyes fixed themselves on his hair. It was red, darker than I

17

had remembered, but red just the same. He was taller than I would have imagined, and strapping big with broad shoulders and large hands. His eyes were a mixture of blue and green, and as they looked into mine, I knew those eyes could belong to no one but Avery James.

"Avery," I cried, overwhelmed with excitement. In my enthusiasm, I grabbed hold of his hands, and probably would have embraced him, but his face turned scarlet and he took a step back. It was an awkward moment, and I longed for the easy camaraderie we had known as children. "It's good to see you, Mistress Elly," he said.

This I could not bear, and I begged, "Just Elly, please, Avery. We were the best of friends once. Have you forgotten those days?"

He said, "No, but times change."

"Not here," I insisted. "This is a magic place. Don't you remember? You told me that yourself." I knew I was babbling, but his indifference was frustrating me. Looking quickly around the clearing, I pointed. "Look, there's the sleeping grass. Remember, Avery? You told me it was an enchanted weed, and if we touched it, it would put us to sleep for a hundred years. Remember how we sat in it and held hands? I think we were both scared to death. I know I was."

He laughed then. "Faith, but you had me fooled! As I recall, you said you didn't believe it and you dared me to sit in it with you. Now, I couldn't be letting you get away with that, but I was shaking in me britches, and that's a fact. I was raised on Irish folklore."

"I know," I said. "And you opened up a whole new world to me. I was fascinated by those stories you used to tell."

The years seemed to be melting away, at least for me, and I yearned to reestablish our old closeness. I nodded toward the pedestal rock. "Let's sit and talk, the way we used to."

We sat down, and I asked him when he had carved our initials on the tree.

"Before I went to Dublin. I've been away too, almost as long as you have. My uncle took me on as an apprentice printer when I was fourteen. I work for the *Herald* in Belfast now."

I was glad he wasn't a farmer. "That's wonderful, Avery," I said. "You mean you actually operate one of those printing presses!"

His smile faded. "Among other things. It's not beyond the grasp of a peasant to learn, Elly."

"I didn't mean it that way," I said. "It's just that all machinery looks complicated to me. You're too touchy. You always were."

My scolding must have jogged his memory, for he laughed. "Elly, you sound just like a cheeky little lass I used to know."

I laughed too. "I remember when you called me that. It was after I'd called you a spawn of the devil." I wished at that moment that we could be children again, carefree and relaxed with each other. "Those were happy days, Avery," I said. "I missed you when I moved to England."

"Were you unhappy there?"

"At first I was. I missed Glengarra and all the people I loved." You, most of all, I thought, looking at the man he'd become and wondering if underneath the little boy I'd adored was still there.

"I missed you too, Elly. The Paradise didn't seem the same without you, so I stopped coming here. Then I moved to Dublin, and my uncle kept me so busy, I didn't have time to be lonely."

"I know. I was busy too. French lessons, riding lessons, music lessons!" I took a deep breath. "I hardly had time to think."

19

He smiled then, the way an adult smiles at a child, and I wished I could take my words back. How silly I must seem to him!

He stood up and glanced quickly at the sun. "It's getting late and I promised Mam I'd be home for supper."

I didn't want to let him go, and impulsively I reached out and touched his arm. "I'll see you again, won't I?"

He looked at me strangely. "The gentry and their tenants don't mix." I must have had a blank expression on my face, for he added impatiently, "We're not the same class, and we're not children anymore, Elly."

I tossed my head angrily. "No, and more's the pity. When we were children, my friendship meant something to you."

My outburst took us both by surprise, and for an endless moment we stared each other down. Then, regretfully, I looked away. I shouldn't have presumed so much. Now I've spoiled it, I thought.

At last he spoke and his words made my heart sing. "I bring me mam money the first Sunday of the month. I'll be here around noontime, if you care to come."

We parted then, each turning in the opposite direction to go home. On the way I thought about Avery and the changes eight years had made in him. The elfin features and gangly body had been transformed as if by magic to the face and form of a prince! Ah, he was handsome, to be sure, but best of all, he was Avery, my old friend and confidant. And the bond is still there, I mused. I could feel it and I knew he could, too.

These thoughts were foremost in my mind that evening as I entered the delicate rococo dining room which my mother had redesigned after a visit to Felbrigg Hall in Norfolk. The pale lilac walls plastered with garlands of oak and ivy leaves in stark white had been a fitting setting for her fragile beauty, and I half expected to see her sitting in her customary place across from my father.

Hugh rose and greeted me heartily. "Elly darling, we thought you'd deserted us tonight." He looked with approval at my gown of deep purple brocade, its skirt standing out fashionably over stiff crinolines. "As always, you look magnificent," he added.

I took his arm, and looking up into his flushed face, I winked and said in an undertone, "The wine kept you company, I see." Then I kissed Papa's thin cheek. "I'm sorry to have kept you waiting. I was out riding."

I took my place, and Hugh said, "Why didn't you ride the mare? Warwick can be wild."

"I like my horses wild."

He smiled. "I saw you from the window. You're quite a horsewoman, Elly."

"Thank you for saying so."

He said no more, and I allowed myself a satisfied smile. Hugh could be domineering, and I was determined not to let him get the upper hand with me.

Secure in my innocence, like a bird who doesn't realize it's been caged, I turned my attention to my father. "Glengarra is just as beautiful as I remembered," I said.

He beamed with pleasure. "Aye, that it is, Elly. But I hope you won't get bored stuck out here in the country after living in London."

Hugh scoffed. "How could anyone prefer London to Glengarra? Cities are all the same. London's no better than Belfast, dirty and overcrowded, not as many Catholics though."

After just seeing Avery, Hugh's bigotry riled me. I waited until the soup had been served and then I said very casually, "What's so terrible about them anyway?"

Hugh put down his soup spoon and stared at me incredulously. "I forget you haven't been living in Ireland." His eyes turned to steel then and he said, "The Catholics, my dear sister, are like locusts in a field. In short, they're a blight!"

"Not all of them," I said, turning to my father for support. "Take the James family, right here on Glengarra. Would you say they were a blight, Papa?" His face was flushed and his eyes were unnaturally bright. "Papa," I said, "are you all right?" He started to cough then and Hugh jumped up, ready to pound him on the back, but Papa waved him away, and clutching a napkin to his mouth, he left the table.

I started to follow, but Hugh said, "Let him be, Elly. It's only a coughing spell."

The maid came with the second course, and when she had left the room, Hugh said, "You mentioned the James family. Have you seen any of them since you got back?"

I said, "I ran into Avery James today when I was out riding, and I'd hardly call him a blight. In fact, he's doing very well, working in Belfast for a newspaper, *The Herald*, I believe."

"*The Herald!*" Hugh shouted, slamming his fist on the table. "*The Herald* is a damn radical paper, and all who have a part in it should be hanged!" Then he pointed his finger at me and said, "Let me tell you something, Elly. You're in Ireland now and you'd best be learning our ways. You're a Kincaid, and you'll not be socializing with the likes of Avery James."

I started to speak, but he cut me off. "Hear me out, Elly. Fa's not up to giving orders, but I am, and if I catch Avery James on this side of Glengarra again, I'll run him off—or maybe I'll run him through."

I had the good sense to know when to back down, and I did. "It was only a chance meeting," I said casually.

I was shocked at the intensity of Hugh's hatred. But Avery knew this already, I thought, recalling his words—"the gentry and their tenants don't mix." I had no intention of following Hugh's orders; in fact, his opposition only increased my determination, but I would be careful, for Avery's sake, not to ruffle Hugh's feathers.

Hugh left for Belfast the day after our heated exchange. "To visit friends," the servant informed me, and I was grateful to those unknown benefactors for taking him out of our midst for a while. I was also informed by the same servant that the master wished to see me in his private quarters as soon as possible.

I found my father, swathed in blankets and sitting before a blazing fire on this, a balmy morning in May. He made an effort to smile when he saw me, and my heart turned over, for he looked so pitifully frail and shrunken in the big wing chair. "Papa, shall I send for the doctor?" I asked, for his appearance alarmed me, and with Hugh away I felt myself solely responsible for Papa's welfare.

He spoke in a hoarse whisper and I had to lean down to understand his words. "I'm fine, Elly. Don't worry. It's just one of my poor days. Old people have them, you know."

I didn't know how old my father was, nearing sixty, I calculated, remembering that he had been almost twenty years older than my mother. "You're sure," I said.

"I'm sure," he answered in a stronger voice. " 'Tis you I want to talk about, Elly."

I moved a small, straight-backed chair closer to him and sat down, feeling the heat of the fireplace penetrate my thin morning gown.

He reached for a silver jewelry box on the table beside him. "These were your mother's jewels. They all belong to you now," he said, and opening the box, he withdrew a magnificent sapphire and diamond necklace. He held it up for my inspection and it sparkled with a dazzling brilliance in the firelight. "She loved this," he said almost to himself. "I gave it to her when Hugh was born." His voice grew suddenly hard. "He might think that entitles him to have it, but I gave it to her, and now I give them all to you."

I was becoming more alarmed by the minute. There was a frenzy about him that I didn't like. "Papa," I said. "We don't need to worry with this now. I think you should get into bed and I'll send a servant to fetch the doctor."

"No, Elly. Let me be. I need to do this now, while Hugh's away."

I thought it best to humor him, so I took the box that he held out to me. As I looked inside, my eyes were dazzled by the array of brooches, bracelets, and necklaces that sparkled against the dark velvet lining. Overwhelmed, I could only say, "They're beautiful. They're so beautiful, I shall be afraid to wear them."

"No, you must wear them, but they are an investment, too, Elly. Should you ever have to leave Glengarra and return to England, you will not go as a poor relation. Your dowry and your mother's jewels will go with you. It is in my will."

His words would haunt me in days to come, but at the time I thought him irrational because of the fever, and I said in a calm, soothing voice, "I'll remember, Papa, but please, let me call a servant to help you to bed."

I ate a solitary supper in my room, and spent a restless night worrying about my father, but the next day he was much improved. We breakfasted together and spent a wonderful morning strolling through Glengarra's gardens. He seemed relaxed and happy, and I couldn't help feeling that it was because Hugh was gone.

Seeming to read my mind at this point, he said, "Hugh's usually gone for several days when he visits his friends. It will give us an opportunity to spend time together, my dear. There is so much I want to tell you about Glengarra and the Kincaid family."

He went on to describe how the land had been deeded to Eugene Kincaid by James I, and that the first house had been destroyed by fire in the early part of the past century. It was his own grandfather, Brendan Kincaid, who had the house rebuilt and formal gardens laid out in the manner of grand English estates. "The conservatory and the greenhouses are my contributions to Glengarra," he said. "But it was your mother who was responsible for the furnishings. Ah, but she had exquisite taste, and an eye for color," he added.

"I know, Papa. I saw no house in England finer than this."

"Aye, but there's more to Glengarra than just beauty, Elly. This has been a peaceful land. There's been no evictions, no exploiting of tenants here. 'Tis been said that Glengarra has always had proud masters, and masters to be proud of. I pray to God that never changes."

"It won't, Papa," I said hastily. Not wanting him to lapse into his depressive state again, I reminded him that he had promised me a tour of the greenhouse. "I want to see those orchids you were telling me about," I said gaily.

He brightened. "And I have gardenias in bloom, too. Those were your mother's favorites. She used to wear them in her hair. You must pick some, Elly, and wear them for me tonight with the sapphires."

To do the jewelry justice, I chose a blue watered-silk gown that bared my shoulders. I have been blessed with heavy, thick hair, and I brushed it back, letting the sides fall in deep waves. The back I wound into an intricate French knot, and I fastened the gardenia in it. I stepped into the gown that Megan held out to me,

25

and she quickly snagged each tiny pearl button with the buttonhook and deftly fitted it into its proper buttonhole.

I said, "Megan, you wield that buttonhook like the queen's lancers."

Bubbling over with mirth, she said, "Aye, but you should have seen me trying to do that with some of me plumper ladies, Mistress. One took a deep breath after I'd done and buttons popped everywhere."

"I'll remember not to take a deep breath," I said.

"Oh, Mistress, with a waist like yours, you have naught to worry about."

I put on the necklace and earbobs and Megan stood back and took me in from head to toe. Clasping her hands together, she smiled and nodded her head in approval. "Never have I seen a more beautiful lady, Mistress. You should be off to a grand ball tonight, dressed as ye are. And dancing with a handsome gentleman," she added, blushing.

For some strange reason, her words made me think of Gavan Mitchell, and I said, "Megan, have you ever heard of Castle Bonnie Brae?"

Her smile immediately faded. "Everybody's heard of Bonnie Brae. 'Tis an evil place, and haunted too. Some say a banshee wails in the tower, crying for some children the master burnt up a long time ago."

I must have looked skeptical, for she added hastily, "And that's not all, Mum. There's a ghost, too—a lady it is. She appears whenever there's a thunderstorm, they say. Nobody knows who she is, but her face appears first at this window, then at that, like she's running through the castle, trying to escape."

Megan's eyes looked ready to pop out of her head, and I was sure she was frightening herself to death, just talking about it.

"There are no ghosts," I said. "And it's only the

wind that wails." I picked up my fan and gave her a smile of encouragement.

"Aye, Mum," Megan answered without conviction as I left the room.

I walked slowly down Glengarra's winding staircase and thought about Bonnie Brae. Mysteries have always intrigued me, and I wondered if I'd ever get an opportunity to see this infamous castle and its equally infamous master. Not likely, I decided, remembering my gentle father's rather violent reaction when Hugh had brought up the name of Mitchell.

Chapter Two

I joined my father, who was waiting for me, and I was happy to see that his good spirits had not deserted him. He was especially pleased to see me wearing the sapphires.

Our conversation at the dinner table was gay and stimulating, and I thought what a charming man my father was, and how attractive he must have been at thirty-five, when he had brought my mother as a child bride to Glengarra.

After dinner we retired to the music room, and Papa persuaded me to play the piano for him. I remembered that he liked to sing, and I played some of his old favorites. He soon joined in, singing along in a rich baritone voice that brought back sweet memories of gatherings in this room when I was a child—my mother playing, my father singing, and Hugh and I, an appreciative audience who clapped and begged for more.

Several songs later Papa leaned over, kissed me on the cheek, and whispered, "It's off to bed I am, me darling, but I want you to know, it's been a perfect day, and it's glad I am we had it."

The sound of clapping hands made us both look up to see Hugh standing in the doorway. "Bravo," he cried, walking toward us. "I do admire musical talent, probably because I have none myself. I never did learn to harmonize, did I, Fa?"

"That you didn't," Papa said caustically.

I wanted so much to prolong the nostalgia the evening had generated and I wanted to draw Hugh into it, too, but his presence acted like a draft on the fire and I hesitated, not knowing what to say.

He leaned his elbows on the piano and his eyes rested on my throat. A strange look crossed his face, and I wished at that moment that Papa had never given me the sapphires.

Papa stood up, and walked toward the door. "Good night," he said curtly.

Hugh turned his eyes away from me and addressed him. "One moment, sir. I have something to ask Elly and I want your approval." Papa stood in the doorway and Hugh continued. "There's to be a ball in Antrim, and I would like Elly to accompany me." He hurried on. "You remember Lord and Lady Fitzgerald, don't you, Fa?"

Papa said, "I haven't lost me memory yet, Hugh."

"Well, they'd like Elly and me to stay a few days with them after the ball. Lady Fitzgerald is looking forward to meeting Elly, wants to take her shopping in Belfast, I believe."

Papa said, "It's up to Elly, Hugh. I'm sure she'd enjoy it, and now I'll say good night."

Aye, she would indeed enjoy it, I thought, and I suddenly realized how very much I'd missed the social whirl of London. I turned to Hugh, eager to hear more about the ball, but his eyes were on our father's retreating back, and a smile of satisfaction crossed his face.

"You look very pleased with yourself," I said.

"I am," he answered, and glancing briefly at my handsome jewelry, added, "No doubt, you are also pleased."

I felt a flash of anger at his words. As the male heir, he would inherit all of Glengarra. These jewels were trinkets in comparison. Did he begrudge me Papa's gift? Nay, not the gift, I thought. In all honesty, Hugh begrudges me only Papa's love. My anger melted, and

I smiled at him. "Tell me all about the ball and the Fitzgeralds. And when is it? I can hardly wait."

His mood suddenly swung, and he looked at me with no trace of envy. "So, you really do want to go."

"Of course. I haven't danced for months, and I love to dance. I was beginning to wonder if Irishmen knew how."

"Better than the bloody British," he said, catching me around the waist and whirling me around the floor, his feet moving in fast and intricate steps which I barely managed to follow.

Breathless, I collapsed on the love seat. "I'll be taking your word for it," I said.

He sank down beside me. "Ah, Elly. 'Tis glad I am to have you home. And that's the only thing Fa and me agree on."

I said, "Hugh, you and Papa should—"

But he wouldn't let me finish. "Forget it, Elly. That's between Fa and me; besides, I want to ask you something." He looked at me intently and said, "Would you change your mind about the ball if I were to tell you it won't be held at the Fitzgeralds?"

I fanned myself languidly. "I don't care where it's held." Then something clicked in my head, and I sat up straight and looked him in the eye. "Where is it to be held?"

"At Bonnie Brae."

"But you told Papa . . ."

"No, I didn't. I said the Fitzgeralds asked us to stay *after* the ball. I never said who was giving it."

A delicious shiver ran up my spine. Gavan Mitchell! The man my father called scoundrel and my brother called friend. I didn't want to deceive Papa, but I did want to go.

Hugh was looking at me. "Well, what's it to be, Elly? Will you go, or stay?"

* * *

Round the bend in the road, Bonnie Brae rose out of the mist. It loomed before us, a dark and forbidding medieval structure without beauty. The rains of centuries had darkened its stone facade to a mottled gray, and its thin, sharp spires pierced the sky like pikes in an enemy's flesh.

I looked at Hugh. "They say it's haunted."

"The villagers are very superstitious," he answered matter-of-factly. "And while we're on the subject of Bonnie Brae, please don't expect too much, Elly. I imagine it's a little on the primitive side compared to what you've been used to."

"Have you never been here?" I asked.

He shook his head. "Gavan's father was a recluse, his grandfather, too, for that matter. There probably hasn't been a guest at Bonnie Brae for twenty-five years."

I was shocked. "What a strange house to grow up in!"

Hugh shrugged. "Gavan was away at school most of the time. Anyway, that's all in the past. I give him five years, and the Mitchell name will be famous, not infamous, throughout Ulster." He smiled smugly. "I wager people who turned down invitations for tonight will pant for them then. As to the castle, he plans extensive renovations after this ball is over, and if I know Gavan, he'll spare no expense turning it into a showplace."

I wondered why Sir Gavan didn't wait until then to entertain, but by this time the carriage was pulling into the long driveway, and a scrawny lad with raised umbrella came forward to open the door and escort us inside.

We entered a cavernous great hall, twice the size of Glengarra's. Its stone walls were hung with ancient weapons and tapestries. Several of the tapestries appeared to be very old, and might have been magnificent once, but the dust of centuries had darkened them.

We were approached by a servant, a disreputable-looking old woman whose speech was poor and whose appearance shocked me. Her thin gray hair looked as if she had not bothered to comb it, and her ankle-length black dress was stained. "Sir Gavan bids me welcome ye to Bonnie Brae," she said slowly in a monotone, as if she had memorized the sentence. She was horribly bent over, and turning her head sideways, she managed to look up at Hugh. "I'll be showin' the mistress to her room, but Sir Gavan says ye should join him in the library with the other gentlemen. The lad'll show ye the way."

The poor lad stood uncertainly in the doorway, soaked to the skin. He seemed reluctant to come any farther inside the castle.

"Show the gentleman to the library," she repeated, and skirting around her, the lad led Hugh from my sight.

Left alone with the servant, I felt uneasy. The woman was looking at me with insolent eyes, as if she were aware of my apprehension, and delighted in it.

"Are you the housekeeper?" I asked for want of anything else to say.

She smiled slightly. "Ye might call me thot."

I was not used to parrying with servants, and the woman's impertinence was getting on my nerves.

"Well then, if you don't know whether or not you are the housekeeper, I must assume you are not," I said.

Her dark eyes flashed fire. "I be here for fifty years, and for the last twenty-five I be the only servant at Bonnie Brae." She turned her back on me then and started slowly climbing the stairs. I followed her, and she muttered angrily to herself, "The floor's not cleaned right. The food's not prepared right. What does he expect? 'Tis lucky he is I got any servants a'tall to come here and wait on his fancy friends. Them's whot has sense won't work in the divil's own house."

I followed her down a long corridor, and she suddenly stopped at a door and flung it open. "This be yere room," she said. "Me name's Starice, just in case ye've been wondering, Mistress." She turned then and shuffled back down the corridor.

I closed the door and looked around. The room was large but sparsely furnished. Its patterned walls had faded to a nondescript color, as had the bed hangings. Heavy velvet draperies in a somber dark green hung at the mullioned windows, shutting out the little daylight that was left, and I lit a lamp and wondered again about this strange household. How could they manage with only one servant? I gathered from Starice's mumblings that extra help had been recruited for this ball, but that Sir Gavan was not pleased with their performances. Oh, well, I thought, Hugh warned me not to expect too much.

With this in mind, I unpacked my own bags when the lad delivered them and I abandoned any hope for assistance in dressing for the evening's festivities.

Taking off my bonnet, I stretched out on the bed and drifted off to sleep.

I was jarred awake by insistent knocks and a raspy voice shouting something unintelligible. Still drowsy, I jumped up and stumbled to the door.

I opened it to find Starice standing before me, a flickering candle in her hand. It cast shadows on her face, making her appear even more ghoulish than before, and I gasped and took a step back.

"Frightened ye, didn't I, me lady," she said. " 'Tis only old Starice come to stoke the fire."

She entered and I turned up the wick in the lamp,

flooding the room with light. "You startled me," I said calmly. "I was resting."

She busied herself with the poker, and without turning around said, "Sir Gavan and the gentleman rode into the village on business. They said they'd be back before the other guests arrive." She turned to leave and then, as an afterthought, added, "Sir Gavan said I should ask if yere ladyship would be wantin a light supper in yere room. He says the buffet will be served late tonight."

I hated the thought of her returning, but I was hungry, so I told her that a light supper would be most welcome.

Presently, a buxom young maid arrived with a meager meal consisting of barley soup and a small loaf of bread. She curtsied and said, "Me name's Bridget. Just ring when you're done, Mistress, and I'll come back and take the dishes away. Then I'll bring hot water and some towels, so's you can wash up before gettin' dressed for the ball."

Bridget was a refreshing change from Starice, being young and comely with apple cheeks and a warm, pleasant manner. Her presence miraculously restored my good spirits, and I mentally scolded myself for allowing my imagination to undermine my common sense.

I finished the supper and Bridget answered my ring, bringing a generous supply of towels and steaming hot water. She left with a smile and a curtsy and I proceeded to wash and get myself dressed.

I wore the peach satin gown that Aunt Celia had brought me from Paris, and that Megan had rhapsodized over the day she helped me unpack my trunk.

I had loved it in London, but now I wondered if it was too daring for a country ball in Ulster. The neckline was banded in a flounce of exquisite cream-colored lace, cut low, baring the shoulders and a good bit of bosom as well. With it I wore my mother's beautiful pearl necklace and dangling earbobs. I tried to subdue my hair which had curled tightly from the rain, and finally, in desperation, I arranged it high on my head and let the escaping curls cascade down my back.

Hugh came to my room to escort me downstairs. He was outrageously generous with his compliments, and I suspected a few tankards of ale accounted for the sparkle that danced in his eyes and the flowery words that flowed from his lips.

"I see your business was conducted in the taverns," I said knowingly.

He looked like a naughty little boy who had just been scolded. "Now, Elly, don't be cross, come along, Gavan can hardly wait to meet you."

"Can he now?" I said. "Then he might have greeted me when we arrived like a proper host."

"Now, don't be holding that against him, Elly. We Ulstermen don't know much about etiquette, but we appreciate our ladies just as much as your London dandies."

"We'll see," I said, picking up my fan and taking his arm.

As we turned the corner of the long corridor, the strains of a waltz floated up and beckoned me down. It had been a long time since I had attended a ball, and I paused at the stairway and leaned over the banister. The great hall was now filled with guests milling about in groups, talking and laughing.

Hugh squeezed my arm. "There's Gavan now, looking up at us from the foot of the stairs. Didn't I tell you he was handsome, Elly?"

A tall, bearded man stared boldly up at me, and I averted my eyes as I descended the staircase on my brother's arm.

"Smile, Elly. I think he's taken with you already," Hugh whispered, and I got the feeling I was on display, like a prize colt. I snapped my fan shut, and wished in that instant that we were children again and I could swat my brother soundly with it.

When we reached the last step, Hugh grinned foolishly and said, "Here she is at last, Gavan." Then he turned to me. "Elly, I'd like you to meet our host, Sir Gavan Mitchell."

I stared into eyes as black as night and felt myself drawn against my will into those deep, dark pools. When he kissed my hand, the touch of his beard on my skin sent a shiver up my arm. I willed myself not to blush as he raised his head and captured my eyes with his own again. "I've waited a long time to meet you, Mistress Elly," he said.

I thought it a strange thing to say, since I'd only just returned to Ireland.

"We'll have to be on our toes, Gav," Hugh said, winking his eye and nodding in my direction. "Our Elly thinks the Irish are barbarians."

"Oh, but we are," Gavan answered, smiling slowly at me and letting his eyes travel from my face to my overexposed breasts. I felt my cheeks burn with a blush I could no longer control, and I was grateful to the two young men who suddenly appeared and joined us.

Gavan and Hugh both looked at the newcomers with obvious annoyance, and Hugh reluctantly introduced them to me as Alex and Clyde Fitzgerald.

They had gone to Trinity with Hugh, they informed me, and, laughing, Clyde proceeded to tell how Hugh had almost gotten the three of them expelled. The long-drawn-out account finally ended, and without taking a breath Clyde Fitzgerald asked me to dance.

"I'd love to," I said gaily, and it amused me to see the agitated look on my brother's face.

We entered the crowded ballroom, and I discovered the Irish were spirited dancers. Clyde Fitzgerald spun me around the floor, keeping perfect time with the lively music, and my good humor miraculously returned. I looked up at him and smiled with pleasure. He was tall and lanky, and a rather homely young man; but he was a surprisingly good dancer and I was beginning to enjoy myself.

When the music stopped, Alex approached and tried to claim me for the next dance, but I laughingly begged off. "Let me catch my breath," I said, feigning exhaustion. "Your brother just danced my feet off."

Alex smiled back at me. "Knowing my brother, he probably stomped all over your feet, so I'll get you a glass of punch, and we can sit down and talk."

Not to be outdone, Clyde offered to bring me something to eat, and they both hurried off to the buffet table.

I felt a hand on my bare arm, and turning around, I suddenly faced Gavan. "You look warm," he said, and I was conscious that my face was flushed and my chest was heaving.

"That was a lively dance," I answered.

"Aye. I was watching you."

He was still holding my arm, and I took a step back, but his hand only tightened. "Come, we'll get you some air," he said, leading me out to a small balcony.

He closed the door, but the faint strains of a violin drifted outside. The music and the star-studded sky lent a heady magic to the summer night, and I felt myself wrapped again in a hypnotic spell.

"Are you cold now?" he asked.

I was almost afraid he might take me in his arms, and more frightening still, I felt powerless to resist him.

He moved back though, and leaned against the wall. Folding his arms, he appeared to study me. "Hugh was right about one thing." He paused. "About the others—I'm not yet sure."

"If it concerns me," I said haughtily, "perhaps I can enlighten you."

37

He smiled then. "Aye, it concerns you. Shall I tell you what he said?"

"Please do."

"He said you were headstrong and beautiful, and that you weren't afraid of anything." His dark eyes met mine in the moonlight, and I stared back, refusing to flinch from his scrutiny. "You are very beautiful," he said. "And probably headstrong, but are you also unafraid?"

When I gave him no answer, he shrugged. "Fear, like truth, can't be hidden for long." Suddenly switching to a lighter tone, he asked me if I liked to ride, and when I replied that I did, he said, "Good. We'll ride tomorrow. I have a fine mare for you."

I was slightly annoyed by his efforts to intimidate me, and I said, "Not too tame a mare, I hope."

He smiled. "There's naught that's tame at Bonnie Brae."

His penetrating eyes made me a little uncomfortable, and I changed the subject. "Will many of your guests be staying overnight?"

He shook his head. "Only the Fitzgeralds, yourself, and Hugh. The rest live close by." A contemptuous look crossed his face and he added, "And they wouldn't stay here anyhow. Haven't you heard? The House of Mitchell is cursed. We are a family of devils. Or didn't you know?" He bent his head down to my eye level and pointed. "See the horns?"

I laughed at his little joke, and he held out his hand. "Will you dance with the devil, Mistress Elly?"

We joined the others on the dance floor, and I gave myself up to the sheer physical pleasure of moving my body as one with his.

I was sorry when the dance ended, for Sir Gavan was an excellent dancer and, I must confess, being in his arms was not at all unpleasant.

The Fitzgerald brothers sought us out though and

insisted we both join them at the buffet. After supper Alex claimed his dance with me, and from then on I was whirled around the floor by a series of energetic partners, and I lost sight of Gavan.

Hugh rescued me from an elderly gentleman who was just about to ask me to dance. "This one's been promised to me," he said, sweeping me away before the old man knew what was happening.

"Hugh, you're terrible," I said.

"Aye, and aren't you glad of it. Or would you be wanting to be led around the floor like this?"

He stiffened up and shuffled his feet in an outrageous imitation, and I laughingly tapped him on the shoulder with my fan. "Stop it, please. You're making a spectacle of us!"

He smiled at me. "Are you enjoying yourself, Elly?"

"Very much so."

"And what do you think of Sir Gavan Mitchell?"

"I'm not sure. He's a trifle arrogant, I think."

He looked at me and then broke into laughter. "He said pretty much the same about you."

"Did he now?"

"Ah, don't be getting your feathers ruffled, Elly. He meant it as a compliment. Gavan admires a woman with spirit."

"You seem to know a lot about him. Have you been friends for a long time?"

"About four years." He laughed. "We met in a tavern . . . in the midst of a brawl, as a matter of fact."

"Very commendable for you both," I said primly.

"Ah, we were just having a little fun and things got rough. I was only eighteen, up from Trinity with my chums, and we tangled with some locals. Gav jumped in and helped us out and we've been friends ever since."

"Isn't he older than you?" I asked.

"Aye. He's twenty-six."

A sophisticated age, compared to my eighteen years, I thought. Perhaps that is the reason he's able to confuse me.

I spent the rest of the evening with the Fitzgeralds, and I made it a point to let Gavan see how much I was enjoying their company.

Guests began to leave in the wee hours of the morning, and when the last had departed, Gavan summoned Starice. The old woman looked sullen, and from the wrinkles in her gown, it was evident that she had been sleeping in it. He spoke to her briefly in an undertone, and when she left the room, she stared angrily at me.

The incident left me more puzzled than annoyed, but I understood when I retired to my room and found a servant waiting. It was the apple-cheeked maid who had brought me the supper tray. "I been told to help you get ready for bed, Mistress," she said.

So Gavan had made it a point to have Starice see to my needs, and she resents it, I thought. How glad I'll be to get away from this inefficient, insane house!

Bridget was standing awkwardly behind me, and it was evident that the child had never acted as a lady's maid before. I met her eyes in the mirror and smiled. "You may unhook the clasp of my necklace, Bridget," I said. "And then I'll stand and let you unbutton the back of my gown."

Bridget fumbled with the delicate clasp but finally managed to unhook it. "How long have you been at Bonnie Brae?" I inquired.

"Oh, I'm not really here, Mistress." She blushed in confusion. "I mean, I'm not here regular, Mistress. Sir Gavan, he hired lots of us from the village to help with this ball. Payin' us good, he is, too, but I'll be leavin' and walkin' home just as soon as I get your ladyship in bed, I will."

"It's too late to be walking home now. Can't you stay the night?"

"Oh, I'm not scared of walkin' home, Mistress, but I sure wouldn't stay the night here, not me, Bridget O'Shea."

"Why not?" I probed.

"Ah, Mistress, I shouldn't be sayin' so much. You're not from these parts, and if the old one hears me . . ."

"You mean Starice?"

"Aye, Mum."

She ran to the door and opened it a crack. Satisfied that Starice was not lurking in the hall, she came back and whispered, "This house is evil, Mistress. Old Sir Gavan was Lucifer hisself, me mam says." Her eyes grew wide with terror then, and she clutched my arm. "When it storms, a ghost appears and floats through the castle."

I stepped out of my gown and smiled at her. "Now, Bridget, that's just a superstition."

Pursing her lips, she said no more, and I slid into the waiting bed, a delicious drowsiness settling over me. I watched with heavy eyes as Bridget busied herself, picking up my gown and hanging it in the armoire.

I never even heard her leave, and the next time I opened my eyes it was morning and Hugh was pounding on my door.

"Have you forgotten we're going riding," he shouted. "Hurry up, Elly. We're waiting breakfast for you."

I dressed quickly and found Hugh, Gavan, and the Fitzgerald brothers all gathered in the dining room.

Clyde seemed surprised that I would be joining them on their ride, and looking at the other three men, he said, "I'll stay back with Mistress Elly if the rest of you want to do some hard riding."

Hugh laughed and winked at me. "You don't know my sister, Clyde. She can match any man in the saddle."

Once we were mounted though, it was obvious that Gavan intended keeping me to himself, and the Fitzgeralds reluctantly rode ahead with Hugh.

"Bonnie Brae is the largest estate in Antrim," he boasted. "And I'm negotiating for the purchase of more land to the north."

It's a wonder you wouldn't spend some money on the castle, I thought.

"The castle, I know, is in a deplorable condition," he said, and I got the uncanny feeling he could read my mind. "Bonnie Brae hasn't had a mistress for twenty-five years, and it shows. I'm planning a complete renovation, inside and outside, and I want it to be right, but when it comes to furnishings, well, I don't know anything about that."

Disarmed by his honesty, I found myself saying, "My mother had quite a talent for decorating. I'm sure you'll be visiting Hugh. Perhaps you can get some ideas from Glengarra."

"Am I to be limited to visiting Hugh?"

He held my eyes captive again with his, and I felt myself blush in confusion. "I meant that you should visit us both, Sir Gavan," I said.

That afternoon a violent storm blew in from the coast, washing out the road and forcing us to stay another night at Bonnie Brae.

Dressing for dinner, I sat before the mirror, arranging my hair. Thunder rolled, ending in a loud clap, and I cringed as lightning streaked across the sky and illuminated the room. It blinked off and on, casting shadows on the walls, and I shuddered as a cold draft fanned the wick. Returning to my reflection, I gasped in horror as another face appeared behind mine in the mirror!

Terrified, I whirled around, to confront—nothing! I

could not bring myself to look in the mirror again, so I remained, my back to it, and watched in frozen fascination as lightning played all about me. Flashing brilliantly, it darted here and there around the room. Then, like a laughing demon, it snuffed out the lamp and scurried back outside, leaving me in total darkness.

Fear, cold and raw, stripped me of all pretension as I groped with mounting panic for the lamp. In my haste I stumbled and fell, and it was then that I heard the wail of the banshee. Sobbing, I huddled on the floor as terrified as ever Bridget or Megan could be.

"Elly, are you all right?"

It was Hugh's voice, and gratefully I answered him. "Aye, the lamp went out. Wait, I'll find my way to the door."

On the way downstairs I approached him casually. "Did you hear a wailing sound coming from the tower?"

He laughed and pinched my cheek. "Superstitions getting to you, Elly?"

"Certainly not," I replied. "It's the wind, of course, and caused by some architectural flaw in the castle. I was merely trying to pinpoint the source."

Hugh's condescending attitude annoyed me, for I hadn't yet gotten my nerves under control. The memory of that face in the mirror would haunt me, I knew, despite the fact that I could very easily rationalize it away.

The woman I had seen was young and beautiful, though frightening with her white face and long, flowing black hair. She had been dressed in white, too, something loose and airy, for it had billowed out behind her.

"Anything wrong?"

"No, of course not."

Hugh was looking at me strangely, and my common

sense suddenly returned, providing me with a logical explanation for my behavior.

Fired by Megan's ghost story, and with a little help from the elements, my imagination had simply taken over. Ghosts and banshees yet! For the love of heaven, Elly, grow up, I chided myself.

We proceeded the rest of the way in silence to the dining hall, where dinner was to be served.

Entering the room, I felt myself drawn back in time to medieval days. A pair of sixteenth-century grotesques stood on either side of the carved stone fireplace and a great wrought-iron chandelier bathed the room in an eerie amber glow. It cast shadows on the huge tapestry with its bestiary of monkeys, boars, and strange giant birds of prey.

Sir Gavan Mitchell stood at the head of the table, and in the flickering candlelight his blazing dark eyes and black beard made him seem the reincarnation of one of his own ancestors. We took our places and he seated himself. Like a feudal lord, he raised his goblet to an unseen servant, who immediately materialized and filled all our glasses with wine.

The meal was tasteless and the servant, like all I had seen at Bonnie Brae, was poorly trained. The child reminded me of a frightened doe, and the object of her fear was obvious, as her eyes kept darting back to her master.

When she left the room, Gavan turned to the rest of us and said, "I apologize for the clumsy wench. Tell me, how do you get good servants?"

I responded a little sharply. "Good servants must be trained, and with patience."

"Something I've very little of," he retorted.

Hugh laughed then and winked at the Fitzgerald brothers. "Our Gavan needs a wife."

I felt myself blushing. "A housekeeper trains servants," I said.

Hugh drained his glass and turned jovially to the Fitzgeralds. "Feel lucky tonight? Three-handed cribbage—I'll take you both on."

Gavan looked at me and smiled. "In that case, Mistress Elly, would you allow me to show you around the castle? Perhaps you can give me some suggestions to improve it."

I forced a smile. "Of course."

We left my brother and his friends to their cards and began our tour.

"I'll give you a little history of the place," Gavan said as we walked down another long, narrow corridor. "The castle was built sometime in the sixteenth century by a Scot. It remained in his family until one of my illustrious ancestors acquired it." He smiled wickedly and added, "Through devious means, I'm sure. At any rate, this is the original part." By now we were in the great hall, and he eyed it critically. Then he turned back to me. "Ugly, isn't it?"

I certainly concurred, but thought it more courteous to remain silent.

"The story goes that my mother hated it, which is understandable, so my father had the west wing built on especially for her. After her desertion he had it sealed off." He laughed then. "A rather drastic way to forget a woman, wouldn't you say? But then, my father was eccentric, to say the least."

He led me from the great hall through a small door that led to yet another narrow corridor.

"This part connects directly to the west wing. Would you like to see it?"

I said I thought it was sealed.

"Not anymore. I had it opened up several weeks ago. I think it's far grander than this, but I'd like your opinion."

I said I'd be happy to give it.

He looked pleased. "You have to understand it's

45

been sealed up for over twenty-five years, so you will have to picture the way it would look cleaned and renovated."

"Of course."

He stopped and opened a door. "It's dark down there. I'll just get us a lamp."

I could see by the dim light in the corridor that the room he entered contained a massive desk and several dark, leather-covered chairs. When he lit a lamp, two large portraits over the mantel caught my eye, and following my gaze, Gavan said, "My illustrious ancestors, the first and second Sir Gavan Mitchell."

I turned my attention to the painting on the left, which I presumed to be of the grandfather, and saw an incredibly ugly man whose face was partially concealed by mutton-chop whiskers. The artist had made no attempt to soften the cruel mouth or add any merriment to the small, beady eyes.

The second Sir Gavan Mitchell was equally unattractive, and in the lamplight his mouth appeared to twitch in a cynical smile as I studied him. The illusion caught me off guard, and I involuntarily stepped back.

"Do they frighten you?"

"Not at all," I said. "I'm just surprised. You look nothing like them."

He glanced up at the portraits and smiled. "I was told I resemble my mother. That's probably the reason my father hated me so much."

He picked up the lamp and we left the room. His willingness to disclose family secrets appalled me, and I didn't know how to deal with it. I suppose my rather formal upbringing had left me unprepared for such candor, and I couldn't help wondering if Hugh was equally brash about his unhappy relationship with Papa.

By now we had reached the end of the corridor, and in front of us stood a massive oak door studded with iron. Gavan set the lamp down on the floor and lifted the heavy wooden bar. He forced it open, and the door groaned, as if to protest our entry.

He held the lamp high, and before my eyes appeared another great hall, this one with a magnificent winding staircase. The floor was marble, and though caked with grime, I could see that it was beautiful. "How lovely," I said.

He seemed desperate for my approval. "You like it, don't you?"

I nodded, and he hurried on.

"I thought you would. My mother was French, and I think it has a French flavor. Some of the chandeliers in the other rooms may have been copied from Versailles," he said proudly, and then shrugged. "I wish I could show you the rest, but, as you can see, it's not a fit place to be taking a lady now."

The curving staircase reminded me of Glengarra's, and struck by the similarity, I said, "I like the staircase. It's a handsome one."

"It is that. Next year I'll give a ball in this wing, and I want to see you descend that handsome staircase."

It was damp in this unused part of the house, and I rubbed my arms. "Let me close the door," he said. "It's cold in there." He set the lantern down on the floor, and at that instant a bat swooped down from the ceiling. I have always been terrified at the thought of a bat getting in my hair, and in my panic I grabbed Gavan around the neck and buried my head in his chest.

"It's only a bat. It won't come near the light. Here, let me close the door."

I backed up against the wall and put my hands over my head, and I did not look up until I heard the massive door clank shut. When I opened my eyes, he was standing before me, very close, and I felt myself drawn hypnotically into his arms.

47

His lips seared mine in a brutal, passionate kiss that was wicked and wonderful all at the same time. I tried to push him away, but his arms tightened around me. Our bodies fused together as one, and I could feel his heart pounding against mine. His lips brushed my neck with soft, gentle kisses that made me tingle with anticipation and a vague hungry yearning.

I felt myself sinking deeper and deeper into an intoxicating state of complete submission, and with a gigantic effort I brought myself back to sanity. "Please, Sir Gavan," I gasped, pushing against him with all my might.

He released me then, and I sagged back against the wall, overcome by weakness and the strange feeling that my body was no longer my own.

The mask slipped back over his face, and he was again calm and completely in control. "I'm sorry," he said. "I meant no dishonor. You're a very beautiful woman, and I am human in spite of what you may have heard."

I avoided his eyes and tried to summon what little dignity I had left. "I think we should join the others," I said.

That night I lay awake, remembering his kisses and the feelings they had aroused in me. How could I have given in to him for even a moment? It's Avery's kisses I want—Avery, who would never insult me with such lust! His dear, familiar face smiled at me from a corner of my mind. I wanted to fall asleep thinking about him, but a dark shadow kept pushing Avery's image aside and it was Gavan's face I saw as I finally drifted off to a deep but troubled sleep.

We left early the next morning, and I managed to avoid Gavan's eyes as we said our farewells.

Chapter Three

Strangford Manor was a welcome change from Bonnie Brae, but this did not surprise me, for I have always found that houses take on the characters of their owners.

One would expect the notorious Mitchell clan to live in a gloomy castle, and by the same token this sprawling country house of weathered gray stone was a perfect match for the lively Fitzgeralds. A profusion of bright red azaleas added a striking contrast to the evergreens that lined the parterres on either side of the entrance, and the whole effect was one of charming informality.

Clyde and Alex had arrived ahead of us and I could see them standing outside as our carriage rounded the bend and pulled up in front of the house. They escorted us inside and introduced us to their mother, who was waiting in the hall to welcome us.

Lady Fitzgerald was a large woman, and she pressed me to her ample bosom with enthusiasm. "What a pleasure to have you, my dear. I have so looked forward to your visit."

I felt immediately comfortable with her, and with the house that had a casual warmth which I found particularly soothing after Bonnie Brae.

The hall where we stood was paneled in rich dark wood, and the staircase, with its massive mahogany balusters, was carpeted in ruby red. At the landing hung a large, vibrantly colored painting of a hunting scene.

Lady Fitzgerald herself showed me to my room.

"You must tell me all about London and the social season," she said as I followed her upstairs. "We haven't been to England in years. Lord Fitzgerald just can't seem to get away. He's frightfully busy here, you see, what with running the estate and breeding his horses, and then neither of us are much for traveling."

We had reached the landing now, and she looked up at the large painting. "We love country life, and anything to do with horses, but we like parties and balls as well," she said. Then she lowered her voice. "Tell me, what did you think of Bonnie Brae?"

She had caught me off guard, and I hesitated. "It's very old and very large."

"And also very frightening, or so I've heard," she said. "The Mitchell family has been notorious in Ulster, my dear, but Clyde says young Sir Gavan is determined to change all that." She paused then and shook her head. "People and horses are no different though, when it comes to breeding. It takes generations and careful attention to bloodlines to improve a strain."

We had reached the top of the stairs, and she paused before the first door. "Here we are, my dear. I'm putting you in my favorite guest room, and I think it'll suit you very well."

"How lovely," I exclaimed when the door was opened, for the delicately furnished and distinctly feminine room was not in keeping with the rest of the house.

She smiled. "When you have a comfort-loving husband and seven strapping sons, you consign your delicate pieces to the guest rooms."

"Seven sons!"

"Aye. Narry a daughter among them." She shook her head. "Not a one has given me a daughter-in-law yet either, the rascals. I've warned them, I'm not keeping house for a bunch of bachelors. I want some grandchildren to bounce on my knee."

She left me to freshen up before tea, and I studied the room. My eyes traveled up the pale blue walls to the magnificent baroque ceiling embellished in intricate designs of gold and white. Two beautiful French chairs upholstered in painted silk stood alongside the carved fireplace. The bed was set in an alcove in the manner of royal French bedchambers, and the hangings matched the brocade of the window drapes. It was a lovely room, and again, I compared it to that dark and dismal Bonnie Brae.

A young maid arrived with water, and I washed my face and hands and hurried downstairs to tea. Only Lady Fitzgerald, Hugh, Alex, and Clyde were present. "Lord Fitzgerald and my other sons are off, attending to estate business," Lady Fitzgerald informed us. "But you'll meet them all tonight at dinner.

The hum of deep male voices met my ears as Hugh and I entered the large, comfortable dining room. Sporting cups adorned the mantelpiece, and large, colorful paintings of horses and pastoral scenes covered the sunny, pale yellow walls. A lively discussion was in progress, and all of the male Fitzgeralds seemed bent on voicing their opinions.

Alex, on seeing us, smiled warmly and hurried over. "Good evening, Mistress Elly," he said. "It's an honor and a pleasure to have you here." He glanced briefly at Hugh and added, "Good to see you too, Kincaid."

Hugh gave him an amused grin. "Thank you, old chum. I thought for a moment there I was invisible."

"Might as well be," Clyde said, suddenly joining us. "Who wants to look at you when your sister's around?"

I was enjoying their banter, and it was fun being the object of their flattery, but Lady Fitzgerald was heading our way, and Alex and Clyde suddenly remembered their manners. "Let us present you to our father and brothers," Alex said.

Lady Fitzgerald's husband and sons all resembled each other, being large, rather homely men with long, narrow faces and ash-blond hair. In Lord Fitzgerald's case though, there was more ash than blond in the thinning locks which he carefully combed to take advantage of every pale strand.

The five older Fitzgerald brothers were introduced to me as Stewart, Thomas, George, Andrew and Richard, and I of course, immediately forgot which was which.

We took our places at table then, I to Lord Fitzgerald's right and Hugh to his left. Lord Fitzgerald was a gracious host, and he put me at ease. He inquired about my father's health and mentioned that he had known my mother's family years ago in England. "How are Celia and Roger Haviland?" he asked.

"They're fine. Right now they're in India," I replied. "My aunt wrote me several months ago that they were going to a village on the outskirts of Bombay to see about disposing of some property there."

He nodded his head. "I seem to remember Roger had a connection in India, an uncle, I believe."

I said, "Aye, his uncle Winslow Haviland, and he recently passed away."

Lady Fitzgerald joined the conversation. "Isn't there some trouble going on in India now? It seems to me I read something in the paper about an uprising of some kind."

I must have paled, for Lord Fitzgerald gave me a reassuring look and said to his wife, "It's just a squabble among the natives, my dear. Celia and Roger are British subjects. They have nothing to fear."

George, or was it Richard, smiled and said, "We have our share of squabbles right here in Ulster."

"Aye," Hugh replied, "Dublin's a hotbed, and if

we're not careful, the bloody upstarts will be taking over Belfast."

One of the older brothers joined in. "You're right about that, Hugh. I hear there's a secret society being formed in Dublin. They're calling themselves the Fenians, and they mean to start a revolution."

Lord Fitzgerald scoffed. "Nonsense. There's been secret societies before."

Clyde said, "Aye, but this time they're being backed with American money, sir."

Alex shouted, "Hang them, I say."

"And I say we change the subject." Lady Fitzgerald's soft voice instantly commanded attention, and she fixed her sons with a no-nonsense stare. "Elly doesn't want to listen to politics, and neither do I."

Lord Fitzgerald hastily agreed. "You're perfectly right, my dear." And turning to me, he said, "Our apologies, Mistress Elly." Then his eyes swept the table, taking in his stalwart sons and resting finally on his wife. "I don't know how Lady Fitzgerald puts up with us," he said.

She favored him with an indulgent smile and turned to the young servant standing at her side. "You may remove the first course now, Nellie, and tell Cook the soup was delicious."

The rest of the meal was equally delicious and beautifully served, and again I could not help comparing this relaxed, well-run home with Bonnie Brae.

After dinner I spent another hour or so in pleasant conversation with the family before retiring to my room. Hugh was returning to Glengarra in the morning, and Lady Fitzgerald and I were planning an early start for our trip to Belfast.

Belfast and Avery, I thought, and smiling to myself, I snuggled down under the covers and gave my ever-fertile imagination free rein to weave exciting and romantic versions of our "chance" meeting on the morrow.

Lady Fitzgerald was a delightful companion, and she made the long carriage ride so pleasant that I was surprised when she said, "There now, we're coming into Belfast. Don't be disappointed, Elly. It's a far cry from London, but there's a wonderful French dressmaker on Castle Street, and a rather good milliner. Aye, like I say, it's not London, but we'll enjoy ourselves nevertheless. Oh, and there's the delightful Ladies' Tea Room. We shall certainly go there. I think you'll agree their pastries are as good as any you'll find in London."

I said, "I'm sure I shall enjoy everything, Lady Fitzgerald. I'm ever so grateful that you invited me to come."

She patted my hand. "You're a dear child, Elly. What I wouldn't give to have a daughter-in-law like you."

I thought it best to say nothing. I liked Alex and Clyde, and their brothers as well, but none of them appealed to me as husbands. Besides, my heart belonged to Avery.

Lady Fitzgerald instructed her coachman to take us to Castle Street. "Fittings are so tedious," she said to me. "We'll finish with the dressmaker first. Then we'll have the rest of the day for shopping."

"Are most of the shops on Castle Street?" I asked, peering out the window as we drove.

"Aye. Everything is. Castle Street is the heart of the business district."

"Hugh tells me there's a radical newspaper called *The Herald*. Would that be on Castle Street too?" I asked innocently.

"Aye, it's only a few doors from the milliner's shop.

54

The poor woman lives in dread it'll be set afire some-day and her shop will go up with it."

I could hardly believe my luck. Surely such a coin-cidence was heaven sent. I smiled to myself, and then quickly arranged my face in a more suitable expres-sion. "How terrible!" I said.

"Aye, terrible for the milliner, but Lord Fitzgerald says t'would be a blessing if *The Herald* was put out of commission."

By this time we had arrived at the dressmaker's, and Lady Fitzgerald, leaning heavily on the undersized coachman, managed to hoist herself out of the carriage to the amusement of two rowdy-looking young men standing on the corner.

Fortunately Lady Fitzgerald was unaware that she was the object of their hilarity. She took my arm and shook her head. "Catholics, no doubt. Standing on the street, laughing like fools, and not a shilling in their pockets."

We entered Madame Duprès's establishment and Madame herself came forward to greet us. "Ah, Lady Fitzgerald. I am so happy to see you. You have brought a beautiful young friend with you today, *n'est-ce pas?*"

"This is Mistress Elly Kincaid from County Down," Lady Fitzgerald said.

Madame nodded her head and smiled knowingly. "The young lady is the fiancée of one of your sons, no?"

"No," Lady Fitzgerald said, and then looked at me and smiled. "I mean, I'm sorry to say she's not, Ma-dame. Mistress Kincaid has just recently arrived from London, and I'm showing her what we have to offer in Belfast."

Madame shrugged and immediately got down to busi-ness. "Come, I have some ex-quee-site new fabrics. I will show you."

We followed her up a narrow stairway to her cutting

room. Bolts of fabrics in an array of colors were piled on tables and stacked against the wall. "These just arrived from Paris a week ago," she said.

I couldn't resist a beautiful piece of cut velvet in a rich dark green. "Mag-nee-fi-cent with your blond hair," Madame said. I wanted it made into a traveling suit with a coachman-style jacket, and she nodded her head in approval. "Very chic. Now, let me just take your measurements."

I helped Lady Fitzgerald select several pieces for a contemplated trip to Wales, and then I began to get edgy, wondering how I could possibly get away to find Avery.

Lady Fitzgerald was leafing through Madame's books, a petulant frown wrinkling her brow. "Dear me, I can't find anything I like. I hate to keep you waiting, Elly."

"Just take your time, Lady Fitzgerald," I said. "Why don't I run down to the milliner's while you're deciding on a pattern? I would like to have a new summer bonnet."

"Well, if you don't mind, Elly."

"Mind? Oh, I don't mind at all," I replied, marveling at how easily I had accomplished my goal. "I'll meet you back here in an hour."

I skipped gaily down the steps and out the door, feeling like a bird let out of a cage.

Walking down Castle Street, I thought about Avery. Wouldn't he be surprised to see me! I paused outside the millinery shop and looked in the window at an assortment of bonnets, none very fashionable in my opinion. Nevertheless, I strode purposefully inside and announced to the clerk, "I'd like something in green, please."

I purchased the first bonnet she showed me without even trying it on and left the shop, leaving the startled woman to stare after me in amazement. Then smiling with anticipation, I opened the door to *The Herald* newspaper office.

All the window shades were drawn, and not a soul was in sight. I called out timidly, "Is anybody here?"

I heard a grunt, and from behind a gigantic piece of machinery, which I assumed to be a printing press, a man appeared. He was middle-aged, and heavyset, and he looked at me with a puzzled expression. "You have something to report, Miss?"

Before I could answer, the front door opened again and Avery came in. "They're breaking windows in the spirit grocer's shop," he announced. Then his eyes rested on me, and a shocked expression crossed his face. "My God, Elly. What are you doing here?"

"I came to town to shop," I said, looking from one to the other in confusion, for both men were staring at me with astonished looks.

Ignoring my presence, the other man directed his attention to Avery. "Are they heading this way?" he asked.

"Not yet. Right now they're busy stringing orange arches across Sandy Row."

This was not the reception I had expected, and I looked at Avery with impatience. "Will you please tell me what is going on?"

"The Catholics from the Pound and the Protestants from Sandy Row are having a little disagreement," he said with sarcasm.

We heard shouts in the street then, and rushing to the window, the three of us peered outside. A noisy gang of men and boys were marching up the middle of the street, brandishing clubs and sticks. I recognized the two loiterers who had stood outside Madame's shop among the group. They carried a crudely constructed banner that read LONG LIVE THE POPE. Avery looked at the other man. "There's going to be trouble, Tom," he said.

"Aye," the other answered.

Avery's expression was grave, and he nodded in my direction. "Keep her here till I get back." Then he turned to me. "You'll be safe with Tom, Elly. I won't be long."

I was terrified, both for Avery and myself. "Don't go out there," I begged, grabbing hold of his arm.

"I have to go, Elly," he said calmly. "We run a newspaper here." Then slipping easily from my grasp, he opened the door and stepped outside.

The big man looked at me with kindly eyes. "Me name's Tom O'Leary," he said. "Now, don't be worrying about Avery, Miss. The lad can take care of himself."

His reassuring manner made me feel better, and I smiled back and offered him my hand. "I am Elly Kincaid from Glengarra," I said.

He looked surprised. "Any relation to Hugh Kincaid?"

"I'm his sister," I told him.

His expression changed again, and a guarded look entered his eyes. "Make yourself comfortable. I'll be in me office." He indicated a chair close by the door but cautioned me to stay away from the windows.

Too impatient to sit down, I wandered over to the printing press. I found it amazing that this iron machine could actually print a newspaper, and looking at its complicated design, I felt a surge of pride that Avery knew how to operate it.

I picked up an earlier edition of *The Herald* that was lying alongside the press and sat down to read it.

I was shocked to find that *The Herald* openly preached revolution, and I could now understand why the landholders objected to it. One article extolled the pike as the queen of weapons, and went on to advocate using it against the cavalry. THE WAR BETWEEN THE PEO-

PLE AND THEIR ENGLISH RULERS HAS JUST BEGUN was the heading for another inflammatory piece.

I threw the paper down in disgust. Why can't we all just live in harmony, I thought. I began to pace the floor, straining my ears for any sound from outside, but an eerie silence prevailed. I wondered if Lady Fitzgerald was still poring over fashion books, blithely unaware of what was taking place, and decided that in all probability she was.

My optimism returned, and I assured myself that the authorities most likely had things under control. The scurvy bunch who'd passed down the street could hardly be taken seriously. But this is a newspaper office, I reminded myself, so any trouble, no matter how trivial, would have to be investigated.

Disregarding Tom O'Leary's advice, I went to the window and looked outside just in time to see Avery walking briskly toward me. Relieved, I hurried to the door to meet him.

My set smile froze when I saw his face. "Is everything under control now?" I asked.

"I'm afraid not. They've called in forces from Ballymena."

My heart sank. "Oh, Avery. What does it mean?"

"It means there's a riot going on, Elly." Then he gave me an encouraging smile. "Don't worry. I'm going to take you upstairs, where you'll be safe. Now, just let me give Tom the news I picked up in the street."

"But Lady Fitzgerald is waiting for me at the dressmaker's," I said. "I told her I'd be back in an hour for tea."

He looked at me incredulously. "Don't you understand? Gangs of ruffians are roaming the streets. Now, wait here while I talk to Tom."

When he came back, I was standing exactly as he'd left me, my face, I'm sure, still wearing the same dumbfounded expression. He took my arm gently and led me upstairs to a loft above the shop. "This is where I live," he said, unlocking the door and escorting me into a cozy one-room flat.

There was a bed, neatly made, and covered with a bright red shawl in lieu of a spread. A chest of drawers stood against the wall. On the other side of the room was a round wooden table, two chairs, and a small, open cabinet with shelves.

Avery walked over to the cabinet and then turned to me with a smile. "We're in luck. I have bread and cheese, and what do you think? Here's a bottle of wine!"

I didn't want him to think me spoiled and hysterical, and I said, "You don't have to pretend for my benefit, Avery. Please, tell me what's going on."

"I will, but let's eat first," he said.

He poured the wine and I tasted the cheese. "Ummm," I said, "this is delicious."

He laughed. "You must really be hungry."

I drank my wine and started to feel relaxed and happy again. Avery was sitting across the table from me and it was almost as if we were a husband and wife dining together in our very own house.

The solemn expression returned to his face, and I was jolted back to reality by his next words. "There's going to be an uprising in Ireland, Elly. This riot, and others like it, are only forerunners for what's to come."

"But why, Avery?"

"Why?" He stood up suddenly and paced the floor, running his hands through his unruly hair. "Because there's no justice in Ireland," he said passionately. "England has us in chains, and we'll never be free until we free ourselves."

"Free ourselves from England? But England is our mother country," I said.

A cynical smile twisted his mouth. "Lord save us from such a mother!" He smashed his fist on the table.

"I say to hell with England. Ireland needs home rule. Then we can forge our own destiny and become as great as America!"

"Oh, Avery," I said. "That's a dream, and a dangerous one at that."

He smiled a crooked smile. "You bet it is, but it's a dream I'd die for!"

His words sent a chill up my spine, and I wondered if I had found him only to lose him again. No, I told myself. I won't think such thoughts, and optimist that I was, I buried all my misgivings with a gay smile and raised my glass. "To dreams! May all of ours come true."

He stood with me and tapped his glass to mine. "To dreams." We drained our glasses and he said, "Someday, Elly, when this is all over and Ireland is free . . ."

My heart stopped, waiting for the words I longed to hear, and when he didn't continue, I said, "Go on, Avery."

"I haven't the right to speak." Suddenly he looked at me with impatience. "Elly, you're so naive. Don't you know that even when we were children our friendship was a misalliance? Your father indulged you when he accepted our friendship, but he patronized me. And as for your brother . . ." A triumphant look suddenly crossed his face. "Did Hugh ever tell you about our little fight in the woods?"

This surprised me. "No, he didn't."

A satisfied smile crept slowly across his face, and he seemed to slip back in time. "Hugh Kincaid didn't approve of a tenant's son playing with his sister, so one day he waylaid me in the woods." He looked me in the eye then. "I sent him home with a bloody nose, so I guess he was ashamed to tell of it."

Aye, I thought, knowing Hugh, he would be mortally ashamed.

"As for my own family," he was saying, "they

61

weren't exactly pleased about our friendship either, especially Mam. His voice rose and thickened with a heavy brogue. "Aye, but yere guardian angel is cryin for ye, Avery. Turnin' yere back on yere own kind, ye are." A contemptuous look crossed his face then, and he added, "Mam complains, but my father just accepts things as they are, and that's even worse. I'd rather be dead than like them. And that's why . . ." He sighed and threw up his hands.

I didn't encourage him to go on. I didn't want to hear about politics or prejudice. I wanted to hear about love. Romantic child that I was, I wanted him to smother me with kisses—kisses that would wipe away forever the brand that Gavan Mitchell had placed on my lips with his scorching, savage touch.

Our eyes locked, and he reached for my hand. I swayed toward him, and in that instant a tremendous crash split the air.

"Good God," he said as we both rushed to the window.

The front street was filled with men, and a loud voice bellowed, "We're coming in, ye bastards."

Someone hurled a brick through the window, spraying the street with a shower of glass, and several onlookers ran and picked up the jagged shards. Brandishing them like swords, they joined the mob who were all carrying some kind of crude weapon.

Avery ran for the door. "Stay here."

"You're not going down there!" I screamed, but he was already gone.

I ran back to the window and watched as the mob disappeared inside. The noise was deafening and I knew they must be destroying everything in sight.

The clamor stopped as suddenly as it had begun, and I opened the door and peered down into what was left of the *Herald*'s office. Papers and overturned chairs littered the floor. The printing press lay on its side, smashed and twisted, looking like some prehistoric giant who'd been clubbed to death. Avery, I thought. Where is he? What have they done to him?

I will never forget the terrible stillness as I picked my way through that shambles of a room. Like a tornado, they had swept in the front and out the back, leaving in their wake complete devastation. Oh, God, please let him be safe, I prayed as I looked around, searching for signs of life.

The silence was suddenly broken by the muffled sound of voices coming from the back of the shop. They're still here, I thought!

Panic seized me, and I stood immobile until I heard Avery's voice.

When I found him, I threw myself into his arms. "Oh, Avery, you're safe." Looking up into his face, I saw a trickle of blood run down the side of his mouth, and I reached up and touched it. "You're hurt," I said.

"I'm all right, but look at this place!"

The police came then, and their attitude was unspeakable. They surveyed the damage and shrugged, asking no questions and taking no notes. It was evident they had no intention of tracking down the perpetrators.

The officer in charge jerked his head toward Tom. "You O'Leary?" And when Tom nodded, the man actually grinned. "Messed your place up a little bit, didn't they?"

"We'll be back in print again."

"Not in Belfast ye won't. Not if ye know what's good for ye."

Avery spoke up then, ignoring the officer's remarks. "This lady is the daughter of Master Thomas Kincaid of Glengarra. She was shopping and took refuge here when the rioting began."

The young officer turned to me in amazement. "Have you a complaint against these radicals, Mistress?"

I couldn't believe what I was hearing. "A complaint? Are you mad? They saved my life! That mob," I cried, scanning the room, "look what they did!"

Ignoring my outburst, Avery spoke to the officer in a rational voice. "See that she has a police escort out of Belfast."

"Shut your bloody mouth. We'll take care of the lady." That said, the policeman turned politely to me. "Where would you like to go, Miss?"

I looked at him with disdain. "Lady Fitzgerald was waiting for me at Madame Duprès's. I should like to join her." Holding my head high, I looked at him with contempt. "The constable's office will be hearing from my father about this outrage."

I turned to Avery and my heart ached, for his face was a mask of indifference. "Good day to you, Mistress Kincaid," he said, turning on his heel and retreating to the back of the shop.

I was reunited with Lady Fitzgerald, and the two of us spent an uneasy night in the Belfast Hotel.

The Fitzgerald name was a prominent one, and the following morning we were given a police escort out of the city.

"Ye'll have no trouble on the country roads," the young officer said as he left us. " 'Tis only that scum from the Pound what's doing the devil's work.

Lady Fitzgerald assumed I had been in the millinery shop when the riot broke out, and I never told her otherwise. Too exhausted to talk, we both dozed on the ride back to Strangford Manor, and once there I insisted on leaving immediately for Glengarra. Again the poor lady was too tired to protest, and she graciously gave me the loan of her coachman and carriage for the trip home.

I slept most of the way and awakened to find myself

in County Down. I looked out the window and thought how sharply this peaceful rural scene contrasted with the ugliness I'd witnessed in Belfast. My thoughts then turned sadly to Avery. I feared for him, for I had seen for myself the unbridled hatred he was exposed to there.

And yet, Tom had said *The Herald* would reopen in Belfast. But how, I thought? The press and all their equipment had been destroyed. I will have to talk to Papa, I decided. Surely, he will not turn his back on him.

When the carriage pulled up in front of Glengarra, I jumped out and ran up the steps. I wanted desperately to see my father, but it was Hugh who met me at the door, his face a somber mask.

"Oh, Hugh," I cried. "You can't imagine. We were caught in a riot. They had to give us a police escort out of the city, and . . ."

He looked at me blankly. "Tell me later, Elly. I have bad news. . . ."

Chapter Four

Standing in the cemetery, a feeling of déjà vu washed over me as I watched my father's casket being lowered into the ground. Memory merged with reality, and I looked across the open grave, expecting to see my father, once again the mourner rather than the mourned, his face and body restored to the fullness of his prime.

I reached for Aunt Celia's hand, but it was Hugh's I touched, and he drew away, a pained expression on his face, as if he wanted to but could not share my grief.

I was jolted immediately back to the present and suddenly I felt completely alone. My father was gone. Never again could I look to him for comfort, and Aunt Celia was in India, in a village so remote, the news of my father's death would probably not reach her for months on end.

"Rest ye in peace," Reverend Wharton intoned, and inclining his head to Hugh and myself, he added, "Joined with your mother he is now, and their happiness is such we poor sinners cannot conceive of it."

I hoped my father was happy, but I was young, and it was hard for me to believe that the life beyond was superior to earthly pleasures. I knew only that I ached to have him back, that gentle wraith of a man who was my strength and comfort.

I looked through my heavy black veil at the band of mourners who huddled in the rain to bid farewell to Thomas Kincaid. We were a pitifully small group, and this added to my sadness. Besides Hugh and myself, there was Sir Henry Drake, my father's solicitor, who was here to read the will and stay on for a few days to assist Hugh with any legal matters; the servants, of course, some of them scarcely recognizable in their Sunday clothes, who wept openly for their beloved master; and one whose presence would have angered my father, Sir Gavan Mitchell.

He conferred briefly with Hugh, offered his condolences to me, and was gone as unobtrusively as he had arrived, immediately following the service.

I glanced at Hugh, now the master of Glengarra, and wondered how he would govern the estate. Would he uphold our father's standards? Or would he allow his greed to plant the seeds for future riots like the one I had witnessed in Belfast? I meant to tell him what I had seen, but it wasn't until almost a month later that I had the opportunity.

Passing the door to Papa's study early one morning, I found my brother alone, poring over a bulky ledger. It seemed odd to see him sitting in Papa's place, and the thought suddenly struck me that now, not only Glengarra, but myself as well, was under Hugh's jurisdiction. Nevertheless, I would have my say.

He looked up as I entered and smiled cordially. "Come in, Elly. Sit down and chat with me awhile. I feel guilty about leaving you alone so much after all you've been through. I've just returned from Belfast and the Fitzgeralds send their condolences."

I nodded and took a seat across from him, and he closed the heavy ledger and pushed it aside, giving his sole attention to me. "I want you to know, Elly, I'll be rewarding the officers who rescued you in Belfast."

I was incensed at the thought of those oafs receiving anything but a sound thrashing, and without thinking I cried, "Reward *The Herald* instead. They're the ones who really saved me."

He studied me with cold eyes. "And just how could that be, Elly?"

I looked at him squarely, refusing to lie my way out. "I was shopping nearby and I stopped in the office to see Avery." Then I told him how the mob from Sandy Row had smashed the printing press and everything in sight, and about how callous the police had acted, ending with, "And so if you're going to hand out rewards, they could use the money to rebuild." I searched his face for some sign of compassion, and finding none, I added, "They are discriminated against, Hugh. I heard the police with my own ears."

He said, "Elly, let me make myself clear on this subject. I have no intention of rewarding *The Herald* for anything. I'm glad they're out of business, and if they ever try to open up again, I hope the mob from Sandy Row runs them out of town for good. As for Avery James, if he helped you in any way, he deserves no reward for it. Didn't Fa give his family a cottage and land to work when they came to Ulster?"

"Ah, Hugh, be fair," I said. "Didn't Glengarra reap the profit from their work?"

"And why not? It's our land, Elly. If that's the way the ingrate feels, I'll evict the lot of them tomorrow."

My heart stopped, and I thought, Now what have I done? "Please, Hugh," I said. "Don't evict the James family. Those aren't their sentiments. I was only trying to get you to see the other side of this."

"Don't talk politics to me, Elly. You don't understand it, and besides, interest in such things is unbecoming in a woman."

My temper flared. "Isn't your beloved queen a woman?"

He said, "Victoria is your queen too, Elly and don't be forgetting it. I don't know what radical ideas you've picked up from the likes of Avery James and Tom O'Leary, but Ireland's destiny is linked to England and

68

these upstarts aren't going to change anything!" He stood up suddenly. "This subject is closed. I've other matters to discuss with you. Gavan wants us to come to Bonnie Brae for a few days. He needs help with his plans for the west wing and with the selection of furniture for the castle. He values your opinion, Elly, and I'd appreciate it if you'd assist him."

My thoughts were still with Avery, and when I didn't answer him right away, he said, "You speak of prejudice, Elly. Should a man be held accountable for what his father or his grandfather might have done?"

I said, "No."

"Good. We agree on something." He smiled and put an arm around me. "Come on, Elly. Let's forget this discussion. Fa wouldn't want us to be quarreling."

I smiled back, but an uneasy feeling overshadowed our truce.

Hugh's downright meanness in refusing to grant Avery any reward or even credit for my rescue riled me, and I vowed to do something myself.

I'd gotten in the habit of taking an early morning ride, and one day I cut through the woods and paid a call on the James family.

A stout woman with beautiful dark eyes answered my knock. Her expression showed surprise, then wariness, and finally resentment as she recognized me. "Something I can do for ye, me lady?"

Feeling ill at ease, I said, "You are Mrs. James, Avery's mother?"

"Aye, I'm Peg James, me lady."

"I came to inquire about Avery," I said, feeling more awkward by the minute. "Perhaps if I come inside."

She said nothing, but held the door open for me, and I entered the small, thatched-roof cottage. Once inside, all my sensibilities recoiled from the squalor I saw, and I stood in the midst of that miserable room and wished with all my heart that I had not come. I tried to avoid staring at the smoke-scarred hearth, the rocker with only one arm, and the crude wooden table still littered with dirty dishes from the previous meal. Avery's quarters above *The Herald* flashed before my eyes. He must consider them a palace compared to this.

Close up, I could see that Peg James looked nothing like her handsome son. Her hair was dark and sprinkled with gray, and she was short and small-boned despite her plumpness. She wore a dress of homespun and the bodice was grease-stained.

"Have you heard from Avery?" I asked, but before she could answer, the back door slammed.

She looked somewhat relieved that we should be interrupted. "That'll be me husband, Patrick," she said.

He, too, appeared shocked and almost fearful to see me. "Is something wrong, me lady?" he asked, pulling off his cap and twisting it in his big hands.

He was built like Avery, and his hair showed streaks of red through the gray, but if he had ever possessed his son's good looks, hard work and time had erased them.

"There's nothing wrong," I said. "I stopped only to inquire about Avery. He was very kind to me in Belfast during the trouble there."

"Avery's not here," he answered, glancing quickly at his wife.

"I understand," I said. "But have you heard from him? Is he still in Belfast?"

Again he glanced at his wife with uneasy eyes. "I don't rightly know, me lady."

I felt as awkward as they, and smiling weakly, I opened my reticule. "Master Kincaid wanted to show his appreciation by leaving this."

Peg started to speak, but her husband silenced her with a look.

I extended the note to Patrick, and he took it eagerly. "Thank ye kindly, me lady. It's grateful we are to Master Hugh for his generosity."

Avery's mother said nothing, but I could feel her hostility. Oh, why did I come? I had learned nothing about Avery and I had patronized and confused his parents.

Feeling like an odious Lady Bountiful, I left the bewildered couple and got into my buggy. I flicked the whip, and the pony bolted down the narrow road in a cloud of dust.

Just as I rounded the bend, I heard a shrill voice cry out, "Stop, please. I must talk to ye, me lady."

I turned around and saw a small girl running down the road. Reining in the pony, I brought the buggy to a sudden halt. She caught up then, and panting for breath, leaned against the wheel. "It's about Avery, me lady. It's . . ."

Her thin little chest was heaving, and I held out my hand. "Come, sit in the buggy and catch your breath." When she was seated beside me, I smiled and said, "You're one of Avery's sisters, aren't you?"

She nodded her head. "I'm the youngest, Mistress. Me name's Tricia." Her eyes met mine, and I saw Avery again at ten, the same copper-colored hair, though hers was long and tightly braided, and the same serious little face, right down to the freckles that marched across the bridge of her nose.

She glanced back at the road, and finding it deserted, spoke in a rush. "Avery's joined the Fenians and Mam says he could get hanged. Please, Mistress, you're a great lady. You won't let them hang Avery, will you?"

The Fenians! Vaguely I recalled the name. I patted her hand, searching wildly for a connection, and then suddenly it came to me. The Fitzgeralds had mentioned the Fenians. They were a secret society. Oh, why did Avery have to get mixed up with them!

The child was looking at me with frightened eyes, and I tried to reassure her. "Don't worry, Tricia. Nothing will happen to Avery. I promise you."

"Thank ye, me lady. I knew ye'd help." Her grave little face brightened just a fraction and then turned sober again. "Mam would tan me good if she knew I told."

"She won't know," I said. "And, Tricia, when Avery comes home, tell him I want to see him. Tell him to send you to the Big House with a note. You'd do that for Avery, wouldn't you, dear?"

"Aye, Mistress. I'd do anything for Avery."

"That's a good lass. Now, you'd best go before you're missed."

She nodded like a conspirator, and was out of the buggy and running down the road in a flash, her raised skirt exposing her long, skinny legs. I sat, deep in thought, letting the buggy block the road. No wonder Avery's family had been so evasive. Hugh would evict them for sure if he knew. But hang a man for belonging to a secret society! I hardly thought so, and in my innocence I attached little importance to it.

Two weeks later I made my second trip to Bonnie Brae. The day had begun with a gentle mist that kissed awake the wild flowers and then evaporated in the bright morning sunshine. Bonnie Brae can't possibly look as bleak and ugly in midsummer, I thought as we approached the steep hill leading to the castle.

Hugh said, "If you see something you don't like, just say so, Elly." Then he smiled with satisfaction. "Gavan wants everything at Bonnie Brae to meet with your approval."

I gave him an exasperated look. "I'm no authority, Hugh. And I hope you haven't presented me as such. If Sir Gavan wants advice, he should consult an architect."

Hugh raised a hand in mock protest. "Don't take me

head off, Elly. Gav knows you're not an architect, and I'm sure he's already engaged one. The man just wants your opinion. Is that too much to ask?"

I made no comment, and he did not pursue the subject. My blustering brother seemed to be treading lightly around me lately. Not at all like Hugh, and I wondered why. If he thinks this contrived little visit to Bonnie Brae is going to change my mind about Gavan, he's in for a rude awakening, I thought. I want no part of the man or his blooming castle, and naively I smiled to myself. This is 1860, Hugh, and even in Ireland women can't be traded like horseflesh.

As the carriage drove up to the front of the castle, we could see that restoration had already begun on the outside. Scaffolding had been erected, and workmen were busy cleaning and repairing the stonework.

This time Gavan greeted us on our arrival and our bags were taken upstairs by two young lads in ill-fitting livery. Our host graciously ushered us into the drawing room which I noticed had been scrupulously cleaned. Gavan was obviously very pleased to see us, and for a moment, I was reminded of a small lad who had not really thought his playmates would attend his party.

"I have much to show you," he said, smiling broadly. "The carpenters have been working day and night to keep to my schedule. I wanted things to be far enough along that you could visualize what I have in mind."

Hugh laughed. "Plenty of time for that tomorrow, Gav. We've had a long ride. As for myself, I could do with a drink!"

"You can always do with a drink," Gavan said jokingly. "But my apologies to your sister." And he turned to me. "Would you be wanting tea, Mistress Elly?"

"That would be nice," I said.

He rang for a servant, and then poured two drinks from the decanter. Looking toward the door, an impatient frown crossed his face and he jerked on the bell cord. "Where is that confounded idiot?"

As if in answer, a young maid appeared. "You rang, Sir Gavan?"

"Of course I rang. What did you think it was?" he snapped. "Bring a pot of tea and some cake or something."

When she had gone, he picked up the glasses and nodded to me. "With your permission, Mistress Elly." Handing one glass to Hugh and bringing the other with him, he sat down beside me. "I need your advice on the garden too. We've never had one at Bonnie Brae, you know." The servant arrived then with the tea and some small cakes and Gavan nodded impatiently. "Put the tray down here by Mistress Kincaid and leave."

As I poured the tea, I could feel his eyes on me, watching my every movement, and a blush crept up the back of my neck. I mentally scolded myself. What is wrong with you? You're not an old maid to be reduced to the vapors by a man's eyes. But this man's eyes are different, I thought, and when he measures me this way, I feel uncomfortable, as if those eyes have laid bare both my soul and my body. That my mind should even entertain such indecent thoughts shocked me, and my cheeks burned with shame.

He smiled faintly and spoke so that only I could hear. "Forgive me for staring, Elly. We Ulstermen are a rough and ready bunch. Not like your Londoners, I fear. You're a fine-looking woman and I can't keep my eyes off you."

I changed the subject quickly to safer ground. "And what did you have in mind for your gardens, Sir Gavan?"

He raised his hand. "Please, I prefer just plain Gavan. As to the gardens, you tell me what plants you like, and I'll order them. I have no preference myself."

Hugh, who had been standing, looking out the window, spoke then. "You'll have to build a greenhouse to suit our Elly, Gav. She fills the rooms with fresh flowers all year round."

Gavan seemed taken with the idea. "Then we shall have one at Bonnie Brae, too. I'll speak to the men about it."

Hugh shook his head. "It's glad I am Glengarra's not in need of renovation. I'd hardly have your patience or your money, Gav."

"Glengarra must be a beautiful place," Gavan said. "And one I hope to emulate, and not only for its appearance." His face took on a wistful look and he added, "I take it, it has been a happy home."

"Aye, it was that," Hugh answered. He was a little in his cups and becoming mellow. "My mother brought the sunshine with her and the only sadness in that house was when she left it. We had some times there, Gav—Christmases like you wouldn't believe, the house all decorated and smelling of pine, the table laden with mouth-watering dishes; roast duck and plum pudding. Ah, 'tis something to remember."

"You were lucky," Gavan said. "I spent Christmas in boarding schools." He paused and frowned. "More should be forgotten than remembered about it." Then he turned to me, and in a lighter vein added, "And how did you manage to put up with this rascal for a brother?"

"I kicked him when he went too far," I said.

Hugh slapped his thigh. "That's the Lord's truth. Our Elly was a spitfire, she was."

Gavan looked at me, and his dark eyes bored into mine. "I wager you're still a little spitfire. Aye, Mistress Elly?"

Hugh said, "Know what our Elly did once, Gav? Smacked me over the head with a croquet mallet."

Gavan laughed. "You were probably cheating at the game."

Hugh rubbed his head. "I think the bump's still there. Ah, my sister was something, and still is," he added, taking another swallow of whiskey. "It'll take a strong man to tame her, but she's a Thoroughbred through and through."

I flashed Hugh a warning look and stared pointedly at the drink in his hand.

He smiled. "See what I mean, Gavan?" Then he clicked his heels and raised his arm in a mock salute. "I'm going, shister dear. As the old saying goes, 'Had me nip, now I'll have me nap.' And a good day to you both."

When we were alone, I covered my embarrassment by saying, "Don't take Hugh too seriously."

"Oh, but I do and I envy him," he said. Suddenly he grew serious. "Hugh Kincaid has everything I want, a gracious home and a gracious lady to preside over it and most of all a name to be proud of."

His words touched me, and I remembered the servant girl's words—*Me mam says old Sir Gavan was Lucifer hisself.* Impulsively I put my hand on his arm. "Most people forget their prejudices in time."

He caught my hand in his and brought it to his lips. "I don't really care about *most* people, only you, Elly Kincaid. Are you prejudiced against the Mitchell name?"

I said, "Ireland is too full of prejudice. I shouldn't want to add to it."

He smiled then. "That makes me very happy." And very slowly he released my hand.

What a strange man, I thought later as I dressed for dinner. Today I had almost liked him. When he had grabbed my hand and held it, I had been afraid he might try to kiss me again, but he had been in every way a gentleman.

Supper that evening was an improvement over the poor fare we had been served on our previous visit, and the maid who served us was more experienced than the clumsy lass who had earned Gavan's displeasure the last time.

Gavan had just returned from a brief business trip to London, and I was interested in hearing about the city that had been my home for eight years.

He mentioned that he had been a guest in the home of Lord Winston Patterson, who was a good friend of one of his business associates, and I said, "Then you must have met Miss Cecily Patterson."

He looked surprised. "You know her?"

"Since we were children," I said. "My aunt and Lady Patterson were friends."

"What a coincidence!"

I made no comment. The fact was I had detested Cecily Patterson and I was sure the feeling was mutual. A shallow, snobbish girl, Cecily had looked down her nose at an Irish tomboy like me.

But she would have regarded this handsome Irish *man* in a very different light, I decided, looking across the table at Gavan. They deserve each other, I thought, and wondered why that annoyed me.

After supper we retired to the card room for a game of whist, but I begged off after a few hands. "You two play without me. Long carriage rides always make me sleepy."

Gavan said, "I'll have a servant show you to your room. Sleep well, Elly."

The little maid whom I had seen on my first visit appeared in answer to Gavan's summons and led me upstairs. To my surprise, the room was totally transformed. New Chippendale furniture had replaced the old makeshift pieces, and the handsome canopied bed was adorned in an exquisite rose brocade. A large Oriental carpet in shades of green and rose covered the floor, and silken drapes in a soft green graced the mullioned windows.

"It's ever so beautiful, isn't it, Mistress?" the servant remarked proudly. "Sir Gavan had it made over especially for you." She giggled and said in a low voice, "The old one like to had a fit. He wouldn't let her set foot in it, he wouldn't. Said she might break something."

"Sir Gavan is redecorating the whole house, Bridget," I said.

The little maid beamed. "You remembered me name! I'm ever so grateful, Mistress. Fine ladies like yourself don't often remember the likes of me." She busied herself, plumping the pillows and turning down the bed. "I hung your clothes up too, Mistress. Like I said, I know naught about being a lady's maid, but I'm learnin', I am." She thought a moment and then added, "None of the other rooms in this wing has been touched, just this one, and Sir Gavan was givin' it to old Starice good, he was, about havin' it finished before your arrival. She's a loony, she is, but she knows things about Bonnie Brae. She kept muttering to herself and saying something about a curse and he better not open up the west wing . . ."

I tried to speak kindly but firmly. "Bridget, a good servant never repeats what she hears in her master's house."

Bridget said no more until I was in bed and the light had been turned down. Then she said very quietly, "Beggin' your pardon, Mistress, but Sir Gavan, he ain't me master. I don't work at Bonnie Brae regular, so I don't owe it me loyalty. You're a good, kind lady and I have to warn you. Don't let Sir Gavan open up the west wing. Starice is a witch and she knows . . ."

"Good night, Bridget," I said, very firmly this time.

Beware the power of suggestion, I told myself after Bridget had gone and I was alone in the dark room, for my eyes were drawn to the open window, where curtains fluttered against a summer breeze. I thought

78

of the face I'd seen in the mirror and the white gown that had billowed out behind the apparition, and I shivered though the night was warm.

I thought of Gavan and his dark, hypnotic eyes that drew me and repelled me all at the same time. *Will you dance with the devil, Mistress Elly?* he had said.

I drifted off to a troubled sleep, and in my dreams I was in the arms of the Prince of Darkness, waltzing in a circle around a great pit. Stealing a glance inside, I saw flames, leaping and crackling within, and then to my horror I missed a step and suddenly I was falling down, down, down into the raging inferno.

I woke up then and sunlight was streaming through the open window. Eager for company, I dressed quickly and went downstairs to find Hugh and Gavan waiting for me. In the cold light of day my nocturnal fantasies seemed ridiculous. Bonnie Brae appeared more gloomy than ghostly and Gavan more an amiable host than my nightmarish Prince of Darkness.

He was gracious and charming as we chatted over a leisurely breakfast in a smaller, more intimate dining room. He spoke of his interest in racing horses, and Hugh said, "Speaking of horses, if you don't mind, I'd like to borrow one of yours, Gav. I'd like to look at some property up the coast."

"You can have the pick of my stable," Gavan replied genially, and then looked at me. "Are you ready for the grand tour, Mistress Elly? I have to warn you though, there's all sorts of debris left about by the workmen. Perhaps you'd better change into riding clothes. I wouldn't want you to be soiling your gown."

"I'm not afraid of a little dirt," I said. "Besides, the gown can be cleaned."

"Good, and I promise you, the bats are all gone now." I colored at the memory, and he smiled. "Much to my disappointment, I might add."

Hugh left for the stables, and I followed Gavan down

the long corridor that led to the west wing. He wore an open-necked white shirt, dark trousers, and boots and with his beard and swarthy complexion he looked like he belonged on the Spanish Main.

The heavy door was closed and he said, "To keep the dust out until the workers are finished."

When he opened it, I saw that the hall had been transformed. The oak paneling had been refinished, the frescoed ceiling restored, and the rosewood staircase that I had so admired in the dim lantern light proved to be even more beautiful by day. Overcome with enthusiasm, I cried, "Oh, Gavan. It's going to be magnificent!"

"I knew you'd like it," he said, and beaming with pleasure, he held out his hand. "Come inside, but take care, there's tools and things flung about."

From the great hall, we moved on to the dining room with its white marble mantelpiece and unusual crystal and rose-quartz chandelier. He pointed to it proudly. "It holds eighteen candles, and it's a beauty when lit." One long wall was completely concealed by dustcloths, but the other was covered in a dark, patterned tapestry, and he motioned to it and said, "I was going to remove this, but I found out from the Pattersons that old tapestries can be cleaned."

He nodded toward the far wall. "How would you like a serpentine-front sideboard over there with a gilded console mirror above it?" Without waiting for an answer, he continued. "And a long mahogany table, a Hepplewhite, I think." Suddenly he shook his head and laughed. "Dashed if I know what any of this means. I memorized it all for your benefit. Would any of this meet with your approval?"

I said, "It sounds very grand. And if anything was copied from the Pattersons, I'm sure it would be in the best of taste."

He said, "You don't sound like you care for the Pattersons."

"I'm afraid it's Cecily I don't care for. She's a little too snobbish for me."

He raised an eyebrow. "Strange. She didn't act snobbish to me."

"She wouldn't," I said curtly, and then could have bitten my tongue when I saw him smother a smile.

Next to the dining room was a study, still furnished and looking like it was awaiting its master's return, with its assortment of pipes in racks and quill pen sticking up from the inkwell. "My father's old study," he said, and hastily shut the door.

The rest of the house had been cleared of furniture, and I wondered why this one remained intact, but I asked no questions, for Gavan's mood seemed to have abruptly changed. He showed me the rest of the wing with none of the enthusiasm and gaiety he had exhibited earlier.

Once outside though, his spirits lifted again and he said, "One of the houses I saw in England had what they called a lilac walk—all different shades and varieties of lilac bushes lining a flagstone path. They say the sight is breathtaking in the spring. What do you think of it?"

I said, "I would love it. Lilacs are my favorite flower."

"I'm not surprised. Somehow, lilacs remind me of you. Now, what else shall we have? A rose garden, I suppose, is a must."

"Aye, no proper gardens would be without one, and plan for it to be close to the house. You'll be wanting to cut the blooms and bring them inside."

He led me to a stone bench and we sat down under the shade of a large tree. I pretended interest in assessing the courtyard, but I could feel his eyes on me and reluctantly I met his gaze. Once again I felt myself drawn into those deep, mysterious pools and held captive by their spell. I heard his voice as if from a great distance. "Elly, I want you to be the one to gather those roses. I want you to be the mistress of Bonnie Brae. I love you and I want you for my wife."

His voice and his eyes held me entranced, and suddenly I was swept into his arms, and when I tried to protest, he silenced me with a kiss. I felt myself sinking into a black pit, and I struggled against him, but his powerful arms would not let me go. His kiss was hard and bruising. Then he parted my lips and explored my mouth with his tongue. I felt outside my body and helpless to resist. His lips moved to the tips of my ears, tantalizing me, and he whispered, "I must have you, Elly. You want me too, I can tell."

I felt his hand on my breast, and I moaned as he found my distended nipple and circled it with his finger, tantalizing me beyond endurance. I gave myself over to wave after wave of sensations I'd not known my body capable of, and then a delicious warmth exploded in my loins, and suddenly my sanity returned.

"No," I cried, and shoved him away. Tears stung my eyes, and my gown clung to my damp body as I stood up and faced him. My legs shook, and my voice trembled with outrage. "You are not a gentleman, and I cannot accept your proposal. You are a scoundrel, sir, and not my brother's friend."

Unperturbed by my outburst, he spoke calmly and with a maddening rationality. "I have not dishonored you or your brother. I want you for my wife." He stood up then and looked down at me in a patronizing way. "Forgive me, Elly. I'm sorry if I frightened you. You're young and innocent and I like that."

I tried to turn away, but he put his hands on my shoulders and made me face him. "There's so much I want to teach you, Elly." Then his mouth curved in a smile, and he said, "And now that I know how passionate you can be, I want more than ever to marry you."

His words mortified me beyond all reason. To think that he had been aware of the shameful feelings he had aroused in me! "You are a cad," I said. "I hate you, and I will never marry you!"

He continued smiling in that infuriating way. "Not now, perhaps," he said calmly. "But I leave the offer open."

Chapter Five

We arrived home, and I immediately retired to my room, seething with indignation and eager to vent it in private.

Arrogant cad! The man's a blackguard, and Hugh's no better, I thought. How my pompous brother infuriated me with his hero worship of Gavan Mitchell! Sitting in the devil's own parlor, bargaining for me like a horse trader? "Our Elly's a Thoroughbred," he'd said with that silly grin on his face. "It'll take a strong man to tame her."

Well, it won't be Sir Gavan Mitchell! I can tell you that, my conniving brother!

Pacing the floor, I nursed my anger, remembering Hugh's reaction when I had demanded that we leave Bonnie Brae. "Come now, Elly. Gavan told me he got carried away a little. Dash it all, lass, the man wants to marry you. He meant no harm. Why, after you're married, you'll be laughing about it."

My temper got the best of me then, and I picked up a hairbrush and threw it across the room. It crashed against a shelf, knocking the head off a small bust of King George. Somehow that made me feel better.

"I'll not be marrying your idol, Hugh Kincaid, and that's final," I said out loud to the empty room.

But I had much to learn about Hugh, and I was soon to discover that he was not above manipulating me for his own purposes.

For the time being though, our quarrel was laid to rest by the news of a tragedy that would prove to have far-reaching consequences for my future, for it closed a door that my father had imagined would always be open to me.

A letter from Uncle Roger's brother, Lord Winston Haviland arrived several days after our return. It sadly informed us of the shocking murders of both Celia and Roger Haviland at the hands of insurgents in India.

This senseless and barbaric attack on my beloved aunt and uncle left me heartbroken and Hugh angry.

He equated the uprising in India with undercover activities in Ireland. "This is what happens when radicals are not put down from the beginning. It should be a lesson to us here. Hang the bloody bastards before they murder us in our beds."

Could this happen in Ireland, I wondered. During the riots in Belfast my sympathy had been with the rebels, but after hearing about my aunt and uncle, I wondered if Hugh could be right. Avery was an idealist. He could easily be duped by violent men. Oh, if only I could talk to him, I thought.

That opportunity presented itself several weeks later when I was sitting on one of the stone benches in the rose garden alone, and deep in thought. An untouched piece of needlework lay in my lap, and my mind drifted back to the afternoon I had sat on a similar bench with Gavan Mitchell.

My outrage and anger at the memory of that humiliating experience had dissipated to the degree that I could now begin to analyze my own reaction to it.

That I had almost succumbed to his outrageous advances was to me the most frightening aspect of the whole sordid situation. By all rights, I should have been disgusted by his performance, but alas, in all honesty, I had to admit that he held a wicked fascination for me. My cheeks burned at the memory of his hands caressing my breast, and I found myself wondering what depravities he had in mind to teach me if I consented to be his wife!

I must have a wanton streak in my character, I thought, or else Gavan Mitchell is indeed the devil he proclaims himself to be.

My agonizing attempts to understand and perhaps excuse my shocking behavior were interrupted abruptly when a small stone landed in my lap. Startled, I looked around, but there was no one in sight.

I picked up my needlepoint and started walking toward the house, and it was then that I saw the little red-haired girl peeping out at me from behind a hedge. "Tricia," I said. "Come out. You don't have to be afraid. There's no one here but me."

Cautiously she stepped out into the garden, and I could see then that she had been crying. "What's wrong?" I asked.

"I can't talk here, Mum. Please, come to The Paradise."

"But you've been crying. Why?"

"I have to go, Mistress. Mam'll switch me for sure if she finds out I'm here."

She slipped behind the hedge again and was gone before I could say any more.

I would have to change into riding clothes and sneak off to the stable without Hugh seeing me, for I could think of no excuse I could give him for going out this late in the afternoon.

I glanced up at the house before going inside, and I thought I saw the curtains move in Papa's old study. But when I passed by the room, the door was open and there was no one inside.

I dressed hurriedly, and as an extra precaution I took the back stairway down. Luck was certainly with me, for I made it out of the house without encountering Hugh or anyone else.

As if sensing my impatience, the groom saddled up my pony with unusual haste and soon I was out of the stable and heading for the woods.

At the clearing I spied Tricia sitting on the pedestal rock. Suddenly a horrible thought entered my mind, and I rushed up to the child. "What is it, Tricia? Has Avery been arrested?"

It was Avery's voice that answered me. "No, he hasn't been arrested."

I turned around and faced him. "Oh, Avery, thank God you're safe! Tricia said—"

"I know what Tricia said." Then he stooped down until he was at eye level with his sister. "Go home now, lass, and stop yere worrying. Everything will be all right."

The little girl looked at him with tears in her eyes. "Avery, you're not cross, are you?"

He took her in his arms and held her close. "How could I be cross with me favorite sister?" Then he brushed her tears away with his fingers and smiled at her. "Go now, and not a word about this. Hear me, lass!"

She smiled back. "I promise, Avery. They can tear out me tongue, but I'll not say a word! Oh, I love you, Avery, and I'll never, never tell."

He shoved her gently. "Off with ye now."

When she had gone, I said, "Oh, Avery, what is it? The child was terrified for you."

He shook his head and smiled a little sadly. "Poor little thing!" Then he smacked his fist against his palm in a gesture of impatience and said, "Ah, we had a big fight at home, Elly. Me father's disowned me for joining the organization." His eyes grew dark with anger. "Acted like a bull with a boil about it, he did, bellowing all over the house. That woke everybody up and then we all got into it. Me brother Colin accused me of putting every man in the family in danger. 'There's

87

spies everywhere,' the fool said. 'And they not only hang the guilty; they hang the fathers and brothers too.' Tricia got hysterical at this and confessed she'd told you what I was about.

"Then Mam jumped all over the poor lass and told her you'd tell your brother. Mam has a sharp tongue, and Tricia thought she'd betrayed me." He smiled weakly and looked at me. "You haven't told anybody, have you, Elly?"

"Of course not," I said, feeling a little hurt. "Don't you trust me, Avery?"

"Aye. I trust you, but a slip of the tongue can happen, and in this case it would mean the end of me, and worse still, the end of the organization. Tricia shouldn't have burdened you with that responsibility."

I said, "Avery, I don't care a fig for the organization, but I'd never hurt you. Tricia knew that and she thought I could help. Oh, why do you want to get involved? It's too dangerous!"

He looked at me with impatience. "You sound like Mam. I have to do this, Elly, even if I die for it." His eyes burned with a martyr's zeal. "I'm a gunrunner," he announced proudly. "And me job's important."

He pushed his cap back and leaned against the tree, and I was reminded of childhood days when he used to regale me with stories of folk heroes and battles and I would feign interest in them for his sake.

"The guns come in from France," he was saying, "marked as farm tools, and we load them onto carts and take them to the church in one of the outlying villages. We've a young priest there who works with us."

He thinks more of that bloody organization than he does of me, I thought, suddenly consumed with jealousy, and on an impulse I reached up and put my arms around him. "All I care about is us, Avery." And

88

standing on tiptoe, I pulled his head down and pressed my lips to his.

He held the kiss for a moment, and then pulled back and looked at me with a startled expression on his face. "Us? Do you know what you're saying, Elly? There can never be anything for us. I'll always love you, but you're a Kincaid and I'm a tenant's son."

I heard only that he loved me, and I said, "Oh, Avery, I love you, too. I always have, ever since we were little."

I gazed up at him, my eyes aglow with happiness, but his held only resignation and an aching regret. "But, Avery," I said. "I don't care that you're a tenant's son."

He gave me an indulgent smile and took my hand. Leading me down to the bank of the stream, where once we had skipped pebbles and chased frogs, he said, "When I was a lad, I used to dream silly dreams. I thought we'd marry and I pictured our wedding right here at The Paradise. We'd stand together on the pedestal rock and make our vows."

His words touched me, and I said, "I can't imagine a more beautiful place for a wedding."

"But don't you see, Elly, that was only a dream. It has no place in reality."

I reached up and put my fingers over his lips. "Hush," I whispered. "Love is reality."

Suddenly his body tensed and his eyes grew wary. "Someone's coming. Wait here."

I watched with bated breath as he moved cautiously up the bank, and then I sighed with relief when I heard Tricia's shrill voice. "Avery, Mam sent me. A man came to the house, asking for you. We told him naught, but Mam's right worried. She thinks he's the authorities. He says his name is Meath."

He relaxed and gave her a smile. "Tell Mam not to worry. He's one of us." Then he turned to me. "I must

89

go now, Elly. Meath is the province organizer. I'm to take him to Dublin with me tonight."

"But, Avery," I cried. "When will I see you?"

"I don't know. That's up to the organization. I have a job to do, Elly."

"Then this is good-bye again," I said with resignation.

He reached down and kissed me, almost reverently, on the lips. Then he touched my hair, very gently with his big hand and he said, "I made up a poem about you once, Elly. Didn't have nerve enough to tell you then. Would you like to hear it now?"

Overcome with emotion, I nodded my head.

"Moonbeams in her hair, me Elly's ever fair." He smiled then. "I was only twelve and not a very good poet, but I loved your hair, I did." His smile faded and he studied my face for what seemed like a long time. "Go with God, Elly." Then he turned quickly, and left me standing there alone in the place we'd called The Paradise.

I remained in the glen after he had gone, remembering all our good times there and wondering how it would all end.

That I should contemplate the future at this particular time and in this particular place was ironic, for our little rendezvous today had already sealed our fates and set in motion events that would irrevocably alter the courses of both our lives.

Our usually loquacious groom was again quiet when I returned the pony to the stable, but my thoughts were too full of Avery to pay any attention to him.

I used the backstairs to return to my room, and again I encountered no one. Mentally congratulating myself on my good luck, I washed the road dust from my face and hands and quickly dressed for dinner.

The evening was warm, and scanning my wardrobe, I chose a gown of soft chiffon in a pale shade of pink. It buttoned down the front, so I could get into it myself quite easily and thus avoid Megan's well-meant chatter. I was quite fond of the lass, but tonight I didn't want to be distracted from my own thoughts.

I wondered if there would be guests for dinner this evening, for Hugh frequently invited neighbors and business associates to dine without consulting me. I would be happy to have Hugh occupied with others tonight, for I felt vaguely uneasy and did not relish being the sole object of his attention.

I entered the dining room, and to my dismay found only Hugh, drink in hand, and with a look of belligerence on his face.

"Ah, Mistress Kincaid of Glengarra, I believe," he said, rising and greeting me with an exaggerated bow.

I could see immediately that he had been drinking, and I resigned myself to an unpleasant meal, for Hugh could be sarcastic when he was in his cups.

"Have a glass of wine with me, Elly," he said, staring at me with glazed eyes.

"No, thank you."

He poured me a glass anyhow, and set it before me. "I'd like to offer a toast."

To pacify him, I raised my glass and waited while he stood, a little uncertain on his feet. "To your happiness, dear sister, on this most auspicious occasion."

He downed his drink in one gulp, and then to my surprise he hurled the glass against the wall. I watched in fascinated horror as the bloodred dregs trickled down, soiling the delicate white plasterwork.

His lip curled as he looked at me. "Barbaric custom, but then, we Ulstermen are all barbarians, aren't we, Elly dear?"

A maid, hearing the crash, hurried into the room. She stooped to pick up the broken glass, but he shoved her aside. "Let it be, and get out. I wish to be alone with my sister."

When she had gone, I placed my unused napkin back on the table and stood up. "I'm going to my room," I said, carefully controlling my voice. "I think you've had too much to drink, Hugh."

"Don't you dare leave." His voice was chilling and surprisingly sober. Taking me in from head to toe, he smirked contemptuously. "Such an elegant and refined young lady! I daresay I should apologize for being drunk in your presence."

I turned away, and with my head held high I started walking slowly toward the door while he continued to talk. "Aye, and it's quite the prude you are, too." Then he clicked his tongue in a mocking manner. "How shocked and incensed you were at Gavan Mitchell's disgraceful behavior when he proposed to you."

I was almost at the door, but I turned and faced him with a fury of my own. "I don't have to listen to this, Hugh, and I don't have to submit to your friend's unwanted advances either."

Before I could reach the knob, he was in front of me and his face was dark with rage. "Aye, but you don't mind submitting to a filthy bastard who grubbed for potatoes on our father's land, do you?"

His words knocked the breath from my body, and I reeled back and stared into his hate-contorted face.

"I saw you in his arms. You, a Kincaid! By God, it made me sick," he said. "I couldn't stay after that, but I heard enough to know what he is."

My mind raced with questions, wondering how much he knew. "He's a Catholic," I said weakly.

"Aye, but he's much more than that. He's a traitor and I'll see him hanged!"

"No!" The word was wrenched from the depths of my soul, and I staggered back against the door.

He ignored my outburst and went on talking, his

eyes glinting with a cruel delight. "If I turn him in to the authorities in Dublin, he'll be jailed and then publicly hanged. We could all go watch it."

I looked at him with horror, and he smiled wickedly. "On the other hand, I could turn his name in to some of the Orange lads here in Ulster. Instead of hanging him, they'd waylay him and give him a pitch cap trial out in a field somewhere. Do you know what a pitch cap trial is, Elly?"

I shook my head numbly.

He pulled out a chair. "Here, sit down and I'll tell you."

He might have been describing a game instead of an insidious method of Irish torture as his voice droned on relentlessly.

"They take a lad's cap and fill it with pitch, then they light it and jam it back on his head. Naturally the lad jumps around like a jackrabbit, trying to pull his cap off and the scorching pitch runs down his face and into his eyes. It's a horrible death, they say."

"*Stop it. Stop it,*" I cried. "For God's sake, Hugh, I love him. Can't you let him go?"

"Not for God's sake and never for yours. I'd see you dead before I'd ever see you again in the arms of that scum." He started to pace the floor and spoke almost to himself. "I blame Fa. This is what comes from mixing the classes. I should have killed the bastard years ago, when I had the opportunity."

I wondered if he was referring to their boyhood fight, and I wanted to remind him that it was Avery who had won it, but we had gone beyond bickering. Avery's very life was at stake now, for I had no doubt that Hugh would follow through with his threats unless we could reach a compromise.

"Hugh," I pleaded. "Don't turn Avery in. I beg of you. I swear, I'll never see him again if that's what you want."

93

He almost smiled. "Aye, that's what I want, and just so you won't change your mind, I want you to tell Gavan you accept his proposal. Reverend Wharton can perform the ceremony here next week. After all, we're still in mourning for Fa, so it would hardly be appropriate to be making a big fuss of it."

I gasped. Marry Gavan next week!

He was looking at me with determination. "Write Gavan a letter tonight and I'll have a servant deliver it to Bonnie Brae in the morning." He opened the door and held it for me. Nodding his head toward the library, he said, "I'll wait here while you write the letter." He looked me in the eye then and added, "Don't think you can better me in this, Elly. The servants know you're not to leave the house, and I've given that simple-minded groom instructions not to let you ride until I rescind the order."

So, I was to be a prisoner at Glengarra, I thought. And even if I could manage to escape, what good would it do? Before I could warn Avery, Hugh would have him captured. Ah, my poor love, I could not bear it if you were to lose your life because of me. I have no choice, I decided. If I am to save Avery, it will have to be on Hugh's terms.

With my back straight and my head held high I strode past my brother and walked into the library. In a matter of seconds I had sealed my fate along with the letter I had written, consenting to Gavan Mitchell's proposal. All too soon I would be Lady Mitchell, mistress of the infamous Castle Bonnie Brae, and wife of its equally infamous master.

My mother's wedding gown of candlelight satin had to be altered slightly to fit me. "She must have been very dainty," I said, sucking in my breath as Madame fastened me into it.

"She looked like a Dresden doll," Lady Fitzgerald said. "Ah, I remember her well, and dear Celia too."

Lady Fitzgerald had accompanied me to Belfast for a fitting with Madame Duprès, and clucking like a mother hen, she voiced her approval as Madame fussed over the gown.

"You favor your mother, Elly," she said. "But hers was a delicate beauty, almost ethereal, while you have the glow of health about you and a vibrancy that poor Laura lacked." A wistful look crossed her face. "Ah, 'tis a pity that Celia couldn't be here to see you today. You are a vision of loveliness, my dear, and Gavan Mitchell is certainly a lucky young man."

"Thank you, Lady Fitzgerald," I said. "I do appreciate all your help."

"Nonsense, Elly. It is a pleasure for me." She frowned slightly. "You're probably the only bride I'll ever assist. Those doltish sons of mine will never present me with a daughter-in-law, though I had hoped Alex or Clyde might win you over, Elly." She waved a plump hand. "Too slow, the pair of them. Let Gavan Mitchell steal you right out from under their noses, they did."

Aye, I thought bitterly. The Mitchells are good at stealing and every other kind of black deed, but I am more a bartered bride than a stolen one, and I couldn't help wondering if Gavan was aware of that fact.

Surely, since I had rebuffed his advances, he would think it strange that I would suddenly change my mind. Or was his ego so monumental that he honestly believed I could not resist him? The thought infuriated me.

"Lady Mitchell, please, stand still!" Madame admonished me.

"I'm not Lady Mitchell yet," I retorted.

"Ah, but you will be very soon, *chérie*," Madame crooned.

Lady Fitzgerald smiled and bobbed her head. "The

95

days do drag when you're in love. I remember my own nuptials. Too elaborate," she clucked. "We were months preparing for it." She giggled like a young girl. "Lord Fitzgerald wanted us to elope. My mother will have a fit, I said. Of course, we didn't. It would have been scandalous." She looked at me and smiled. "So you see, Elly, you're lucky. You've had a very short engagement."

I smiled woodenly and wondered what she would say if I told her the truth.

"Short engagements are romantic," Madame said. "I met Philippe one week and married him the next."

Lady Fitzgerald looked astonished. "How extraordinary!" she exclaimed.

Madame rolled her eyes. "*Oui.* Not knowing a husband very well makes for an exciting marriage, *n'est-ce pas?*" She looked at me and winked.

I blushed, and Lady Fitzgerald must have decided that this line of conversation had gone far enough and swiftly changed the subject. "How are the renovations to the castle coming along, Elly? I hear it's going to be a showplace."

"Fine," I answered.

"Is Sir Gavan opening up the west wing?" Madame asked slyly.

I nodded and shivered slightly as Bridget's frantic face flashed before my eyes. I heard her voice again, pleading with me. *It's something about a curse. Please, Mistress, don't let Sir Gavan open up the west wing. Starice is a witch and she knows . . .*

Dear God, I thought. What am I letting myself in for? The Mitchells and Bonnie Brae have been gossiped about for a century. Surely there must be some truth to the rumors.

I looked at Lady Fitzgerald and Madame Duprès, who were both staring at me with strange expressions on their faces. They know, I thought. They're just too polite to say so.

It was a small wedding. "Out of respect for our late father," I overheard Hugh tell the Fitzgeralds.

You conniver, I thought. If you had any respect for our father, you'd not be forcing me to marry into a family he despised!

"Ella Victoria Kincaid, do you take Gavan Tyrone Mitchell to be your lawful husband?" Reverend Wharton's deep voice sounded majestic. A hush settled over Glengarra's flower-bedecked drawing room, and all eyes turned to me as I dutifully made my responses in a small, unsteady voice.

It's done, I thought. I've promised to love, honor, and obey this man for the rest of my life.

I heard Gavan's voice as if from a great distance and then I felt his hand, warm on my cold one, placing the ring on my finger.

"I now pronounce you man and wife," Reverend Wharton said.

My veil was lifted and I looked up into the dark, unfathomable eyes of my husband. His lips brushed mine very gently, and then Hugh interrupted the moment of privacy by slapping Gavan on the back and exclaiming heartily, "Congratulations, old man. Now we're brothers-in-law."

Still smiling broadly, my brother turned to me and embraced me heartily. His kiss landed on my cheek as I quickly turned my head. A wounded look flashed momentarily across his face and then he laughed loudly and said something to Clyde Fitzgerald.

Lady Fitzgerald engulfed me in her arms, and I clung to her, feeling at that moment an aching need for my mother or Aunt Celia. "Don't forsake me," I whispered as she released me.

She looked at me with genuine concern, and then her plump face broke into an indulgent smile and she whispered in my ear, "All brides feel as you do, Elly. It's a little scary to be leaving your home and family." Then she turned to Gavan, who stood beside me. "You're a lucky young man, Sir Gavan, but I'm sure you already know that."

"I do indeed, Lady Fitzgerald," he answered stiffly.

Not at all put off by his aloofness, she tapped him coquettishly with her fan. "We'll leave you newlyweds to yourselves for a month, but after that we'll be expecting to see you at Strangford Manor. There's one party after another during the hunting season, and Lord Fitzgerald and I will be devastated if you don't accept every one of our invitations."

That settled, Lady Fitzgerald fluttered away like a big, colorful butterfly in her rose and black silk. Gavan winked at me and said in an undertone, "Married not quite five minutes, and already I've received my first invitation to Strangford Manor. I must say, Lady Mitchell, you've wrapped me in a cloak of respectability!"

Hugh proposed a toast to the bride and groom, and I looked at my glass of champagne and thought how quickly bubbles burst and we are left with the taste of vinegar on our tongues.

Gavan placed his hand possessively on my waist. "We have a long ride ahead of us, Elly."

"I'll change now," I said, and slipped away.

Chapter Six

"Wake up, Elly. We're almost home."

Home! The word penetrated my sleep-drugged brain, and I smiled in anticipation of the familiar warmth and beauty of Glengarra.

The gentle rocking motion of the carriage dulled my senses, and I almost slipped back again into the world of slumber, but a vague, discordant note jogged my memory, and I opened my eyes.

The figure of a man, barely discernible in the darkness, loomed over me, and I must have gasped, for he said, "Shh," in a low voice.

I moved to sit up, and discovered to my surprise that the man was Gavan, and that I was lying across his lap, cradled in his arms.

"Did you have a bad dream?" he asked.

Confused, I thought myself still in the dream, for why else would I be lying in Gavan Mitchell's arms?

"Home?" I repeated dully, sitting up and looking out the window into total darkness.

"Up there, at the top of the hill."

Peering out again, I came fully and suddenly awake, for rising up in the distance, and silhouetted against the moonlit sky, was not Glengarra, but Bonnie Brae!

As we drew closer, I could see the eerie glow of candles flickering in the windows, and I faced reality with a shudder. This was now my home!

I turned and looked at the man beside me. His face in the shadows held a sinister look, and I drew away.

"Don't be shy now, lass. We're married, all proper

and legal," he said, drawing me back into the circle of his arm. His lips brushed my ear, and he whispered, "Don't resist me, Elly. I've dreamed of this night. Relax, forget all your scruples, and just trust me."

I felt myself falling under his spell again as my body grew limp and I leaned back against him.

The carriage gave a sudden jolt and stopped. I was blinded by a bright light, and Gavan cursed. "That damn idiot. Stand back with that lamp," he shouted to the lad who stood outside the carriage.

The door was opened and a hand reached in to help me out. Gavan followed, continuing to berate the lad. "Hold that lamp high. Do you want to blind me?"

At Gavan's command the lad raised the lantern above his head and lighted our way up the stone steps. The door miraculously opened for us and we entered the west wing's great hall.

Behind the massive door stood the bent figure of Starice. The old woman cackled and stared up at me with mocking eyes. "Welcome home, Lady Mitchell."

She was uglier than I had remembered, and her smile turned my blood to ice. Our eyes momentarily locked, and instantly I knew she was challenging me to usurp her place here in this house. I stiffened and in my best lady-of-the-manor voice answered her. "Thank you, Starice."

Gavan spoke to her gruffly. "We'll be needing supper sent upstairs. Has the cook something prepared?"

"Begging your pardon, Sir Gavan. There's a gentleman in your study. He said he has important business to discuss."

He glared at her with impatience. "Have you no sense at all? I don't want to be bothered with anyone tonight."

"He wouldn't leave, Sir Gavan, he . . ."

"Oh, all right."

He turned then to me. "I'm sorry, Elly. Starice will

show you upstairs. I promise I won't be long." He kissed me lightly on the forehead. Then he cupped my chin in his hand and looked into my eyes. "Remember what I told you in the carriage." My cheeks burned at the memory, and he smiled wickedly.

I followed the deformed figure of Starice slowly up the winding staircase. Surely I must be possessed, I thought, for though part of me wanted to flee this house, and this man, another part of me wanted to stay and allow myself to be swallowed up in his spell.

I made no effort to speak to Starice, and she, too, was silent. The old woman had declared herself my enemy, of that I was certain, but for the moment she was the least of my worries.

She opened a door at the top of the stairs and stepped back to let me enter. The furnishings from the room I had occupied on my last visit had been moved here, and it gave me a welcome feeling of familiarity.

"You may leave now, but please bring the supper up in half an hour," I told her.

Her lips scarcely moved, and it wasn't until after she had shut the door that I realized what she had said. "I be here long after ye're gone too."

The young lad who had held the torch brought up my portmanteau and I opened it and took out the white satin nightgown and chiffon peignoir that Madame Duprès had designed for me.

I decided to undress now, before Gavan came upstairs, and hastily I removed my traveling suit and boots. I would have to do something about the servant situation here immediately, I decided as I struggled to get out of my clothes.

Haste and nervousness turned my fingers to butter, and I thought how I would love to bring Megan here as my personal maid, but I knew she would never come to Bonnie Brae.

I slipped the dainty, lace-trimmed gown over my

head, and its smoothness felt sensuous against my bare skin. Trying to keep my mind blank, I reached up with shaking hands and pulled the pins out of my hair. It tumbled down my back in wild disarray, and looking in the mirror, I blushed, remembering Madame Duprès's words—*Not knowing a husband very well makes for an exciting marriage,* n'est-ce pas?

Feeling suddenly modest, I reached for the peignoir. It was an exquisite creation of whisper-soft chiffon gathered onto a yoke of embroidered satin. I buttoned it all the way up the high neck and started nervously pacing the floor. My innocence was confounded by distrust, for I was convinced that Gavan was not a moral man.

Furthermore, I didn't even know what was considered moral between a husband and wife. Aunt Celia had told me very little, but I had gathered from her embarrassed and confusing talk with me that all would be fine when I fell in love and married a gentle, considerate man like my uncle.

But Gavan is neither gentle nor considerate, I told myself, and while he may be the man I married, he is certainly not the man I fell in love with.

The loud knock on the door made me jump, and I said sharply, "Come in."

Expecting to see Gavan, I was startled to see Starice. She stood framed in the doorway, her hideously twisted body jerking with excitement. "Sir Gavan has been shot!" she shouted.

I ran to the door, the voluminous folds of my dressing gown billowing out behind me. The old crone stood rooted to the spot, blocking my path. Her face was contorted in an expression of absolute terror as she stared up at me. Thinking she was having some sort of fit, I grabbed her by the shoulders. "Tell me where he is," I demanded.

She muttered something unintelligible, and I shoved

her aside and ran down the stairs. Catching a glimpse of myself in the hall mirror, I thought I knew why Starice had acted so terrified when she saw me, but I had more important things on my mind at the moment.

Following the sound of voices, I hurried down the corridor to find utter pandemonium, as servants, more than I dreamed Bonnie Brae possessed, milled around, wringing their hands outside their master's study.

Over the din I could distinctly hear Gavan, and a feeling of relief washed over me. He was alive, and not too seriously hurt, I wagered from the tone and timbre of his voice. "Get that bloody chair over here, you fool. All right now, grab my arms, but don't touch the damn leg!"

I entered the room and saw that Gavan was being assisted into a chair by two burly servants, probably stable hands. His left leg was stretched out stiffly before him and an ugly circle of blood stained his dove-gray trousers.

His face was bathed in sweat and contorted in pain. I knelt down beside him. "Oh, Gavan," I said, "whatever has happened?"

He looked at me with surprise and annoyance. "Elly, this is no place for you. It's nothing, just a flesh wound."

"But why? Who?"

His dark eyes looked murderous, and he muttered more to himself than to me, "That bastard! I'll see him swing for this." Then he waved his hand impatiently. "Just a disgruntled squire, Elly. Sold his land to me, now he wants it back.

I looked up at the two rough-looking men who stood nearby. "Has a doctor . . ."

Gavan cut me off and spoke sharply. "Aye. Everything's been done that needs to be done. Now, for God's sake, go back to your room, Elly. I don't want you here."

His hands were clenched into fists, and I gathered he was in great pain, but I still saw no need for him to address me in such a manner before the servants. I stood up, suddenly embarrassed to be seen in my night-clothes, my feet bare and my hair streaming down my back.

It was obvious he considered me dismissed, and without further ado, he bellowed commands to the servants. "Have a bed brought in. I'll sleep here tonight. You, there, pour me a glass of whiskey . . ."

As I left the room, I passed Starice. Her small beady eyes gleamed maliciously at me, and a faint smile of triumph creased her thin lips.

Once in my room, with the door closed, I dissolved into tears. All the frustrations and heartaches of the day crowded in on me, reaching a climax with this latest terrifying development.

Someone had hated Gavan so much that he had tried to kill him. Again I wondered what sort of man I had married. Still smarting from my humiliation downstairs, I was not overly eager to find excuses for him.

Turning down the lamp, I got into bed, but sleep would not come. What if the bullet had found its mark? The thought startled and upset me. Would I have considered myself a captive bride rescued by fate, or a widow who lost the chance to be a wife? Relief or regret? Which emotion would I be feeling at this moment if . . . I buried my head in the pillow and refused to think about it.

A new day had dawned when next I woke, and I met it with determination. Like it or not, I was mistress of this castle, and I would be treated as such. I would demand respect, both from Gavan and that old witch downstairs.

Once my social-climbing husband had indicated to

me that he wanted a gracious home. Well, he will have one, I thought, but on my terms!

I rang for a servant, and presently a skinny, mouse-faced lass appeared. "You be needin' somethin', Lady Mitchell?" she whined.

Her manner and appearance did little to put me in a charitable mood, and I looked at her with annoyance, taking in the grubby hands and mop of tangled hair, which I'd wager was inhabited. "What is your name?" I asked.

"Megan, Mistress."

For a moment, I was speechless. What an insult to the efficient Megan of Glengarra, I thought. "A lovely name," I said tartly. "And one that will require some living up to. My maid at Glengarra was also named Megan."

Her dull eyes registered nothing, and she nodded her head stupidly.

"I want you to bring me hot water and clean towels," I said. "And, Megan—do you live in the village?"

"Aye, Lady Mitchell."

"Good. Then after you bring the hot water, I want you to go home and scrub yourself clean. I want you to wash your hair and brush it. Then you may come back to Bonnie Brae."

"But Starice . . ."

"I will speak to Starice."

"Aye, Lady Mitchell."

She returned after a considerable time, and I dispatched her home with a stern admonition not to return unless she had followed my instructions.

I washed quickly and dressed, choosing a plum-colored gown with a high neck and long sleeves. Braiding my heavy long hair, I coiled it at the nape of my neck. Wisps of curls managed to escape, though, to frame my face and soften the effect. At least I don't look like a debutante, I thought, feeling the need to appear older than my eighteen years. Silently begging help from my mother and Aunt Celia, I set out to accomplish the task that lay ahead of me.

Slowly and with dignity I walked downstairs. Though I was aching to know Gavan's condition, pride made me cautious of another rebuff. A flesh wound, I'd heard, was not a serious thing, and more than likely he was feeling much better this morning. I hope his disposition has improved as well, I thought.

I remembered that the dining room was located at the south end of the entrance hall. It was a small room compared to the huge dining hall of the east wing and more suitable for everyday use.

When I had last seen it about a month before, the ceiling was in the process of being plastered and the walls had been covered over with dustcloths. Gavan had told me the room was now complete, even to the furniture, which he said had arrived only this past week.

He had seemed particularly proud of the room, and I was curious to see it. I would eat my breakfast, I decided, and then seek out my ill-tempered husband.

I entered the room, and my breath caught in my throat! A huge mural covered one whole wall, and my eyes blurred as I gazed at it, for the scene that stretched before me in all its grandeur was one I remembered well—that first breathtaking view of Glengarra as seen from the top of the hill. Spellbound, I continued to stare at the painting. It was so real that I felt if I could step inside and walk up the winding path, I would be home again.

Overcome with emotion, I sat down and tried to collect my thoughts. He had meant it as a surprise, for I recalled the dustcloths that had concealed this very wall on my last visit. I was deeply touched, and vaguely puzzled. What an enigma he is! I mused.

My eyes traveled around the rest of the room, which

had been beautifully done. The tapestry on the other long wall had been cleaned, and its vibrant colors of ruby, sapphire, and emerald glowed like jewels. The chairs were covered in crimson velvet, and a handsome Persian rug in red, gold, and blue covered the floor. An unusual and magnificent chandelier in crystal and rose-quartz glittered above the dark Hepplewhite table.

My gaze returned to the mural, and I feasted my eyes upon it. Making a hasty decision, I pulled the bell cord, and when a servant appeared, I said, "You may serve breakfast in Sir Gavan's study. I'll eat there with him."

Threading my way through a maze of corridors, I located the study, and was relieved to see that the door was open and Gavan was alone. He lay propped up on a cot in the middle of the room, looking miserable and unapproachable, like a great, wounded lion.

I stood in the doorway and called softly, "May I come in?"

"Please do."

I pulled up a chair and sat down beside him. "Are you feeling better this morning?"

"Not much," he said, and shrugged, dismissing the subject. "At any rate, I must apologize for my ungentlemanly behavior last night." His old arrogance suddenly returned, and he smiled briefly. "But then, I'm no gentleman, as you so well know."

I said, "Gavan, I saw the mural. It's perfectly beautiful, and I want to thank you for it."

His sullen, dark eyes measured me. "Then do it properly," he said.

A little taken aback by his challenge, I leaned forward timidly and brushed his lips with mine. Instantly I felt his strong fingers on the back of my neck, and he returned the kiss, parting my lips and searing them with a hot flame that streaked through my body. His fingers twisted in my hair, pulling out the heavy pins that held it in place.

"Beggin' yere pardon, Sir Gavan."

The shrill voice exploded in my brain like the screech of an owl, and I jerked back, freeing myself from his embrace.

Starice stood in the doorway and behind her stood an elderly, bespectacled man wearing a faint smile of benign amusement. "The doctor has arrived," she announced.

My face scarlet, I reached up with frantic hands to wind my hair back into its knot. Gavan, however, only appeared annoyed that the doctor was late. "It's about time. I could be dead by now."

"Horses doon't have wings, you know," he replied with a genial smile, and approaching the bed, he began with calm deliberation to open his bulging medical kit.

Suddenly recalling my presence, Gavan said to the doctor, "This is Lady Mitchell." Then he turned with a half smile to me. "Dr. McTavish. His horses are older than he is."

Dr. McTavish took my hand. "I'm honored, Lady Mitchell." Then he patted it in a consoling manner. "All will be fine. Your husband's strong as a bull and twice as stubborn."

Gavan cut in gruffly. "Let's get on with it, then." Turning to me, he spoke in a gentler tone. "You may go now, Elly, but send Starice in."

Dr. McTavish concurred. "It's best that you not be here, Lady Mitchell. I'll have to remove the bullet. The servant can help, and I'll see you on my way out."

I almost collided in the corridor with the maid bearing our breakfast tray. "Never mind now," I said. "The doctor is with Sir Gavan. You may leave the tray on the dining room table, but go fetch Starice first. The doctor will be needing her help."

I returned to the dining room, and when the servant

brought the tray, I picked halfheartedly at the lukewarm food. I should have been hungry, but my appetite had disappeared along with my brave resolutions.

Looking longingly at the mural, I ached for Glengarra and the carefree life I had known there. Bonnie Brae is steeped in evil, and will never rise above its bizarre past, I told myself.

Feeling as if I had been dropped down into an alien world, I wondered if I would ever be able to cope with Bonnie Brae's strange inhabitants and their twisted personalities.

In an avalanche of self-pity I wept for myself, and for all those I had loved and lost; my beloved Avery, my family, including Hugh, for I considered him no longer my brother.

I pushed the plate of uneaten food aside and decided to go back to the study. I had no idea how long such an operation would take, but the doctor had not seemed unduly alarmed, and Gavan's condition had certainly not affected his strength or carnal desire.

The door was closed, and I stood outside and paced the floor.

"It's all over now" I heard Dr. McTavish say, and I stood still, my heart pounding with sudden fear.

Then I heard Gavan's voice, and a feeling of relief washed over me. "It's out?"

"Aye, it's out, lad. You rest quietly now."

"The hell you shay." Gavan slurred his words drunkenly, and I leaned close to the door and listened. "I've just taken me a wife, you old fool. I don't want to rest; I want me a wedding night!"

"Aye, so I saw when I came in the door, but you let your bride be, laddie, till that leg heals. You're young and hot-blooded, but I doon't think ye want to be walking with a limp for the rest of your days."

The door was suddenly opened and Starice came out, carrying a basin filled with bloody water. I averted my eyes, but not before I saw the sickening smile that crossed her face.

Dr. McTavish came immediately behind her, and when he saw me, he said, "I wouldn't go in yet, Lady Mitchell. I've given him a strong dose of laudanum and he's a little out of his head. He'll drop off to sleep in a few minutes."

"Is he going to be all right?" I asked nervously.

"Aye, if he follows instructions." He shook his head and regarded me gravely. "The bullet struck a bone and he must remain immobile and in the splint I've fashioned for at least six weeks. If he moves the leg, the bone will separate and he could be crippled for life." He smiled at me in a fatherly way. "But I know you'll not let that happen, Lady Mitchell. Then he chuckled to himself. "You'll have your hands full with him, I'm afraid, but I'll be back tomorrow to lay the law down to him, I will."

After Dr. McTavish left, I returned to the study. I drew up a chair and sat down, intending to keep a vigil at Gavan's bedside. I had heard lurid tales about laudanum. A woman in London had jumped out the window after dosing herself with it. Granted, I thought, that story was more or less idle gossip. Nevertheless, I didn't want Gavan to thrash around and injure his leg again.

At that moment he stirred and flung the blanket back, exposing a broad, naked chest and powerful arms. I had never seen a half-naked man before, and I could not tear my eyes away. I wanted to reach down and touch the silky coal-black hair that started at the base of his throat, fanned out over his chest, and feathered down in a thin line to his navel.

How would it feel, I fantasized, to have that hard, bare chest pressed up against my own naked breasts? Then the thought struck me that he might be completely naked, and I quickly pulled the covers up to his chin and sat back down in the chair, twisting my hands in my lap.

That I should even entertain such licentious thoughts shocked me and made me wonder what was happening to me!

"Bastard," he muttered, and I jumped and looked quickly at him. His eyes were closed, but his face was contorted in an ugly scowl. "I'll see you in hell before I'll give that land back," he said.

He's reliving yesterday, I thought, and I watched as he moaned and twisted his head.

Suddenly he opened drug-crazed eyes and stared directly at me. "Shut up, you old witch," he shouted. Raising himself up on one elbow, he stared past me, his eyes blank. "Curses be damned. I'm master now and I'm opening up the west wing."

He was extremely agitated, and I knew he was back in the past, speaking to someone else. "Hush," I said, gently pushing him back on the pillow.

His eyes met mine and I recoiled in fear from what I saw there. "The past is done. You breathe one word," he said menacingly, "and I'll have you flogged the way my father did!"

He grew quiet then, and shaking uncontrollably, I collapsed in the chair. What did it all mean? Frantically I tried to recall his exact words. He had been speaking to Starice, of that I was certain. There had been something about a curse, and apparently she hadn't wanted him to open up the west wing. His threat chilled me. He would flog her, he said, and his father had done the same. Dear God, Papa was right. The Mitchells are fiends!

I slept fitfully that night, trying to keep my imagination from running wild over the mysteries surrounding Bonnie Brae. I awoke with a throbbing headache and a yearning for a hot tub to calm my nerves and soothe my aching muscles.

I rang for a servant and proceeded to wait, and then wait some more, until I became so agitated I cried from frustration. My nerves were as tightly laced as a dowager's corset, and I wondered crazily if Starice might be behind this new humiliation. *Bonnie Brae and all in it are conspiring to drive me insane,* I thought, pulling off my nightgown and dressing myself without the benefit of a wash, much less a bath!

My confrontation with Starice was equally frustrating. Megan had left, she informed me, and intimated it was somehow my fault.

"I informed Sir Gavan this mornin' we'd be shorthanded, now that Megan's gone. Yere ladyship found fault with the lass, I told him, but help's not easy to come by at Bonnie Brae."

"From now on I'll engage the staff," I told her. "Furthermore, I want you to call all the servants together in the dining room at ten this morning. I shall acquaint them with rules and regulations which will henceforth be followed to the letter in this house."

Her evil old face twisted with suppressed rage, and I met her eyes without flinching. "As ye say, Lady Mitchell," she spat out, and slithered away, leaving me shaken but unbowed.

I ate a hasty breakfast and then paid a call on Gavan. I hoped the laudanum had worn off, for I didn't think I could stand to hear any more disturbing revelations.

I entered the room to find him sitting up in bed, and I noticed with relief, as I approached him, that he wore a burgundy robe, and that his eyes were clear, and he appeared rational.

"Good morning," he said, regarding me with obvious pleasure.

"You look a hundred percent better than you did last night," I said, giving him an encouraging smile.

He frowned. "You saw me last night?"

"I sat up with you until a servant relieved me."

"Whatever for?" he snapped. "I'm no invalid and won't be treated like one."

His ill humor bounced back to me and I caught it with ease. I have already had a confrontation with one devil this morning, I thought. I'll not be taking on another! "As you wish," I said sarcastically. "Believe me, it won't happen again." I turned and started to walk away, but he reached out and caught my arm. "Let me go," I said, tears welling up in my eyes.

"No, not until you accept my apology."

"I accept it," I said wearily, brushing the tears quickly away before I faced him.

He shook his head. "I'm sorry, Elly. This is so far from what I planned." He stammered. "It's just, it's just . . . Never mind, it's over now. I feel fine, and when that old fool of a doctor comes, I'll dance a jig around him." He smiled. "I'll be up and good as new by tomorrow, and our honeymoon can finally begin."

Oh, my God, I thought. He doesn't know. He thinks he's going to be up and around tomorrow, and the doctor's going to tell him it'll be six more weeks before he can get out of that bed.

"Gavan," I said, quickly changing the subject and deviously seeking his approval while he was in a good mood. "I would like your support in my dealings with the servants."

He gave me a disinterested look. "Starice mentioned something this morning about that." He raised an eyebrow and looked at me with amusement. "She said you gave one of them a severe tongue-lashing and the wench quit." His eyes mocked me. "Didn't you tell me once that servants should be treated with patience?"

I fumed but refused to justify myself in his eyes. "If you believe Starice, that's immaterial to me, and if you're satisfied with the caliber of servants she's been recruiting, then it's useless to go on with this conversation."

113

He laughed. "What a little spitfire you are, Elly! Lord, no, I'm not at all satisfied with the servants in this house, and if you can make improvements, you have my blessing and my gratitude." A guarded look crossed his face then, and he said, "I wouldn't fire them until you get replacements though. The villagers are very superstitious and they have some silly notions about Bonnie Brae."

"Very well," I said, "but I don't anticipate a problem. I thought I'd enlist Lady Fitzgerald's help. Her staff may be able to recommend some of their friends in Belfast. We don't need to depend on the villagers."

He said, "Fine. That sounds like an excellent idea. The less I see of the villagers, the better."

I glanced quickly at the mantel clock. "I've called a meeting of the household staff for ten, so I'd better be on my way."

He reached for my hand and pulled me toward him. "Aren't you going to kiss your husband good-bye?"

I leaned down and kissed him lightly, and this time he released me with a smile. "Tomorrow I'll show you how to do better."

I heard Dr. McTavish's voice and made a hasty retreat before he should see me. I had no intention of being present when Gavan received the doctor's ultimatum.

Chapter Seven

As expected, Gavan did not take the doctor's warning with good grace. He did take it seriously though, for his male vanity would not allow him to do otherwise.

"I gave your husband my prognosis, Lady Mitchell," Dr. McTavish told me. "And I doon't think you need to worry now." He smiled slightly. "Sir Gavan's a fine specimen of a man, and proud of it, too. He'll not be taking any chances walking with a limp."

Then the old doctor's bright blue eyes crinkled, and he shook his head. "When you're young, six weeks seems an eternity, but like I told your husband, lass, it'll all be over before you know it." Taking my hand, he patted it reassuringly. "Too bad this had to happen, and on your honeymoon, too, but you young people have another fifty years to make up for it."

He took his leave then with a smile and a promise. "I'll check on Sir Gavan again in a couple of weeks."

A feeling of panic overwhelmed me. This pudgy, down-to-earth little man was the only sane person I had encountered since coming to Bonnie Brae, and now he was leaving me. For two long weeks I would be left alone in this dismal house to cope with an ill-tempered husband and a demented old woman.

Feeling abandoned, I stood watch at the window until the good doctor's buggy was swallowed up in the mists that seemed to hover perpetually over Bonnie Brae.

In the days that followed, I devoted myself exclusively to my husband. I read poetry to him, played cards with him, and ate my meals with him in his makeshift bedroom. My efforts, however, did little to improve his disposition, and I found it hard to overlook his boorish behavior.

"That's enough for tonight," he said irritably, throwing down his cards in the middle of our game. "You don't have to keep trying to amuse me, Elly."

I tried to remain calm. "I'm not trying to amuse you, Gavan. I'm trying to find mutual interests. We hardly know each other. Games and books that are shared can—"

He interrupted me impatiently. "Christ, once this bloody leg's healed, I'll have no need for parlor games or lovesick poetry. I'm a man of action, Elly. I like games that involve some danger, and as for making love—I'd rather do it than read a damn poem about it!"

"Good night," I said sharply, picking up the cards and flouncing out of the room.

As I turned the corner of the corridor, I heard him bellowing for Starice. "Get in here, you old witch. I need the damn bottle."

I retreated to my room and slammed the door, my chest heaving with indignation. Pacing the floor, I mentally denounced Gavan Mitchell with every step. Impossible, ill-mannered, ill-bred . . . Oh, I couldn't think of enough bad words to describe him!

I picked up my hairbrush, raised it above my head, and then paused. Why was I letting this man get the best of me? I lowered the brush slowly and gently applied it to my hair, letting its stiff bristles massage my scalp and ease my frazzled nerves with every methodical stroke.

From now on, I decided, he can take out his frustrations on himself. No longer shall I play the part of the attentive little wife.

But what shall I do with myself, I wondered. I could ride, I thought, but the weather had been miserable lately.

Suddenly a very intriguing thought popped into my head. As mistress of this monstrous castle, haven't I the right to explore it? I need to give it a thorough inspection anyhow if I'm to train new servants.

The more I thought about it, the more excited I became. I'll go from top to bottom and wing to wing. I'll cover every inch of this infamous castle, I told myself. And if there are secrets here, perhaps I'll unearth them!

I got ready for bed without assistance. The servant problem was still in limbo, since Gavan's convalescence had necessitated my devoting all of my time to him. Starice, in the meantime, had replaced Megan with another incompetent, and I made as little use of the girl as possible.

I turned down the lamp and got into bed. Hurricanelike winds and a sudden onslaught of rain rattled the old windows like bony fingers knocking, and I shivered, though the night was unseasonably warm for October. Emotionally drained, I paid it no heed, and quickly fell into a deep, dreamless sleep.

Sometime later, a loud clap of thunder made me sit bolt upright in the bed, and I squinted as flashes of lightning blinded me. The casement window blew open, sending the curtains to flutter wildly in the wind, and splashes of rain hit the floor and even sprayed across my bed.

Jumping up, I ran to the window and pulled it shut while splashes of rain stung my face and soaked my thin gown. Wiping my wet hair back with my hand, I turned around—and standing in the corner near my bed stood the apparition!

My blood turned to ice and a scream stuck in my

throat as the vision stretched out her hands and came toward me.

Her lips were moving in silent speech, and the enormous dark eyes stared into mine. Closer and closer she came, as the lightning flashed fiercely on and off, off and on, and then finally I was plunged into total blackness.

Every bone in my body ached in rebellion against the hard, damp floor. There was not even a rug on this side of the bed to act as a cushion. Confused, I stood up and massaged my neck. Why had I been lying on the floor?

Still in the vague world of half-sleep, my thoughts meandered around in my brain. A storm? Aye, I thought. There had been a storm, and the window had blown open, and I had gotten up to close it. . . . I gasped in sudden remembrance—the white gown billowing out behind her, smudged dark eyes in a chalk-white face, and lips that had moved as if she were speaking to me; the apparition!

That had to be a dream, I told myself. There are no thunderstorms in October, and I certainly don't believe in ghosts.

I got up and rang for the maid. This is one morning I'll have a bath with water that's hot, and not tepid, I decided. The new maid was as slow as Megan, but not as dirty, so that was something in her favor. Perhaps she could be trained, I thought, if I ever get the time to do it. "Come in," I called in answer to her knock.

"Good morning, yere ladyship."

Without looking up, I said, "Good morning—" and stopped abruptly. "I'm sorry. I seem to have forgotten your name."

"It's Bridget, yere ladyship. Don't ye remember me?"

118

The cheerful voice was vaguely familiar, and I turned around to find the pleasant, apple-cheeked lass who'd attended me on my earlier visits to Bonnie Brae. "Bridget," I exclaimed with genuine warmth. "I'm happy to see you, but when did you come back? I thought you said . . ."

"I know, yere ladyship. I said I didn't work regular at Bonnie Brae, but as of now I do." Her plump face broke into a smile. "We heard in the village 'bout you and Sir Gavan gettin' married, we did." Then her eyes narrowed, and her face wrinkled with disgust. "We heard about the old one too. How she was hiring the worst sluts she could find for maids, just to make yere ladyship miserable. I says to me mam, says I, 'I don't fancy workin' at Bonnie Brae, but Mistress Kincaid's a real elegant lady, and hearin' this gets me Irish up real good. I gotta mind to go right up there and hire on.'

" 'Go way with ye,' " me mam says. 'You'd live up there with a banshee in the tower and a ghost that appears whenever there's a storm?'

" 'The new Lady Mitchell says there's naught to fear,' says I." Her confidence wavered slightly and she turned trusting eyes to mine. "Ye did say that, didn't ye, Lady Mitchell?"

"Aye, Bridget," I answered, hoping for her sake that I sounded convincing.

"Now, what can I do for ye, yere ladyship? Would ye be wantin' a hot bath?"

"That would be heavenly," I said. And then with a swell of gratitude, "It's good to have you back, Bridget. I've missed you."

She beamed. "Thank ye, Lady Mitchell."

As she turned to leave, I said very casually, "By the way, Bridget, did we have a thunderstorm last night?"

"Did we ever! A bloomin' hurricane, it was too. You must be a sound sleeper, Lady Mitchell." She giggled then, and covered her mouth coyly with her hand.

119

"They say the old one was beside herself. Hid in a broom closet, she did, and wouldn't come out till it was all over."

She curtsied awkwardly and closed the door, and I was left to wonder about last night. Had my imagination again played tricks on me? Perhaps it was the fluttering curtains that I saw, and in my dreamlike state I mistook them for something else.

At any rate, there had been a storm. And Starice is afraid of them, I mused, pondering the implications that presented.

Bridget's proclivity for kitchen gossip didn't seem quite so objectionable to me as before, and my optimism returned. I now have an ally in this house, I told myself, and I will deal with whatever problems confront me.

I spent the better part of the morning carefully inspecting the rooms on this, the second floor of the west wing. The suite I occupied was the only one completely furnished. Selected pieces from the original furnishings had been left in some of the rooms, and I was particularly intrigued by a beautiful, antique gilded desk. Remembering that Gavan's mother had been French, I wondered if it could possibly be one of the rare pieces designed by André de Rochemont.

The French cabinetmaker, along with most of his clientele, had been an unfortunate victim of the Reign of Terror, but his unique creations had been preserved and were now much sought after by collectors.

All this I had gleaned from Aunt Celia, who had been an avid collector. I ran my hand along the underside of the desk, feeling for the artist's identifying mark, and my fingers touched a small, flat button. Startled, I pulled back my hand as a secret compartment popped open. Too excited for caution, I reached into the deep, narrow space and pulled out a sheaf of papers tied together with ribbon.

Sitting on the floor, I eagerly examined my discovery. They were letters, all of them written in French. The paper had yellowed and the ink was faded, but I managed to make out a few words here and there. They were all addressed to Lady Gabrielle Rousseau Mitchell and appeared to be letters to Gavan's mother from her father in France. But why would they be hidden in a secret compartment?

Gathering them up, I tied them again with the faded lavender ribbon and returned them to their hiding place. I would try to read them again when I had more time, I decided. I closed the door and continued with my inspection.

Five large bedrooms, each with adjoining antechambers and dressing rooms, were situated on this floor, and all had been cleaned and freshly painted, waiting only to be carpeted and furnished, which Gavan had informed me would be done as soon as I had approved his selections.

"I want you to be satisfied with everything at Bonnie Brae," he had told me in the carriage after our wedding.

How different he had seemed then! So much so, in fact, that for a brief moment I had become as excited as he, and I had almost believed there might be grounds for some compatibility in our strange marriage. But once in the shadow of Bonnie Brae he had become once more the changeling, as dark and mysterious as the house itself.

I climbed a narrow stairway to the third floor, which I could see had been planned as a nursery. Colorful nursery-rhyme characters bordered the walls of the large, square room at the top of the stairs. Ideal for use as a playroom, I thought, passing through it to four smaller rooms which would nicely serve as children's bedrooms and quarters for a nursemaid.

A mute and striking testimonial to dreams gone awry, I thought sadly as I wandered through empty rooms that had never heard the laughter of children. Would these rooms fare any better with the new master and mistress of Bonnie Brae? Not wanting to dwell on such disturbing thoughts, I put them out of my mind and left the third floor quickly.

Once downstairs, I summoned Starice and requested the keys to every room in the castle. "I'm inspecting the house," I told her, "and I believe some of the rooms in the old section are kept locked. I shall need to inspect them too."

"Them's what are locked are not used, yere ladyship," she answered slyly.

"From now on all the rooms at Bonnie Brae will be used," I retorted, and held out my hand for the keys.

She handed them over reluctantly, looking up at me with narrowed eyes. "Take care, Lady Mitchell," she said, her voice oozing venom. "Them that seeks usually finds."

I took the keys from her clawlike hand and steeled myself not to recoil when fingers cold as death brushed mine.

"Thank you," I said coldly, walking back through the great hall and to the door that separated the west wing from the older part of the castle.

I closed the iron-studded door behind me and stood in the corridor, recalling the night, here in the shadows, when Gavan had assaulted my innocence with passionate kisses that had left me a shaken and not unwilling partner to his lust.

I hurried down the long corridor, making my first stop the study, where the portraits of Gavan's ancestors had peered down on me that night with such disdain.

After several tries I found the proper key, and the door swung slowly open.

I was surprised and a little disappointed to see that the portraits were gone. As I entered the room, the door started to swing shut, and feeling vaguely uneasy, I propped it open with a chair. Even without the portraits the room seemed to be filled with the presence of those two evil-looking men and I wanted to be able to leave quickly whenever I had a mind to.

I took my notebook and pencil out of the pocket of my skirt and glanced around the room, making hurried notations for the servants: "Needs thorough dusting, take up carpet and beat, wash windows, clean drapes."

I wandered aimlessly around the room. There was nothing more for me to do here, and yet for some unknown reason I felt a compulsion to remain. A strong feeling took hold of me, propelling me toward the built-in bookcase, and I stood in a trancelike state, staring at it. Lots of old castles, I knew, held hidden passageways. Ireland's history of sieges and warring factions within had made escape sometimes the better part of valor.

My curiosity aroused, I set to work to satisfy it. I removed all the books from the reachable shelves and knocked sharply against the wall. I stirred up a mountain of dust and mentally added the bookcase to my list of neglected chores, but the wall held firm.

I was about to give up, when the same strong intuitive feeling that had led me to the bookcase made me cautiously run my foot along the baseboard beneath it. I heard a click, and tasted the thrill of discovery as the bookcase swung open and I found myself staring down a long, narrow passageway.

With reckless abandon I stepped inside. I had progressed only a few steps when I was plunged into darkness. With my hands stretched out on either side of me, and touching the walls, I groped my way another several feet. I knew I should turn back, but my curiosity urged me on. For some inexplicable reason I had to know where the passage came out.

I tried not to think that creatures other than myself were in all likelihood occupying this narrow space along with me. To scatter them, and perhaps to break the tomblike silence for my own satisfaction as well, I began to knock on the walls as I moved cautiously forward, going deeper and deeper into the tunnel.

Suddenly my head struck stone, and I groped blindly for the latch that would spring open and release me to the other side, but I was facing a solid brick wall!

A blind alley! Terror such as I had never known before overtook me. My body broke out in a cold sweat and my teeth chattered uncontrollably. I felt myself close to something so diabolically evil that I turned in panic and ran from it.

The stone walls felt slimy to my touch, and I jerked back my hands, refusing to let them guide me as before. I butted into them then, first one side and then the other, and the sharp rocks scratched my shoulders.

I was crying and mumbling out loud, "Dear God, please let the door still be open!"

With burning eyes I peered ahead, frantically searching for that thin shaft of light, and when I saw it, I began to laugh hysterically with relief and gratitude.

Stumbling through the opening, I breathlessly pushed the bookcase back into place and sank to the floor, my legs too weak now to hold me.

I remained there for some time, hugging my knees to my chest, and rocking back and forth like a child who has awakened from a nightmare and can't yet believe she is safe.

Still shaken and a little humbled by my experience, I slipped quietly back to the west wing. I glanced furtively around, and finding no one, I made an unlady-like dash up the stairs and into my room.

Catching sight of my reflection in the full-length mirror, I gasped. A ragamuffin with smudged face and frightened eyes stared back at me. The hem of my gown was black, and one sleeve hung in shreds, with my bare arm showing through it. Thank God, nobody had seen me!

I pulled at the gown with frantic fingers, not even caring that I was ripping it apart in my haste to get it off. I couldn't tolerate having it on another minute. When it lay a heap of rags on the floor, I picked up the pieces and tossed them into the fireplace.

Then I tackled my hair and brushed it until my scalp tingled and I was certain no spiders or other dwellers of that dark hole could have attached themselves to me.

Finally I washed all over with water from the pitcher, and climbed naked into bed.

I was angry with myself, not for entering the passageway—I'd always had an insatiable curiosity and the soul of an explorer, though, I must admit, I should have outgrown such adventures a long time ago—but for the paralyzing terror I had experienced in the passageway. That part I could not understand.

There was no reason for it, and coupled with last night's alarming hallucination, I wondered, are insidious forces at work in this house to undermine my sanity?

Sure, and the game little lass who earned Avery's respect a long time ago would be ashamed of you now, I told myself. I smiled, remembering how I'd jumped impulsively into the sleeping grass and dared him to do likewise. I'd been a daredevil then; I'd not let Bonnie Brae make a coward of me now.

* * *

125

I had my dinner in the dining room alone. Determined to uphold the standards Aunt Celia had imbued in me, I was formally attired in a garnet silk gown and my neck and ears were adorned with rubies, family heirlooms which Gavan had bestowed on me as an engagement gift.

I had not been to visit him, nor did I intend to do so until he requested my presence and apologized. I might then go back to taking my meals with him, but there would be time for little else, as I planned to be extremely busy reorganizing and restaffing Bonnie Brae.

I still had Starice's keys, which I had brought with me, thinking to return them after dinner. When the dessert, a particularly unappetizing-looking pudding, was served, I said to the maid, "Tell Starice I would like to see her, please."

"Starice is in her room, yere ladyship, and she won't come out for nobody, she won't. But the master would like to see you as soon as you're done eating."

"Thank you," I said, pushing the pudding aside. "You may clear the table now, Mary."

Walking down the hall toward my husband's room, I met up with Bridget, who was heading back to the kitchen with a tray full of dirty dishes.

"Good evening, Lady Mitchell. I was after serving Sir Gavan his supper." She lowered her voice and moved closer to me. "They say the old one had a fit today, actin' all loony and scared out of her wits, she was." She rolled her eyes and tapped her head with her index finger. "Touched in the head, she is. Thought she heard somebody knocking on the walls, and that really set her off." She gave a short laugh. "Guess she thought it was Old Nick coming to get her."

I smiled a little patronizingly and said, "Hurry along now, Bridget. Cook will be waiting for those dishes."

She bobbed a curtsy. "Aye, yere ladyship."

I continued on down the corridor, smiling with satisfaction to myself. One small victory for my side, I thought, amused that I had inadvertently turned the tables on old Starice.

"Well, what have we here? A visit from my wife!" Gavan regarded me with a sarcastic smile as I stood in the doorway.

"I believe it was you, sir, who sent for me," I replied coldly as I approached his bed.

"And so I did. What's going on here? Blast it all, Elly. I can't have all the servants quitting on us at one time. Can't you at least try to get along with Starice? She came in here, asking me to retire her!"

"I only asked for her keys," I said angrily. "I wanted to inspect the house. Is that so outrageous? I am mistress here, am I not?"

"Of course you are, but you have to remember, Elly, she's an old woman and she's been in charge of Bonnie Brae for a long time. I'll admit, she's a little crazy," he said, and then added, "Small wonder, being around my father for fifty years."

Suddenly he caught my hand and held it tightly. "Put up with her until I'm on my feet, Elly. Then I promise you, I'll retire her." He released my hand and ran his fingers up my bare arm. "Enough about Starice. Where have you been? I've missed you."

I took a step back. "Missed me? If I remember correctly, you found my card games and poems boring!"

He reached out and pulled me back roughly. "Aye, the card games and the poems were boring, but not you, Elly. Never you!"

"You're hurting me," I said, struggling to free myself.

"Then sit down," he answered, and I had no recourse but to sit beside him on the bed.

He ran his fingers again up my arm and drew circles on my bare shoulder. His touch was as light as a feather, and I felt myself blush, but I did not push him away. "Don't you know what it does to a man to have a beautiful wife so close?" he asked softly. His fingers moved to my upper arm and suddenly tightened. "And me, with my leg strapped to this damn board!" he finished angrily.

I didn't know what to say, so I murmured weakly, "I'm sorry, Gavan."

He smiled. "Not nearly as sorry as I am, and again, I apologize for my bad temper. Will you forgive me again?"

"Of course."

"Good. You look very beautiful tonight," he said gallantly. His eyes strayed to my throat, and he smiled. The rubies become you, and I'm pleased to see you wearing them."

"Thank you," I said. "They're exquisite."

He waved my gratitude away with his hand. "Now, what were you doing all day while I was languishing here in bed?"

"I was exploring the castle."

His expression was a guarded one. "Oh, and did you find any deep, dark secrets?"

I mentally decided not to mention the letters, nor to let him know that I had actually gone through the passageway. "No, but I did find what looked like a secret passageway behind the bookcase in your father's study."

His eyes were hooded. "Really!"

"Did you know about it?" I asked.

"Lots of these old castles have them. They were used as escape hatches." Then he smiled wryly. "I spent as little time as possible in my father's study, or in his company, for that matter."

"Do you know where it leads?" I asked eagerly.

"They all lead outside. That was the purpose of them, but this one was probably sealed when the west wing was added on."

Of course, I thought. A perfectly logical explanation for my so-called mystery.

"I wouldn't go in there," he continued. "Those places are damp and probably crawling with mice and insects."

I shuddered in remembrance. "Ugh!"

He smiled indulgently, confident, I'm sure, that a genteel young lady like myself would never do anything so rash.

"There's a beautiful antique desk upstairs in one of the bedrooms," I said. "It looks French. Did it belong to your mother?"

"I have no idea. My mother left when I was an infant."

"What was her name, Gavan?" I asked innocently.

"Gabrielle Rousseau."

"A lovely name."

"Aye, but one I'm eager to forget, Elly." His face hardened and his eyes narrowed. "After all, she ran away and left me, and with him, too."

We spent the rest of the evening together in rather pleasant conversation. He agreed that I should write to Lady Fitzgerald to apprise her of our situation here, for we would be accepting no social engagements for quite some time, and also to enlist her assistance in addressing the servant problem at Bonnie Brae.

I said good night, and still on his good behavior, he gave me a chaste kiss and squeezed my hand. "I suppose you'll soon be off to Strangford Manor for a few days. Just don't forget to come home."

I promised him I would not, and I retired that night with an easier mind. Things are taking a turn for the better, I thought.

I was looking forward to seeing Lady Fitzgerald, and I felt confident that with her help, the servant problem would soon be solved. It had already improved, I felt, with the arrival of Bridget. And now Gavan had promised to retire Starice! That was more than I had dared hope for, and I snuggled down under the covers, feeling a little less apprehensive than usual.

As I was drifting off to sleep, a nagging thought suddenly surfaced in my mind like a shark on a tranquil sea. If the passageway stopped at the west wing, how had Starice heard me knocking on the walls?

Chapter Eight

Lady Fitzgerald handed me a cup of tea. "You poor child! Who would have thought such a thing could happen?" She shook her head, and the corkscrew curls at the sides of her face danced with indignation. "Lord Fitzgerald says Ireland's in the clutches of barbarians. Why, these agrarian societies are just running amok!"

"Lady Fitzgerald, the man who shot Gavan was another landholder," I said, but my words went in one diamond-studded ear and out the other. In Lady Fitzgerald's eyes, secret societies were at the bottom of everything bad that happened in Ireland. "At any rate," I added. "Gavan's much better and the doctor promises him he'll be up and around in another couple of weeks."

"Thank heaven for that." She took a sip of her tea, and jumped immediately into the next subject. "Now, as to your servant problem, consider it settled."

Lady Fitzgerald leaned forward and lowered her voice like a conspirator. "I've discovered a wonderful little woman in Belfast by the name of Maire McGee. Mistress McGee will do all your recruiting for you, Elly, and you can be confident, she'll send you a well-trained staff." She chuckled with self-satisfaction and tapped a finger to her lips. "Mum's the word though, Elly. We wouldn't want everybody to know about Mistress McGee."

We arrived in Belfast that afternoon, and seeing the city again filled me with sadness. I thought of the naive girl who had arrived here once with a head full of romantic dreams and how quickly they had been shattered.

"There's *The Herald*'s old office," Lady Fitzgerald said, and looking, I saw that the windows had been boarded up and hate-mongers had scribbled crude messages across them. I turned my head away in disgust.

We turned down one of the side streets and stopped in front of a modest cottage.

"Here we are, Elly dear. Now your troubles will soon be over," Lady Fitzgerald chirped.

Would that all my troubles could be as easily settled, I thought, as an hour later we returned to the carriage with Mistress McGee's assurance that a full staff would be dispatched to Bonnie Brae in two weeks.

"What a miracle worker you are!" I exclaimed as we settled ourselves into the carriage. "I don't know how I would manage without you."

She reached over and squeezed my hand. "Nonsense, Elly. You're the daughter I never had. It's been my pleasure, and I want you to know you can always count on me."

I wished at that moment that I could confide in this warm, motherly woman. But how could I tell the aristocratic Lady Fitzgerald that I loved a Fenian? And what would this prim and proper lady say if I were to add that my husband was a devil who could arouse in me shameful visions of tantalizingly erotic delights.

She cleared her throat, and I suddenly realized that I had been lost in my thoughts. "I'm sorry, Lady Fitzgerald, I was . . ."

"Thinking about that husband of yours, I know, Elly." She tittered behind her gloved hand. "I was a young bride myself once. Absence makes the heart grow fonder though," she added with a smile. "And you two lovebirds will be kissing and cooing again tomorrow."

Oh, Lord, I thought. If she only knew!

We did a little shopping, and then made haste to return to Stangford Manor in time to take a short rest before dinner.

"You'll love our dinner guests this evening," Lady Fitzgerald said to me on the way home. "Lord and Lady Cunningham are absolutely charming. He's the fifth Earl of Dunsmore, and his wife, Lady Cunningham is the daughter of the late Sir John Wickford. It was before your time, of course, my dear, but Sir John was a rather famous London architect, and his daughter is a veritable authority on castles."

We gathered before dinner in Strangford Manor's comfortable drawing room with its restful decor of gold and blue. Alex, Clyde, and two of their older brothers, whose names I frantically tried to recall, were present, along with Lord and Lady Fitzgerald, who introduced me to their guests.

Lord Cunningham was a slightly built man in his mid to late forties. He had a rather long, thin nose and very gentle, pale blue eyes.

His wife had an equally long, aristocratic nose, dark hair, very white skin, and piercing brown eyes. She was a plain woman and in her prim black-velvet gown she could have passed for a governess. I was prepared for her wit, for Lady Fitzgerald had informed me of her intelligence, but not for the warmth that shone in her dark eyes as she acknowledged our introduction.

"Lady Mitchell is the recent bride of Sir Gavan Mitchell of Bonnie Brae," Lady Fitzgerald explained.

Lady Cunningham's eyes lit up. "How wonderful! Bonnie Brae is a fascinating old castle. I'm familiar with it, of course, but I've never actually seen it."

"My husband is presently restoring the castle," I said.

She nodded her head. "A monumental task, my dear,

and don't I know it! My father was an architect, and he worked on several old castles in Scotland. He let me go with him on his inspections when I was a little girl, and I was positively entranced by them!" She smiled, and looked at her husband. "I still am entranced, and one of these days . . ."

He laughed, and turned to Lord Fitzgerald. "Anne has been after me to buy one, but I can't abide the drafty old things."

Lady Cunningham gave her husband a playful tap with her fan. "They're drafty only if they're haunted," she said.

"Haunted!" Clyde repeated, joining the group. "Have you ever been in a haunted one, Lady Cunningham?"

"Aye, in Scotland," she answered. "But I didn't see the ghost myself. They appear only to certain people, you know."

My heart skipped a beat, and I said, "You believe in them, then?"

"Of course, but there's naught to fear. They're the spirits of very unhappy people, people who have left something undone in their lives, something they must come back to rectify."

Lady Fitzgerald shook her head. "Well, I'd not fancy meeting up with one, harmless or not!"

Clyde grinned. "Alex will surely haunt Strangford Manor someday, then. The lad never finishes anything he starts."

"Stop your nonsense, Clyde," Lady Fitzgerald scolded.

I wanted to talk to Lady Cunningham about ghosts, but I didn't want the discussion to degenerate into an excuse for Alex and Clyde to poke fun at each other, so I would have to wait and hope to catch Lady Cunningham alone after dinner.

I gathered from the dinner-table conversation that

Lord Cunningham had extensive holdings in both Ireland and Scotland, the Irish lands having been acquired at the time of his marriage to Lady Cunningham.

I overheard him mention the Fenians in an aside to Lord Fitzgerald, and I strained my ears to eavesdrop on that conversation while still trying to keep up with Alex and Clyde, who were flirting with me despite my newly acquired married state.

Lord Fitzgerald's words were lost in the hum of other conversations, and I was unable to ascertain any new information about the Fenians.

After we left the gentlemen to their port, I did, however, garner a sizable amount of information about castles and the ghosts who haunt them.

The ladies retired to a small salon off the dining room, and Lady Fitzgerald lost no time in bringing up the subject that was foremost in both our minds.

She pounced on Lady Cunningham the moment the servant had left the room. "Now that the men are not around to poke fun, Lady Cunningham, you must finish that story about the ghost in the Scottish castle."

Lady Cunningham took a sip of her port and smiled. "As I said, I didn't see the apparition myself, but I did have extensive discussions with one who did." She patted her lips daintily with a napkin, and continued. "The sightings took place at Dinsmooth Castle, a sixteenth-century edifice, very similar in appearance to your Bonnie Brae, I imagine," and she inclined her head toward me. "Candle-snuffer roofs, crow-stepped gables?"

I said, "Yes."

She nodded her head. "Very typical of the Scots Baronial style." She continued. "As to the ghost story, it came to light when my husband's brother purchased land off the coast of Scotland about twenty years ago.

"He commissioned my father to set about restoring the ruins of an old castle on the property. Shortly after

135

it was completed and they had moved in, a fierce-looking red-bearded gentleman began to appear to my sister-in-law."

Lady Fitzgerald fanned herself rapidly. "Dear me!" she exclaimed. "Who was he?"

"It turned out, when we researched the history of the castle, that the original owner had acquired his wealth by plunder. In later years he built the castle and assumed a cloak of respectability until his death in 1622. His spirit could not rest in peace though, for in his youth he had plundered an abbey and made off with valuable religious artifacts, and, inadvertently, the relic of a saint!"

"How shocking!" Lady Fitzgerald exclaimed.

"Quite," Lady Cunningham agreed. "And it wasn't until the relic was recovered and returned to the church that his spirit was allowed to rest in peace."

"How was the relic recovered?" I asked.

"The spirit led my sister-in-law to the cave where he had hidden it," Lady Cunningham replied.

Lady Fitzgerald gasped. "I'll never be able to sleep tonight, but do tell, Lady Cunningham—did the ghost speak and tell her where to find it?"

"No, but after we found out what he had done, my sister-in-law felt a strong compulsion to have the cave searched, and there it was!"

I recalled my own strong compulsion to enter the passageway, and my hand shook as I placed my empty wineglass on the table. Who was Bonnie Brae's ghost, and what was the apparition trying to tell me? "An exciting story," I said. "But I would be interested to know how you researched the history of the castle."

"By poring through records and journals," she replied with a smile. "But that was twenty years ago. Several books have appeared since then, and if you're interested in researching Bonnie Brae, I have a fine book on Irish castles. Yours would be in there, I'm sure."

"I would love to read it," I said.

She promised to send me a copy, and the subject was dropped, as the gentlemen had returned from the dining room.

Alex and Clyde insisted that I join them in a game of cards, but I begged off, as I planned to leave for Bonnie Brae early in the morning.

I left Strangford Manor with appeals from Lady Fitzgerald that I return soon again. "As soon as Sir Gavan's recuperated, Elly, you both must come for a nice, long visit."

I promised we would, and she stood outside my carriage, her head stuck in the window, as if she couldn't bear to have me go. "Thank you so much, Lady Fitzgerald," I said. "It was a wonderful visit, and I shall certainly miss you."

"Then visit us soon again," she said, stepping back at last and letting the driver release the impatient horses. I waved my handkerchief out the window until we had left Strangford Lough's driveway behind us.

All the way home I thought about Lady Cunningham's ghost story, and her theory about the existence of spirits. Who was Bonnie Brae's apparition, and what did she want of me?

I would not mention this to Gavan, I decided, for it was clear he did not relish discussing his family.

As Bonnie Brae came within sight, I wondered about the Scotsman who had originally owned the castle. Gavan had told me once that the Mitchells had acquired it by devious means. Could the apparition be a member of the Scotsman's family?

As we pulled into the driveway, I noticed that Dr. McTavish's buggy was parked in front of the house, and as I alighted from the carriage, the front door opened and Dr. McTavish hurried outside like an agitated little squirrel.

"Dr. McTavish," I called, and he looked up quickly, and then headed toward me.

"Madam," he blurted out, "I am not a religious man, but blasphemy such as I have just been exposed to makes me extremely uncomfortable."

"Sir Gavan?" I said.

"The same," he answered, shaking his head as he removed his hat.

"All's not right with his leg?" I asked.

"All's fine with his leg, but the man expects miracles. Furious he is because his leg is weak and it pains him to so much as put his weight upon it. Thought he'd stand up and be running like a jackrabbit, he did, the young fool!"

He took a deep breath and wiped his bald head with his handkerchief. "I gave him the name of a doctor in Belfast. He did some work during the Crimean War to speed up recoveries, using a new method. It utilizes massage, hot baths, and special exercises," he explained. "If your husband can't let nature take its course, let him try this!"

"Dr. McTavish," I said. "Please don't take offense. Sir Gavan and I are both grateful to you."

His kindly eyes softened. "There lass, doon't be concerning yourself with me. That's a raging young bull you have in there. Let him go to Dr. Beecham's clinic for a couple of weeks. If nothing else, it'll tire him out and calm him down."

I could hear Gavan ranting and raging as I hurried down the corridor to the study. Servants scurried about like mice as he bellowed out orders. "Get me Starice," I heard him shout, and a white-faced maid ran out of the room.

One look at Gavan, and I understood the maid's haste. He was Satan personified, with his blazing black

138

eyes and flaring nostrils. Standing up, his tall, powerful figure loomed menacingly over the room as he leaned on one crutch and waved the other.

Upon seeing me, he dropped the crutches, took a step forward, and stumbled, crashing into the wall. He grabbed a small table for support and leaned against it, sweat pouring down his face. I rushed up to him. "Gavan, let me help you," I said.

Grimacing in pain, he spoke through clenched teeth. "Hand me those damn sticks, and then get out of here, Elly."

I gave him the crutches, and stepping aside, I let him maneuver himself over to the bed. He sank down on it with obvious relief, and refusing to be put off by his ferocious scowl, I calmly began straightening the covers.

Caught off guard, he looked up at me with a half smile. "You don't scare easily, do you?"

"I thought you already knew that," I said.

His words took on an unfamiliar, almost wistful tone. "Aye, that I did. Otherwise, I should never have brought you to Bonnie Brae."

Reaching for my hand, he drew it up to his lips and planted a gentle kiss on my open palm. No longer fierce, his dark eyes looked into mine, and I sensed within them a mute appeal for compassion. It was as close as we had ever come to bridging the gap of mistrust that had always haunted our relationship.

I wanted to prolong this brief, tender moment, but it shattered like exploding crystal at the sound of Starice's shrill voice. "Beggin yere pardon, Sir Gavan. The lass said ye wanted to see me."

He answered her with anger. "Haven't I told you to knock before barging in here? No, I don't need you now. Come back later."

She grunted and shuffled away, but not before giving me a murderous look in retaliation.

Still frowning, he turned on me with sarcasm. "I trust you had success finding replacements for Bonnie Brae's unsuitable servants?"

"I did, indeed," I said emphatically. Then I showed him Maire McGee's signed agreement, with references attached, attesting to the qualifications of the servants I had hired. He seemed impressed, and nodded his head in approval.

"I think this refutes Starice's contention that no decent servants can be found to work at Bonnie Brae," I said smugly.

He regarded me sternly, like an adult who is forced to deal with a recalcitrant child. "I don't want you to say one word about this to Starice. I shall be the one to tell her about her retirement." He paused, and then to my amazement, added, "She will be relocated to a small cottage on the grounds and free to come and go as she pleases."

So, she has triumphed after all, I thought, visualizing the old woman's gloating face popping out to taunt me wherever and whenever she so desired.

Considering that subject closed, he went on to another. "That old fool, McTavish, wants me to go to another quack in Belfast for treatment."

I nodded, still trying to understand his commitment to Starice.

"I might consider it," he mused. "Anything would be better than this." He paused, stripping away my prim, high-necked traveling suit with hungry eyes. "And when I come back, Lady Mitchell, I'll make it all up to you," he said.

My traitorous body tingled with anticipation as he caressed me slowly with his eyes, letting his glances roam intimately over me. I felt a warm blush creep into my cheeks, and he gave me a wicked smile. "And that's a promise, Lady Mitchell . . ."

* * *

140

Gavan and I left Bonnie Brae in separate carriages the following day, he for Belfast, and I for Strangford Manor, where he insisted I should stay until his return. I did not argue the point, for I knew he was in no mood to be crossed.

I tried to tell myself that Lady Cunningham's ghost story played no part in my decision. After all, I reasoned, it was more pleasant at Strangford Manor, and Lady Fitzgerald had certainly made it clear that I would be welcome.

On that point I was not mistaken, for my surprise return filled her with delight. "It's just wonderful to have you back again," she chirped as we sat once more in her comfortable drawing room, drinking tea. Gavan had refused to leave his carriage to join us, turning down Lady Fitzgerald's invitation with the excuse that he must make haste to Belfast.

"Sir Gavan cannot bear to have anyone see him this way," I explained, hoping she had not taken offense.

She rolled her eyes and laughed. "Men! They're all alike, my dear. Never want to admit to any weakness, even when it's only temporary like your husband's."

She helped herself to another petit four. "Umm, try the lemon ones, Elly." Wiping her fingers daintily on her napkin, she cooed, "I'm so glad you came back. Lord and Lady Cunningham left early this morning, and with you gone, too, the house seemed positively ghostly." She placed a plump hand over her mouth. "Oh, and speaking of ghosts, wasn't that an exciting story Lady Cunningham told?"

I sipped my tea. "Very exciting."

She hesitated, but only for a second. "Elly, I've never mentioned it before, but there has always been talk of a ghost at Bonnie Brae. You haven't seen any signs of it, have you?"

141

"I'm not sure I believe in ghosts, Lady Fitzgerald," I replied cautiously.

"All the same, I'm glad you're not alone up there with Sir Gavan away."

I let the subject drop, and we chatted about other things until she suddenly remembered that Lady Cunningham had left something for me. "Dear me, now, what did I do with it? It was that book about the castles, Elly. Remember, Lady Cunningham was going to mail it to you? Well, she found a copy in our library. I must confess, I didn't even know it was there." She giggled girlishly. "I'm afraid I'm not much of a reader, Elly. The library is Lord Fitzgerald's domain." She pursed her lips and frowned for a moment. "Now, where did I . . ."

"You'll come across it," I said, not wanting to appear too eager.

Her expressive eyes suddenly lit up. "I remember now. It's right here," she said triumphantly, jumping up and retrieving it from a desk drawer.

She handed the book to me and then immediately lost interest in it. Chattering away about other things, she ended the conversation with, "You look fatigued, Elly, and I'm a silly goose for not letting you rest after your journey. Now, you go right ahead, dear, and take yourself a lovely nap."

I was glad of the opportunity to escape, not to nap, but to read, for I was hoping the book would give me a clue as to the identity of Bonnie Brae's troubled spirit. I opened the book and read:

Castle Bonnie Brae was built in the year 1625 by a Scot who settled in Ireland under the English scheme for the Plantation of Ulster. Sir Angus McBain and his descendents occupied the castle for more than a century. The building was severely damaged by General Monk's troops in

1648, at which time Sir Angus was killed. The castle was rebuilt by his son, John, and subsequently occupied by his grandson, and great-grandson, who retained ownership until his death at the age of eighty in the year 1769.

Ownership then passed to a nephew, James McBain, a spendthrift and a gambler. He married Lady Jane Cabot, daughter of the second Earl of Clofton, an heiress from the south of Wales. He gambled and lost his wife's inheritance, along with most of her family jewels, including a rare ruby necklace. This so depressed Lady Jane that she committed suicide by jumping from the castle's tower.

Deeply in debt, James McBain sold the castle in 1780 to Sir Gavan Mitchell, about whom little is known. Ownership has been handed down in a direct line within the Mitchell family to the present day.

I closed the book and thought about what I had read. It was plain that the author had avoided exposing himself to libel by recounting the more lurid exploits of the Mitchell clan; hence the sketchy account of their stewardship of the castle.

I was particularly intrigued by the discovery that the ruby necklace had belonged to the Cabots and not to the Mitchells, and that the tragic Lady Jane Cabot McBain had jumped from the tower in despair over the loss of it. Could she be the ghost of Bonnie Brae? And if so, what does she want of me? I mused.

I spent a wonderful week at Strangford Manor. Despite her size, Lady Fitzgerald was an accomplished horsewoman, and our rides gave me an opportunity to appreciate the countryside in all the splendor of those crisp October days.

The men in the family were busy attending to the affairs of Strangford Manor, for Lord Fitzgerald was no absentee landlord. He believed, as had my father, that landholders had a responsibility to govern their estates fairly and profitably.

I was satisfied, though, to be relieved of the company of men for a while. Alex and Clyde were amusing, but at times I wearied of their fawning devotion.

At least that's something I'll never have to worry about with Gavan. I smiled to myself. Strange, but when I was away from him, I could tolerate his moods and temper tantrums with humor rather than with anger. Was I becoming immune to them? Or had I exaggerated their importance? I remembered the mural, and I asked myself, could a man who showed such perception and sensitivity really be a devil?

Yet while my heart was mellowing like the fields of golden grain soon to be harvested, fate had conspired again to deal one final, shattering blow to the eternal triangle of Gavan Mitchell, Avery James, and Elly Kincaid.

Dinner, as I remember it that evening, was particularly gay, like the calm before the storm, but I was blithely unaware of anything save the warmth and conviviality I felt on that occasion.

The whole family was present, and the older sons, whose names I had finally conquered, had overcome their shyness, and I found them to be gracious and friendly.

Alex and Clyde were at their best—witty, but not cutting—and their affection for me had resolved itself into a brotherly one, which pleased me enormously.

After dinner we retreated to the library, where Lord Fitzgerald and Stewart gravitated to the chess board for a match, and Clyde persuaded me to join him in a game of whist against Alex and Thomas. "You'll be sorry," I warned him. "I'm unlucky at cards."

Lady Fitzgerald looked up from her needlepoint. "They should be the ones to worry, not you, Elly. When you're unlucky at cards, you're lucky in love."

Alex and Clyde groaned in unison, and we all laughed.

Andrew bid us an early good night, as he was leaving for Ballymena early in the morning on business, and George and Richard settled down in front of the fire to read. It was a tranquil family scene and one I wanted to press like a flower and keep with me during the long winter nights at Bonnie Brae.

"We'll draw first for the deal," Clyde said.

"I declare," Lady Fitzgerald remarked. "This thread breaks if you look at it. They certainly don't make things the way they used to."

"You deal, Elly. One card at a time, facedown," Alex instructed.

"Checkmate," Stewart cried triumphantly.

"I never did understand that game," Lady Fitzgerald remarked.

"Diamonds are trumps," Thomas said.

George suddenly stood up. "Read this," he cried, handing his newspaper to Richard. "It says here that they've arrested some of those Fenians in Dublin!"

Richard scanned the article. "That editor, O'Leary from *The Herald*, was one of them!" he announced.

"Good riddance," Alex said.

"They'll hang them," George predicted.

"And so they should," Alex added. "Go on, Elly, it's your turn."

My heart turned to stone, and their faces blurred before my eyes. I heard a loud ringing in my ears and their voices grew faint.

"What's wrong, Elly? Don't you feel well?"

"She's white as a sheet."

"Get the smelling salts."

A whiff of something sharp cleared my head, and their worried faces came back into focus. Lady Fitzgerald took charge. "Alex, Clyde, help Elly over to the love seat. George, hand me that pillow for her head." She patted my hand. "Feeling better now, dear?"

"I'm all right," I said weakly. "I don't know what came over me."

"Some subjects are just not fit for sensitive young ladies' ears," she said, admonishing her tall sons with a withering glance.

"We're sorry, Elly," Alex offered.

"We're boors," George said contritely.

"No, please. It's not any of your faults. I'm just overly tired, and the sherry went to my head," I explained.

"You just come along with me, dear," Lady Fitzgerald said. "A good night's sleep is what you need."

I allowed myself to be pampered and fussed over and tucked into bed, but a good night's sleep was the farthermost thing from my mind. I had to see that newspaper and assure myself that Avery's name was not listed.

I paced the floor, I prayed; and never had the night seemed so long. I waited until they were all safely in bed, and then I checked the time by the mantel clock, and when an hour had passed, I crept silently on bare feet downstairs to the library.

I felt around in the darkness, moving cautiously until my hand touched the silken drapes at the window. Pulling them open, I let a beautiful harvest moon shine into the room and light my way.

I spied the newspaper on a table and snatched it up quickly, stuffing it under my nightgown. Then with a pounding heart I left the room and felt my way back upstairs with agonizing slowness, bargaining all the way with God. "Please, let Avery be safe, and I promise You, I'll never think about him again."

Once in my room I leaned back against the door and clutched the paper to my breast. Like a lead weight it pressed against my heart, making me gasp for breath.

I stood there, savoring for one last minute the bliss of my innocence, and then I carried the paper over to the lamp and read: "Six Fenians were captured today as they attempted to smuggle guns into Dublin. Tom O'Leary, John Clancey, Avery James . . ."

Chapter Nine

I spent a sleepless night, reading over and over the account of Avery's capture. Refusing to indulge myself in tears, I paced the floor until dawn before reaching the decision to enlist Hugh's aid.

Although I did not want to see my brother, I realized he was my only hope. Hugh had connections, and I was sure he could get Avery off with a light sentence. And after all, I reasoned, didn't he owe me at least that much?

I would return home, and then set out for Glengarra, and though I should probably be insulted, I didn't see how I could be refused!

I engineered my hasty departure from Strangford Manor by insisting that I had to prepare for the arrival of Maire McGee's new staff. It was a flimsy excuse, but the only one my weary brain could come up with.

Lady Fitzgerald, I'm afraid, had another motive in mind, and I rather suspect that after my departure, Alex and Clyde were treated to a stern lecture on the impropriety of flirting with their mother's married guest! Be that as it may, I thought. All I wanted was to get home, and as quickly as possible.

I must admit that Bonnie Brae's stables surpassed even Glengarra's, for Gavan's lively team of blacks rivaled any I had seen in Ireland, or in England either, for that matter, and they covered the relatively short distance between the two estates in record time.

Entering Bonnie Brae's massive gate, I looked up at the tower and visualized a beautiful young woman stepping out onto the crow-stepped gable and suddenly hurling herself down in a dizzying spiral to what at that time would have been the bawn. She would have hit the ground with a terrible impact, I realized, and the thought made my stomach turn over.

I pushed the hideous picture out of my mind as the carriage stopped, and Brendan stepped down to open the door for me. "Leave the trunk be," I instructed him. "And take care of the horses. We leave immediately for Glengarra."

He drove the carriage around to the stable, and I went to my room and gathered up my mother's jewelry. I didn't know how Hugh would secure Avery's release, but if a bribe was required, I would be prepared to offer it.

I had Bridget pack a hearty food basket for the long journey ahead, and we set out on the open road again, this time heading south into County Down.

Eight hours later, just as the sun was sinking in a blaze of orange glory, my white, fairy-tale mansion came into view. It was the mural come to life, and I marveled anew at the artist's ability to capture Glengarra and transport it to Bonnie Brae.

As we passed between the giant oaks that lined the drive, I wished with all my heart that my gentle father could rush outside and welcome me home again.

I smiled wistfully, remembering that wonderful day, just six months earlier, when my heart had been filled with love for my long-lost family, and looking back, I recalled that it was then I had vowed to heal the rift between my father and my brother. How sadly had I failed! And now there was a new rift to be healed.

The carriage pulled up in front of the house, and my burly driver handed me down and stood, looking uncertainly toward the luggage on top. "I'll have a servant sent out for it," I said, adjusting my bonnet and walking resolutely up to the door.

I lifted the knocker, feeling the chill of an autumn breeze as I stood there, waiting to be welcomed. But it was I who was taken by surprise when the door opened, and I found myself facing an unfamiliar young servant. Where was Conor, who had been Glengarra's butler ever since I could remember?

I returned the lad's rather insolent stare with a royal rebuff. "I am Lady Mitchell, Master Kincaid's sister. Kindly have someone assist with the luggage." Sweeping grandly past him, I began to peel off my gloves. "Where might I be finding Master Hugh?" I inquired.

"Master Hugh is in his study, yere ladyship."

"Don't bother to announce me," I said quickly, heading for the room that in my mind would forever be, not Hugh's study, but Papa's.

The door was ajar, and I could see my brother, standing with his back to me, staring out the window. I was about to knock, when he turned, and on catching sight of me, a startled expression crossed his face, making him jump and slosh the remains of his drink down the front of his waistcoat.

He recovered himself quickly and executed a mocking bow. "Lady Mitchell, this is a surprise!" He paused for a moment, looking perplexed. "Where's Gavan?" he asked.

"Gavan's in Belfast; I came alone."

He gave me a self-satisfied smile. "Well, well, so you've come to apologize." He waved his hand. "There's no need. We'll not speak of it again."

I smothered my outrage for Avery's sake. "Hugh, what's done is done. Let us begin again."

"My sentiments exactly. That calls for a drink," he said jovially. He reached for the bell cord, and a maid, who must have been standing right outside the door, instantly materialized.

She was a buxom wench, and comely, but she had the look of a barmaid about her, and I could well imagine that Hugh had plucked her right out of a tavern. "You be wantin' something, Master Hugh?" she asked, giving him a seductive smile.

"A glass of wine for Lady Mitchell," he said, returning the smile. "And don't be forgetting, Molly, I'll be needing you later tonight." Their eyes met, and there was no mistaking the intimacy in the look they exchanged. She curtsied and left the room, leaving behind a sickening odor of cheap perfume.

"You seem to have a lot of new servants," I said casually. "Where are the old ones?"

He took a drink and shrugged. "I let them go. They were Fa's servants, not mine."

And you didn't want them sitting in judgment on you, I thought, looking at him with mounting disgust. He had a bloated look about him now, and the once-handsome, boyish face mirrored his decadence.

The maid returned with my wine, and when she had been dismissed, I knew the time had come to state my case, for Hugh would soon be too drunk to listen.

"I've come for your help, Hugh," I said simply.

He raised an eyebrow. "My help? Now, what could Hugh Kincaid possibly do for Lady Gavan Mitchell?"

"Avery's been arrested," I said.

His eyes narrowed. "And what is that to me? Or to you either, for that matter?"

"I kept our bargain, Hugh. Oh, I know you did too," I added quickly. "I thought I was guaranteeing Avery's safety, but he got caught anyway. You have influence; you can get him off with a light sentence." My voice rose in desperation as he continued to stare at me with a strange, incredulous look on his face. "I brought Mama's jewelry," I said in a rush. You can use it for bribes. It's worth a great deal, and Gavan need never know. Oh, please, Hugh, do this for me and I'll be eternally grateful. . . ."

"Silence!" His blazing eyes bore into mine, and I

151

reeled back as if he had struck me. "Spare me this disgusting display," he said. "I don't want to ever hear his name again." His face turned purple with rage. "He will get what he deserves, and there's nothing you or anyone else can do about it."

"You turned him in!" I cried as the truth suddenly dawned on me.

"I had a duty to turn him in," he proclaimed self-righteously.

"A duty? What about your duty to me? You gave me your word!"

"I was protecting you from yourself. Do you think I could stand by and watch you drag our name through the mud?"

"And what are you doing to the Kincaid name?" I cried hysterically. "You, with your drinking and your whoring right in this house—you're defiling the very memory of Papa and Mama!"

My words must have stunned him, for he took a step back. All the color drained out of his face, and he said quietly, "Go home to your husband, Elly. You'll find no help for a Fenian here."

His words tolled the death knell of hope for me, and I put down my untouched wineglass and stood up. "I'll leave first thing in the morning," I said. "Until then, I'll remain in my room, and I don't want to see you ever again for as long as I live."

He ignored me, and with great deliberation concentrated his efforts on pouring himself another drink.

I left him there and retreated to my old room, where, among the vestiges of happier days, I contemplated the bleakness of the future.

Dawn found me oddly rested, for I had slept well despite the sounds of revelry and drunken laughter that had drifted upstairs and occasionally disturbed my slumber.

My brother and his companions had either passed out or taken themselves to bed, but in either case, they would be oblivious to my presence for several more hours.

Wary of alerting Hugh's new servants, I rummaged through my trunk and pulled out riding clothes. Without benefit of a wash, I dressed quickly and slipped down the back staircase.

An early morning frost covered the grass, and my boots crunched as I made my way to the stable, where I was surprised to find a familiar face.

"Mistress Elly," the young groom exclaimed, and then blushed in embarrassment. "I mean, I mean . . ."

"Lady Mitchell," I added with a smile, hoping to put him more at ease.

"Aye, yere ladyship. I just forgot." He shook his head. "Seein' you here again took me back some, it did." He brightened then. "Shall I saddle up yere old pony for ye, Miss—I mean, Lady Mitchell?"

"Saddle Warwick," I said. "He's faster."

Once mounted, I dug in my heels, and Warwick clattered across the cobblestones and headed for the open road, galloping like a winged, fairy-tale horse.

I slowed him to a trot, as the tenant cottages with their thatched roofs began to appear. Farmers working in the fields waved to me as I passed them, and I waved back, my heart already heavy with the certainty of what I should find there.

Dismounting before the familiar gate, I walked through a yard still littered with the vestiges of a hasty departure. Bits of cloth clung to a bush, and an old iron pot, dented and dirty, lay on the step, a pitiful reminder of their poverty. How had they been evicted? Recalling stories that I hadn't wanted to believe, I envisioned a mounted constabulary poking, and shouting, and driving Avery's family like cattle off the land.

My throat ached with tears I could not shed, and I let Warwick take me back to Glengarra, my heart heavy with the thought that another door had just been shut in my face.

When I returned, I found Brendan in the stable, grooming the carriage horses. I dismounted and motioned him outside, where our conversation could not be overheard. "I must go to Dublin," I said.

"Aye, me lady. When would you be wantin' to leave?"

"Immediately, and, Brendan, I'd rather you didn't mention to the other servants where we are going."

He shook his big head solemnly. "I'm not about to gallywag with the likes of them, yere ladyship."

Our eyes met, and I knew at that instant that I had a friend in this big, open-faced man named Timothy Brendan Kelley.

I hurried back inside, slipping quietly through the tomblike silence that covered Glengarra like a shroud. Surely some of the servants must be up and stirring about by now, and I gingerly pulled the bell cord and waited, hardly knowing what to expect.

My call was answered by yet another new servant, a plain lass whose pockmarked face and emaciated body would hardly have qualified her to have been a participant in last night's revelry.

Her name was Fiona, she informed me, and aye, she would bring me hot water for washing. The kitchen was a bit of a mess, she implied, as Master Hugh had entertained several gentlemen last night, and they had kept the cook busy preparing a late supper that had lasted, she confided wide-eyed, until the wee small hours of the morning.

She had taken a deep breath then, and reluctantly agreed to bring me a light breakfast and a cup of tea.

154

She returned quickly with the food and hot water, and I dismissed her, preferring to make my hasty preparations without assistance.

The next time I rang I received no answer at all, and my trunk was hauled downstairs and back onto the carriage by Brendan, with scant assistance from Glengarra's uninterested staff. Hugh never showed his face, and for that I was grateful.

As we drove away, I looked back, and my heart ached for the gentleness and beauty that had once been a part of this lovely land. From out of the past I heard my father's voice. "Glengarra has always had proud masters, and masters to be proud of."

I brushed away the tears that blurred my vision. "Good-bye, Glengarra," I whispered as the house disappeared from sight. "I shall remember you always. . . ."

We spent the night at a roadside inn, where the accommodations were poor but infinitely preferable to my previous night's stay at Glengarra.

Brendan Kelley proved to be a godsend, for this giant of a man's commanding presence earned him immediate attention and instant respect. "Mind ye be givin' Lady Mitchell a clean room, or I'll be havin' yere hide in the morning," I heard him whisper in an aside to the surly innkeeper.

I smiled to myself as, bowing and scraping, the man approached me with, "Beggin' yere pardon, yere ladyship. We don't get many guests this time of year, but me wife'll be havin' yere room ready in no time a'tall."

"That will be fine," I said, "and in the meantime you can bring us some supper. We'll eat over there." I nodded my head toward a table in the corner of the room.

Brendan returned from the stable then, and when I

155

informed him of my arrangements for supper, he protested. "I'll be takin' me meal in the kitchen. It wouldn't be fittin' for the likes of me to be dinin' with you, Lady Mitchell."

"You'll do no such thing. I want your company, and if it'll make you feel any better, I order you to eat with me tonight."

"Aye, if ye say so, Lady Mitchell," he mumbled, looking fiercely at the innkeeper, as if it were all somehow his fault.

Appearances to the contrary, I found Brendan Kelley to be a gentle man with the face of a peasant and the soul of a poet. And moreover, he knew Dublin like the back of his hand.

"Dublin used to be me home," he explained, and then went on to describe the city to me in all its contrasts. "There are some sections so mean and ugly, the devil himself would not live in them." Then his eyes grew sad, and he added, "None's so poor as the poor of Dublin's fair city."

I sensed in his words a sympathy for Ireland's stepchildren, and I ached to shift my burden to his big, capable shoulders, but I dare not. He was Gavan's man, and I could not ask him to betray his master's trust.

He spoke of the authorities' stop-gap measures to keep the poor from revolting with their "penny dinners" and makeshift shelters, and then went on to describe the lush beauty of the rhododendron forest growing in a sheltered slope on the grounds of Howth Castle.

I wanted to ask this remarkable man to tell me his own story, instead of Dublin's, but I hesitated, lest I impose upon our friendship.

Supper came, and it was adequate if not appetizing. Brendan ate with gusto, but I was too tired to manage more than a few bites, and preferring to satisfy my need for sleep rather than for food, I took myself off to bed.

We left early the next morning, and four hours later Brendan was manipulating the prancing team across the Half-Penny Bridge, and into the lusty city.

We rumbled through streets so narrow that I held my breath lest we should collide with a loaded cart, or trample one of the many urchins who darted from one side to the other like mice in a maze.

Contrasting with the squalor, we passed magnificent buildings that I later learned were the Four Courts, the Custom House, and Trinity College. The picturesque beauty of St. Stephens Green lay but a stone's throw from the misery of the night shelters, rat holes that Brendan had described as breeding grounds for future revolutionaries.

He stopped the carriage in front of the Dublin Inn. "It's a suitable place for a lady to stay," he assured me. "And I'll be close by in the servants' quarters if ye should be needin' me help."

He left me then, and I signed the register and was shown to a room on the second floor.

All my brave resolutions collapsed when the door closed and the futility of my mission suddenly overwhelmed me.

How could I, a sheltered and overly protected female, expect to accomplish such a monumental feat? I knew nothing about pawning jewels, bribing guards. Why, I didn't even know how to find the jail!

Feeling utterly alone and miserable, I pulled off my bonnet and threw myself across the bed, letting the hot tears of despair flow freely at last.

Memories, bitter in their sweetness, tugged at my heart. I saw Avery, a neglected, ragged child, his face, shining with the conviction that despite the odds against him he was second to none. I saw him again, his face grim with childish determination as he challenged me with a power higher than mine. "God's on me side," he said.

Oh, Avery! Where is your God if not in me, for there is no one else to save you.

I got up then and poured cold water into the bowl. I dipped my handkerchief in it and gently patted my swollen eyes. Then I combed my hair and slapped the bonnet back on my head. Tying the streamers, I looked at my reflection in the mirror with sudden determination. I will not let Avery down, I told myself, and picking up my purse, I left the inn.

The cab driver opened the hatch and called down to me, "This be Kilmainham Prison, me lady. Are ye sure in yere mind that ye be wantin' to stop?"

"Aye," I said, looking up through the opening into his disapproving face.

He got down and opened the door. "Shall I wait?" he asked as he handed me out.

Grateful for the suggestion, I nodded my head and fixed my eyes on the austere gray stone building that loomed before me.

My heart pounded as I approached the sentry who stood at the gate. "State your business," he said in a clipped voice that sent a chill down my spine.

"I've come to see a prisoner. His name is Avery James," I said.

"And your name?" he asked.

I stumbled over the words. "Lady—I mean, just tell him it's Elly Kincaid."

"I'll tell the likes of him nothing," he said, giving me a malicious grin. "It's the warden of Kilmainham Prison what gives out visitors' passes. Now, what's your relationship to the prisoner?" When I didn't answer, he grew impatient. "Are you his wife, his sister?"

"No."

"I see," he remarked, giving me a smug smile. "Sorry, only blood relations get to see the prisoners."

"Just a minute," I said, suddenly recovering my courage. "My father was Master Thomas Kincaid of Glengarra. Avery James was a tenant on our land. I must see him."

He hesitated a moment, looking doubtful. Then he shrugged and said, "Wait here, please."

He disappeared inside, and I stood, staring up at Kilmainham Prison, where the ghosts of Emmet, Tone, and Tandy surely dwelled, and I prayed that these bleak, forbidding walls would never house the restless spirit of Avery James.

The sentry was gone a long time, and the cab driver, who stood waiting across the street, finally came over, and with kindly concern offered to have me wait inside the cab.

"No, thank you. I'm fine," I insisted, though the air had grown damp, and a dark sky threatened rain.

At last the sentry returned, and my heart turned over. "The captain would have issued you a pass," he said, pausing for effect. "But the prisoner refuses to see you."

My stricken face must have given him enormous satisfaction, for he smiled and added, "He says to tell you that as far as he's concerned, Elly Kincaid is dead, and he has no wish to see Lady Gavan Mitchell."

I turned away and walked slowly across the street to the waiting cab. So, he knows about my marriage, and in his mind I am as guilty as Hugh.

I returned to the inn with a heavy heart, but I wasn't ready to give up yet. I would go back to Kilmainham tomorrow, and this time I would ask to see Tom O'Leary.

I would hand the jewels over to Tom, and Avery need never know I had any part in it. There was enough there for all six of them to bribe their way out, and my only regret was that my mother's jewels would end up in the pockets of corrupt men. But at least they will have been used to save lives, I thought.

Wearily I climbed the short flight of stairs to my room at the Dublin Inn.

As soon as I opened the door, I noticed that the shades had all been drawn and a large chair had been moved from a corner of the room to the center, facing the window. Feeling vaguely disturbed, I closed the door behind me, and as I turned, I saw the figure of a man rise slowly out of the chair.

I gasped as he turned and faced me. "Gavan!" I cried, struggling to catch my breath.

His face, in the shadows, struck terror in my heart, and I backed into the door as he advanced toward me. "I should kill you," he said, his eyes staring into mine with demonic fury.

I groped for the doorknob, but he crossed the room swiftly with no trace of a limp, and gripping my shoulders with steel fingers, he dragged me away from the door and shoved me into the chair. Towering over me, he said in a menacing tone, "Don't you dare try to leave. I want to hear the truth from your own lips. I've already heard part of it from your drunken brother!"

"What have you heard?"

"That you married me to save your lover from the gallows. Is that true?" he demanded.

"Aye," I said softly, wanting to add something, but I didn't know what.

His jaw tightened, and the blood drained from his face. "And without my consent you left my home and traveled in my carriage, and with my servant, all the way to Dublin. *For what?*" he shouted. "What did you plan to do down here?" he demanded again.

"I wanted to use my mother's jewelry to bribe the guards to help them escape," I said, my voice shaking with near hysteria.

"You've just come from the prison, haven't you?"

I nodded numbly.

"And did you succeed?" he asked with a sneer.

"No. They wouldn't let me in, I thought—"

"You thought what?"

"I thought I'd try again tomorrow," I sobbed.

He reached down and pulled me roughly out of the chair. "You're my wife. Do you understand? You'll not be traipsing around Dublin making a fool of me. Is that clear?" His fingers dug into my flesh, and he gave me a shake. "Answer me! Do you understand?"

"Aye," I cried. "I understand."

He released me then. "Get packed. You're leaving Dublin immediately, and give me your key."

I handed it to him and he glared back at me. "Don't disobey me, Elly. You're going home now if I have to drag you through that lobby by your hair!"

He left then, and I heard the key turn in the lock.

Gavan was a violent man, and I had mortally wounded his pride. I recalled his savage face and blazing eyes, the pressure of his hands on my arms. I heard again the ominous tone in his voice—*I should kill you!*

I jumped as the door suddenly opened then, and he entered the room, followed by Brendan.

"Carry Lady Mitchell's trunk out to the carriage," he commanded, and taking my arm in a firm grip, he propelled me out of the room and down the stairs without speaking a word.

He handed me into the carriage and spoke in a cold voice. "I've put you into Brendan's care. I shouldn't think you'd want to make any trouble for him."

"I have too much respect for Brendan to expose him to your wrath," I said.

161

Chapter Ten

Starice was eager to inform me, immediately upon my arrival home, that she no longer worked at Bonnie Brae.

"Sir Gavan has retired me," she announced, her ugly face staring defiantly into mine. Then her mean little eyes glittered, and looking like an evil troll, she gave me an impish smile. "But I'll not be far, yere ladyship. I'll be in that wee cottage, right across from the cemetery, for the rest of me days."

I couldn't resist sarcasm. "How very thoughtful of Sir Gavan."

A contemptuous look crossed her face, and she changed before my eyes from imp to menacing witch. " 'Tis me reward." Then she stared vacantly into space and added, "For services rendered."

"I'm sure you've been a faithful servant," I said. "You were here even before Sir Gavan's mother arrived, weren't you?"

Her crafty eyes evaded mine. "Yere a curious young woman, Lady Mitchell. Ye'd like to know about that, and other things as well, wouldn't ye? Well, ye'll hear naught from me, but I'll give ye a warning, I will." She stopped, her eyes fixed straight ahead in a glassy stare, as if she were going into a trance. "Let the dead rest, and the past be. There's some secrets too dark to know."

I tried to put her words out of my mind. She's just a crazy old woman, I told myself, but her warning had touched a raw nerve in me. I justified my interest in the Mitchell family's past by reminding myself that it was not idle curiosity on my part, but rather an attempt to understand the present Sir Gavan Mitchell that drove me to unearth Bonnie Brae's dark secrets, but would I be better off for not knowing?

The dark side of my husband's personality had terrified me in Dublin, and I dreaded the thought of being isolated at Bonnie Brae with a madman. "I should kill you," he had said, and I shuddered, wondering what was in store for me on Gavan's return.

My heart ached for Avery, but there was nothing I could do for him now. The trial was to be held in another couple of weeks, and I could only hope that a merciful judge would spare the Fenians, men who held freedom for Ireland dearer than their very lives.

The new servants had not yet arrived, and the cold, dreary days of late fall kept me indoors. Bored and restless, I wandered through the west wing's empty rooms, amusing myself by making a mental list of what should be required to furnish them, when my eye fell on the gilded French desk and I suddenly remembered the letters.

I opened the secret compartment and took the packet out. Sitting down on the floor, I untied the faded lavender ribbon and began to sort through the dozen or more letters in my lap.

Scanning the dates, I arranged them in order, the first having been written in June of the year 1833, and the last January 1834. Interspersed with these letters from Père Rousseau were several mementos from Gabrielle Rousseau's life in France; a prayer book, inscribed on the flyleaf:

> *Ma petite Gabrielle,*
> *Voyage toujours à l'ombre de Dieu.*
> *Grandmère*
> *1822*

163

"Travel always in the shadow of God." A pious wish from a loving grandmother, I thought, and yet Gabrielle Rousseau had grown up to marry the second Sir Gavan Mitchell, a man whose coarse and evil nature could not be hidden, even in a portrait.

I flipped the little book's pages, and a pressed rose dropped into my lap along with a slip of paper containing a poem. It had been translated into French, but I recognized it as Lord Byron's:

> There be none of beauty's daughters
> With a magic like thee;
> And like music on the waters
> Is thy sweet voice to me.

The classic keepsakes of a romantic young woman, I thought, gathering the rose and the poem and replacing them in the prayer book. What could have possessed Gabrielle Rousseau to marry a Mitchell, and then to run away and leave behind her own innocent son to be honed into his father's corrupt image?

I picked up one of the letters, and suddenly the room became cold and an eerie feeling that I was not alone took possession of me. With nervous hands I gathered up the papers from my lap and stuffed them haphazardly back into their hiding place. Then I ran out and across the hall to the safety of my own room, locking the door behind me. It wasn't until later that I recalled that in my haste I had forgotten to close the secret compartment.

I rang for Bridget, more for the comfort of her chatter than a need for her services. Her plump wholesomeness had a way of dispelling my morbid fantasies, and I felt relieved as soon as she entered the room.

"I brought ye a nice cup of hot tea, Lady Mitchell," she said with a smile. "Was that what ye rang for?"

"You're a mind reader," I said gratefully, and she blushed and looked very pleased with herself.

"Me mam always said I had a sixth sense. Come with a caul over me face, I did, and that's a sign, they say. Leastways, I know I can spot them's that works for the divil by their smell, and that old one . . . Makes the hairs stand up on back of me neck, she does."

"Sir Gavan has retired Starice, Bridget. You don't have to worry about her anymore."

"So I heard, Lady Mitchell, but she's still roamin' around Bonnie Brae like she owned it. Like to scare the daylights out of me just now, she did . . ."

"You saw Starice just now?"

"Aye, the old witch disappeared around a corner just as I come up with yere tea."

Bridget's words puzzled me. Starice didn't like to be in the west wing, and there was no reason for her to come upstairs. "She'll soon get used to staying in her own cottage," I said with more confidence than I felt.

When Bridget left, I went to the window and looked outside. I had a clear view of the family cemetery, and so close that it was almost a part of it stood Starice's cottage. What a fitting location! The ghoul and the ghosts, I thought, letting my imagination run wild to picture Starice calling forth all of Bonnie Brae's evil spirits to cavort in the moonlight outside my window while I slept.

No sign of Gavan, and as for me, I hoped his business kept him indefinitely in Dublin; but since I knew that was impossible, I prayed my murderous husband's inevitable return would not occur until I should feel somewhat protected by the presence of a houseful of servants.

I retreated to the morning room after breakfast to write a letter to Lady Fitzgerald, thanking her for her

165

hospitality and hoping to smooth over any misunderstanding that my departure from Strangford Manor may have occasioned.

"Beggin' yere pardon, Lady Mitchell. You have a visitor." The young lad who was temporarily acting as butler stood before me with a small silver tray bearing the calling card of Lady Cunningham.

"Send Lady Cunningham in immediately," I said, feeling a surge of pleasure at this unexpected visit.

A moment later she bustled in, arms outstretched and her face warm with a smile. "Lady Mitchell, do forgive me for barging in like this. I hope I'm not presuming on our short acquaintanceship."

"I'm delighted to see you," I said eagerly. "Believe me, I can't think of a more pleasant surprise."

"Lord Cunningham is still in Dublin on some dreadfully boring business, so I decided to return to Strangford Manor, and I just couldn't resist stopping by on my way."

"Well, I'm certainly glad you did. Sir Gavan is in Dublin on business too, so I'm hungry for companionship and news."

"News? Well, of course, you're buried out here in the country, so you wouldn't know, but those Fenians escaped!"

I clutched the arm of the chair. "They escaped? You're sure?"

"Of course. It's the talk of Dublin. Cheated the hangman, they did, poor devils. In a way I'm glad. Let them go to America, where all things are equal, or so they say. Ireland's had enough hangings. Don't you agree?"

My heart was pounding and I wanted to cry for joy. "You're sure," I said. "*All* of them escaped."

"Aye. It was a plot, and a daring one at that. I'm sure money changed hands, but—"

166

"You mentioned America," I said. "Is that where they've gone?"

"I'm sure. It was probably American money that got them out. They'll probably go over there and become rich and respectable. It's been done before, you know."

I nodded, still numb from the shock of this new development. He's lost to me forever now, but then, hadn't he been lost to me from the very beginning? At least in this new land he'll be what he's always wanted to be, the equal of any man. Oh, my darling, my dear, sweet rebel!

Lady Cunningham was looking at me strangely, and I suddenly realized that she must have asked me a question. "Forgive me, Lady Cunningham. My mind's been wandering."

"Don't fret so, Elly. May I call you Elly?"

"Please do, Lady Cunningham."

"Good. And you must call me Anne. I imagine Ireland, and now Bonnie Brae, have been quite a shock to you. Lady Fitzgerald has told me that you grew up in England and only recently returned home."

"Aye, just six months ago."

Her eyes were warm with sympathy. "And in that short time you've lost your father, your aunt and uncle, left Glengarra, which I understand you loved, and been transported here to the infamous Castle Bonnie Brae." She waved her hand and smiled. "Aye, I know all about Bonnie Brae, Elly, and I'm sure, even with a loving husband's help, it hasn't been easy for you."

"You know . . ." I hesitated.

"I know it has a ghost," she said gently. "And I think you've seen it."

I nodded, relieved at last to admit the truth to myself. "I didn't want to believe it, but . . ."

"I understand perfectly. You're an educated young woman. You've been led to believe that ghosts and banshees, and all manner of evil spirits are the products

167

of superstitious minds, but that's not true, dear. There's a very prestigious society in England that has dedicated itself to the study of this phenomenon. I myself am a member."

"I've never told anybody about it," I said, "and I wouldn't want Sir Gavan to know," I added quickly.

"Naturally, dear. Men are very uncomfortable about things they can't control. Even Lord Cunningham, modern man that he is, has a hard time accepting some things."

Her warmth, and her calm, logical manner gave me confidence. "You don't know what a relief it is to be able to talk about it."

She reached over and squeezed my hand. "I know, and you were wise to keep your own counsel. Even Lady Fitzgerald, and I love her dearly, does not really understand, Elly. I guess I've always been a little unorthodox, something women are not supposed to be."

I told her then about the incidents surrounding the apparition's appearance and my suspicion that the spirit was that of Lady Jane Cabot McBain.

She looked pensive. "But what could she want of you?" She sipped the tea that Bridget had so thoughtfully brought us, and said, "There's more to the history of Bonnie Brae than was contained in the book you read. Please don't take offense, but the Mitchells were villains, as were the ancestors of a great number of illustrious families in Ireland."

I admitted that I had heard some things about the family before my marriage.

"It is said that old Sir Gavan Mitchell cheated McBain out of his fortune, but who's to know the truth? At any rate, McBain laid a curse on the Mitchells after his wife's suicide."

"What was the curse?" I asked.

"Insanity. The curse predicted that all Gavan Mitch-

168

ells, from here into eternity, would carry the curse of madness."

I involuntarily shuddered and she gave me a sympathetic smile and shook her head. "I don't believe in curses, Elly. That part is superstition."

But Gavan's father was mad, I thought, and if Lady Cunningham had seen Gavan's performance in Dublin, she might not be so quick to dismiss the curse.

Lady Cunningham—I still could not think of her as Anne—removed her bonnet. "I do hope someday they design a bonnet that doesn't make a mature woman look like a fool. I can't stand these things that tie under my chin."

Her thick black hair was parted in the middle and braided around her small head, giving her the deceiving look of a spinster, but her vibrant personality shone through in her dark, inquisitive eyes. "Now," she said with a smile. May I request a tour?"

Lady Cunningham's knowledge of old castles made it seem that she, and not I, was conducting the tour, and I marveled at the astuteness of this woman who knew so much about architecture.

Bonnie Brae, built in 1625, was hardly considered an ancient edifice, but Lady Cunningham told me that the keep, or tower, appeared to be older. "In many instances these abandoned, ancient keeps were already on the land when the planters came, and they merely added on to them."

She was not interested in touring the west wing, since it was a modern addition. "Did you know it was built to impress your mother-in-law?" she asked.

I feigned surprise, wanting to hear her version.

"Old Sir Gavan met his wife when she was only fourteen. She was a great beauty, they say, the only daughter of a French merchant. She accompanied her father on a business trip to Ireland, and that's how she met Sir Gavan. Father and daughter spent several days being entertained at Bonnie Brae, and the young woman—'' She paused and frowned. "Her name has slipped my mind."

I supplied the name eagerly, anxious to hear more about this fascinating subject.

She snapped her fingers. "Of course, Gabrielle Rousseau. How could I forget such a beautiful name."

"You were saying," I prompted.

"Aye, well, the young woman was apparently quite outspoken, and she made no secret of her dislike for the castle. Perhaps it was her dislike for Sir Gavan Mitchell." She paused, and then in her own outspoken way continued. "He was not blessed with charm or good looks, nothing like your own handsome husband, and he was old enough to be the child's father. Nevertheless, he built on the west wing, and three years later he brought the young woman back here as his bride."

I opened the heavy, iron-studded door that led to the main wing, and said, "Gavan doesn't like to talk about it. His mother left, you know, when he was still an infant."

"She was very young. It was probably all too much for her."

"There's a secret passageway in here," I said, stopping in front of the old study.

"Most old houses had one kind or another. Some were underground. They usually led to the sea."

"Gavan said this one was sealed when the west wing was added on."

We entered the room and I showed her the entrance behind the bookcase. "This is typical," she said, showing scant interest.

"I felt a strong compulsion to enter it," I confessed,

and after hearing about your sister-in-law, I wondered if . . ."

She looked skeptical. "Secret passageways are fascinating, but usually just cold and dirty."

Her main interest was the tower, as that was the oldest part of the castle, and since I had never been there myself, I was eager to explore it too.

As we started up the tower stairs, Lady Cunningham took note of the pointed ogee windows at the landings, and explained that they must have been added in the past century, when much gothicizing of castles was in vogue. "For, I feel certain this tower dates back to the thirteenth century," she said. "Which could mean, Elly, that your apparition might be someone we have no knowledge of a'tall."

Each of the three stories contained tiny cell-like rooms, some of which had been utilized for storage. While Lady Cunningham was examining the windows, I turned my attention to a mountain of old furniture that had been piled on top of the other and jammed into a corner.

I recognized some chairs that had formerly been used in the main wing. They held no interest for me, but like Aunt Celia, I had a mania for antiques and I shoved them aside, hoping to discover a rare find among the older pieces.

What I found was the missing portraits of Gavan's ancestors. I was surprised to find them relegated to the tower, but I was not prepared for what I found when I turned the paintings over.

The portraits had been mutilated beyond repair, and I knew at once that this was no accident. Someone had viciously slashed, or maybe stomped, those hideous faces into oblivion with an insane frenzy.

"Can you make it to the top?"

I heard Lady Cunningham's voice and jammed the portraits back behind the chairs. "I'm coming," I said.

The view from the narrow window in the turret was worth our climb, and even on this gray November day we could see for miles. Framed in the gothic window, and stretching out to sea, Bonnie Brae's lands took on the look of a medieval empire.

There was only one room at the top, and Lady Cunningham gasped when she saw it. "This was a torture chamber!" she declared.

Iron chains were cemented into the walls, and the sight of them made me eager to leave this horrid place, but my companion was examining every inch of the room with a practiced eye.

The thought of someone being imprisoned here disturbed me greatly, and I couldn't bear to look at the evidence of it. I turned to the window, and looking down, I thought with a sickening remembrance that this was the last view of Bonnie Brae that Lady McBain had seen before plunging down, down . . .

Lady Cunningham suddenly stood beside me and encircled me with her arm. "Do you feel faint, Elly? Please, come away from the window, dear." She led me over to the landing and had me sit on the step. "Forgive me, Elly. I get carried away with this sort of thing, and I forget that others don't share my fascination with ancient history. It was a barbaric time. I've seen enough. Come, let us go back."

As we closed the tower door and stepped outside, I looked up to the window in the main house and thought I saw Starice peering down at us, but when I looked again, she was gone, and I decided it had been my imagination.

"Are you sure you're all right now?" Lady Cunningham asked, and I nodded.

The poor woman blamed herself for taking me to the tower and exposing my gentle sensibilities to the harsh reality of medieval life, but it was so much more than that.

"I felt a powerful aura of evil up there," I explained. "It was like—" I paused, and then suddenly I knew what it was like. "It was the same feeling I experienced in the passageway, an uncanny, terrible sense of diabolical evil. I don't know how else to explain it, but it was strong, and it came from outside myself, if you know what I mean."

Lady Cunningham frowned. "Did you experience that sensation of evil when the apparition appeared to you?"

I shook my head. "No, no, I'm positive I didn't. I was frightened," I said slowly, trying to remember my exact feelings. "I think I was frightened because I was seeing something I didn't believe in." I stopped and thought back carefully to both times when the apparition had appeared. "No," I said emphatically. "I did not feel any evil."

"Then you may have two spirits," Lady Cunningham said. "One that you see, and one that you don't see. The second presence is one that you only feel."

Her words disturbed me, and I shivered. "It is chilly today," she said. "Let us go inside."

We spoke of other things over lunch, Lady Fitzgerald's annual Christmas ball for one. "Oh, I do hope you and Sir Gavan will be able to come. The Fitzgeralds entertain so beautifully, and she'll really be disappointed if you're not there, Elly."

"I don't know," I said evasively. "Sir Gavan travels quite a bit on business, you know."

"Not at Christmastime, my dear!" She smiled. "I forgot, you're still a bride, and you think you must clear every invitation through your lord and master first." Shaking her head, she made a face. "If it was left to the men, there would be few balls either given or attended. Lord Cunningham, and he's the sweetest man in the world, would much rather hunt than dance." She leaned forward as if she were telling me a great secret, and said, "I just accept an invitation and then tell him about it!"

I smiled and rang for the maid to bring us our dessert. I am hardly a typical bride, I thought, and Gavan is certainly not the average husband, and as for our marriage, I had no earthly idea what will happen now that Gavan knew the truth about it.

Lady Cunningham insisted that she must leave immediately after lunch, and I accompanied her outside to her carriage.

"I'm sorry if I distressed you, Elly," she said, taking my hand.

"Not at all, Anne. It's been a relief to discuss these things. I'm awfully glad you came."

The footman assisted her into the carriage and I stood outside, talking to her through the window. I was reminded of the day Lady Fitzgerald had stood outside my carriage, reluctant to have me leave Strangford Manor, and as the carriage pulled away, I understood her feelings.

The companionship of other women was dear to us because we lived in a world of men. They governed it, controlled it, and no matter how capable we were, a father, husband, brother, or even a son was presumed to be more capable.

I thought of my predecessors, Bonnie Brae's unfortunate mistresses. The sins of the Mitchell men had weighed heavily on these poor women. Lady McBain had killed herself because the first Sir Gavan Mitchell had stolen her fortune, and recalling the brutal face I had seen in the portrait, I doubted if his own wife had known much happiness or peace of mind.

As to the second Lady Mitchell, her husband had brutalized her to the point of driving her out of the castle and abandoning her child.

And what will be the fate of the third Lady Mitchell? I wondered.

I walked slowly back to the house, and my thoughts turned to Avery, who had held freedom more precious even than love. He had tried to tell me about it once, but at the time I had not understood. Good-bye, my dear, sweet Avery. I wish you freedom, I wish you equality, and above all, I wish you love.

I spent the rest of the afternoon rearranging books in the library and wandering impatiently about the house. It seemed gloomy now, without Anne Cunningham's vivacious presence, and my bored mind searched about for something interesting to do.

Suddenly I remembered the letters in the secret compartment, and bolstered by courage borrowed from Lady Cunningham, I marched myself upstairs with a firm resolve to finish translating the letters.

Entering the room, I noticed immediately that the secret compartment was open, and I remembered then that I had left it that way myself. What had caused me to flee this room in terror?

Conscious now, after Lady Cunningham's visit, of the need to analyze my feelings during these supernatural experiences, I tried to recreate the incident in my mind.

I had been sitting on the floor, looking at the prayer book, reading the poem, examining the rose, and then . . . I had picked up one of the letters.

Immediately I recalled feeling the hair prickle on the back of my neck, the taste of ashes in my mouth, and the deadly chill that had suddenly invaded the room. I *had* felt another presence, and it had been an evil one.

I plunged my hand into the secret compartment. With mounting panic I felt around inside the empty space. The packet was gone!

I rushed back to my own room and locked the door. Starice, I thought. Bridget had mentioned that she had seen the old woman in the corridor. Had Starice taken the letters? And if so, why? And then I had to ask myself the final question. Had it been Starice's presence I had felt in the room, or someone else's?

I nearly jumped out of my skin at the knock on the door. It opened slowly, and I released my breath with a gasp of relief when Bridget's beaming face appeared. "I come with a message, Lady Mitchell. Sir Gavan says ye should join him in the main dining hall in an hour."

I stared back at her with a shocked expression on my face.

"Ye didn't know Sir Gavan was home, yere ladyship?"

I shook my head vigorously. "When did he . . . ? Why wasn't I . . . ?"

She giggled. "I thought yere ladyship knew. Sir Gavan arrived home in the wee small hours of the morning." A puzzled expression crossed her face, and then she smiled again. "I guess he didn't want to disturb yere ladyship. He went right up to his old room in the main wing, he did, and there he's been all day."

Thoughts raced through my mind while she talked. He was right there in the main house when I was showing it to Lady Cunningham. Why didn't he make his presence known then?

"I brought hot water for the hip bath," she said, reaching behind her and picking up two steaming buckets. "Oh, and something else." The puzzled look returned to her face. "Sir Gavan said yere to wear a white gown and the ruby necklace." She emptied the buckets into the tub. "Meet him in the main dining hall and wear a white gown and the ruby necklace," she repeated by rote, obviously eager to make sure she had followed instructions.

"Very well, Bridget," I said. "You may go now."

The warm bath, usually so effective, did little to soothe my frazzled nerves. Why was he using the main dining hall? That gloomy, medieval room with its gargoyles and bestiaries had depressed me from the very beginning. It was a setting reminiscent of feudal lords and their subservient ladies. Was that why he had chosen it?

I wrapped myself in a towel and searched my wardrobe for a white gown. I thought to ignore the request, but decided not to antagonize him, since it appeared he was in one of his difficult moods.

The only white gown I owned was a ball gown of French silk, cut low to expose a wide expanse of bosom. I pulled it out and put it on, and when she returned, Bridget buttoned me up the back and fastened the ruby necklace around my neck.

I swept my heavy hair up off my neck with jeweled combs, and it framed my face in a mass of curls.

"Ye look just beautiful, Lady Mitchell," Bridget exclaimed. "Like a bride ye are."

Aye, I thought, the bride of Satan. Leaving the room, I walked regally down the stairs, and though my head was held high, my hands shook as I opened the great iron-studded door and left the west wing.

Chapter Eleven

"Come in, Lady Mitchell. I've been waiting for you."

Gavan stood at one end of the long banquet table, measuring me with mocking eyes. In the flickering candlelight his handsome face took on a wicked look, and yet I was strangely drawn to him, like a moth helpless to resist the flame.

He wore a waistcoat of dark red velvet that heightened the blackness of his hair and beard, and with his classic features he resembled more a French count than an Irish lord.

He approached me and kissed my hand. "You look lovely tonight, Lady Mitchell." His eyes roamed over me, and a slight smile creased the corners of his mouth. "So virginal in your white gown." He raised his hand to my throat and flicked the ruby necklace. "The touch of scarlet is appropriate too." His black eyes were cold as they stared into mine. "Take your place," he said abruptly, and nodded his head to the other end of the long table.

He followed, and pulled out the intricately carved, high-backed chair for me. Returning to his place at table, he clapped his hands like some mighty Bedouin king, and immediately the servant girl who had briefly attended me before Bridget's arrival appeared. She filled our wineglasses and made a hasty retreat, eager no doubt to escape lest she do something to earn the master's disapproval.

"A toast," Gavan said, lifting his glass, and I raised mine warily, not knowing what to expect. "To your

Fenian." His eyes held a malicious gleam as he stared down the long length of the table at me. "He's escaped with his cohorts, and Ireland's loss is America's gain, for nevermore shall they set foot on Irish soil."

I returned his stare with unflinching eyes. Thanks to Lady Cunningham, I would not be giving him the satisfaction he sought. "To the Fenians," I said boldly, raising the glass to my lips. A murderous look crossed his face, and the wine turned bitter on my tongue. Be careful, a voice within me warned, and at that moment the maid returned and I was grateful for the brief interruption while she served the first course.

We picked up our spoons and began to taste our soup. In the silence that followed, my mind raced ahead, trying to anticipate his next move. We were playing a deadly game of cat and mouse, and although my tormentor's first thrust had missed its mark, I knew that would only whet his appetite for final victory.

"Your guest supplied you with gossip as well as the current news, I take it." His voice carried only a hint of sarcasm, but my guard went up immediately.

"I imagine you're referring to Lady Cunningham," I said indifferently. "She wanted only to see the castle. She's somewhat of an expert on them."

"So I understand. Unfortunately I was introduced to the lady's husband in Dublin." His scowl deepened. "She certainly lost no time getting here once she knew I was away."

"Gavan, really," I said. "I doubt that her husband even mentioned that you were in Dublin. Lady Cunningham was simply on her way to spend some time at Strangford Manor and she thought she'd stop by and see Bonnie Brae."

"How convenient for her, and for you too, since it gave you an excuse to do some snooping of your own, didn't it?"

I was astonished at the turn this was taking, and I

looked up with as much impatience as Gavan when the lass returned to remove our hardly touched soup plates.

An overcooked leg of lamb, potatoes, and several more unappetizing-looking dishes followed. The awkward little maid took an interminably long time to serve them, and the silence grew unbearable while we waited. At last she left us, and we resumed the conversation.

I said, "I was not aware that you objected to my exploring the castle."

"What I object to," he countered in a menacing tone, "is motive—yours and your knowledgeable friend's."

I was baffled. "What motive could we possibly have?"

His voice turned cold as he answered. "Let's try morbid curiosity, and add to Lady Cunningham's the desire to exploit and sensationalize Bonnie Brae for her own purposes."

I was shocked. "Gavan, Lady Cunningham would never be a party to anything of a sensational nature." What did he mean?

"The lady is a member of a silly London society dedicated to the purpose of investigating what they so auspiciously refer to as "supernatural phenomena." His eyes flashed and he glared back at me angrily. "They're a bunch of addle-brained nincompoops who have nothing better to do with their time, and I do not relish them sticking their big noses into my affairs!"

"I'm sorry," I said. "But I'm sure your fears are groundless. Lady—" I bit my tongue, for I was about to say, *Lady Cunningham would never betray a confidence.* "Lady Cunningham would never exploit a friendship," I countered.

He ignored me. "I imagine she filled your head with harrowing tales of Bonnie Brae's dark history, and you, gullible and genteel lady that you are, ate them up, I'm sure. It must have given you a wonderful feeling of superiority, didn't it?"

I shook my head, wondering what this was leading up to. "I'm sorry if I displeased you by showing Lady Cunningham the castle, and I can assure you, it won't happen again."

He smirked. "What a little hypocrite you are, Lady Mitchell! And how commendable that you should now agree to keep Bonnie Brae's secrets a secret." His eyes, fierce and hard, met mine, and I felt a chill as he said, "Since you are now, by virtue of our happy marriage, a Mitchell, I have decided to shatter Lady Cunningham's tired old rumors with facts." He paused dramatically, making me wait while he took another sip of his wine, and then he smiled and continued. "As soon as you have finished your dinner, we shall go together to the tower, and I will tell you far more harrowing tales than the weak ones you feasted on this afternoon."

If I had been wary of entering the tower in broad daylight, I was terrified of doing so at night, and with Gavan as my guide, but I dared not refuse.

Taking my hand, he led me through the pantry and down a short corridor that ended at a small, old-fashioned door.

"You see," he said smugly. "You ladies needn't have gone outside to enter the tower. It can be reached quite easily through the house." Taking down a large lantern that hung from the wall, he lit it and added, "This will help, but it will still be dark inside. Seeing it at night, though, will give you more of a feel for the place, don't you agree? After all, the poor devils who spent time in the tower had no light."

He unlocked the door and stepped into the black abyss. Extending his hand, he smiled and said, "Come, let another expert instruct you on our tower."

All my instincts told me to run away from him, and

away from this house, but pride would not allow me to give in. I took his hand and was drawn inside, and when he closed the door, a silent scream erupted in my throat. My skin crawled and I was faced with the irrational fear that I would never leave this place.

"The first two floors are used mostly for storage now," he said.

I was thankful that I had concealed the mutilated portraits. I didn't think I could bear looking at them in the lantern light.

"Prisoners were kept on all three floors though," he added.

My curiosity was aroused, and I said, "Are you referring to the skirmish with General Monk's troops?"

He gave a short laugh. "I don't know what went on here in the seventeenth century. I'm talking about my father and my grandfather's time. Their prisoners weren't prisoners of war."

His words shocked me. "Who were they, then?"

"Anybody who displeased them—tenants, servants . . . Their screams could sometimes be heard along that small corridor, the one we just left."

"Dear God," I murmured.

"I warned you what to expect." He held the lantern high, illuminating old trunks and chests that lined one wall. "That large trunk in the corner belonged to my father's first wife."

This surprised me. I had not known that Gabrielle Rousseau was a second wife, but it seemed highly plausible, given the difference in their ages. "What was the first wife's name?"

"Honoré. She died young, as did my grandmother."

"Did your father have children by his first wife?"

"No. According to Starice, she was barren, and of course my father was not pleased about that. At any rate, she conveniently died, allowing him to replace her with a more productive wife."

I was very interested in hearing about the Mitchell women, as I considered all of them to be candidates for Bonnie Brae's ghost. "And what of your grandmother? You say she also died young?"

"Aye. She was murdered here in the tower, possibly on the very spot where you are standing."

I automatically stepped back, and overcome with shock, I said, "Your own grandmother died in this tower!"

"Don't waste your sympathy on her. She was as notorious as my grandfather, maybe more so." He leaned back against the wall and gazed directly into my eyes as he talked. "The Lady Devil, she was called, and by all accounts that's exactly what she was. She liked to punish her servants by locking them in the tower."

His eyes never left my face, and I couldn't believe what I was hearing. He had stated the fact with as much nonchalance as if he had said that his grandmother liked to embroider or weave.

"Sometimes she'd forget to feed them," he continued. "And other times she'd return to torture them. She came back once too often and was clubbed to death by one of her victims."

I must have paled, and for a fleeting second the hard lines on his face softened. "You're not going to faint, are you?"

"Certainly not," I said, taking a deep breath and meeting his eyes without flinching.

His mask slipped quickly back into place. "Let's climb to the tower, then. There's more."

I was panting for breath when we reached the top, but Gavan showed no effects from the long climb. Like a tour guide delivering a lecture, he went right into his spiel.

"My grandfather, the first Sir Gavan Mitchell, was very secretive. Where he came from, and how he accumulated his wealth is a mystery to this day, but by the time he arrived in Belfast, he had amassed enough of a fortune to allow him to outmaneuver McBain and acquire, not only Bonnie Brae, but all the rest of the poor fool's assets." He paused and added dramatically, "Including the Scotsman's beautiful young wife."

"Jane Cabot McBain?" This was a new twist to Lady Cunningham's story, and one I was not prepared for.

He smiled. "No doubt Lady Cunningham told you the beautiful Jane committed suicide by leaping to her death from the tower window." He shook his head and smiled smugly. "Not so. The truth of the matter is she was pushed!"

I gasped. "Pushed!"

"Aye. It seems my grandfather promised to return Bonnie Brae in exchange for the lady's favors." He set the lantern down on the floor and continued the narrative in the same abstract tone. "The old bastard's body was as ugly as his soul, so that was quite a sacrifice to ask of the lady. She complied, and he, of course, reneged. I'm sure he found it very amusing to have humiliated such an aristocratic lady, but unfortunately for the lady, her husband did not find it at all amusing, especially since her sacrifice had been in vain."

In the darkness he reached for my hand and propelled me very firmly toward the window. Standing behind me, he quickly swung open the casements and encircled me with strong arms. "Look down there," he said.

A full moon bathed the ground below in an eerie light, and I gulped the night air into my lungs to clear my head. His arms tightened across my breasts, and I knew he could feel my wildly pounding heart.

"Quite a severe punishment for an unfaithful wife, wouldn't you say?" he asked in a mocking tone.

His arms became a vise around me, and I felt my feet being lifted off the floor. I squirmed against him, the panic within me rising to a crescendo, and suddenly he laughed.

Depositing me none too gently on my feet again, he gripped my shoulders and turned me around to face him. "Did you think I was going to toss you out the window too? What for? You're not an unfaithful wife— at least not yet!"

My anger overrode my fear. "Your insinuations are insulting, sir."

He seized my shoulders again and glared down at me. "Take care, Lady Mitchell. There's more than one way to be unfaithful." His eyes glittered in the moonlight, and his words hung in the air like harbingers of doom. "Thinking about one man and lying with another; that's the worst way!"

Closing the window, he picked up the lantern, and in a perfectly normal tone of voice said, "Well, now that you know the real history of Bonnie Brae, we can leave."

Once out of the tower and back in the comparative warmth and safety of the house, I began to feel a mounting sense of indignation.

We returned to the dining hall, and drawing myself up with dignity, I looked directly into his eyes and spoke in the cold, polite voice of a stranger. "Thank you for the tour. It's been an exhausting day, so I shall say good night, sir. I'm going to bed now."

His voice was equally cold and equally polite. "You'll go to bed when I tell you. Now, sit down and drink some wine. You look chilled to the bone."

My eyes smoldered with resentment, but I took the glass he held out to me. Before he could propose another toast, I drank it down quickly.

185

He raised an eyebrow and smiled. "Done like a true Kincaid!"

I returned his sarcasm with sudden anger. "My brother is not, and never will be a true Kincaid."

"Why so touchy? I've rattled all the skeletons in the Mitchell closet for you. Hugh's drinking problem is mild in comparison."

I regarded him coldly. "So you did, but I wonder now where you received such incriminating information. Surely . . ."

"Surely not from the perpetrators themselves, you were about to say." He refilled both our wineglasses, and looked at me with a strange, haunted expression on his face. "The Mitchells, Mistress Kincaid, were like no family your sheltered and repressed little mind could envision. They were proud of their exploits, and they reveled in their own evil. As a mere child I was exposed to tales more horrible than any I've told you." A faraway look came into his eyes, and he said, "I could make your hair stand on end if I told you some of the things that went on here when I was a lad."

I stared back at him in horror and sudden pity, picturing the small, defenseless child he once had been.

He drank his second glass of wine quickly and poured himself another. When he spoke again, all his old arrogance had returned. "You're not keeping up with me. Drink up, Lady Mitchell."

I finished the wine and placed my hand over the empty glass before he could refill it. Standing up suddenly, I felt light-headed and I prayed I could walk out of the room without staggering or stumbling. "Good night," I said as I walked slowly toward the door.

I never once looked back, and having left the room, I hurried down the long corridor to the security of the west wing and my locked bedchamber. Breathing heavily, I reached for the handle on the iron-studded door when I felt his hot breath on the back of my neck. Dear God, he'd been behind me all the while, walking on silent cat feet like a panther stalking his prey.

I felt his arms go around me, and his lips crushed mine in a bruising kiss. "This is our long-postponed wedding night," he said, slipping his hand possessively inside my bodice and caressing my breast. Flames of desire swept through my treacherous body even as my lips protested. "No, Gavan, no!"

His eyes, so close to mine, looked fierce. "Don't you ever say no to me, Elly. You and your sly brother may have pulled the wool over my eyes, but I'm your husband, and by God, you'll not forget it!"

Sweeping me up into his arms, he carried me back through the great hall and up the stairs to his bedroom in the main wing. He threw me on the bed and smothered me with wild, hungry kisses that left me weak.

Slipping the low-cut gown down to my waist, he devoured me with his eyes. I tried to cover myself with my hands, but he pulled them away. "You're beautiful, Elly, and you're mine. I'll take you to heights you've never known before." And bending his head, he whispered, "I'll make you forget your Fenian and his simple, peasant ways."

I felt the soft brush of his beard on my bare breasts and the flick of his tongue. I put my arms around him and drew him closer, giving myself up in wild abandon to erotic pleasures beyond any I had ever known.

Like a rag doll, I let him turn me over and unbutton the back of my gown. Consumed by passion, I did not protest when he slipped even the last vestige of clothing from my body, and trembling with an unknown yearning, I lay still as he parted my legs to take me.

His hard, pulsing member tore through my maidenhead, and the almost unbearable pain was shattered in a series of sensations so intense that I heard myself moan in a strange, undulating voice that came from deep within the core of my very being. Instinctively I moved with him, pressing him to me closer and closer in a wild frenzy of exquisite torture that reached almost unbearable heights, until with one last, giant thrust he brought me to a climax that burst within me like a shower of exploding stars, and I lay weak and satiated beneath him.

He collapsed on top of me, our naked, sweating bodies fusing together as one, and then he raised himself up, and though I could barely discern his face in the moonlight, I sensed bewilderment and an uncharacteristic remorse in the words he murmured. "I'm sorry, Elly. I didn't know you were a virgin."

Opening one eye, I squinted through the glare of a bright sun that streamed through the window and bathed my face with its warmth. The unfamiliar room momentarily disoriented me, and then I suddenly remembered last night. Had it been a dream? I moved my hand gingerly to the other side of the bed, and feeling nothing, I sat up suddenly and let my eyes travel over the room.

My clothes lay in a rumpled heap where Gavan had tossed them, and I sank back on the bed, my cheeks burning with the memory of my own wanton behavior. How could I have given in to Gavan when I love Avery?

Remembering Avery's chaste kisses, I cursed my traitorous body for the hunger that even now made me yearn for Gavan's burning lips and practiced hands.

I jumped with anticipation at the sound of the discreet knock on the door. A white cap, disheveled hair, and a face I didn't even recognize peeped around the door like a puppet on a string. "Beggin' yere pardon, Lady Mitchell, but there's a slew of servants waitin' to see ye in the hall downstairs."

Thank God, we'll soon have a permanent staff, I thought, noting the rumpled gown and smudged face of this latest jewel from Starice's grab bag. "You must be new," I said.

"Aye, me lady. Old Starice, she hired me while you and the master was away. Me name's Megan, yere ladyship."

I shook my head, wondering if Glengarra's Megan was the only clean one in Ireland. "Tell the servants to wait. I'll be down directly, and please have Bridget bring hot water to my bedroom in the west wing." And then, as an afterthought, I said casually, "Has Sir Gavan had his breakfast?"

"Sir Gavan? Aye, he's had breakfast and been gone hours ago, yere ladyship."

I felt a stab of disappointment, and the words were out before I could take them back. "Where did he go?"

She looked at me blankly. "I don't rightly know." Her brow furrowed in an effort to remember something, and then she added, "But I'm thinkin' that he left ye a note by Bridget, yere ladyship."

When she had gone, I got up. Catching sight of myself in the mirror, I saw that my initiation into womanhood had altered my appearance. Wearing nothing but the ruby necklace, I stared back at a naked harlot with wildly disheveled hair.

I thought of all the married women I knew, from Aunt Celia to Lady Fitzgerald, and I was certain, without a shadow of a doubt, that none of them had ever behaved so scandalously.

Pulling on my rumpled clothes, I hurried to the west wing, and like a wayward maiden returning from a rendezvous, I sneaked back into my virginal bed and pretended to be asleep when Bridget knocked.

"Just leave the note and fill the tub," I said in a drowsy voice, wanting no part of Bridget's small talk today.

As soon as she left, I jumped up and grabbed the note from the dresser.

"Dear Elly," I read.

I apologize for last night. You'll be rid of me for six or seven weeks, as I must make land purchases in the west.

Gavan.

Tears of frustration stung my eyes, and I stepped angrily out of my clothes and into the hot tub. I felt again the strange sensation that my body was no longer my own, and I scrubbed myself vigorously, wanting to erase his touch.

How dare he leave without facing me! How dare he bring me to the brink of terror in the tower and then ravage me in his bed! He was a devil like all the Mitchells, and I had let him possess me and make me forget a commitment that was fine and good. Oh, never would I forgive him for making me betray my love for Avery!

I dressed myself in a plain plum-colored gown that buttoned up the front to a straight high neck, and I wound my unruly hair up into a knot. Then I went downstairs to face Maire McGee's handpicked staff of servants.

They were an impressive group, consisting of an experienced housekeeper, a butler, footman, and three healthy looking, well-scrubbed maids.

I explained to the housekeeper, a Scottish woman by the name of Mrs. Stewart, that we already had servants in the house whom I expected she would also train, and that I had no wish to dismiss them unless she found them uncooperative. I added that Bridget was to remain as my personal maid, and that she would answer only to me.

In the weeks that followed, I was pleased beyond measure with Mrs. Stewart's results. She, and her very efficient staff, worked wonders at Bonnie Brae, and once again time lay heavy on my hands.

I had heard nothing from Gavan beyond the brief note announcing his departure, and he had now been gone six weeks.

The weather had turned unseasonably warm for December, and my short walks around the castle grounds did nothing to satisfy my restless spirit. I needed open fields before me and a strong mount under me. I needed to feel the wind on my face, and to hear the music of thundering hooves in my ears, but pride made me hesitant to face Brendan.

I had not seen him since our trip to Dublin, and I did not know what explanation, if any, Gavan had offered for his sudden appearance and our hasty departure. Finally, the call of the Gypsy being too strong to resist, I folded my pride like a fancy, useless fan and donned my riding habit.

Much to my relief, Brendan smiled when he saw me, and his big, rough face fairly glowed with warmth, making the raised scar that zigzagged from the corner of his right eye and across his broad nose seem even whiter. " 'Tis a beautiful morning for a ride, Lady Mitchell, and I've a fine new mare for ye to try." Wiping his hands on his already stained shirt, he turned to a stableboy who was grooming one of the stallions. "Fetch the new mare out here."

Brendan's easygoing, friendly manner made me feel comfortable, and I forgot that he'd been a witness to my humiliation in Dublin. Perhaps, knowing his master, he thought nothing of it, I mused. I judged him to be a man in his late forties, and I wondered if he had been at the castle when the last Lady Mitchell had escaped her husband's ire by running away. "Have you been long at Bonnie Brae?" I asked him.

"Nay, yere ladyship. Sir Gavan brought me here just five years ago." A strange look crossed his face, and he said, "Do ye recall the sordid section of Dublin that we passed through?"

I nodded. How could I ever forget the squalor that lay hidden, seething with ugliness and want, in the midst of such splendor?

"That's the part of Dublin I come from." His expression hardened, and he rubbed his hand over the scar on his face. He seemed to have forgotten I was there, for his eyes took on a faraway look, and he spoke softly, as if to himself. "Cutthroats and blackguards all, but I, Brendan Kelley, can still command them." A triumphant look crossed his face then, and he smiled. "Aye, without me, Sir Gavan would never have penetrated the walls of hell!"

The stableboy brought the horse out then, and Brendan suddenly returned from his haunted past. "There she be, Lady Mitchell, a fine little bay filly she is, and I've no doubt ye'll be takin' a fancy to her."

"She's beautiful," I said.

"Aye, she is that, but she has a proud heritage too. She was sired by a grandson of Copenhagen." He patted the horse's nose and explained. "Copenhagen carried the Duke of Wellington to victory at Waterloo."

"Has she been named yet?" I asked, and when Brendan shook his head, I smiled. "Then I shall call her, Gypsy."

That day marked the beginning of a new freedom for me, for with Gypsy at my disposal, I would no longer be confined to the house and I looked forward to widening my horizons at Bonnie Brae.

As I cantered away from the stables, heading east toward the windswept moors that bordered Bonnie Brae's coastline, I wondered about Brendan's strange meanderings. What had he meant when he said that he could still command the cutthroats that dwelled in the dark recesses of Dublin City, and what had Gavan to do with any of it?

I pushed the disturbing thought from my mind, determined to enjoy the freedom the day afforded me, for with Gypsy as my silent companion I was now able to see, and, unfortunately, to also be seen beyond the castle and its immediate environs.

Chapter Twelve

Remembering Glengarra's beautiful green hills, I found little to admire in the starkness of the moors that stretched before me, and turning Gypsy the other way, I decided to ride west toward Bonnie Brae's tenant farms, when I spied two figures emerging from the bogs.

Though they were some distance from me, I recognized immediately the small, bent form of Starice. Curious as to the identity of her companion, I held Gypsy back and waited, partially concealed by the tall marsh grass. They were arguing, and their voices carried.

"Ye owe me, Starice, on the ashes of them's ye wronged." The speaker was a disreputable-looking old man with long white hair that hung to his shoulders.

Starice's shrill voice pierced the air. "Yere crazy, Lauren Devlin. I had nothing to do with it."

They passed closer, and I could see that the old man's long hair was matted and dirty, and his clothes were little more than rags. "Ye were the divil's whore, Starice," he said.

"Aye," she shrieked. "And I'll be meetin him in hell soon enough, so I don't need ye to remind me of it."

She carried a basket overloaded with what looked like weeds, and in her agitation she swung it, dropping half of its contents onto the ground. Too engrossed in her conversation to notice the loss, she passed by, looking like a little black spider, hugging the ground, her skinny arms and legs protruding from her shawl-clad body.

When they were out of sight, I dismounted and

picked up one of the weeds that had fallen from her basket. The long stalk of grass looked familiar, and suddenly I recognized it.

This was the same sleeping grass that grew in The Paradise, where Avery and I had played as children, and I smiled, recalling Avery's hushed words. "It's an enchanted weed, and it can put ye to sleep for a hundred years!"

I had a picture of the cackling old witch brewing it up in a steaming caldron, and then I laughed at myself for being childish.

I did wonder, though, about Starice's companion and their strange conversation. Apparently this half-crazed old man believed that Starice owed him some favor, and she was reluctant to give it. But what had he meant about the ashes of those she had wronged?

I mounted Gypsy and rode back at a leisurely pace, but when I came to the cemetery, I stopped. I suppose some might find it macabre, but I have always found graveyards fascinating. Tombstone inscriptions can provide keyhole glimpses into past lives, and it would be interesting to read those commemorating the Mitchell clan, I thought.

Tethering Gypsy to a tree, I climbed a slight hill and entered the cemetery. Years of neglect had left it overgrown by weeds and with some of its markers tilted and close to being uprooted from soil erosion.

The most recent grave was, of course, that of Gavan's father, and his headstone was a simple marker, bearing his name and the dates February 19, 1789–April 2, 1860.

He was forty-five years old when Gavan was born, I mused, and Gabrielle Rousseau couldn't have been more than eighteen.

His first wife lay beside him.

Honoré Carlyle Mitchell, born December 11, 1792, died June 16, 1817.

No epitaph to mark her passing, no "beloved wife," or even, "rest in peace," for poor Honoré, I thought. A short life, and surely a miserable one, but how could it have been otherwise when she had married a wicked old tyrant like Sir Gavan Mitchell the second.

A sudden strong wind whistled through the naked trees, and I looked up at a sky suddenly grown dark. Almost immediately the atmosphere changed to one of danger, and looking around, I realized that I was in an isolated spot, and at a distinct disadvantage being on foot. I turned to go back, and then froze as a disembodied voice called my name.

My eyes darted from right to left and back again, but no living soul did I see, and although common sense told me it was only the wind, I could not overcome the spooky feeling that somebody was watching me.

"Lady Mitchell."

The scream stuck in my throat as the grinning face of the old man I'd seen on the moors suddenly emerged from behind a large monument and confronted me.

His watery blue eyes danced with mischief, and he laughed, the short, nervous laugh of the insane. "Scared ye, didn't I?"

"Not really," I said cautiously.

He looked disappointed. "Ye saw me?"

"Oh, no. You had a good hiding place," I added.

The mischievous look suddenly disappeared, and his watery old eyes turned crafty. "What ye be doin' in Bonnie Brae's graveyard?"

"Just visiting," I said, starting slowly to walk away from him.

Sudden anger flashed across his face, and my intuition told me he could be dangerous. Dear God, just let me get out of here and safely back to Gypsy, I pleaded.

"Did ye pray for them?"

The question startled me, and I groped for an answer that would satisfy him.

"Don't be wastin' prayers on the Mitchells because the almighty has damned them," he said in an agitated voice. "Damned them to everlasting hellfire," he shouted, moving closer to me. "All the Mitchells will burn, me lady, burn, burn, burn!"

He jumped up and down, laughing with a fiendish glee, and I picked up my riding skirt and ran, my heart pounding in my chest.

The rain started then, big pelting drops that splashed in my face, and mixed with my tears. His laughter followed me, and I stumbled blindly through the downpour, trying to find my way out of the cemetery.

My riding hat blew off, and the wind whipped my wet hair into my face, but still I ran, my throat aching and my lungs near to bursting. My soaked riding habit weighed me down, and stopping for a moment to catch my breath, I looked around, trying to get my bearings. I had lost all sense of direction, and I wondered with a sinking feeling if I had merely been going round and round in circles.

Then a terrifying thought suddenly struck me! If I don't soon find my way out, I will be doomed to spending the night here!

My stomach turned over and bile rose up in my throat. Clamping my hand over my mouth, I began to run again, faster and faster like a half-drowned, half-crazed rat in a maze, when suddenly my foot caught on an upturned root and I sprawled headlong into the dirt.

My head hit the sharp corner of a marble marker, and hugging the upraised mound of a grave, I felt myself sinking into a black pit, when suddenly the blessed sound of a human voice rang in my ears.

The voice was deep and strong and robustly alive, and I knew at once the caller was neither ghostly nor insane. "Lady Mitchell, Lady Mitchell!"

It was Brendan, and I was overcome with relief and

joy. Raising myself up, I tried to shout over the wind. "I'm here. Help me." My voice was weak and I cried tears of frustration. Would he go away and leave me here?

Despair almost overtook me, and I thought to lay my head back down on the grave and let sleep overtake me, but I could not give up so easily, and using my last ounce of strength, I forced myself to stand.

I saw him then, only several yards away. "Brendan, help!"

When he reached me, I collapsed in his strong arms, letting the blackness overtake me.

I opened my eyes, and saw with relief the rose silk bed hangings that told me I was back at Bonnie Brae, safe in my own bed.

The drapes were drawn and the room was in shadows, and it felt so wonderful to be warm and dry that I almost drifted back into slumber again, but my head throbbed, and I reached up and touched it. "Oooo," I said aloud as my fingers pressed against the tender raised spot.

"Did ye want something, me lady?"

I jumped at the sound, and then looked up into Bridget's concerned face.

"Thanks be to the Almighty! It's glad I am to see ye awake, Lady Mitchell. Ye give us all a scare, ye did. I been sittin' here all night, and ye been tossin' and turnin' and cryin' out something awful. Mrs. Stewart took and sent for the doctor first thing this morning, she did."

I started to sit up on hearing this, but she pushed me gently back and adjusted the covers. "Now, ye be lyin' still, Lady Mitchell. Mrs. Stewart says ye might be havin' a cushion."

I was confused, and Bridget wasn't helping matters. "A cushion? What are you talking about, Bridget?"

She sat down on the bed and patted my hand. "Now, don't be gettin' yereself riled up, Lady Mitchell. All I know is, big Brendan brought ye home, soaked to the skin and with yere head all bloody. Like to scare the livin' daylights out of me, it did." She took a breath and continued. "He went out to look for ye when ye didn't come back from yere ride. It was rainin' cats and dogs by then and Brendan got worried. He saw yere horse tied up outside the cemetery, and that's how he found ye."

Her eyes grew wide, and she said, "Nobody goes near Bonnie Brae's graveyard, Lady Mitchell. The divil's own demons are buried there."

My memory returned with her words and I shuddered, remembering the terror I had felt. But it's over now, I told myself, and I certainly don't need a doctor. "I feel fine now," I said.

"Now, don't ye be frettin', Lady Mitchell. Mrs. Stewart said the first sign of a cushion is vomiting, and ye was doin' plenty of that last night."

"What is a cushion?" I said, mystified.

She tapped her head. "Comes from being hit here. Rattles a body's brains, it does."

I could hardly control my laughter. "You mean a concussion," I said.

She was nonplussed. "Aye, like I said, a cushion."

I gave her a reassuring smile. "All I have is a little bump, no *cushion*. But I'll tell you what I'd like to have."

She was instantly alert to my needs. "What can I get ye, Lady Mitchell? A cup of tea? Some warm broth?"

I laughed. "No. I'd like a big dish of strawberries."

Bridget looked stunned. "Strawberries in December, yere ladyship?"

How silly of me, I thought. "Pay me no mind,

Bridget. I don't know what I was thinking of. I just had a sudden craving for strawberries."

A strange expression crossed her face, and she gave me an indulgent smile. "I'll bring ye a nice breakfast, and some strawberry jam. How does that strike ye, Lady Mitchell?"

I said, "Fine," and snuggled down under the covers. Yesterday's adventure had lost some of its terror in retrospect, and now, in the safety of my room, I decided that the old man was obviously daft, but probably meant me no real harm.

It was Mrs. Stewart who brought up my tray. "Guid morning, Lady Mitchell. Ye look weel noo," she said in her soft Highland voice. "But ye were a paire sight when Brendan brought ye home—soaked to the skin ye were and bluidy fae the cut on yere head. I was a'feared ye had a concushion."

She was a tall, rather plain woman in her late fifties, a little on the prim side, but I liked her, and I admired the calm and efficient way she had taken over the management of Bonnie Brae. "This looks delicious," I said heartily, trying to convince her I was perfectly well, for she was looking at me with deep concern.

Piling pillows behind me, she set the tray on my lap. "Juist tak yere time and enjoy yere meal, yere ladyship."

I picked up a piece of warm toast, thickly spread with strawberry jam. "Ummm, delicious," I said, savoring the slightly tart taste on my tongue.

She turned to leave and hesitated at the door. "Dr. McTavish is doonstairs." Before I could protest, she quickly added. "With Sir Gavan gone, yere ladyship, we ken no what tae do. I thought it best the doctor hae a look at that bump on yere head."

"Oh, all right," I said with resignation. "Send him on up."

I pushed the tray to the foot of the bed. Either I ate

200

too fast, or I do have what Bridget calls a *cushion* in my head. Feeling weak, I lay back on the pillows, and in a few minutes Mrs. Stewart returned with Dr. McTavish.

"Well, well, lassie, and how aire ye feeling today?"

He greeted me with a warm smile, and I was secretly glad to see him.

Mrs. Stewart discreetly faded from sight, leaving us alone and I answered him candidly. "Not so good, Doctor. I felt fine when I first woke up, but now I feel sick to my stomach again. Do you think I could have a concussion?"

He came over and carefully examined the bump on my head. "Dinna loook like much of a bump, Lady Mitchell." Then he smiled. "I don't think ye have a concussion a'tall."

"But I never feel sick to my stomach," I said.

He continued to smile. "Are yere periods regular, lassie?"

I sat up suddenly. "I'm three weeks late, but you don't think . . ."

He nodded. "I think it's more likely ye'll be havin' a bairn than a concussion, Lady Mitchell."

After Dr. McTavish left, I remained in bed, my thoughts muddled in confusion. A baby, dear God, I was going to have Gavan's baby!

Now look what he's done, I thought. And where is he? Oh, I don't even know if I want a baby, and surely Gavan won't want it. How could he, when he hates me so much! Poor baby, I thought, feeling suddenly protective toward the little thing.

As the days wore on, I gradually began to accept the inevitable. Let him stay away, I thought. At least I'll have something of my own to love and care for.

I had received a long letter from Lady Fitzgerald

and she had enclosed an engraved invitation for us to attend her gala Christmas ball.

"I won't take no for an answer," she had said. "You two lovebirds have been alone long enough now. We all miss you, Elly, and we'll be heartbroken if you don't come."

How was I to tell her that my bridegroom was not to be found, and I would probably spend Christmas alone at Bonnie Brae?

In the end, though, I wrote back and said that Gavan had been called away on business and if he returned in time, we would be happy to accept the invitation.

I became more and more depressed as Christmastime grew near. I thought back to all the wonderful Christmases I had known in England.

I had exactly ten days to prepare Bonnie Brae for what I was sure would be its first real Christmas, and once begun, I entered into the project with surprising enthusiasm. I sent a note by messenger to Strangford Manor, asking Lady Fitzgerald to accompany me to Belfast on a shopping spree and, of course, I received an immediate and enthusiastic reply in the affirmative.

We arrived in Belfast in a flurry of snow, and though Lady Fitzgerald worried that it might hamper our return, I had no such qualms. We were using Bonnie Brae's phaeton, driven by two of Gavan's strong black stallions, and with Brendan in the driver's seat, I felt we had naught to fear.

I purchased brooches for both Bridget and Mrs. Stewart and a cameo for the housekeeper, for I doubted she would wear anything fancier. But what to get for Brendan, I thought. And finally, at Lady Fitzgerald's suggestion, I settled on a handsome pipe and leather tobacco pouch.

"Now, what will you be buying for that dear husband of yours?" Lady Fitzgerald asked, and my mouth hung open in shock.

I didn't even know if Gavan would be home for Christmas, and I certainly wasn't feeling disposed to give him a present. But Lady Fitzgerald could not be expected to know the peculiarities of our situation.

"Here's a handsome watch," she said, looking into the glass-topped display case.

"An exquisite piece," the jeweler noted with an eager smile. He took it from the case and flipped the small gold lid open, showing us the face of the watch. "It opens in the back too," he said. "For me lady's picture, and of course it can be engraved with his initials on the front and "From your loving wife," or whatever you may wish on the back."

The very thought horrified me, and I said, "No, my husband already has a watch."

"Perhaps a stickpin, then," he offered. "That also makes a handsome gift."

"That's true, dear," Lady Fitzgerald said, nodding her head with approval.

At least it can't be engraved and there's no room for my picture, I thought, reluctantly settling on a fine diamond-studded one.

We left the jewelers and picked our way along a sidewalk lightly powdered with white. Lady Fitzgerald clung to my arm, taking mincing little steps. Snowflakes sparkled on her green velvet cape, and the plumes on her bonnet danced in the wind. "Snow is pleasant only when one looks at it from the inside," she said.

I squeezed her arm. "That's cheating. Now, tell the truth, doesn't it put you in the holiday spirit?"

"Not at my age." She smiled though. "But there was a time when I found it romantic. Lord Fitzgerald and

I used to take out the sleigh and ride all over Strangford Manor. What a sight that was in the moonlight!"

What a good marriage they've had, I thought, and wondered suddenly if I could have had that kind of marriage with Avery.

"This is a special Christmas for you and Gavan—your first," she was saying. "When the children come, you'll have to share each other. Not that that isn't wonderful too." She laughed. "Just a little more hectic, as you'll discover someday, Elly."

Like this time next year, I'll discover it, I thought, feeling suddenly frightened at the prospect. I couldn't imagine myself a mother, and I certainly couldn't imagine Gavan a father!

I bought colored paper and feathers and lace imported from France to make decorations for the tree. Brendan packed them all carefully in the carriage while we retreated to our favorite sweet shop for hot chocolate and a bit of lunch.

I spent the night at Strangford Manor, and much to my amusement, Alex and Clyde treated me as reverently as if I had been their maiden aunt.

"Have I grown old and ugly in just two months?" I teased, finding that I missed our former relationship.

They assured me that such was not the case, and with wary eyes in their mother's direction, they gradually resumed their old, innocent flirtation, giving my bruised ego a much-needed lift.

We awoke the next morning to a pristine, snow-covered world, and after a hearty breakfast I took my leave of a family that had become very dear to me.

"We'll see you on the twenty-sixth," Lady Fitzgerald said as she kissed me good-bye, and I nodded, knowing that I would have to come up with some last-minute excuse to explain my absence.

Bundling myself into the carriage with lap robes that had been warmed by the fire, and with a hot brick to rest my feet upon, I started out in comfort for the trek to Bonnie Brae.

We drove through a winter wonderland marred only by the tracks our carriage wheels made in the snow, and even Bonnie Brae, as we approached it, took on a rakish dignity in the midst of a background of such pure and untouched perfection.

Mrs. Stewart bustled me inside to warm myself by the fire, and Bridget hastened to bring me a hot cup of tea. Their concern touched me, for just having left the security and warmth of Strangford Manor, I felt lonely.

I retired early, and must have just drifted off to sleep when I heard someone crying. I sat up in bed, drawing the covers around me and listened. Someone was in need of help.

Drawing on my robe, I lit my lamp and opened the door leading to the hallway. It seemed to be coming from the east wing, and I hurried downstairs with no thought other than that I must help whoever was in such a pitiful state.

I unlatched the iron-studded door and hurried down the long, dark corridor to the main wing of the castle. The light from my lamp cast eerie shadows on the walls, and I gasped and then realized it was my own figure I saw in the enlarged silhouette.

Once in the great hall, I followed the sound to the dining room, and then realized with a sinking feeling that it was coming from the tower.

The banshee! If I thought I had heard it once a long time ago, I knew now that I had been mistaken. This was like no sound I had ever heard. The villagers said it cried for the children the old master had murdered, I thought, but traditionally, it also signified a death in the house. Whose, I wondered, and when?

I suddenly realized I was alone in this section of the

castle, and a feeling of panic overwhelmed me. I turned and ran as if the devil himself were chasing me, back to the safety of the west wing.

I was shivering when I got back into bed, and although I no longer heard the sound, sleep did not come for a long time, and when it did, it was filled with a terrifying dream about the banshee and the baby.

In the morning, although I couldn't remember exactly, I recalled the gist of it and I prayed more fervently than I have ever prayed before. "Please, don't let it be the baby. I'll be a good mother. I swear it. Just don't let it be my baby!"

Apparently no one else heard the banshee, for nothing was mentioned, and I tried to put it out of my mind by concentrating on holiday preparations.

I consulted with Mrs. Stewart, who was enthusiastic about the tree-lighting ceremony. "Bless ye for yere gooodness, Lady Mitchell. T'will be a bonnie Christmas after all. I'll be telling the servants aboot it. Ach, ye ken be sure they'll be pleased."

I sent for Brendan and asked him to scout the woods for a tree. "We'll put it here, under the staircase," I said, indicating a spot in the west wing's great hall.

He looked at me blankly, and I suddenly realized that he had no earthly idea what I was talking about. The Christmas tree was a German custom, and it had been introduced to England only fairly recently by Prince Albert. "We had them in London," I said. "They're decorated with candy and paper ornaments and they add a festive touch to the house. Any large evergreen will do," I explained.

He measured the area with his eyes. "Aye, and I'm thinking I know just the right tree. There's a giant pine up the northernmost tip of Bonnie Brae. I'll ride up there first thing in the morning and have a look at it."

Soon the house began to acquire the hustle and bustle I'd always associated with the holidays.

Tantalizing odors emerged from the kitchen as Cook baked nut cakes and plum pudding, along with Mrs. Stewart's old Scottish recipe for bannock cakes, those delicious little oatmeal cookies that are baked on a griddle.

The days flew by and on the day before Christmas Eve, Brendan brought in the tree. It took three men to set it up, and they left a trail of pine needles on the floor from the kitchen to the great hall, but I think it was the most perfect tree I have ever seen.

It took the four of us, Bridget, Brendan, the stable-boy and myself the better part of the day to trim it, and I wished I had made twice as many decorations.

"But we can fill in with candies and nuts," I assured Bridget, who was overawed at the spectacle.

"It looks gorgeous just as it is, yere ladyship," she said, looking up at the tree with eyes full of wonder.

"Just wait until the candles are lighted," I told her.

"Aye, what a sight that'll be!" Brendan added, coming down from the ladder and gazing up at our masterpiece. "Bonnie Brae's never celebrated Christmas far as I be knowin'." His eyes met mine and he said softly, "We're mighty grateful to ye, Lady Mitchell. Some of us as well have never celebrated Christmas."

It is I who should be grateful to them, I thought, for they have given more than they have gotten, and for the first time in my life I think I really understood the meaning of the Christmas spirit.

I spent the next morning making additional decorations out of a roll of heavy silver foil which I had purchased in Belfast. My Cornish governess had shown me how to cut intricate designs out of paper, and as a child I had spent hours folding and cutting in preparation for trimming our tree.

I was engrossed in my work and didn't hear the door to the morning room open.

"Merry Christmas."

I dropped the scissors and looked up to find Gavan standing in the doorway.

Chapter Thirteen

For the past eight weeks I'd carried within me a mental image of Gavan, but it paled beside the flesh-and-blood man who stood before me. His eyes were fiercer, his hair blacker, and he was far taller than I had remembered. He looked wildly handsome and distinctly masculine in his mud-splattered riding clothes, and caught off guard, I stared up at him without speaking.

An expression of disappointment (or more than likely it was impatience) flashed across his face, but he covered it quickly with a cynical smile. "The warmth of your greeting overwhelms me, Lady Mitchell."

His sarcasm scraped my nerves raw, and all the frustrations of the past two months welled up inside me. "Why should you expect a warm greeting? I've heard nothing from you for two months. You might have been dead for all I knew!"

He gave me a calculating look. "Perhaps that would have suited you better." Crossing the room, he slumped down in a chair and regarded me with a half smile. "Fate almost obliged you, too, Lady Mitchell, but alas, the masters of Bonnie Brae are all devils, as you so well know, and devils are not easy to kill."

"I don't know what you're talking about," I said irritably. "I'm not in the mood for riddles."

Close up, I could see that his slumped-down sprawled-out position was not an affectation. His eyes were glassy and rimmed with dark circles and his unkempt appearance bore witness to a long and arduous journey.

"Suffice it to say that I was unavoidably detained," he said, rising. "And now, if you'll excuse me, I need to catch up on some sleep." He executed a mocking bow, and added, "I hope to be more presentable when I see you at dinner, Lady Mitchell."

He left the room, and I found it impossible to continue making the decorations, for my hands were shaking so much that I could not use the scissors. What had he expected? Did he think I would throw myself into his arms and weep with joy because he finally decided to come home? Two months with no word from him, and even now he offers no explanation beyond a silly riddle!

I got up and started pacing the floor. I didn't care where he was or who he was with, but if he had any idea of picking up where he left off two months ago, he could think again!

The tree-lighting ceremony and the accompanying festivities had been scheduled for this evening, and I forced myself to continue with the preparations. I wasn't going to let Gavan Mitchell spoil the servants' Christmas, or my own either, for that matter.

Megan, who had blossomed under Mrs. Stewart's tutelage into a neat and willing worker, interrupted my thoughts. "Beggin' yere pardon, yere ladyship, but Mrs. Stewart said to give ye these apples."

The large basket she held was overflowing with luscious-looking bright red fruit. "Thank you, Megan. They're to go on the Christmas tree," I explained.

She smiled broadly. "That Christmas tree is a sight to behold, yere ladyship. Niver have I seen such a grand and glorious thing. Do all the fine houses in England have them?"

"Aye, most of them do. 'Tis a German custom and one that the British have taken quite a fancy to." I had

210

never seen Megan so animated. Her thin, mouselike little face fairly glowed, and on an impulse I asked, "Would you like to put the apples on the tree, Megan?"

Her eyes widened and she hesitated. "Oh, I don't know as I could place them properly, yere ladyship. I wouldn't want to be spoiling it."

"Nonsense, Megan. Just put them wherever you think they should go. The Christmas tree belongs to us all. Now, run along and ask Mrs. Stewart to show you how to thread them with string."

She executed an awkward curtsy and hurried off, leaving me with a warm feeling in my heart. Bonnie Brae's old walls will ring with laughter and song for at least one night, I thought, and then wondered nervously if Gavan would object.

I chose my dinner gown carefully, knowing I would also be wearing it for the celebration with the servants later in the evening. I wanted to look festive but not formal for this occasion, and I finally decided on an emerald-green watered silk. It had a modest neckline which I secured with a gold filigree brooch, and very full, bell-shaped sleeves.

Bridget braided my hair with narrow green satin ribbon and coiled the huge knot at the nape of my neck.

"Yere hair's like spun gold. So fair ye are, Lady Mitchell. Like a Christmas angel, ye look, and like a Christmas angel ye are," she said, fluffing my skirt out over its crinolines.

I had already given Mrs. Stewart, Brendan, and Bridget their individual gifts after we had trimmed the tree and Bridget was still excited about hers.

"I can hardly wait to show me mam the brooch," she said for the tenth or more time. "Niver did I expect to own a piece of jewelry, and certainly not one so fine

211

as that brooch. What did ye say the pearls were called, yere ladyship?"

"Seed pearls."

"Aye, seed pearls," she repeated in a hushed voice. "Just to imagine, Bridget O'Shea wearin seed pearls!" She patted her ample bosom. "Close to me heart, I'll be wearin' it, and thinkin' of yere ladyship every time, I will." She frowned suddenly in annoyance. "Wait till the tonguewaggers in the village hear about the celebration at Bonnie Brae. That'll give the old biddies somethin' to chin about, it will—a Christmas tree, and a whistle bowl. Bet they niver heard tell of either one of them!"

I suppressed my laughter and said, "It's called a *wassail bowl*. It's a drink, Bridget, made with ale, spices, and roasted apples. The word *wassail* means *be thou well* in old English."

She nodded her head and smiled. "I'm not much for strong drink, yere ladyship, but I'll sure try a taste from that whistle bowl."

I entered the west wing's dining room to find Gavan there ahead of me, but despite my nervousness I felt far more in command this time than at our last dinner together. Tonight it was I who was on familiar ground and Gavan who was the stranger.

This room, where I had eaten my solitary dinners for the past two months, bore my imprint, not only in the giant mural of Glengarra and in the arrangements of holly and greens that graced the table and mantelpieces, but in the efficient new servants, whose allegiance was to the mistress rather than the master of Bonnie Brae.

"Good evening, sir. I hope you rested well," I said, as if to a guest. I smiled sweetly up at him. "Your red waistcoat is very appropriate. I thought of sending one of the servants up with a request that you wear it tonight, but I see it wasn't necessary."

My sarcasm brought a startled look to his face, but he quickly recovered himself and gave me an amused smile. "I'm happy that you approve of my choice." Then he glanced quickly around the room. You've outdone yourself, Lady Mitchell. Bonnie Brae has never looked so festive. The tree is magnificent, but where did you get it?" he asked.

"Brendan said he found it at the northernmost tip of Bonnie Brae's territory."

"I see."

I wondered if he was angry with Brendan for cutting it down, and I added quickly, "I asked him to do it. I hope you don't mind."

"Why should I mind? Bonnie Brae is your home."

It seemed an appropriate time to bring up the celebration. "Since you were not here," I began, "I went ahead and made arrangements to give the servants a little party tonight." I paused, and when there was no outburst, I continued. "I didn't know what customs you observed at Bonnie Brae, so I just followed my own family's traditions."

To my surprise, he seemed pleased. "And am I invited to this party?"

"Of course. As the master of Bonnie Brae, I would hope that you'd take charge of the celebration."

He shook his head. "I'll leave that to you. I don't know much about such things."

Nevertheless, when we had all gathered in the great hall for the lighting of the tree, Gavan slipped very naturally into his role as master and host of the evening. He introduced himself to the new servants, and expressed both the master's and the mistress's wishes to all for a Merry Christmas.

I nodded to Brendan and he, along with several of his stable hands began to light the candles on the tree.

When all were lit, servants scurried about, extinguishing the other lights, and we gazed up at the tree in all its glory.

Like twinkling stars, its candles flickered, making my paper cutouts glitter like spun silver and Megan's apples glow like rubies in the soft light.

Voices suddenly rose in an old Irish carolers' song:

God bless the master of this house,
Likewise the mistress too.
May their barns be filled with wheat and corn,
And their hearts be always true.

A merry Christmas is our wish
Where'er we do appear,
To you a well-filled purse, a well-filled dish,
And a happy bright New Year!

Thankful I was for the dim light, for the carol had touched me deeply. Stealing a glance at Gavan, I thought how the candlelight softened his face, taking away for a time the harsh lines and arrogant look I knew so well.

This little-known Irish carol was followed by "Good Christian Men, Rejoice," and "God Rest Ye Merry Gentlemen," two rousing carols that had always been particular favorites of mine, and when this part of the program was over, everyone's attention was turned to the long table that had been set up in the great hall. It was laden with mouth-watering delicacies the likes of which I'm sure some present had neither seen nor tasted ever before.

"Shall I invite them to the table?" Gavan asked me in a whisper.

"Not yet. Our new butler has prepared a wassail bowl for us," I said.

At that moment I saw Mrs. Stewart raise her hand,

and the butler marched into the hall, carrying a large, steaming bowl which he placed in the center of the table.

I whispered to Gavan, "The master and mistress of the house must taste it first. That's the custom."

He turned to me with a half smile. "What's in it?"

"Hot ale, spices, and toasted apples," I said. "And if it's anything like my Uncle Roger's recipe, it'll be delicious."

He smiled and offered me his arm. "Then by all means, let us observe the custom, Lady Mitchell."

In draining our cups, we pronounced the wassail a fitting drink to end the ceremony.

"It is now customary," I told Gavan, "for the master and mistress to leave, so the servants can enjoy the rest of the evening on their own."

Amid much bowing and curtsying and with hearty good wishes ringing in our ears, we threaded our way through the smiling, happy crowd.

"My compliments to you for a magnificent celebration," Gavan said, leading me into the drawing room.

"Thank you," I answered stiffly.

Now that we were alone, the good fellowship that had so recently been engendered was suddenly lost.

He walked over to the fire and poked at the smoldering embers. At his touch, they crackled and blazed, sending out tiny sparks that flashed and then withdrew into the central flame again. For some unknown reason this display upset me, and I turned to the window and looked out at the snow.

"Must I always be apologizing to you?"

His voice was low and close to my ear, but I continued to stare out the window. "You don't have to apologize at all, Gavan," I said.

He moved away, and I could hear the clink of glasses as he poured drinks from the decanter. "Dammit, Elly,

I'm not in the habit of reporting on my comings and goings. If I worried you, I apologize."

I turned and faced him. "I was not worried," I countered hotly.

"All right, then, let's say you were angry."

"Ignored is what I was."

He threw up his hands. "Then I apologize for making you feel ignored." He held out one of the glasses to me. "Here, have a glass of wine. It'll calm your nerves."

"My nerves are perfectly calm," I said through clenched teeth. "And I don't want any wine."

"Come on, drink it," he coaxed.

"No, the doctor said I shouldn't—" I stopped, realizing I'd already said too much.

"What doctor? Why?" His eyes bored into mine. "Have you been sick?"

I felt my lip quiver, and the tears that had been held back for two months filled my eyes and then spilled over. "I'm going to have a baby," I sobbed, and without looking at his face, I ran out of the room.

I slipped quietly up the backstairs, leaving behind the merry laughter that still filled the great hall. Oh, to be so carefree again, I thought, wallowing in my own misery.

Crying uncontrollably, I undressed and got into bed. I felt completely and utterly alone, and that feeling was still new to me.

Before my life had changed so drastically, there had always been someone to turn to: my mother and father, or Aunt Celia and Uncle Roger, sometimes even Hugh, for he had shared some unhappy times with me. But now I had no one, I thought, and sobbing miserably, I buried my head in the pillow.

I did not hear the door open, and when I felt a hand on my shoulder, I stiffened, but very gently he turned me over, and in the darkness he kissed my tear-stained face.

"Does it make you so unhappy to be carrying my child?" he asked.

I couldn't see his face, but I could feel the tension in his body as he waited for my answer. "I want the child," I said, "and I'll love it, but . . ."

Before I could finish, he put his hand over my mouth and crushed me to him. Speaking in a husky voice, he said, "Don't be a fool, Elly. Maybe you gave your heart to the Fenian, but you gave your body to me, and between us we've made a child. That's as close as two people can get!"

He parted my lips and kissed me, and like the smoldering embers of a fire I felt my body ignite and answer him with a deep hunger that ached for fulfillment.

Our coming together was gentler and more tender this time, and afterward I lay in his arms, spent and oddly happy as the clock struck midnight on Christmas Eve.

When I awoke, it was already dawn, and Gavan lay sleeping beside me. He was stretched out on his back, covers flung aside, exposing his broad chest with the fascinating black hair that trickled down to his navel.

I had an irresistible urge to stroke it, and very timidly, lest he awaken, I leaned over him. It was then that I noticed the scar. It was high up on his left side, running in a straight line almost to the center. I was certain it had not been there before, and besides, it was red and angry-looking, which told me it had to be new.

"Do you approve?"

I jumped at the sound of his voice. "You only pretended to be asleep," I said, blushing with embarrassment.

He laughed and pushed me down beside him. "We're married, Lady Mitchell. You're allowed to look." Then quickly yanking my covers off, he added, "Of course I demand the same privilege."

I squealed in mock outrage and slapped him with the pillow, and it didn't take long for our wrestling match to turn into a love match which was heightened to a new and rather risqué experience in the bold, bright light of day.

Together we soared to peaks of indescribable ecstasy, and at last, with passion spent, we lay quietly beside each other, at peace with ourselves and all the world.

"Merry Christmas, Gavan," I said softly.

He brushed my lips with a gentle kiss. "Merry Christmas, Elly."

He lay back down and I reached out and rubbed my hand over the silken hairs on his chest. When my fingers touched the scar, I said, "What's this?"

"Nothing, just a scratch."

I sat up and looked down at him. "It's too deep to be a scratch. Where did you get it? You didn't have it before."

I felt him stiffen, and the old guarded look returned to his face. "I said it was nothing. Don't worry about it."

He got up then and starting dressing, and I turned over and pretended to go back to sleep. He's angry that I questioned him about the scar. Oh, why must everything about him be a secret, I wondered, feeling irritated.

But then, to my further surprise, he came around to my side of the bed and kissed me. Without a trace of anger in his voice he said, "I'll go back to my old room and change. If you can make it downstairs in an hour, sleepyhead, I'll have breakfast with you."

Would I ever be able to understand his mood swings? I wondered.

I rang for Bridget and answered her cheery greeting with a wan smile. My stomach was feeling queasy again, but I refused to give in to it; besides, it usually passed rather quickly, and then I would feel fine for the rest of the day.

"Some soda mint tea'll be takin' care of that quite nicely," Bridget said. I must have had a shocked expression on my face, for she apologized quickly. "Beggin' yere pardon, Lady Mitchell. I don't mean to be oversteppin' me place, but ever since ye had a cravin' for the strawberries . . ."

She paused uncertainly, and then hurried on in her breathless way. "Me oldest sister, Fiona. She had the morning sickness bad with her first one, she did, and that's what me mam give her."

I forced a smile, only to prove to Bridget that I was not offended. "I always did say you were a mind reader."

She seemed relieved. "Not really, yere ladyship. I'm just a keen observer. At least that's what Mrs. Stewart says I am. Now, would ye be wantin to try the soda mint?"

"If you say it works, I'll try it," I told her.

She turned to leave and then paused in the doorway. "Remember when ye hit yere head in the cemetery, Lady Mitchell?"

"I remember."

"Well, old Starice, she come to the kitchen that night with some medicine for ye. 'Course Mrs. Stewart, she threw it right out the door soon's the old witch left." Bridget's usually pleasant face turned deadly serious then. "Cook's old cat lapped it up and he slept without wakin' for three days straight, yere ladyship." Her deeply concerned blue eyes looked directly into mine,

219

and she slowly shook her head. "Poor thing ain't been right since."

She curtsied and closed the door, leaving me alone to mull over her words.

Of course it was the sleeping grass. Hadn't I watched Starice carry the deadly weed home in her basket? She knew what it was, and she'd gone to the moors to gather it.

I shuddered, remembering my own mental image of her cackling with fiendish delight and bending over a steaming caldron. Had that been fantasy or premonition? At the time the picture had amused me; it no longer did. Thank God, I thought, for vigilant and loyal servants!

Bridget returned with the soda mint tea and hot water for my bath. I accepted both, along with her concern, in deep gratitude. "Whatever would I do without you, Bridget," I said.

"Ye won't have to do without me, Lady Mitchell. I'll be here long as ye want me, lookin' out for yereself and the little one," she said emphatically.

I decided not to mention the incident to Gavan. It sounded too far-fetched, and of course there was no proof. Bolstered by my faith in Bridget and Mrs. Stewart, I put the incident behind me and went downstairs to breakfast. It was Christmas. Gavan was home, and for the time being things were going well.

I entered the dining room and, as usual, he was waiting for me. He gave me an admiring appraisal and smiled his approval.

A sumptuous breakfast buffet was awaiting us at the sideboard, and Mrs. Stewart hovered over it, rearranging the serving dishes.

Gavan came forward to greet me. "Merry Christmas, my dear. You look lovely in that gown." He winked his eye and nodded his head toward Mrs. Stewart. Then he kissed me sedately and whispered, "But lovelier without it."

"Stop it," I hissed. "Merry Christmas, Mrs. Stewart," I said over his shoulder.

"Ach, and a blessed one to ye both," she answered. "I'll be off to services now, yere ladyship. Sir Gavan hae graciously offered me tae use the carriage, but dinna ye worry, Megan will be after gettin' anything ye need."

When she had left the room, I said, "It was good of you, Gavan, to offer her the coach."

He chucked me under my chin. "I'm not the ogre you think I am, Elly."

"We're both ogres for not going to church ourselves," I said.

He held up a hand in mock horror. "A Mitchell in church! Why, all the good pious souls would drench me with holy water and run for their lives!"

"That's just an excuse," I told him, helping myself to two plump sausages.

"Next Christmas you and our son can go, and perhaps you'll pray for me." He sounded very serious, and I looked at him quickly, but he was already smiling. "I'm certain it will be a son, and while we're on the subject, would you object to calling him Emmet?"

I was surprised. I had assumed he would want the name carried on. "You don't wish to call him Gavan?"

His smile vanished. "There will be no more Gavan Mitchells if I can help it."

He seemed so intense and I didn't want him to lose his good humor. "I love Emmet. It's a beautiful name."

Later I was to wonder why he wanted no more namesakes, and I vaguely recalled that Lady Cunningham had mentioned something about a curse on the Gavan Mitchells.

We took our places then, and when I reached for my

napkin, I found a small box had been concealed underneath it.

"Open it, it's your Christmas present," he said.

I thanked God for Lady Fitzgerald and the jeweler who had talked me into purchasing the stickpin. "Not until I get your present. It's upstairs. Just wait."

When I returned to the dining room, I was out of breath.

"Why did you run? I could have waited a minute," he said.

I laughed. "Well, I couldn't. I'm a child when it comes to presents."

"You're a child when it comes to many things," he said, pulling me into his lap. "An exasperating but adorable child!"

"I am not. How gorgeous!" I cried, opening the box and gazing in awe at the large, sparkling diamond that nestled like a star against its midnight-blue cushion. "It's the biggest, most beautiful diamond I've ever seen."

He smiled at my enthusiasm with typical masculine indulgence. "Here, let me put it on you." I held out my hand, and he slipped it on over my plain gold wedding band. "We were married before we were engaged. Now we are both," he said simply.

I looked down at the huge stone on my finger, and then at Gavan, who had just opened my gift. He was staring at the stickpin with a strange look on his face. "The jeweler will exchange it if you'd rather have something el—"

My words were smothered by a kiss that was long and strangely chaste. He held me close, and I could not see his face, but his voice was low and husky with emotion. "I wouldn't think of exchanging it. It's the first Christmas present I've ever received, and I'll cherish it."

"I come for a word with ye, Sir Gavan."

The familiar voice startled us both, and we broke apart so suddenly that I was almost dumped on the floor. I started to get up, but Gavan wouldn't let me. Rage contorted his face as he shouted, "Get in the kitchen, and if you ever enter a room without knocking again, I'll send you to an asylum!"

So quickly did the intruder vanish then, it was almost as if we had imagined her presence. Yet the brief interruption had served to shatter Gavan's mood and deny me a much-needed opportunity for a glimpse into my husband's past.

His mercurial moods always amazed me, and I watched his sudden fury mount out of all proportion to the offense.

"Who the hell does she think she is? Barging in here without knocking. I've told her about this before. By God, I'll put the old witch where she belongs!"

I got up from his lap and smoothed my skirts, thinking that I should take advantage of this unexpected opportunity. "Please, Gavan, it's not worth getting upset about. Perhaps now, though, it's time to ban her from the house."

He looked at me with the eyes of a stranger. "Bonnie Brae will always be Starice's home. That much she's earned, and if I ever hear you've deemed otherwise, you'll answer to me!"

Chapter Fourteen

Gavan's dark moods disturbed me, but as we settled into married life that winter of 1861, I must admit that I was not unhappy.

My arrogant and domineering husband had another side to his nature, and in those early months of my pregnancy I found he could be caring and sweetly solicitous to my needs.

Our social life blossomed after the Christmas ball at Strangford Manor, for Lady Fitzgerald's position was such that none would dare snub us after it became obvious that she had taken the young Mitchells under her wing.

Consequently we received more invitations that winter than we cared to accept, and my "delicate condition" came in handy as a readily accepted excuse. To give the devil his due, though, Gavan's charm was mesmerizing. Men liked him and women of all ages adored him. He had completely captivated two of the most upright and conservative women I knew, Lady Fitzgerald and Mrs. Stewart. In their eyes he could do no wrong, and there were times when I childishly resented his coup de grâce in accomplishing this.

Now that we had been launched into Ulster society, Gavan was eager to finish furnishing the castle.

"Next year we'll give a Christmas ball, the likes of which nobody in Ireland has ever seen," he predicted, and I suddenly realized that his family's ostracism had affected him far more than he cared to admit.

Emmet, as Gavan insisted on calling our unborn

child, made his presence felt early in the new year, and as the months passed, his gymnastics made his mother decidedly uncomfortable. By the spring I swore he was standing up and turning around, which Gavan declared to be a sure sign the child was male.

His interest in Emmet was more than just a natural desire for an heir; he seemed to be looking forward to taking an active part in the child's development, and I wondered if perhaps his own lonely childhood was responsible for this.

The only time he had ever touched on the subject had been the night when he had taken me to the tower, and intimated far more than he had revealed about those dark days, but I had learned not to probe, for it made him angry and was to no avail.

The scar on his chest was another secret that Gavan preferred to keep, and after he had rebuffed my one attempt to question him about it, I made no further inquiries. Perhaps it is better that I don't know, I decided.

I was aware of the dark side of my husband's personality, but for the present, life was good, and I did not want to disturb these halcyon days with ugly suspicions.

It had been a long and bitter-cold winter with one snow following another into April, but finally the spring of 1861 was ushered in on a balmy day in May. Sun drenched the snow-spotted fields with a healing warmth, and looking out the window, I spotted a bright yellow crocus lifting its face to be kissed.

Grabbing a cloak, I hurried downstairs, feet flying despite my cumbersome body.

"Please tae be careful, yere ladyship," Mrs. Stewart warned. She stood at the bottom of the staircase, looking up at me with concern. "Ye dinna want to fall now, with the bairn so close tae coming."

I paused, and holding the banister, I resumed my descent in a stately manner. Sometimes Mrs. Stewart made me feel like a child with an overly protective nanny, but I loved her for her gentle concern. "I'm fine, don't worry about me," I said as I reached the bottom of the stairs.

"Aire ye going oot?" she asked, noticing my shawl.

"Only for a little walk. I won't go far—I promise."

"Juist tae be careful, and cover yere head," she called out as I closed the door.

Both Mrs. Stewart and Bridget were looking forward with great eagerness to having a baby in the house. Bridget had asked to act as nursemaid, and I had agreed, knowing that there would be no one who would give my baby better care than Bridget O'Shea.

I walked slowly down the winding pathway. The sun was warm on my back, and I watched a robin press his ear to the ground and then struggle mightily to pull up an unwilling worm.

"Did ye hear the banshee?"

The voice was one that I would never forget, and a chill ran up my spine. Turning around quickly, I saw the old man crouching on the ground beside a bush.

"What are you doing here?"

He smiled a toothless grin and stood up. "I be tendin' the grounds, Lady Mitchell. Spring be comin', and there be lots to do."

"Leave at once," I told him. "You have no right being on this property."

The idiot's smile froze on his face, and a crafty look crept into his eyes. "Sir Gavan give me the right. He hired me as groundskeeper. Afore the winter, he did."

I was shocked. Could it be true? Why would Gavan do such a thing when it was plain the man was crazy?"

"Somebody's gonna die," he said, scratching at his

226

filthy clothes. "Ain't no escape when the banshee wails."

I turned from him in disgust and walked back toward the house.

"Die, die, die," he chanted after me.

Once inside, I went to look for Gavan, and as I walked toward his study, I heard voices, his and Brendan's.

"He's dangerous, Sir Gavan. Let me call on me mates."

"Not this time, Brendan."

"They did a good job for ye in Dublin, didn't they?"

"Aye, but I can handle this myself."

When they saw me standing in the doorway, they stopped suddenly and stared.

"What is it, Elly?" Gavan said with impatience.

"I wanted to talk to you about something."

"See me later. I'm busy now," he said abruptly.

Brendan backed out of the room. "I'll be takin' me leave, Sir Gavan." Then he turned to me. "Come in, Lady Mitchell. I was just goin'."

Gavan glared at me as if I were a child who had interrupted the grown-ups' conversation. "And what is so important that it can't wait?" he asked after Brendan had disappeared.

"Did you hire that man outside as a groundskeeper?"

"What? Oh, you mean Lauren Devlin. Aye, Starice asked me several months ago to give him a job."

"Gavan, he's filthy and crazy to boot. And just because Starice asks you . . ." Too exasperated to finish I let the sentence hang.

Leaning back in his chair, he raised an eyebrow and fixed me with a cynical stare. "Why, he's one of your poor, Lady Mitchell. His family were once tenants here. Surely you of all people wouldn't want me to refuse him!"

His sarcastic allusion to Avery's family angered me. "It's not because he's poor, Gavan. It's because he's insane and dangerous!"

He waved my misgivings aside with impatience. "I tell you, he's harmless, Elly. Now, don't worry me with nonsense. I have real problems to think about."

I turned on my heel and flounced out of the room. His superior attitude infuriated me. *The foolish woman is just having hysterics. Don't worry me with nonsense, he says. The master has real problems to think about.*

Later he tried to make amends and said all of the wrong things. "I'm sorry if I lost my temper, but I've got a lot on my mind right now, Elly."

"So have I, and I resent you treating me like a silly goose when I come to you with something important."

"I treat you like a silly goose only when you act like one. I told you, he's harmless. That should be enough for you!"

"Oh, should it now? And are you saying I should defer my judgment to yours just because you're a man and I'm only a lowly woman?"

He smiled. "Something like that."

I don't know which affected me more, the smile or the statement, but rage boiled up inside me like an erupting volcano, and all the strides we'd made in coming to terms with our marriage were swept away at that moment. I stared back at him coldly. "Then we have nothing more to say to each other."

Our quarrel festered and the distance between us grew wider with each passing day. We had shared my bedroom in the west wing every night since Christmas Eve, but this night I locked the door on him and his voice, carefully controlled, came to me from the other side. "If it wasn't for your condition, Elly, I'd break this door down and show you who's the master of Bonnie Brae. As it is, you can have your bed to yourself.

228

I'll not sleep in it until you get down on your knees and beg me to!"

You'll be in hell before I get down on my knees and beg you for anything, I thought.

May passed, and by the middle of June, we had progressed to speaking only when necessary.

"I must take a trip—a shipment of cattle is arriving," he said by way of explanation. "Brendan and I will be going to the north end to see about it tomorrow."

I was surprised that he would go now, for the baby was expected in three weeks. But nothing must interfere with his empire, I thought, looking at him with disdain. "Your cattle does not concern me," I said.

"No, it doesn't. I merely wanted to say that I'd have no objection if you wanted to invite Lady Fitzgerald to stay with you while I'm gone."

The suggestion, coming from him, rubbed me the wrong way. "I didn't realize I needed your permission to invite a guest to Bonnie Brae."

His control snapped, and he slammed his fist down on the table. "You need my permission for everything. Do you understand? I'm your husband, or have you forgotten that?"

"I wish to God I could!"

"I should be back in a few days," he said coldly.

"Stay as long as you like. I don't need you here," I told him.

A strange, almost stricken look momentarily appeared on his face, but it had been occasioned only by a wound to his pride, as his reply confirmed. "Emmet is my heir and the future master of Bonnie Brae. What you want doesn't matter. It's my place to be here!"

"Emmet, Emmet," I cried in a singsong voice. "Have you ever thought of the possibility that this child might be a girl!"

229

He had never looked more satanic. "The Mitchells have sons," he said with finality.

This exchange had been followed by a stony silence that we refused to break, even to say good-bye, for I stubbornly refused to play the role of dutiful little wife, standing on the step and waving, as my husband galloped away in a cloud of dust. I did, however, observe their departure from the window at a discreet distance.

And so once more I was left alone at Bonnie Brae, and much as I would have enjoyed Lady Fitzgerald's company, I would have to do without it now. My pride would never allow me to give Gavan the satisfaction of knowing I had complied with his wishes.

Looking back on the days when we had been almost happy, I suddenly understood that they had been a delusion. We were mismatched in every way except one. Moreover, the strong physical attraction that drew me to Gavan Mitchell had from the very beginning seemed wrong, and compared to what I had felt for Avery, downright immoral.

"Dear, sweet Avery," I whispered sadly, "where are you now?"

Rousing myself from a nostalgia too poignant to contemplate, I turned my thoughts to mundane affairs.

I had been meaning to store banquet cloths and other seldom-used table linens in an empty closet which I had noticed just off the kitchen.

Gathering up the linens, I carried them downstairs. The closet was small, and extremely shallow, and I wondered what it could possibly have been used for in the past. At any rate, I decided, shelving would have to be added if it was to be of any use at all, and I went in search of one of the male servants for assistance.

In the kitchen I found the cook, Katy, who looked at me with surprise, for I seldom visited, preferring to leave this part of Bonnie Brae's operation strictly in Mrs. Stewart's capable hands.

"I would like to have some carpentry work done on that small closet in the hall," I said. "Are Francis or William about?"

Her eyes fairly bugged out of her head, and her mouth hung open, giving her a stupid look.

"Starice wouldn't let us use that closet, yere ladyship. Lord, but the poor soul was scared to death of it, she was. Wouldn't go near it, and gave strict orders nobody else should either."

"Starice had some strange compulsions about the west wing," I said, dismissing her comments. "Just send Francis or William to me as soon as you find them, Mrs. Burke."

Francis, a middle-aged tenant who also did odd jobs around the castle, appeared in answer to my summons, and I explained what I wanted done.

"I've got some boards in the stable what'll do the job, Mistress. Let me just go get them," he said.

When he had located the boards and his tools, we went together and looked at the closet. I showed him where I wanted the shelves to go, and then, leaving him to his work, I went outside for a stroll.

The garden, which Gavan had laid out last summer to my specifications, was beginning to show promise. Most of the trees and shrubs were still small, and some varieties would not bloom for yet another year, but the roses were magnificent, and I sat down on the stone bench, breathing in their fragrance and remembering a summer afternoon when we had sat there together and Gavan had proposed to me.

His advances had shocked and at the same time quickened me with desire, and even though I hated him, remembering made me yearn once more for the thrill of his kiss, the magic of his touch, and slowly, for no reason at all, tears filled my eyes, and spilling over, dropped like splashes of rain on my lap.

I got up and walked slowly down the flagstone path

between the long rows of bushes which would blossom next spring, giving us a "lilac walk" like the one Gavan had seen and admired in England.

A sudden breeze charged the atmosphere and I looked up to see a sky turning dark in the wake of a summer storm. I stood and watched the gathering clouds, not caring that the wind undid my hair and whipped it about my face.

Rolls of thunder shattered the air with a magnificent overture, bringing all the raging elements together in a spectacular display that was both violent and beautiful.

Transfixed, I was oblivious to everything but the storm until I heard someone shouting my name over the wind. "Lady Mitchell, Lady Mitchell . . ."

I came out of my trance as Mrs. Stewart appeared beside me, holding the shredded remnants of an umbrella in one hand while tugging at my arm with the other. "Please tae come inside Lady Mitchell. Ye'll catch yere death of cold oot here in the storm."

"It came up so fast," I murmured, trying to excuse my own stupidity. Soaked to the skin, and obviously frightened of the lightning, the poor woman nodded and pulled on my hands. I felt guilty for dragging her outside on my account, and locking arms, we bowed our heads against the wind and slowly made our way back to the house.

Colin, the butler, met us at the door and assisted us inside. He was a rather prissy young man, and he looked at us with dismay. "Dear me! Whatever are ye doin' outside? 'Tis stormin' something fierce!"

Mrs. Stewart pursed her lips. "Ach, Colin, dinna be haeing the vapors aboot it. 'Tis juist a summer storm." She handed him what was left of the umbrella. "Put this in the trash." Then she turned to me. "Ye'd best be getting oot o' those wet things, Lady Mitchell."

"I will, Mrs. Stewart, but make sure you do the same. I'll never forgive myself if you catch cold."

We both went to our rooms to change, and it wasn't until a day later that I heard what had happened to Francis during the storm.

He came to see me, and looking sheepish, said, "I be wantin' to explain why I didn't put the shelves in the wee closet for ye, Lady Mitchell."

I had almost forgotten that I'd asked him. "It doesn't matter, Francis. You can do it today."

"Nay, yere ladyship, let me explain about the closet."

Francis was a great one for detail, and I nodded, prepared to listen to a long, boring account of how the wood was too thick or too thin, or there was some other such trivial problem to deal with.

"I had the boards all measured and cut, ye see, and I didn't know if ye wanted them painted before or after they was up. Ye'd gone outside for a walk, Cook said, so I just thought I'd nail them in and then paint."

"That will be fine," I said, wondering if this was all that was keeping him from getting to work on it.

"Aye, so I thought, yere ladyship," he added in his maddeningly tedious way. "So I started to nail the board to the wall and that's when the lightning struck me hand!" He paused dramatically, and when I didn't comment, he continued with renewed excitement. "Throwed me clear out of that wee closet and into the hall, it did, and me whole arm burned like it'd been set on fire."

I was skeptical. There was no window in the closet, so I didn't see how lightning could possibly strike him, but I wasn't about to argue the point. "I'm sorry. It was a bad storm, but I'm glad you're feeling all right now."

"Aye, yere ladyship, me arm's fine now."

"Good, then perhaps you can work on the shelving today. It's cooled off, so I don't expect we'll be having another storm."

233

He readily agreed. "That's just what I thought, yere ladyship, and I goes down there with me tools and all, and what do ye think?"

"I can't imagine."

"There's another wall, a brick one, behind that wee closet, and nails won't go through brick, yere ladyship."

The ghost of an idea clicked in my brain, and eager to be rid of him, I said, "Don't worry about it, Francis. I've decided not to use the closet anyway, but thank you just the same."

When he had gone, I gave my imagination free reign.

Suppose the secret passageway had not been sealed off when the west wing was built, as Gavan claimed. Suppose instead, it had been extended, ending in an opening concealed in this closet. Wouldn't this account for the fact that Starice, whose hearing must certainly be impaired, could hear me rapping from this wing?

The other part of Francis's story was more disturbing. Certainly lightning could not enter a windowless closet, but Francis was not a liar and neither was he possessed of a vivid imagination. Therefore, I would have to assume that the force which had stunned him and driven him out of the closet must have come from the same evil entity that I had sensed inside the passageway.

Lady Cunningham's words came back to me. *You may have two spirits. One you see and one you only feel.*

For the next several nights I slept fitfully, dreams disconnected and convoluted, passing through my subconscious like scenes from the window of a moving train. I saw Gavan on horseback, his long black cape flying as he rode like the wind, trying to escape someone, or something. He kept looking back, but his pursuer remained behind him in the shadows.

I saw the apparition standing at the foot of my bed. Again her hands were stretched out to me in a silent plea for I knew not what, and then she bowed her head and wept silently.

I saw Starice holding a basket overflowing with stalks of sleeping grass. She tossed them into a blazing fire, and suddenly Lauren Devlin appeared beside her. He was grinning and jumping up and down, and then he tossed something into the fire too. Looking close, I saw that it was a baby!

I woke up then, drenched in sweat and trembling all over.

The next day I was full of nervous energy. If only I could ride, I thought, but of course I couldn't, so I went up to the nursery and rearranged it, moving the baby's crib from one side of the wall to the other. I took all the nappies and baby blankets out of one drawer, refolded them, and put them in another drawer. If I could, I would have rewashed them and hung them out on the clothesline.

And then you'd be sent to the loony bin, I told myself, using Bridget's favorite expression. I couldn't help but smile, imagining the servants' shocked faces if the mistress of the house were to actually do such a thing.

There were times, I thought, and this was one of them, when I envied servants. They performed real work and had the satisfaction of doing it well, and they never had time to be bored or to brood.

"Lady Mitchell! Whatever are ye thinkin' about, movin' furniture around in yere condition?" Bridget stood, hands on hips, looking at me from the doorway.

"You're a worse scold than Mrs. Stewart," I said with a sigh. "Besides, I only pushed it and it's light as a feather."

Bridget giggled. "Speaking of bein' a scold. I was

just after givin' it to that old Lauren Devlin, I was."
She nodded her head in satisfaction. "I shook me finger
at him and I says, 'See here, ye be gettin' yereself
cleaned up, or I'll be takin' those rags off ye and
cleanin' ye meself.' Then I looks him right in the eye,
and I says, 'I'll use me scrub brush, too, and I'll scrub
the skin right off'n yere skinny hide, I will!' "

I laughed at the thought of it. "Oh, Bridget, you're
priceless. But, tell me, did Mrs. Stewart hear you say
all that?"

She blushed. Bridget greatly admired Mrs. Stewart,
but the Irish girl's earthiness would have shocked the
prim Scotswoman, and we both knew it. "I hope not,"
she said, and we both burst into laughter.

As always, after a conversation with Bridget I felt
better, and I spent the rest of the morning arranging
flowers for the great hall.

I heard a carriage enter the driveway and wondered
if Gavan was returning early. But no, I thought, he
wouldn't be coming by carriage. I ran to the parlor
and looked out the window, and to my surprise and joy
I saw Lady Fitzgerald's skinny little footman valiantly
trying to assist her plump figure out of the carriage.

I threw open the door and rushed outside. Embrac-
ing her, I smelled the sweet, old-fashioned scent of the
lavender she wore. "What a nice surprise this is!"

"A surprise? Well, I hope it's not a surprise. Gavan
said you invited me?"

I said, "Gavan? You saw Gavan?"

"Why, of course. He and his man stopped at Strangford Manor on their way north. He said you told him
to ask me . . ."

"Of course I did," I assured her hastily. "But I was
afraid you might be too busy to come."

"Never! Like I told that nice young man of yours,
Elly, I'm available whenever you need me."

That nice young man is a tyrant, I thought. And you

236

wouldn't think him so charming if you saw him without his mask. At any rate, I was delighted to have her and I took her arm and led her inside the house.

"I declare," she said, stepping into the great hall. "What a magnificent castle."

I'd forgotten she'd never been to Bonnie Brae. "I'll take Strangford Manor any day," I said. "It's warm and alive, just the opposite of Bonnie Brae."

Her blue eyes looked into mine with compassion. "A house reflects its owners, Elly. As we all know, Bonnie Brae has had an ugly, troubled past, but you and Sir Gavan are young. Why, soon these old walls will ring with the laughter of children." She looked around her and sighed deeply. "Love will bring this old castle to life again, my dear."

I squeezed her hand. "I hope you're right. And thank you, Lady Fitzgerald."

She linked her arm in mine. "Give me a cup of tea, and we'll talk. Gavan said you've been depressed, and I'm here to cheer you up."

We chatted over tea and Mrs. Stewart's jelly cakes, which Lady Fitzgerald adored. "I'll have just one more little cake. You say it's a Scottish recipe, Elly?"

"Aye, from our housekeeper, Mrs. Stewart."

"Delicious. You must let me have it." Her huge bosom jutted out like a tray attached to her body, and she casually brushed a crumb from it. "As I told Sir Gavan, Elly, women become quite upset during the last stages of pregnancy. It's a perfectly natural thing. Why, I remember just before Alex was born, or was it Clyde? No, maybe George. Well, no matter, it was one of them. Anyway, I simply made poor Lord Fitzgerald's life miserable. I snapped at him over every little thing."

She leaned closer and lowered her voice. "The truth of the matter is, I detested him!" Looking down at my bulging belly, she gave me a sympathetic smile. "I suppose it's our way of getting back at the men for putting

237

us through all this discomfort. But it doesn't last long. After the baby comes, we forgive and forget."

What in the world had Gavan been telling her? It galled me that he had won her over to his side so completely, but I could understand it. Hadn't he almost won me over, too, with his devilish charm?

A cramping pain gripped me suddenly, and I winced, but Lady Fitzgerald didn't notice. It's indigestion, I thought. I shouldn't have eaten the cakes. It can't be anything else. The baby's not due for another three weeks, but I felt it again, and this time it was stronger.

It would serve Gavan Mitchell right if the baby came and he wasn't here, I told myself.

Chapter Fifteen

Emmet Thomas Mitchell was coming into the world three weeks early, and from what I could ascertain from the whispered exchanges and knowing glances of Lady Fitzgerald and Mrs. Stewart, he was coming feet-first.

Dr. McTavish had been summoned, and he miraculously arrived in time to take over and assure the two frantic women that all would be fine.

He stood at the head of my bed and spoke in a calm, gentle voice. "I'll be giving ye a wee bit of ether for the pain, Lady Mitchell." Then he patted my hand. "There's a brave lass." Turning to Mrs. Stewart, he said, "I'll try to turn the bairn. Canna ye give me a hand with the ether?"

She nodded her head, and Dr. McTavish poured a few drops of it onto a towel. "Put this over her face, but only for a second. Ye ken?" She nodded, and when he said, "Noo," she pressed the towel under my nostrils briefly, and I breathed in the heavy, sickening odor. It dulled the pain, but made me feel strange and I rather think I was out of my head most of the time after that.

I thought I saw Gavan in the room. He had a horrified look on his face, and started demanding that Dr. McTavish "do something immediately," whereupon Dr. McTavish replied, "For God's sake, Mon. If ye don't want to lose the bairn and yere wife, get out of here and let me do what has tae be done."

I thought I saw the apparition standing in the shadows. She was smiling, and her presence did not alarm me, for I felt she was here to help. I turned to Lady Fitzgerald and said, "See her? There she is, over in the corner!"

She mopped my brow with a cool cloth. "Aye, love. Take heart."

Mrs. Stewart was putting the towel over my face, and I thought I had slipped back into the swollen waters of The Paradise. I was a child again, and I didn't want to drown. "Help, Avery, help."

I opened my eyes and saw Gavan's white face above me. I'm not drowning; I'm having a baby, I remembered as a terrible pressure bore down on me.

"Puish," Dr. McTavish cried, and with my last ounce of strength I did. Through blurred eyes I saw him hold up my baby, and I heard it cry.

"Ye hae a fine wee laddie," Dr. McTavish said, and I looked around the room for Gavan, but he was gone. I must have only imagined he was here, I thought, starting to cry. Through my tears I saw the worried faces of Mrs. Stewart and Lady Fitzgerald. "The wee laddie's fine, yere ladyship," Mrs. Stewart assured me, and I heard Dr. McTavish say, "It's because of the ether."

I felt hands kneading and pressing my stomach and I heard Mrs. Stewart say, "There's the afterbirth. She'll no hemorrhage, noo."

Their voices grew fainter and fainter, and through my drowsiness I called out for Gavan, but they didn't hear me.

I wanted him more than I could believe possible. This was our child. Together we had given it life, and I wanted to share the wonder of that with my son's father, but he didn't care. He wasn't even here. . . .

I slept for nearly two hours, or so they told me, and when I awakened, I felt wonderful and I wanted to see my baby.

Mrs. Stewart placed him in my arms, and when I looked at his dear little face, a feeling of love such as I had never known before came over me. I removed the blanket and looked at his tiny body, gazing in wonder at the miniature hands and feet, so perfectly formed, the skin, softer than satin. I nuzzled him to me and drank in the smell of his newness.

His hair was black, like Gavan's, and his eyes were midnight blue.

I looked up at Mrs. Stewart. "Did you ever see such dark blue eyes?"

She smiled down at him. "Aye, Lady Mitchell. All newborns' eyes are blue. They change later, ye ken. Some stay blue, some turn broon. This wee lad's 'ill probably turn black lak his da's." She paused then and gave me a strange look. "Should I be askin' Sir Gavan to come in, noo?"

I was surprised. "When did he arrive?"

"Before the bairn was born. He was right here in the room the whole time."

Then I hadn't imagined it!

She smiled. "Dr. McTavish wouldn'a let Sir Gavan near the bed till right afore the bairn come oot, so, he sat hisself doon in the corner of the room. Ach, a worried mon, he was."

"Mrs. Stewart," I said. "Get me a mirror and my hairbrush, please."

I handed her the baby and started to sit up. Putting him down in his basket, she rushed over to me. "Dinna raise yere head, Lady Mitchell. Dr. McTavish'll be gieing me a guid tongue-lashing fae no watchin' ye."

I kept my head flat on the pillow, and she brushed my hair out like a fan over it. "Now, give me the baby and tell Sir Gavan to come in," I told her.

He entered the darkened room and tiptoed across the heavy carpet. "We're both awake," I called. He looked the way small boys look when entering a church,

241

apprehensive and out of place in such august surroundings.

As he approached the bed, I could see his face relax. "You look—much better," he said.

I smiled. "I certainly hope so. Have you seen our son?"

"Aye, just after he was born."

"I'm sure he looks better now, too." I rolled the blanket down, exposing the little face.

I wondered why he hadn't kissed me, and why he looked . . . How did he look? Tired? Noticing the fine lines around his eyes, I would have to say, aye, he looked tired, and almost sad too. But why should he be sad? The baby was a boy; that's what he wanted, wasn't it? The child was healthy, if maybe a little small, but he'd come early. Of course he would be small.

Feeling a mother's protective instinct, I pulled the blanket up, shielding the little face from his father's gaze. "He's perfect," I said. "And now, if you don't mind, I'd like to rest."

"Certainly." He leaned down, and to my surprise brushed the top of the baby's head with his lips. Then he kissed me softly on the cheek and murmured in a choked voice, "Thank you, Elly, for my son."

After he left I stared at the wall, and tears rolled down my cheeks. I cried for something lost, but what could be lost?

In the days and weeks that followed, I was busy falling in love with my son. Everything about Emmet delighted me. It wasn't considered fashionable to nurse, and a wet nurse had been engaged, but I resented the time she spent with him and wished, instead, it were my milk that was nourishing him and making him gain weight.

"You'll be glad someday you didn't," Lady Fitzgerald remarked when I told her my feelings. "Why, if I had nursed all seven of mine, my bosom would be down to my knees."

Looking at the huge appendage that jutted out in front of her, I had to laugh, just picturing such a thing. "I shall miss you," I told her, for she had informed me that she would be returning to Strangford Manor after the christening.

Putting down her needlework, she hesitated a moment. "You and Gavan need to be alone, Elly."

I didn't know what to say. If only I could confide in her, but I couldn't. There were too many things about Gavan and me that I didn't even understand myself.

Then she said a strange thing. "Gavan loves you very much, Elly. And to be loved is sometimes better than loving."

Bridget came into the room then with the baby, who'd just had his bath, and the conversation took another turn. I was glad for the interruption. Dear Lady Fitzgerald, I thought. She wants to help, but she just doesn't understand.

Emmet's christening was to be a grand affair. The private baptism at a nearby country church would be followed by a lawn party at Bonnie Brae.

Gavan had made the arrangements himself, paving the way for his son's acceptance into the fold by a generous donation to the church. I was looking forward with eagerness to the celebration, though it would signal the end of Lady Fitzgerald's visit. Her presence had relieved the tension between Gavan and me, and I wondered what would happen when she was gone.

Gavan was cordial to me, but distant, and my intuition told me that something besides our old quarrel was bothering him, but I could not imagine what it could be.

He, too, was looking forward to Emmet's christening, but his reasons had little to do with religion. This was an opportunity to entertain and to show off the future heir of Bonnie Brae.

The house was now completely furnished, the final pieces having arrived shortly before the baby's birth, and although they were handsome and certainly expensive, they failed, at least as far as I was concerned, to change the face of Bonnie Brae.

A skeleton is no less hideous dressed in a ball gown, I thought, and for me the corruption and decay that the castle represented was still evident. Gavan, however, was pleased with the results.

He took personal charge of the preparations for the party, rarely consulting me, but courting the opinions of both Lady Fitzgerald and Mrs. Stewart.

"What do you ladies think? Should the buffet table be placed indoors or outdoors?"

"I prefer an indoor buffet, Sir Gavan. There's always the possibility of a shower, and then you have servants scurrying around, trying to move dishes into the house at the last minute."

"Aye, and I dinna lak tae see bowlies of food settin' oot under a hot sun."

"You're absolutely right, ladies. Thank you. We'll have the buffet indoors."

When the day came, tables were set up on the lawn and guests carried plates from the lavish indoor buffet to enjoy the mild August afternoon. It was a festive occasion.

Emmet Thomas Mitchell, now duly a child of God and member of the Church of England, had been handed over to Bridget to be put to bed, and I looked forward to enjoying the company of old friends.

Alex and Clyde were a welcome sight, and my wilted

ego perked up like a dew-kissed rose under their honeyed words.

"They say motherhood makes a woman more beautiful. I'd say that was true, wouldn't you, Clyde?"

"Aye, I'll not argue with you there. Come, sit down, Elly, and talk to us. We've missed you for true."

"We have that. The lassies in Belfast are a dull lot this season."

I laughed. "That's because you two don't give them a chance to talk."

Alex wrinkled his nose. "They have no sense of humor. Don't even laugh at our jokes. But enough about us, Elly. Did you hear the latest?"

"Probably not. What is it?"

"They found a body in Belfast Lough last week."

"How exciting," I said. "Who was it?"

"They're not sure yet, but they think it might be Squire Daly."

The name meant nothing to me. "Who's Squire Daly?"

Alex and Clyde looked at each other in amazement before Clyde answered. "Squire Daly's the man who shot Gavan!"

I felt suddenly nervous. "Gavan never told me his name," I said.

Clyde shrugged. "He probably wanted to forget it himself. Anyway, somebody shot Squire Daly. Now, that's ironic, isn't it?"

I said, "When do they think he was killed?"

"A long time ago, two months at least."

I made an excuse about checking the buffet and left them. Gavan and Brendan had been up around Belfast Lough just about two months ago, I recalled. Had they really gone for cattle or had there been another reason for their sudden departure?

Scraps of conversation came back to me.

"He's dangerous," Brendan had said. "Let me call on me mates."

And Gavan had answered, "Not this time. I'll handle it myself."

I remembered the scar on his chest and his reluctance to explain it. Could there be a connection? Knowing Gavan's temperament, it would not be hard to imagine him exacting revenge. Gavan conducted himself like a feudal lord, and feudal lords were a law unto themselves.

I forced myself to smile and exchange pleasantries with guests who stood milling around the garden in groups, talking and laughing, but my legs became suddenly wobbly, and I steadied myself by reaching for the back of a chair.

"I was afraid this would be too much for you." Gavan was suddenly beside me, and before I could protest, he had swept me up in his arms and was carrying me into the house.

A path was cleared for us by anxious guests. "Let them through. Lady Mitchell has fainted!"

"Put me down," I spat out. "You're making a fool of me. I'm perfectly fine!"

Depositing me on the chaise in the drawing room, he regarded me with cold eyes. "If you get up from here, I'll put you to bed. You're in no condition for all this excitement. I should have known better." Then, with a sarcastic smirk, he added, "Your admirers can pay court to you in here while you're resting."

Lady Fitzgerald rushed over. "Is Elly all right?"

"Aye, but I want her to stay off her feet for the rest of the day."

Lady Fitzgerald nodded her head vigorously. "You're absolutely right, Gavan." She turned to me then and said, "You do look pale, Elly."

"I'm fine," I assured her. "It was probably the sun."

"Well, you do exactly as Gavan says."

"Oh, she will," he answered smugly.

I'm sure the color came back to my face after that remark, and I thought, Oh, if I weren't positive you'd carry out your threat in front of all these people, I'd get up and go right back outside and dance a jig with both Alex and Clyde!

I did not have time to continue mulling over my problems, for I became the object of much attention then, with someone offering me a shawl, and others just their advice.

"Put this over your shoulders. You must guard against drafts, my dear. You modern young women take too many chances.

"I stayed in the bed for six weeks after my Gerald was born, and I never set a foot downstairs until he was three months old. Of course, that was thirty years ago."

"Drink a teaspoonful of whiskey in your tea every day. You'll soon get your strength back."

Blessed relief is in sight, I thought, noticing Alex and Clyde and two of their older brothers coming into the room. They pulled up chairs, and the ladies reluctantly wandered off to find a place to continue their discussion safely out of the range of male ears.

Alex brought me a plate of delicacies from the buffet table, which we all shared, and we enjoyed a lively conversation punctuated by much laughter. I looked up to find Gavan standing in the doorway, his eyes dark and piercing as he stared relentlessly at us, and I drew the borrowed shawl tighter about my shoulders.

Emmet, having awakened from his nap, was brought downstairs by Bridget. Gavan took the baby from her arms and held him up for all to see. "Let me present my son, Emmet Thomas Mitchell," he announced. Handing the child back to his nurse, he raised his glass and proposed a toast, "To the future master of Bonnie Brae."

247

His eyes glittered with an unnatural brightness, and I suddenly recalled the curse of insanity that had been levied against the first Sir Gavan Mitchell.

Lady Cunningham had shrugged it off. "I don't believe in curses," she had said.

But Gavan's father had been insane, and hadn't it been rumored that his grandfather, in a fit of rage, had burned an entire family alive in their cottage?

An eerie feeling washed over me. Was Gavan destined to follow in his ancestors' footsteps, and was that the reason he had refused to hand down the name to his son?

I recalled his moods, the erratic changes in his personality, his secretiveness, and now, a new, terrible suspicion haunted me. Was my husband a murderer?

The party lost its glow, and the conversation, which up to now had seemed witty and stimulating, grated on my nerves. Alex and Clyde appeared suddenly superficial and trite and their older brothers dull. I was relieved when Lady Fitzgerald appeared and took her sons in hand with the statement that it was time to go home.

Other guests followed the Fitzgeralds' lead, offering their congratulations and bidding me good bye, and in a matter of minutes the room had emptied itself of its chattering, laughing occupants, leaving me alone with my thoughts in the deepening shadows of the setting sun.

Taking advantage of Gavan's preoccupation with the departing guests, I retreated to my room. I dreaded the thought of facing Gavan across the dinner table later this evening alone and without Lady Fitzgerald between us.

I fell into an exhausted sleep, and when I awoke, the room was in darkness. Groping for the lamp, I lit it and then rang for a servant. I had no appetite for food or a confrontation with Gavan, so I refrained from making an appearance in the dining room.

It was Megan who answered my summons, for with Bridget now acting as Emmet's nurse, our little mouse had been pressed into more responsible duties.

"Megan, I want you to take a message to Sir Gavan." Knowing she was slow-witted, I made it short and simple. "Tell Sir Gavan that I'm tired and won't come down for dinner this evening."

She left and I felt myself relax. Picking up my knitting, I automatically worked the design, needles clicking away as rapidly as my thoughts.

I decided to go to the nursery and spend some time with my little son, but as I opened the door, I found Megan, her small fist raised, ready to knock on the door.

"Oh, yere ladyship, I was just about to knock. Sir Gavan sent me back with an answer to yere message." She frowned and paused, seemingly to collect her thoughts. "He says to tell ye, Lady Mitchell, that dinner is at eight o'clock, and if yere not downstairs by that time, he'll come up and escort ye down hisself."

She nervously wiped her hands on her apron. She looked absolutely terrified, and I felt a sudden sympathy for her. Gavan, in one of his black moods, could be a hair-raising sight. "Thank you, Megan," I said calmly. "You may go to your quarters. I won't be needing you anymore tonight."

I closed the door and slowly descended the stairs. His conduct was insufferable, but I dared not risk pushing him over the edge.

I entered the dining room, and he greeted me, wearing a sarcastic smile. "Good evening, Lady Mitchell. I understand you're tired. All charmed out, I imagine, by displaying so much of it for our guests." He paused and his eyes glittered dangerously. "The Fitzgerald brothers, I noticed, were quite taken with your gaiety."

Refusing to let him goad me, I stared back in stony silence.

"I see you have none left for your husband. Too bad." Giving me a mock bow, he pulled out my chair. "But sit down anyhow, and let me at least have the pleasure of your company."

We ate in a silence that stretched my nerves to the breaking point. Unable to stand it any longer, I pushed my hardly touched plate aside, and said, "I'm sorry, Gavan. I'm not hungry, and I have a splitting headache."

He laughed. "The classic excuse! Can't you at least show some originality?" His eyes narrowed. "Why don't you try the truth? Why don't you say why you want no part of your husband and the baser instincts he arouses in you?"

He stood up then and glared down at me. "You don't have to say, because I already know why, Elly. It's because you prefer to moon over a childish attachment that you perceive to be pure and noble and beyond my understanding."

Why was he harking back to Avery?

His eyes grew colder and harder, and I felt his hate reach out to me. "I told you once you'd have to beg me to come to your bedroom. Well, I take that back, Elly. You're my wife and the mother of my son. I don't need to possess your heart, I can possess your body anytime I want. Go upstairs and wait for me in bed. And don't lock that door," he warned. "Or I'll break it down!"

I fled upstairs, seething with rage. He is a tyrant like all the Mitchells, I thought. How could I ever have expected anything more?

I didn't lock the door. What good would it do? He would only break it down and embarrass me before the

250

servants. I undressed and got into bed, feeling like a slave. My body stiffened in resentment.

It was several hours later that I heard the doorknob turn. He undressed in the darkness without saying a word, and I felt the mattress sink as he got in beside me. A strong odor of whiskey reached my nostrils as he pulled me toward him and bruised my lips with a kiss.

His practiced hands roamed over me, but it was as if my body were dead. I felt nothing, and when he entered me, I felt a searing pain, more intense than when he had taken my virginity. I gritted my teeth, refusing to cry out. Dr. McTavish had hinted that the first time might be painful, but I would never give Gavan the satisfaction of knowing he had touched me in any way at all.

It was the first time we had come together without joy, and I think the awareness of it must have unsettled him, for he got up, and without a word left the room.

After that night we avoided each other. I took my meals on a tray in my room, making no apologies to Gavan for doing so, and he ignored my absence from the dinner table.

Lauren was much in evidence, working every day in the gardens, and I understood from Bridget, who kept a sharp eye on him, that he had been given a key to the tower.

"Sir Gavan hisself gave it to him, Lady Mitchell, so he could be storing his tools there, but I says to the crazy old fool, 'Don't ye be settin' a foot inside the house, 'cause I'll smell ye, and I'll be settin' ye in a tub of soapy water, I will.' " She laughed. "That oughta keep him out!"

"Where does he sleep?" I asked. "In the stable?"

"Nay, yere ladyship. Starice give him a room in her

cottage. That'll be two ghoulies together," she remarked dryly.

One stormy night I heard the banshee again, and getting out of bed, I ran upstairs to the nursery, frantic lest Emmet should be in danger. But he was sleeping peacefully, and hovering over his cradle, I saw the floating shape of the apparition. I had no fear of her now, for I sensed her goodness just as strongly as I sensed the evil of the second spirit, which I was now convinced inhabited Bonnie Brae's secret passageway.

Leaving my unknown benefactor to protect Emmet, I returned to my room and slept without fear.

The following morning I saw from my window a lone rider approaching Bonnie Brae at great speed. A short while later Megan came to my room to tell me that Sir Gavan wished to speak to me in his study.

I found him seated behind his desk, his expression grave. "Sit down, Elly," he said solemnly. "I have something to tell you."

I made no move to take the chair he indicated. "I'd just as soon stand," I said.

His glance held a hint of exasperation, but he spoke in a calm manner. "A messenger has just arrived from Glengarra. It seems your brother has met with an accident."

"He's hurt?"

"I'm afraid he's dead, Elly."

I sat down quickly. "Hugh is dead?" Numb with shock, I stared back at him, and then finally managed to ask, "How did it happen?"

"There was a fight. He was stabbed."

My mind couldn't take it all in, and conflicting emotions raged within me. I had hated Hugh, but he was my brother, and now he was dead.

Gavan continued in a steady, quiet manner. "It happened in a tavern. He'd been drinking heavily, it seems. He didn't suffer. It was all over very quickly."

I continued to stare vacantly at him, and he got up and walked over to me. I stood then, and moved away from him toward the door.

"They need someone to go to Belfast to positively identify the body. I'll do that," he added quickly, "and in the meantime you get yourself ready. I'll have Brendan drive you to Glengarra, and you can wait for me there."

He rang for Mrs. Stewart then, and when she appeared, he said, "Help Lady Mitchell pack a trunk. She's going to Glengarra. There's been a death in her family."

Chapter Sixteen

I still could not believe that Hugh was dead!

I suppose somewhere deep inside me I had secretly hoped that someday the ideals of my father, and all the Kincaids who had ruled Glengarra in the past, would surface in Hugh. Now that could never be, and his place in the annals of Glengarra would forever remain an ignoble one.

I cried for that more than for the loss of Hugh, for I had lost my brother a long time before.

Mrs. Stewart understood none of this, and she tried in her kindly way to comfort me. "Aye, 'tis hard, I ken, tae lose a brother, Lady Mitchell, and mair's the shame at his age, but the guid die young, they say."

It didn't take long for me to pack, as I expected to be gone for only a short while. I hated the thought of being separated from Emmet, but I had to concede that he was better off at Bonnie Brae, for I didn't know what I would find at Glengarra.

I put on my bonnet and Mrs. Stewart handed me a shawl. "It's September noo," she reminded me in her dear, nannylike manner. "Ye dinna want to catch cold. Ye'll be needin' yere strength for what lies ahead, Lady Mitchell."

"Aye, that I will," I answered, giving her a smile of gratitude for a sympathy that was sincere, if not misplaced.

My trunk was carried down, and I slipped upstairs for a final peek at my son.

Bridget was folding freshly laundered nappies, and

she tiptoed across the room to me. "He's asleep, but I'll be wakin' him to say good-bye to his mam."

"No, don't," I whispered. "I just want to see him before I leave."

He was lying faceup in his cradle. His little mouth was turned up at the corners, almost like a smile, and I motioned to Bridget, who stood beside me.

"Dreamin' of the angels," she said, looking down at him with eyes full of love.

Why did I feel apprehensive? The child was the picture of health, and Bridget was here to give him all her loving care.

"He only just went to sleep," she said with regret. "The little rascal was wide awake for his da."

"Sir Gavan came to the nursery?"

"Aye, like he does every morning, but earlier today because he was leavin', I guess." She suddenly remembered the reason for our departure. "I'm right sorry about yere brother, Lady Mitchell. Don't be worryin' though. I'll be taking good care of the little master here."

"Thank you, Bridget," I mumbled. I was still digesting the news that Gavan came every morning to the nursery.

Hurrying downstairs, I found the carriage waiting for me, Brendan at the reins, and the team of blacks prancing, impatient to be off.

Gavan was already mounted on horseback, and on seeing me he trotted the stallion over to where I stood. Making no move to dismount, he looked down at me from the animal's great height and said, "I'll stop at Strangford Manor and tell the Fitzgeralds. Alex and Clyde were his boyhood friends. They'll be wanting to attend the funeral."

I hadn't thought that far ahead, and I merely nodded.

"I should arrive at Glengarra by Wednesday. You

see to the minister and arrange the funeral for Thursday. I'll take care of everything else when I get there."

I thanked him, and without another word he turned his mount north and galloped away, leaving me standing in the driveway.

Out of the corner of my eye I saw Lauren Devlin approaching me, and I steeled myself for more of his ramblings.

"The banshee dinna wail for this one," he said, shaking his head and frowning with annoyance. "It's for Bonnie Brae the banshee wails. He pointed a bony finger toward the castle. "Somebody in there will die."

"Stop it, stop it," I cried, unable to stand any more, and the next thing I knew Brendan had come down from his perch and miraculously appeared beside me.

Towering over the old man, he lifted him up like he would a child with one hand. "I catch ye bothering Lady Mitchell again and I'll be putting ye up in that tree for the ravens to peck at."

I said, "Please, Brendan. Let him go."

The huge arm came immediately down, and as soon as Lauren's feet touched the ground, he was scurrying away like a frightened rodent.

"Pay him no mind," Brendan said. "He's as loony as old Starice, but there's naught to fear from either of them."

I nodded my head, wishing I could be as sure.

The sun was setting when we arrived at Glengarra, and the fiery orange ball vaguely disturbed me. A crazy thought popped into my head that it might fall, and I visualized it bursting and enveloping everything on earth in its hellish flames.

As we entered the driveway, I was sickened by the neglect that assaulted my eyes; the knee-high grass was littered with debris, and once carefully tended flower beds were now overgrown, their delicate blossoms choked by encroaching weeds.

Glengarra's condition had deteriorated in the year since I had seen it last, and I shuddered to think what I would find inside.

The carriage stopped in front of the house, and Brendan hopped down and stuck his head in my window. "Please to wait in the carriage, Lady Mitchell. I'll be going up to the door first."

I nodded, grateful for his understanding. The caliber of servants now at Glengarra could be such that I might welcome Brendan's protection.

I could not see who opened the door, but Brendan was admitted inside and several minutes later he returned. "There's only a maid," he told me, "and not much of a one at that. She says her name is Molly."

The barmaid, I thought with disgust. "We'll manage, Brendan," I said. "Please come inside after you tend to the horses. I'll likely be needing your help."

"Aye, and I'll be giving it, yere ladyship."

Molly was waiting in the hall. She, too, had changed in a year's time. There was a dissipated look about her now, and her once pretty face had hardened.

"Where are the rest of the servants, Molly?" I inquired.

She gave me an insolent look. "How should I be knowin'? I ain't mistress here."

Brendan had come in behind me and he overheard the exchange. "Keep a civil tongue in yere head, gel. Lady Mitchell asked ye a question."

She tossed her head in resentment. "I s'pose they took off after they heard about the master."

"And probably not with empty hands," Brendan said.

I hadn't thought of that, and I wondered suddenly why Molly had remained. Somehow that question bothered me more than the possibility of missing valuables.

"Thank you, Molly, for staying," I said, forcing myself to act cordially toward her. "Is there food in the house? We've had naught to eat since early morning. A cold supper would do fine," I suggested, not wanting to tax her capabilities.

Her face turned sullen, but she said, "I'll fix something."

I had Brendan carry my portmanteau upstairs to my old room. Everything seemed to be in order, if not clean. The furniture was covered with an accumulation of dust, and cobwebs hung from the corners. I doubted if the room had been touched since I had left it a year ago.

"I'll see to the horses now, Lady Mitchell," Brendan said.

I nodded wearily and started to untie my bonnet. I dreaded seeing what the rest of the house looked like.

He seemed to read my mind. "Don't ye be worryin' none, yere ladyship. We'll have this place in order afore yere brother's funeral." He thought a moment and then added, "Not wantin' to overstep me place, Lady Mitchell, but might I be makin' a suggestion?"

"I'd welcome a suggestion, Brendan."

"If I was to go to the tenant cottages hereabouts, I'm thinkin' there'd be many a family that would be rememberin' yere father's kindness, and they'd be willin' to help out for a few days, actin' as temporary servants, as it were."

"Oh, Brendan," I said. "That's a wonderful suggestion!" I smiled with relief. Whatever would I do without this resourceful man!

His big face broke into a warm smile. "Then I'll be attendin' to it first thing in the morning, yere ladyship."

After Brendan left for the stables, I went downstairs and my worst suspicions were confirmed. My beautiful Glengarra had been abused and stripped. The handmade Persian carpet in the drawing room was riddled with stains, likewise the matching cream-colored love seats in the music room; silverware, bric-a-brac, paintings, anything that would bring a price had been carted away.

My eyes filled with tears at the desecration of the home I held so dear.

Later, seated alone at the dining room table while Molly shoved a platter of cold meat and slices of stale bread in front of me, I fixed her with a cold eye. "I want the names of the servants who left. I'm reporting them to the constable. The house has been stripped of valuables."

Sudden fear flashed across her face at mention of the constable. "They took only a few trinkets. Hugh sold the good stuff."

Her familiar use of my brother's name added to my irritation, and I regarded her coldly. "Master Hugh would have no reason to sell his own possessions."

She sneered at me. "He had card games every night in this room, and most of the time he lost." My shocked expression must have pleased her immensely, for like a vicious animal, she closed in quickly for the kill. "He spent all his money, and that's why I stayed here to see you."

Her eyes narrowed, and her lip curled. "I'm owed something, and I mean to get it. He's left me with a brat, and I wants me share!"

I didn't believe her about the money. Hugh had investments and rent from the tenants. But a baby! Kincaid blood mixed with the blood of this slut. Oh, God, how could he?

She was watching me intently, and I didn't want to

lose control. "How old is this baby you claim to have, and where is it?"

"He's four months old and stayin' with me sister in town. I'll bring him out here so ye can see for yere-self," she added, looking angry.

"Do that. And now you can clear the table," I said. "This food's not fit to eat, and I don't want you to serve it to Brendan. Fix him a hot meal. Do you understand?"

She gave me a hateful look. "Aye, I understand, Lady Mitchell."

Sick at heart, and weighted down by this new problem, I wandered from room to room, trying to concentrate on happy times, but my thoughts doggedly returned to Molly and the baby who could be, and probably was my brother's child.

For the rest of my life this bastard grandson of Thomas and Laura Kincaid would haunt me. I felt no warmth for the mother, but I knew I could not turn my back on Hugh's son. I would have to make some arrangement for supporting the child.

Once again I stood in Glengarra's cemetery as Reverend Wharton conducted graveside services for the last Kincaid. The rain, which seemed always to accompany my family's burials, poured down on our small group—Gavan, Alex, Clyde, and myself. Looking up, I spied Molly, standing at a distance under a tree.

What she had felt for Hugh I would never know, but her presence in the cemetery took me by surprise and made me feel a sudden pity for her.

As Hugh had left no will, I, as the only living relative, was sole heir. After Hugh's creditors—and I imagined them to be legion—had been satisfied, the balance of the estate would revert to me.

I intended speaking to my father's solicitor about setting up an annuity for Hugh's son. All of this would have to be cleared first through Gavan, for as my husband, he held control over my affairs.

We returned to the house after the funeral, and the temporary help that Brendan had recruited among the tenants had prepared a plain but substantial meal for us.

The house was clean, thanks to the efforts of a few hardworking women, myself included, and the indomitable Brendan.

As always, after the dead have been laid to rest, the living begin to anoint themselves with guilt. Over and over again I asked myself, "Could I have done anything to prevent this tragedy?"

I looked across the table at the solemn faces of Alex and Clyde. Death, in all its starkness, had stilled their laughter.

Hugh had been their contemporary, their boyhood chum, and though they had drifted apart in later years, his passing had affected them deeply and made them aware, I'm sure, of their own mortality.

Alex made an effort at polite conversation, and Gavan and Clyde rather gratefully pursued the topic. My thoughts were on other matters, and in deference to my grief they made no attempt to persuade me to join in.

In spite of the occasion and the sad changes it reflected, I was glad to be home. Glengarra would always be a refuge for me, and I suddenly wished that I could stay.

The thought enticed me. I needed peace and time to make choices. It was obvious that my marriage had been a mistake. Based on deception, plagued by secrecy and suspicion, torn apart by dissension . . . how could it ever succeed? And yet there had been times when I had felt it might. . . .

261

I suddenly became aware that the conversation had stopped. All three men were staring at me, and I said, "I'm sorry. I wasn't listening."

"That's all right, Elly," Alex assured me. "We were just saying that we'll be leaving for Strangford Manor."

I suppose I responded with all the right phrases. Still somewhat in a daze, I followed the men out of the dining room and into the great hall, where I kissed them good-bye and thanked them again.

Gavan went outside with Alex, but Clyde remained. He reached for my hand and looked at me with sad eyes. "Elly, I just want you to know that we tried to help Hugh. Alex and I came down here a couple of times, but he wouldn't listen to us." He sighed with resignation. "Gavan tried too. If he couldn't help him, nobody could! I guess our old mate was just sick, Elly."

I looked at him sharply. "Gavan tried to help Hugh? When?"

"I don't know about lately. I was referring to last winter. You know, when Gavan was stabbed, and he spent a couple of weeks here with Hugh." A strange look crossed his face. "I'm not telling tales. You did know about that!"

I nodded quickly. "Of course."

He left then, hurrying outside to join his brother, and I watched from the window as the three men held an animated conversation in front of the waiting carriage.

Clyde's slip about Gavan raised even more questions in my mind, but I was weary of lies and half truths. I had Emmet to consider now. I feared for him at Bonnie Brae. There was an evil there that distorted and twisted all who came under its spell, and I did not want that evil to touch my son.

When Gavan came back inside the house, I said,

"Could we sit down and talk briefly before the lawyer arrives? There are some things we must settle first."

He followed me into the drawing room, and though I remained standing, he seated himself in a large wing chair. Looking at me with indifference, he settled himself comfortably. "I'm listening."

"Molly tells me she had a child by my brother. I wish I could say I don't believe her, but I do." His expression never changed, and I wondered if he had known about it, but he made no comment. "I would like to provide for this child from the estate."

"That could be arranged."

He certainly wasn't making it easy for me, and I leaned against the mantel for support. "Then you would agree to such an arrangement?"

He regarded me with the eyes of a stranger. "What you do with this estate is immaterial to me. You are Glengarra's heir, not I."

"But you have a legal say, Gavan. You know you do," I countered.

He raised an eyebrow. "As your husband I have many legal rights. I do not always choose to make use of them."

Walking over to the window, I looked out at the pitiful remains of my father's rose garden, and without turning around, I said, "In that case, you shouldn't mind if Emmet and I take up residence here at Glengarra."

He was on his feet immediately, and his strong hands gripped my shoulders and turned me around roughly to face him. "Did I hear you correctly, Lady Mitchell?"

I nodded, dumbstruck at his sudden change of mood, and I felt a shiver of fear as I looked into his eyes.

"You will take my son nowhere. Do you understand?"

His fingers dug into my arms and he shook me with

263

such violence that I screamed, "Stop it, Gavan. Have you lost your mind?"

He released me so suddenly that I almost fell. All the color had drained out of his face, and his eyes looked blacker and more terrifying than I had ever seen them.

"That remains to be seen," he said in a menacing tone. "Just remember this, Lady Mitchell. If I am insane, so also is my son, but you shall not have him. He is a Mitchell and he belongs at Bonnie Brae. Perhaps you do not."

Turning on his heel, he walked away from me, but he paused in the doorway. "I suggest you return to Bonnie Brae and pack your things. You can live at Glengarra alone." A diabolical smile crossed his face then. "Or sell it, and take yourself to America. Perhaps you can find your Fenian there!"

Dear God, what had I done? I might have known Gavan would never let me go without exacting a price.

My father's solicitor arrived shortly after our quarrel, and at first Gavan refused to be present, but Sir Henry would not discuss anything with me alone.

Since we were leaving for Bonnie Brae the following day, Gavan relented, but although Sir Henry addressed himself more to Gavan than to me, my husband made few comments and signed the necessary papers without reading them.

The annuity matter was dispensed with first. Sir Henry's disapproval shone in the stern set of his jaw, but he made no comment.

After all business matters had been concluded, he simply remarked that Hugh Kincaid had not taken kindly to advice. He added, "Fortunately he was not aware of some of the investments your father had made, and those should give you sufficient capital to pay off his debts." He looked pointedly at Gavan. "Should you

264

desire to sell the estate, I may have an interested buyer."

"I'm allowing my wife to make that decision," Gavan said. "She may want to sell it and travel. Then again, she may want to keep it for herself."

He isn't giving me much choice, I thought with foreboding.

Sir Henry merely looked puzzled. "Well, you know where to reach me."

The old lawyer left, and I went upstairs. I heard a door slam, and shortly thereafter the thunder of hooves. Looking out my window, I saw Gavan race across the meadow on one of his blacks. He was riding hard, as if the devil himself were after him, an analogy that contained more truth than I wanted to believe.

He did not appear for supper, which was little more than leftovers from the afternoon meal, for we would all be leaving in the morning. I told Brendan to inform his makeshift staff that they were welcome to take all of the remaining food home with them, for the house would be closed on the morrow.

My last duty would be to inform Molly of my decision, and to ensure privacy I asked that she report to me in the master's Study.

While I waited for her, I opened the huge ledger that had seemed to occupy so much of my father's and then my brother's time.

It was a rent ledger, and I leafed through it idly until one name leapt up at me from the page: Patrick Colin James. Dates and amounts collected were listed meticulously in a small, neat hand, and at the end, the word *evicted* was printed in bold letters.

I slammed the ledger shut. The ruling class, I thought with sudden disgust. What gives us the right to control other people's lives?

I looked up then and saw Molly standing in the doorway. Her whole bearing was one of bitterness and resentment. "You sent for me?" she asked.

I sighed. "Sit down, Molly. I have something to tell you."

"I'll hear it standin' up."

I explained about the annuity, and in spite of her anger, I think she was relieved. I wrote down Sir Henry Drake's name and address, and she stared at the paper blankly when I handed it to her.

Realizing that she could not read, I explained. "It's the lawyer's name and address. You must go to his office every month for the money."

She folded the paper and stuffed it in her bosom. Then, holding her head high, she looked down on me, and there was a proud and wild sort of beauty to her as she said, "I ain't thankin' ye for it. Me son's a bastard, but he's Hugh Kincaid's bastard!"

I never heard Gavan come back, but I was informed when I came downstairs in the morning that he had eaten his breakfast and gone to the stables to speak to the two grooms who would be retained to care for Glengarra's horses.

The furniture was covered, and I locked the remaining valuables in the safe.

I dismissed with deep gratitude and a generous stipend the tenant wives who had come to our rescue. One matronly widow with a smile that had weathered both famine and prejudice said, "Speaking for the lot of us, yere ladyship, yere da was a kind and good master. The likes of him don't pass this way often."

On a sudden impulse I took her aside and asked, "Would you be knowing whatever happened to the James family?"

She nodded slowly. "They went back to Sharonhill, their old village."

I locked the front door, and this time I did not look back as the carriage drove away, leaving Glengarra behind. Should I come back, it would mean the end of my marriage and the loss of my son. I did not want Glengarra under those terms.

Gavan and I sat across from each other in stony silence for most of the long trip, speaking only when necessary.

"There's an inn up ahead. Do you want to stop for something to eat?"

"If you don't mind, I'd like to get home. I'm anxious about Emmet."

My anxiety mounted with each agonizing mile on this endless, narrow road that went uphill and downhill with monotonous regularity.

Once I had loved gazing on the pastoral beauty of County Down, but now I watched eagerly for the rougher terrain of Antrim. For the first time in my life I longed to see the spires of Bonnie Brae rise up and pierce the sky.

The rain had stopped, but gray clouds still hung menacingly overhead. I closed my eyes, shutting out the dismal view, but my own thoughts were not much brighter. . . .

I must have slept, for when I opened my eyes again we were indeed in Antrim, jostling over rocky roads that soon would lead us to Bonnie Brae.

I glanced over at Gavan. His eyes were closed, and I thought again how innocent and vulnerable he looked in sleep.

As I watched him, he stirred, and I quickly turned my gaze to the window just as Bonnie Brae's tower appeared through the trees.

Something bright caught my attention, and I pressed my face to the windowpane, but I saw only gray stone against an equally gray sky.

I could hardly wait to hold my precious baby in my arms again. Soon, I thought, keeping my eyes fixed on the approaching castle.

The bright flash appeared again. Looking up, I saw that flames like serpent's tongues were flicking in and out of one of the slits in the top of the tower.

"Gavan," I screamed. "For God's sake, wake up. The castle's on fire!"

Chapter Seventeen

Gavan rushed out of the carriage as soon as it pulled up in front of the house, and I followed. Pushing past the startled butler, he shouted, "The castle's on fire. Get the servants out."

It's all right, I kept telling myself. The rest of the castle is safe. It's only the tower.

Panting for breath, and hampered by my long skirt, I lagged behind Gavan, who had already disappeared at the top of the stairs.

As I climbed to the third floor, Gavan appeared on the landing with Bridget. She was leaning heavily against him, and I noticed with a sinking feeling that neither of them had the baby.

"Where's Emmet?" I asked, trying to control my panic.

Gavan had a wild look about him. "I don't know." Shoving Bridget suddenly toward me, he shouted, "Get her outside."

I looked into Bridget's vacant eyes. "Where's Emmet?" I demanded.

"She can't tell you, Elly. I think she's drunk. Just do as I say. Take her outside. I'll find Emmet."

He ran back upstairs, leaving me with Bridget, whose dead weight sagged against me. Her eyes had rolled back in her head and her mouth hung open.

I couldn't believe that Bridget would do this, and then I suddenly remembered: Bridget didn't drink!

Her head lolled on my shoulder, and as I looked at

her, the truth struck me like a physical blow. She wasn't drunk. She'd been drugged!

Starice and the sleeping grass, I thought. If it could put a cat to sleep for three days . . .

Bridget outweighed me by thirty or more pounds, and looking down the long flight of stairs, I knew I could not hold her up. She would drag me with her and we would both plunge from top to bottom.

Unconsciously I raised my hand and slapped her hard, once, twice, three times. "Bridget, for God's sake, wake up," I screamed.

Her eyes popped open, and she looked at me with a sudden disoriented surprise. "Lady Mitchell, wha-wha . . ."

"Never mind," I said, taking her arm in a firm grip. "We're going downstairs now, Bridget. Be very careful. One, two, three, four." I counted each step as slowly and painfully we made our way to the bottom.

The door connecting the two wings was open, and smoke poured out of the east wing into the great hall. I hurried Bridget outside, and we stood on the step, gasping for air.

There was a beehive of activity on the front lawn, with servants and nearby tenants straining to pull a portable pump on heavy wheels over the grass. Others stood in clusters, gazing up at the tower in awe.

Mrs. Stewart ran up to us, and I said, "Take care of Bridget. Don't let her go to sleep." And before she could answer, I was back inside the house again.

Smoke now filled the great hall, and I pulled my shawl up over my head and held it over the lower part of my face. I raced up the steps, shouting all the while for Gavan, but an eerie quiet hung over the house like a shroud.

I checked all the rooms on the second floor and then made my way back up to the nursery. Seeing the empty crib, my hysteria mounted, and I shouted aloud,

"Damn you, Starice. What have you done with my baby?"

The smoke was getting heavier, and it stung my eyes, making me fall halfway down the long staircase, but I picked myself up and ran through the connecting door to the east wing.

Passing the old study, I stopped, remembering the secret passageway. I ran inside and started pulling books out of the bookcase like a wild woman, crying hysterically all the while.

A horrible feeling washed over me as I released the spring and the secret door swung open. Recoiling at the sight of the gaping black hole that stretched before me, I stopped, hesitating to enter that dark and evil place.

But Emmet may be in there, I thought, and without remembering to prop open the door, I stepped inside, finding myself immediately engulfed in absolute darkness as the door swung shut again.

Something slithered over my foot, and I screamed. Placing my hands on either side of the damp walls, I shuffled my feet to frighten the mice, but it wasn't the mice I was afraid of, for suddenly I knew that Emmet was not here—but something else was.

The evil presence that Lady Cunningham had warned me about had lured me here, and like a fool I had walked into its trap.

I turned and ran back to the entrance. With superhuman strength I pushed and pounded on the door, but the lock would not spring open, I had to get out! I had to find Emmet!

Hysterical now, I screamed at the top of my lungs. "Damn you, damn you to hell! You will not win, do you hear me? You will not win!"

I kept screaming at it and cursing it, alternately pounding and kicking the door, when suddenly it opened and Gavan's startled face peered into mine.

271

"Good God, Elly. I thought you were outside."

He reached for my hands and pulled me back into the room. The air was thick with smoke now, and we were both coughing and struggling to breathe. "Get outside," he commanded in a hoarse whisper, but I shook my head violently.

I wasn't leaving until we had found Emmet. Covering his mouth, he grabbed my hand. "Come on. We don't have time to argue."

He pulled me with him through the corridor and into the dining room. Picking up a heavy brass candlestick, he smashed the window with it and we both stood for a moment, filling our lungs with air.

"This is Starice's work," I gasped.

He shook his head violently. "No, she wouldn't do this." Then he looked at me with angry eyes. "Your maid was drunk. God knows where she left him."

"Not drunk, drugged!" I answered, and then stopped suddenly. My blood had turned to ice, and I dug my fingernails into his arm. "Listen," I said. "It's the cry of the banshee."

We stood, straining our ears, and after an eternity I heard again the long, thin wail. I felt myself slipping into lethargy under its spell. It's no use now, I thought. The banshee's crying for Emmet. He's gone. My baby's gone. . . .

My head reeled, and my cheek stung as Gavan's open palm struck my face. "Come out of it, Elly. That's no banshee. The baby's in the tower!"

We ran into the kitchen, and with superhuman strength Gavan pulled the massive tower door open with one hand.

We stepped into the tower, and what I saw then, I shall never forget.

Standing on the stair landing and holding a blanket-wrapped bundle was Lauren Devlin! The two upper floors of the tower must have been engulfed in flames, for his grinning face was illuminated by a red glow from above.

On spying Gavan, he suddenly laughed, and with maniacal glee shouted, "Welcome, Sir Gavan. It be a long time comin', but I'm evenin' the score at last."

Gavan was calmer than I have ever seen him. "We'll talk about it, Lauren. What wrong have I done you?"

" 'Tis an old score, long before yere time." He nodded with smug satisfaction. Then he smiled. "But it be settled today."

"Come down, and give me the child," Gavan insisted.

"Nay," Lauren shouted, stamping his foot in anger. His madman's eyes glittered with insane fury, and I panicked.

"Gavan," I said in a choked voice, but he silenced me with a look.

"She knew," Lauren said, pointing a finger at me. "Dinna I tell ye the banshee wailed for Bonnie Brae?"

"Oh, please," I whimpered, half crazy myself with the pain of it. To be so close, and yet so helpless in the face of this madman!

Gavan pushed me behind him, out of Lauren's sight. "This is between us, Devlin," he said, taking a step forward.

"Don't come any closer!" Lauren screamed, backing up one step "Or I be hurlin' this babe upstairs into the fire, and ye'll niver be knowin' why."

"You move down two steps, and I'll move back two steps," Gavan said, still in that calm, soothing voice.

I marveled at Gavan's composure. My thoughts ranged from beseeching Lauren with tearful pleas to attacking him with violence, but I instinctively knew that Gavan's way was the right way.

Lauren stepped down and Gavan moved back. Our son was a little farther away from the flames but no closer to us. Emmet was quiet now, and I choked back a sob. Perhaps his little lungs had already collapsed from the smoke.

Gavan must have been thinking along similar lines, for he urged Lauren on. "Tell me. What is this great wrong that has been done to you?"

"It were the Devlin family that old Sir Gavan burnt up." His eyes turned glassy, and he seemed to be back in another time. "I'd been out, pickin' berries for me mam, and when I come back, they was lockin' the doors and putting the torch to it. Me mam, all me little sisters . . ."

He stopped suddenly and stared, not at us, but above us. Looking up, I saw a billowing white figure floating over our heads.

In that brief, unguarded moment Gavan struck! Like a charging bull, he raced up the steps, and shoving the old man aside, he grabbed the silent bundle from his arms just as sparks showered down on us.

A terrible explosion rocked the tower then, and Gavan shouted, "Get out. Get out!"

We stumbled over the threshold just as the upper floors collapsed, burying Lauren in a hail of fire.

There's much I still don't remember. They say I was in shock when we emerged, both of us covered in soot and looking like chimney sweeps.

I vaguely recall sitting on the grass, crying for my dead child. Tears rolled down my cheeks, and they must have made lines of white on my blackened face.

"It's a'over noo, Lady Mitchell. Dinna cry nae maire." Mrs. Stewart's kindly face looked into mine. She patted my hand and spoke to someone beside her. "I dinna think she hears me."

"She'll be comin' around," the other said. " 'Tis the shock of it all."

"The wind's picked up," someone else said. "They'll niver save Castle Bonnie Brae now."

Let it burn to the ground, I thought. It took my son. I never want to see it again.

"Perhaps if she saw the bairn," Mrs. Stewart said.

Oh, no, I thought. I couldn't bear it.

"Sir Gavan give it right away to the doctor. Piece a'luck him ridin' by and stoppin'."

"Luck? Do ye no ken the hand of God in this? 'Tis a miracle, it is!"

My brain was starting to thaw. What were they saying? Could it be possible? "My baby," I screamed. "Is he alive?"

Mrs. Stewart rushed over and knelt down beside me. "Aye, yere ladyship. The wee bairn is safe. 'Tis a miracle from heaven."

Closing my eyes, I gave a silent prayer of thanksgiving to God, and to the unknown spirit of my benefactress, the apparition, for it was through her efforts that Emmet had been saved.

I was taken to a nearby tenant's cottage, and there in the kitchen I found my son, wrapped in a clean blanket, and gurgling happily at the antics of the tenant's young children, who were gathered around him.

The tenant's wife smiled and curtsied. "Welcome to Dan Hennigan's cottage, Mistress Mitchell. I'm Annie, his wife." She turned to her children. "Off with ye now. The mistress is wantin to see her baby."

They looked at me with surprise, and I could imagine their thoughts. This soot-covered creature is the mistress of Bonnie Brae!

I picked up my precious little son and held him close. Brushing my lips over the soft tuft of baby hair, I wished with all my heart that Gavan could have shared this moment with me, but he was back at Bonnie Brae, battling the fire. "It was your da who saved you, Emmet," I whispered, rocking him gently in my arms until his eyes closed in sleep.

I laid him down in the crudely made wooden cradle and turned back to the housewife. "Dr. McTavish examined him?"

"Aye, yere ladyship. He said the little lad was untouched, but poor Sir Gavan's hands . . ."

"What about Sir Gavan's hands?"

"All cut and bleedin' they were."

I vaguely recalled a second explosion and glass raining down on us like hailstones. "Is Sir Gavan still here?" I asked.

"Nay, yere ladyship. Soon's the doctor bandaged him Sir Gavan went back to help put out the fire. The nursemaid's here though," she said. "Poor lass, she was some sick, she was."

"Bridget?"

"Aye, that's what they called her. She's sleepin' in me second room. "The doctor give her medicine and the poor lass like to heave up all her insides."

"May I see her?" I asked.

"Aye, yere ladyship."

Bridget lay in a corner of the room on a straw-covered pallet. Her eyes were closed, but I noticed with relief that she was breathing.. I knelt down beside her and took her hand in mine. "Bridget, oh Bridget. What happened?"

Her eyelids fluttered and then opened. "Oh, Lady Mitchell. It were Lauren." Her eyes grew suddenly wide, and she became excited. "Me little one . . ."

"Emmet's fine, Bridget. He's here with us."

Tears rolled down her cheeks. "He put something in me tea. He told me so. I was layin' on the floor. I couldn't move, and he laughs like a hyena, and he picks up the baby." Her voice broke and she sobbed bitterly.

"It's all right, Bridget. You couldn't help it." I

brushed her tears away. "Shh, all's well. Go to sleep."
I tiptoed out of the room and gently closed the door.

Annie Hennigan's two older sons had come home to
report the bad news. Though men had constantly taken
turns manning the pump, strong winds and low water
pressure had allowed the fire to get a head start in the
upper floors of the tower, and now it was completely
out of control.

It had even spread to the west wing, and one of the
lads announced with boyish excitement, "The whole
bloomin' castle's burnin' up!"

A sudden fear seized me. There were valuables in
that house. Suppose Gavan had gone back inside! I
turned to Annie Hennigan. "I must go back. I'm worried about my husband."

She gave her sons a disapproving glance. "Pay them
no mind, yere ladyship." But our eyes met, and she
added, "If ye be wantin' to go, me lads will take ye
back."

Outside, the air was pungent with the smell of smoke,
and light from the fire lit up the sky, turning night into
day.

The two young lads—they couldn't have been more
than ten and twelve—were full of excitement. They'd
talk of this night for years to come, telling their children that they had been there when Bonnie Brae, the
legendary dwelling place of ghosts and banshees, had
burned to the ground.

I gave Bonnie Brae a cursory glance as we arrived
at the scene. I was intent on locating Gavan.

I soon spotted him, deep in conversation with Brendan and several other men who'd been manning the
pump, and my relief turned once again to bitterness.
He saw me but made no move to communicate with
me. Nothing has changed, I thought, and turning my
head away from him, I joined the spectators who stood
on the lawn, watching the castle burn.

Some scenes are etched on our memories so deeply that they never fade, and as long as I live I will remember Bonnie Brae in its death throes.

Twisted and blackened, the old castle writhed like a giant monster as flames consumed it. It was horrible but majestic. I stood on the hillside and watched it burn without pity.

Furniture from the west wing littered the lawn. Evidently nothing from the rest of the house had been saved. My clothes are gone, I thought, and my jewelry.

Once all efforts to contain the fire had been abandoned, the spectators started to drift away, relieved that their own thatched-roof cottages had been spared.

The portable pump which had proved no match for the wind and the tower's great height stood idle as the team of volunteers sprawled exhausted on the ground to watch the fire burn itself out.

Generous tenants had offered their humble homes to shelter all of us made homeless this night, and I walked with Mrs. Stewart and Megan back to the Hennigan cottage.

"Bonnie Brae will rise again," Mrs. Stewart remarked by way of encouragement, but I hoped with all my heart that it would not.

Gavan and Brendan, along with the volunteer fire crew, remained until the fire had indeed burned itself out, and they were back the next day to sort through the debris.

The constable's office sent men to the scene to search for Lauren's body and make a report of the arson. A routine matter, merely a formality, they so informed Gavan, but of course at the time they had no way of knowing that they would unearth a deadly secret, one that Bonnie Brae had kept hidden and one that I, in my innocence, had threatened to lay bare.

* * *

Several days later Gavan accompanied me to Strangford Manor with Bridget and the baby. He was on his way to Belfast to meet with his lawyer and file a claim for the loss of Bonnie Brae.

The safe and most of the furniture from the west wing had been saved, along with my jewelry which was found in the debris, safely contained in its steel box.

We, of course, had escaped with nothing but the clothes on our backs, Gavan's in worse condition than mine, and I'm afraid we made a rather sorry-looking picture as we presented ourselves at Strangford Manor.

Explanations were hastily given, and the whole family expressed their shock and dismay at our misfortune.

Typically these dear friends opened their home and hearts to us. Alex and Clyde came to Gavan's rescue and supplied him with clothes.

"We wouldn't want you to be arrested in Belfast for vagrancy, old man," Alex quipped when Gavan thanked them.

The ever-resourceful Lady Fitzgerald managed in a matter of hours to secure a wet nurse for Emmet. The woman was the cook's niece, and she didn't need persuading to come to Strangford Manor.

"You look exhausted, both of you. Hot baths and sleep, that's what you need," Lady Fitzgerald told us. She bobbed her head up and down with determination, and even my taciturn husband had to laugh.

"Madam, I bow to your wishes." Then he turned to Alex. "Have your man draw me a bath before your mother dumps me in the watering trough."

Clyde laughed. "I wouldn't put it past her. Our mother would make a tough general look like a pansy."

Lady Fitzgerald smiled back at the three of them. "Go on with you," she said.

I looked at Gavan, and I thought, no wonder he's so fond of Lady Fitzgerald. She's the mother he never had.

My own bath, sprinkled with oil of roses, was pure heaven, and I luxuriated in it.

Leaning back in the oversize tub, I closed my eyes and let the tensions of the past slip gently away: Hugh's death, his illegitimate son, and the stalemate between Gavan and me.

Someday soon I would have to deal with them, but for now I wanted a reprieve. I was at Strangford Manor, wrapped in the warmth and love of true friends, and for the time being I would lay my troubles to rest.

I slept for four hours, and when I awoke, I felt like Cinderella, for my tattered, smoke-filled clothes had miraculously disappeared, and in their place were fresh, lavender-scented undergarments and a lovely old-fashioned gown in rose-colored silk. It had a dainty lace collar and long, tight sleeves.

The dress fit perfectly, and I later learned it had been in Lady Fitzgerald's trousseau. "I kept it, Elly," she confided, to remind myself that once I, too, had an eighteen-inch waist."

We enjoyed a superb dinner, and though none of the sad events of the recent past were mentioned, I think Hugh's death brought us all closer together.

It touched me to know that Alex and Clyde, and Gavan, too, had tried to help my brother, and I began to come to terms with my own feelings. Hugh had been sick, I realized, and at last I found it in my heart to forgive him.

We had just retired to the drawing room, and Alex had started to shuffle the cards when the butler informed Lord Fitzgerald that a Constable O'Rourke had arrived and wished to have a word with Sir Gavan and Lady Mitchell.

I suppose it had to do with Lauren's death and the arson investigation, but I thought it rather strange that the constable would follow us to Strangford Manor to give his report.

"Take the constable into the library," Lord Fitzgerald told his servant, and then turned to Gavan. "Confounded nuisance, tracking you down like this, but I suppose there's no putting the fool off."

Constable O'Rourke was a stocky, rather rough-looking man, more accustomed, I imagined, to settling farmers' disputes than in dealing with the aristocracy. He apologized profusely for interrupting our evening, and Gavan looked at him with impatience. "Aye. Well, sit down and let's get on with it, then."

When we were seated, O'Rourke added, "I thought it best to be gettin' in touch with you now, seeing as there'll probably have to be an inquest, and . . ."

Gavan scowled. "An inquest? What on earth for? The man died in the fire. That should be obvious." He gave him a sarcastic look. "I take it you've recovered the body?"

O'Rourke nodded patiently. "Aye, me lord. We recovered the man's body, all right, but we also recovered a woman's!"

I was confused. Everyone had been accounted for. Who could it be?

Gavan said nothing, and the constable looked uncomfortable. He pulled on his mustache and nodded to me. "Beggin' yere pardon, Lady Mitchell, but what we recovered was actually the skeleton of a woman, somebody who died a long time ago and was still in the castle."

Gavan looked annoyed. "Are you sure of what you're saying?"

"Aye, Sir Gavan. The medical examiner did an examination. It was him what determined the skel—the body was a woman's. There was a weddin' ring with engravin' on it, too, so we have an identification." He reached into his pocket and brought out a wide gold band. Handing it to Gavan, he watched my husband's reaction with obvious anticipation.

Gavan held the ring toward the light and scrutinized the underside. Both the constable and myself were staring intently at him now.

I held my breath as an incredulous look appeared on his face, and then very slowly Gavan read, "GRM. Gabrielle Rousseau Mitchell." Turning to the constable, he said, "I'm afraid the body is my mother's."

Chapter Eighteen

The constable fingered his mustache. Looking extremely uncomfortable, he hesitated, but only for a moment. "I'm right sorry to hear that, me lord, but it's me duty to inform you that the medical examiner also determined the cause of death to be from a severe beating."

I gasped, and Gavan turned sharply to the constable. "Was it necessary to subject my wife to this?"

O'Rourke measured Gavan, and he did not look so much like a country bumpkin anymore. "This is a criminal investigation, Sir Gavan, and on two levels. I'll be needing to ask Lady Mitchell some questions later on."

"Get on with it, then," Gavan said gruffly.

Constable O'Rourke stood up and walked around in front of us. He directed his first question to Gavan. "When did your mother disappear, sir?"

"I don't know. I was an infant. Starice, the former housekeeper at Bonnie Brae, could tell you exactly."

"Can you tell me this woman's full name and where I might find her?"

Gavan eyed him coldly. "Starice is all I know. I doubt if she has another name." He seemed detached and continued mechanically. "She's a Gypsy who was taken in by my father. She was at Bonnie Brae for over fifty years and now she's living in a cottage on the grounds."

That Starice was a Gypsy did not surprise me. I had always known there was something foreign and different about her, but Gypsies were outcasts, and I found it strange that Gavan's father would have taken one into his home.

Constable O'Rourke produced a small notebook from his pocket and wrote something in it. "Excuse me for asking this next question, Sir Gavan, but would you be having any idea who might have murdered your mother?"

Gavan wore a haunted look and all the color had drained from his face. "My father," he said stiffly. Turning his head, he looked straight at me. "My father had a violent temper, an unfortunate family trait."

Constable O'Rourke had the good grace to make no comment and to busy himself with his notebook. When he had finished writing, he said, "As to the other matter—the facts are fairly obvious. One thing though. I understand the nursemaid had been drugged. Is that correct?"

Gavan seemed lost in his own thoughts, and I answered, "Aye. Dr. McTavish confirmed it."

O'Rourke turned his full attention to me then. "Where do you suppose a lunatic like Devlin would acquire such a drug?"

"From Starice," I answered simply. "She went to the moors to collect sleeping grass. I saw her gathering it there myself." Let him ask her about it, I thought. I shan't protect the old witch. She's as guilty as Lauren.

Gavan suddenly cut in. "Starice was always making up potions and such. It was all superstition. Nobody was ever harmed by them." He turned angry eyes in my direction and continued. "I've known Starice all my life. She is eccentric, but in no way would she have been a party to Lauren's scheme."

O'Rourke then asked us both to tell him about our confrontation with Lauren in the tower. He jotted down several notes as we related the incident, and then he snapped his notebook shut and replaced it in his pocket.

"Thank you, Sir Gavan, Lady Mitchell." He extended his hand, but Gavan was staring blankly into space.

I nudged him and jolted out of his trance, he rose and mechanically shook the constable's hand.

"I'll be needing you to come to my office and sign some papers," O'Rourke said. "Your mother's body can then be released for burial."

Gavan nodded. "I must go to Belfast tomorrow, but I'll be in touch with you in a day or so."

When we were alone, I reached out to touch him. "Gavan, I . . ."

He stepped quickly aside and cut me off. "I'd like to be alone, Elly. Make my apologies to the Fitzgeralds, and tell them I'll be gone early in the morning."

He looked so strange that I hesitated. "What shall I tell them?"

"Tell them the truth, for God's sake. Bonnie Brae has no secrets now."

Poor Gavan! Little did he know that Bonnie Brae's final and most startling secret had yet to be revealed.

Had he known, we both might have been saved much unhappiness and soul-searching. . . .

But perhaps we are the stronger for not having known.

I didn't see Gavan again until two weeks later, when he returned to Strangford Manor.

He seemed withdrawn, and informed me almost as an afterthought that his mother's body had already been buried in Bonnie Brae's cemetery and the inquest into her death had been held.

"They determined that death was caused by the hand of person or persons unknown." He sneered and then added, "My father managed to get away with murder up to the bitter end. I imagine he's laughing in hell about it."

"Was Starice at the inquest?" I asked.

"Naturally, but she knew nothing. My father told everybody that my mother had left him. No one would dare question his word."

I said, "What about the sleeping potion?"

He regarded me with cold eyes. "I knew you'd hark back to that. If he got it from Starice, it was without her knowledge. That seems clear to the police—to everybody except you." He turned away from me with a disgusted look on his face. "Your interest in the downtrodden doesn't extend to ugly old women. Does it?"

I gave him no answer. His attitude toward me was that of a stranger's. I understood his shock and dismay at the discovery of his mother's body, and it was certainly obvious that his father had been her murderer, but why had this made him withdraw from me?

We were alone in the house except for the servants. All of the Fitzgerald men were out attending to business, and Lady Fitzgerald, on Gavan's arrival, had taken herself off to visit a sick tenant.

In the two weeks that Gavan had been gone I had given serious thought to our predicament, and I had decided to suggest that we return to Bonnie Brae, gather up all the servants, and move to Glengarra.

I could not leave Gavan alone now. He was my husband, and the events of the past three weeks had been traumatic ones, especially for him.

"Since the inquest is over and your mother's been laid to rest, there's no further need to stay in Antrim," I said. He was watching me closely, and I took a deep breath. "I think it would be best if we all moved to Glengarra until you decide to rebuild."

I expected a sharp answer, perhaps a sarcastic innuendo. *You're inviting me to live with you at Glengarra, Lady Mitchell?*

Instead, he turned to me with haunted, unreadable eyes. "Thank you for the offer, but I must decline."

286

"But where . . . ?"

He waved me off. "You go to Glengarra. Take Emmet with you. I'll not stand in your way, Elly."

His answer stunned me. This was a far cry from the rage he had expressed when first I had suggested moving without him to Glengarra. Never would I take his son, he had said.

And so I have won, I thought, but I tasted no victory, only ashes and a vague feeling of irredeemable loss.

I couldn't believe he meant it, and swallowing my pride, I said, "I'd be willing to try, Gavan."

He gave me a haunted look, and my blood chilled when he said, "History has a way of repeating itself. You'd best go, Elly, while you still have the chance."

We left Strangford Manor the next morning, on a bleak and cold December day. Bridget, Emmet, and I rode in the carriage and Gavan followed us on horseback.

The trees were now stripped of their leaves and the hard brown fields had a destitute look about them. In three weeks time it would be Christmas again.

I closed my eyes and centered my thoughts on that happy time. I tried to recall my childhood Christmases, but they had faded over the years.

The holidays spent in England had been full of merriment and warmth, steeped in tradition and lavish in its celebration of the event, but my thoughts refused to dwell there either. It was the Christmas just past that I remembered.

I saw the glittering tree, the smiling faces of the servants, and I heard their voices. "God bless the master of this house. Likewise, the mistress too . . ."

" 'Tis a blessing the fire never reached the stable," Bridget said. "Sure would be a shame to lose this team of horses, it would."

Reluctantly I opened my eyes. Silence didn't last long around Bridget, and I nodded my head.

"I says to me mam, them black horses at Bonnie Brae got wings on their feet." She laughed. "Me mam ain't niver been out of the village, yere ladyship. She thinks Belfast is the other side of the moon, and when I told her Strangford Manor was just outside the city, she like ta died. Be takin' ye better'n a week ta get there, says she."

I smiled and suddenly wondered if Bridget would object to moving to Glengarra. She was evidently close to her mother, and saw her frequently. What would I do without her? I thought. Her chatter could be nerve-racking, but there were times when I welcomed it, and she was loyal to a fault.

"Bridget, as you know, we can't stay at Bonnie Brae," I said. "So Sir Gavan and I have decided to move to my family's estate in County Down."

Gavan had already informed me he would be leaving for England on business as soon as we were settled, but I saw no need to explain his absence to the servants.

She looked upset, and I decided I would not try to persuade her. It would be her decision to make. "You may come with us, in fact we're offering all the servants a place at Glengarra, but if you prefer to stay, I will understand."

She shook her head violently. "I go where yere ladyship and this little fellow goes. I almost lost him once, but niver again!"

I reached across the seat and patted her hand. "I'm glad, Bridget. You'd be sorely missed."

Her face was wreathed in smiles. "That's why I like workin' for ye, Lady Mitchell. I tole me mam, I did, Lady Mitchell always makes a body feel good, I said. She's a grand and beautiful lady, but she doesn't look down her nose at nobody!"

"Go on with ye," I said, sounding enough like Bridget to send her into peals of laughter.

We arrived at Bonnie Brae at noon, and were dropped off at the Hennigan cottage, where Mrs. Stewart and Megan were staying. Brendan and several of the male servants had been living in the barn, and Gavan went to speak to them.

Megan, as I had expected, was agreeable to going to Glengarra. She knew she could not remain indefinitely with the Hennigans, and to return to her old life in the village would be impossible now that she had upgraded herself.

"A credit to Mrs. Stewart, I am," Megan was fond of saying. "If it weren't for her, I'd be back in the village, wearin' rags and scratchin' meself."

And so Mrs. Stewart's announcement affected Megan deeply, as, I must confess, it did us all. "I thank ye fae the offer, Lady Mitchell, but I've decided to gae back to Scotland noo."

She had one brother left in Glasgow, she said. "And he be seventy. I'm sixty-five, and it's time tae come hame. I'd lak tae spend a few years maire in the land of my birth."

I could not ask her to stay, though I would miss her dearly, this gentle soul who had arrived at Bonnie Brae and graced that cold and discordant place with her serenity and common sense.

After dispatching a tearful Megan to the carriage, I gathered the small, gray-haired woman into my arms. "I shall miss you," I said.

"Ach. Maire's the pity we canna hae all those we love in one place, but ye'll be always in my heart. Guidbye, Lady Mitchell. Tak guid care of Sir Gavan, and the little lad."

Her gentle blue eyes looked into mine, and then she said something that would haunt me in the months ahead. "Yesterday is gone, lass. Dinna lose tomorrow by looking back."

We would be traveling in two carriages. All of our former staff with the exception of Mrs. Stewart would be moving to Glengarra, along with Emmet's wet nurse and the woman's own five-month-old baby.

I had assumed that Gavan would ride beside the lead carriage, but after each occupant's few belongings had been packed, he took me aside. "I must return to Belfast immediately, Elly." His eyes rested on the group of servants waiting to enter the carriages. "You won't need me at Glengarra with all this help."

I felt a stab of bitter disappointment. He wasn't going with us. He was saying good-bye!

He handed me an envelope. "These funds should be sufficient for several months."

Too shocked and hurt to speak, I stared up at him vacantly.

He continued. "I may go to England for a while. I have some business concerns there, and . . ." Shrugging, he added, "Maybe I'll decide to stay. . . ."

I wanted to scream, *Don't go. Come to Glengarra. We'll try again,* but I only stared up at him with a dull ache in my breast.

He smiled, almost wistfully. "Bonnie Brae was never a happy home, Elly. Maybe I won't bother to rebuild."

"You'll keep in touch. You'll let me know . . ." I said feebly.

"Of course. Take care now." He placed his hands on my shoulders and kissed the top of my head quickly.

I turned away so he wouldn't see the hot tears that suddenly appeared and streamed down my cheeks.

Through the blur I saw him go over to Bridget and take the baby from her arms. I couldn't bear to watch, and I turned my head and hurried into the waiting carriage.

When Bridget and the baby had joined me, I looked

out the window and saw that Gavan had already mounted his horse. He spoke briefly to Brendan and then turned his great stallion in the opposite direction and galloped away.

I leaned my head back on the seat and closed my burning eyes. Bridget, Megan, and the other nursemaid were chattering among themselves, but I didn't hear them. Gavan's words were ringing in my ears. *I might decide to stay. I might decide to stay.*

The staff settled in well at Glengarra. It was as though Mrs. Stewart's gentle but firm presence hovered over them, and nothing less than perfection was permitted. Their beloved tutor might be in Glasgow, but her name was a household word at Glengarra.

This took an amusing turn when astonished locals were informed that their merchandise or their methods were not up to Mrs. Stewart's standards.

"Who's this Mrs. Stewart?" I overheard one of Glengarra's old stable hands ask. "I ain't niver seen the woman. But it's 'Mrs. Stewart won't like this" *and* "Mrs. Stewart won't allow that' from the whole bunch o' them up at the manor house."

Working together, they accomplished wonders, and in a matter of weeks the proud old house showed signs of recovery.

The year of abuse and neglect had left scars, some, like my memories, not easily erased, but perhaps time will mellow them, I thought, running my hand over the deep abrasions in a rare George VII inlaid mahogany sideboard.

The house sparkled with cleanliness, though, and delicious aromas emanated from the kitchen, a goodly portion of which had a distinctly Scottish flavor.

Now that all was in order, I spent most of my time in the nursery. Emmet, at six months was the joy of my life. He laughed easily and spouted the most delightful gibberish that Bridget, and I, too, interpreted as a sign of great intelligence.

"He'll be talkin' plain before we know it, yere ladyship. Me sister's babies niver did this till they was a year old. The last one's two and it's the Lord's truth, he don't talk as good as Emmet."

Brendan approached me one morning as I was leaving the nursery. "Would ye be wantin' me to get a tree, yere ladyship?"

I stared at him stupidly. "A tree?"

He looked embarrassed. "Next week's Christmas, and I thought—well, the little fella would probably enjoy it." He paused and then added, "Aye, and the rest of us as well."

I had completely forgotten Christmas, and without much enthusiasm, I said, "Certainly, Brendan. See if you can find a nice one."

"I'll do me best." He shook his head and smiled with nostalgia. "The north tip—aye, that was the place for tall trees. Sure and it was a beauty I got there last year."

Taking advantage of the opportunity, I said, "Brendan, speaking of the north tip. I understand Squire Daly was found murdered there last summer."

Twisting his cap in his hands, and looking uncomfortable, he answered. "So, they say." His expression suddenly changed, and his piercing eyes met mine and held. "When a man stalks another man with murder in mind, it has to end with a murder, and sometimes it's his own. Squire Daly murdered hisself." His expression quickly reverted to a benevolent one, and he ended the discussion with a smile. "I'll be after scoutin' for a nice tree."

So Squire Daly had stalked Gavan even after wounding him at Bonnie Brae! That would account for Gavan's chest wound and his long recuperation at Glengarra.

In my heart I had condemned my husband for Squire Daly's murder, but as the ever-loyal Brendan had pointed out, could a man be blamed for acting in self-defense?

In all honesty, I thought not, and my own disloyalty about the incident gnawed at my conscience.

We decorated the tree, sang the carols, and filled the wassail bowl, but something was missing. Even Emmet, with all his adorable baby ways, could not raise my spirits, and I lay in bed on Christmas Eve and wondered why there was such an empty feeling in my heart.

What did I want? I asked myself. Avery? Would I be happy with him in America? The idea was so far-fetched, I couldn't place it in the realm of reality, and yet I would always love Avery. Wouldn't I?

Would I be happy if Gavan were here? But hadn't I come to Glengarra to escape him? It was in this very house after my brother's funeral that I had decided I wanted to return to Glengarra. The fire had had nothing to do with my decision.

I wept silently. Where is the peace and comfort that I thought I would find here?

Suddenly my thoughts turned to the apparition, that gentle spirit who had roamed the halls of Bonnie Brae, searching for her own comfort and peace. Was she Gavan's mother? In the light of recent developments, I thought it highly likely that she was.

But why had she appeared to me and not to Gavan? And what had she been trying to tell me?

My tired brain could supply only questions, and finally I drifted off to sleep.

We were snowed in for most of the winter, but several times Brendan hitched up the sleigh and I rode into the village. Hugh's child was constantly on my mind during these excursions, and I found myself eyeing each passerby, hoping and then dreading the thought that one of them might be Molly.

The bank statement which Sir Henry sent to me confirmed that Molly was cashing the checks, and I could only hope that they were being put to good use. Her attitude toward me had always been resentful, and though there were times when I felt an irresistible urge to see my nephew, I knew I could not indulge the whim.

Never would I forget the discomfort I had caused both myself and Avery's family when, in my brashness, I had paid them an unwelcome call.

And so I gave up my outings to the village and tried to busy myself indoors, and just when I had become convinced that winter would never end, it did.

I woke up one morning early in April to hear the chirping of birds, and looking out my window, I saw that the snow was quickly melting under a bright sun.

Would that the winter in my heart could melt as well, I thought, for nothing gave me joy save Emmet, and even with him I felt a longing for something more.

Gazing out over Glengarra's meadow to the woods beyond, I felt a compulsion to visit The Paradise. I had not been there since the day I had said good-bye to Avery, and without thinking I automatically reached for my riding habit.

I dressed quickly, and feeling alive with anticipation, I skipped down the backstairs, heading for the stable. I hadn't been on horseback since Emmet's birth, and I suddenly realized how much I had missed it.

Brendan greeted me with a smile, and at my request brought out Warwick. "My old companion in crime," I said, patting the stallion's nose. He whinnied, and I laughed. "There, you do remember me, don't you?"

"That's a fine animal," Brendan said.

"Aye. He was my brother's horse. Hugh was afraid for me to ride him, but I did it anyhow. One look at this old boy, and the mares all looked too tame for me."

Brendan shook his head. "Yere brother was proud of yere ridin', Lady Mitchell. Used to talk about it when he came up to Bonnie Brae. 'No man can sit a horse better'n me sister,' he told me once."

Ah, Hugh, I thought. If only the drink hadn't gotten to you.

When I was mounted, Brendan looked up at me with eyes that seemed to read my mind. "Nothing like a brisk ride to clear a body's head and chase the cobwebs out," he joked.

I headed directly for the woods, feeling a compulsion to stand in the glen and feel its magic once more. For a long time now I had not been able to see Avery's face clearly in my mind, and it saddened me to think that someday it would fade completely from my memory. Perhaps at The Paradise I can recapture him, I thought.

Entering the forest, I noticed a slight drop in the temperature. In the denseness of the woodland, snow still covered the ground, but the little brook was running, and here and there sunlight filtered through the still-bare trees.

I dismounted, and following the old, familiar path, I led Warwick through the brush. When I came to the clearing, I stopped short, looking about me with surprise.

The glen seemed different, smaller, and not nearly so impressive without the lushness of ferns and heather to enhance it.

The pedestal rock that once had filled our imaginations to the brimming with visions of druid priests and echoes of magical incantations had probably been crafted by centuries of rain wearing it down, which would account for its steplike formation.

The sleeping grass that had held such an evil fascination for us was dried up now and stiff with winter's frost.

My eyes traveled to the large tree and the childish scrawl that staked our claim. "Elly and A.J."

I stared at it for a long time. The names did not belong together, and neither did we, I suddenly realized.

Our love was a misalliance, I thought. Something that could never be, except in the eyes of children. And suddenly I saw with crystal clarity that that is what our love had been. The love of children!

Now I understood why it was that I could recall Avery so clearly as a boy but never as a man. My memories were childhood memories, dear and sweet, and full of love, but not the love of a man for a woman or a woman for a man.

Dear God, how could I have been so blind? Avery knew it, and he had tried to tell me. "There can never be anything for us. I'll always love you, but you're a Kincaid and I'm a tenant's son."

He loved me; of course he did. But his love had been for the cheeky little girl who had shared the loneliness of childhood with him. He had never loved me as a woman.

I sat down on the pedestal rock. Gavan had known it too. "You prefer to moon over a childish attachment that you perceive to be pure and noble and beyond my understanding," he had said.

Oh, dear God, how I must have hurt him! What we had felt for each other had been love, not lust, but I had been too naive to realize it.

I had been a child in a woman's body, chasing after

a romantic fantasy. Wrapping myself in the past, I had let the present pass me by, and in so doing, I had lost the future. *Yesterday is gone. Dinna lose tomorrow by looking back.*

Dear Mrs. Stewart. She had tried to warn me. But she hadn't known that already it was too late.

For some unfathomable reason Gavan's mother's death had marked a turning point in our relationship. I had sensed his withdrawal that night in the Fitzgerald library, and it had become more apparent in the days that followed.

My heart ached with regret as I finally admitted the truth. I was in love with my husband, but he no longer loved me!

Taking Warwick's reins, I walked slowly out of The Paradise, never to return. I like to think, though, that in this mystical place a little girl in a starched pinafore, and a boy with flaming hair still climb the pedestal rock and mix their laughter with the bubbling brook.

Once in the open, I gave Warwick his head and we raced recklessly over fields still coated with dangerous patches of ice. The air had turned brisk, and I welcomed its cold sting on my face.

Chased by his own demons, Warwick thundered across the meadow, leaving tufts of frozen earth in his wake, and neither of us blanched as we soared over snow fences in jumps that would have unseated all but a few experienced riders.

"I chased the cobwebs out of my head," I told Brendan cynically when I returned to the stable.

He eyed my mud-splattered riding habit and disheveled hair. "Ye might be wantin' to go up the backstairs. Ye have a visitor inside."

Of all times, I thought. It was probably Reverend Wharton. He'd made several calls, hinting about how he hadn't seen me in church of a Sunday lately.

He'll take me as I am, I thought, forgetting the stairs and striding down the corridor to the morning room, where I heard the murmur of voices.

I opened the door and held my breath. Gavan was seated on the love seat, bouncing Emmet on his knee!

Chapter Nineteen

He looked wonderful, and I was instantly conscious of my mud-splattered clothes and disheveled hair. I pulled the tangled mass up and tried to secure it with pins, but he said, "No, don't. You look beautiful, Elly, just the way you are."

Smiling warmly, he walked across the room to meet me, holding Emmet in his arms, and I thought that he looked different. There was a tranquility about him that I had never seen before, and his eyes were no longer guarded.

"This little fellow is wonderful, Elly. I can't believe how he's grown," he said.

Emmet reached out for me, and I took him from Gavan. Burying my face in the baby's hair, I answered, "Aye, but it's been almost five months since you've seen him."

He looked away. "I know, Elly. I've come to talk about that. I've been in England, but I've just returned from a trip to France."

"Well," I said. "Your travels must have agreed with you. You look content."

"I am content, Elly. More so than I've ever been in my entire life."

His admission disturbed me. Something, or someone, must be responsible for such a radical change. My thoughts centered on Cecily Patterson. Gavan had been entertained by her family before we were married, and the sly Cecily had done her best to charm him then, I recalled.

"I trust you renewed your acquaintance with the Pattersons while you were in London," I said.

He hesitated a moment and then repeated, "The Pattersons? Aye, I spent some time with them."

Cecily would not be above flirting with a married man, and no doubt Gavan, with all his disappointments, would have been ready for a sympathetic ear. Did he plan to return to England, and was he here to ask for a divorce? I wondered.

I reached for the bell cord. "I'll have Bridget take Emmet back to the nursery. Then we can talk."

He seemed ill at ease, another radical change in my arrogant husband's personality. "Aye, and I could use a drink, if you don't mind."

I said, "Of course. Sherry's in the decanter, but if you prefer something stronger, there's a bottle of brandy behind the Old Testament, over there on the second shelf." I nodded my head toward the bookcase, and he smiled.

"I remember. Hugh always hid one there." Walking across the room, he retrieved the bottle. "Would you like the sherry?" he asked.

"No, nothing for me."

Bridget came into the room then, and I handed her the baby. "It's time for his nap, but he doesn't seem sleepy."

She giggled. "Sure and the little lad's been havin' a time with his da. Splashed him with water from his bath, he did, and the two of them laughing fit to die." She gathered Emmet in her arms and smiled. "Come along, Master Emmet. Ye be takin' a nice nap for Bridget and then ye can play with yere da again."

It was irrational to be annoyed, but I couldn't help it. Emmet was not usually receptive to strangers, and yet after all that time he accepted Gavan with open arms!

We took chairs across from each other, and the silence became oppressive as Gavan continued to study the drink in his hand, turning the glass slowly and staring at the amber liquid. "This is a little hard to say, Elly."

Just say it, I thought. Ask for the divorce and be done with it.

He drained the glass and set it carefully on the table. "What I am going to say may shock you, but I want there to be absolute truth between us."

I doubted if anything more could shock me, but I waited patiently for him to continue.

"Two months ago I received a message from Starice. She wanted to see me. She was dying, Elly."

His dark eyes searched mine for some sign of pity, but alas, I had none to give. Starice had been my enemy, and I could not play the hypocrite.

He said, "I know you've never understood, but I owed her much." He took a long swallow of brandy. "So I came back to Ireland two months ago."

My resentment grew. He came back for Starice but couldn't take the time to see his wife and son.

He spoke softly. "She wanted to tell me the final secret of Bonnie Brae."

"What more could there be?" I cried, feeling hurt and angry, and wanting to hurt him too. "Your father murdered your mother and buried her body somewhere in the house. Surely that is the ultimate secret."

He was too engrossed in his story to notice my resentment. "Aye, Elly, that was a dark and terrible secret, but it was done to hide another secret." He paused dramatically and looked at me with eyes that were no longer haunted. "You see, I'm not a Mitchell!"

The full impact of his words didn't strike me right away, and I merely stared at him with a blank expression.

He stood up then and started pacing the floor. "Do you know what that means?" I'm a bastard, Elly. I

301

don't even know my real father's name, and I don't care. All I care about is that I'm not related to those mad devils, those twisted, diabolical old men." His face contorted, and his next words seemed to be wrenched from the very depths of his soul. "I couldn't stand to look at their faces, and one night I tore their portraits from the wall and stomped them into oblivion. God, how I hated them!" He paused a moment, and then added, "But their blood is not my blood, nor Emmet's either."

He turned tormented eyes to me. "The yoke of the living dead has been lifted from me, Elly. Don't you understand? I'm not a Mitchell. This means I don't have to be afraid anymore."

He turned his head, but I saw tears glistening on his cheeks and he murmured softly, "I don't have to be afraid of losing my mind."

The real meaning behind his words eluded me. I only knew that he had not asked me for a divorce, not yet, at least.

"Starice had lied to the constable," he said. "She had known all along that my mother was dead, but she kept my father's secret. It was her secret as well," he added sadly. "Because she was an accessory."

He shook his head. "Poor thing, she was another of my father's victims."

Reaching over, he took my hand. "It's not a pretty story, Elly, but may I tell it to you the way Starice told it to me?"

I nodded, suddenly ashamed of my pettiness.

"It began when Starice was a young girl. One of the tenants complained to my father that he had been missing some chickens. He blamed the theft on a band of Gypsies who were camped out on the moors.

"My father rode out to the encampment with several

of his men to exact payment from the Gypsies and force them to move on.

"Starice, at the time, was fourteen years old, and very beautiful. When my father saw her, he told the Gypsy leader that he would accept the girl as his payment.

"Unfortunately for the Gypsies, Starice's father refused, which, of course, infuriated my father. He had his men set fire to the caravans, and in the ensuing melee, carried the girl off.

"She was a virgin and little more than a child, but that made no difference to him. He locked her up in the tower and subjected her to every kind of perversion his depraved mind could conceive.

"When he had broken her spirit, he kept her on as a servant in the house. I imagine it gave him a devilish delight to openly torment his sickly wife with his mistress.

"Starice's life was hell in those days. There was not only my father to contend with, but my grandfather as well, and the old man was a worse lecher than his son, she said.

"My father's first wife finally died, trying to give him an heir, and Starice stayed on, even after my father had tired of her. He became even more brutal then, she told me, and once he threw her down the stairs, crippling her for life.

"I asked her why she didn't run away, but she said there was no place for her to go, and besides, she deserved the punishment—she thought she could buy her way into heaven with it.

"Years later my father went to France and brought home a young bride. My mother was seventeen, and he was forty-five.

"At first he was so taken with his beautiful young wife that he hid his true nature, but after I was born two months ahead of time, he knew, despite the mid-

303

wife's assertion to the contrary, that I could not be his son.

"He hounded my mother to confess, but she always insisted that he was the father. I suppose she feared he'd kill me if she told the truth."

He poured himself another brandy. "Shall I go on? It gets worse."

"Tell me, Gavan," I answered. "And then never speak of it again."

He drained the glass, and I noticed that his hands shook when he replaced it on the table.

"One night he came home drunk and started questioning her again. He'd confiscated a letter from my mother's father in France, and reading between the lines, he felt his suspicions to be confirmed."

Gavan paused, and an expression of such deep pain crossed his face that I was about to ask him not to go on, but the words died in my throat as an inner wisdom told me he needed to come to terms with the past.

Gaining control of himself, he continued, "My father, in one of his rages, was the devil incarnate. Starice used to hide me from him when I was a lad," he added as an afterthought.

Tears filled his eyes then, and impatiently he brushed them away. "He beat my poor mother unmercifully. Starice tried to intervene, but he was like a mad dog. While he was struggling with Starice, my mother managed to break away and run for her life downstairs. Of course he caught up with her and she fell, either dead or unconscious at his feet."

Gavan's eyes grew dark with suppressed rage. "Starice said there was a secret passageway in the west wing, and he dragged my mother into it."

I gasped, suddenly understanding the evil that permeated that place. "The secret passageway behind the bookcase ended in the west wing," I said. "In a closet right outside the pantry."

He nodded. "Starice said he placed my mother's body in the passageway and sealed it up that very night, creating a six-by-six-foot tomb. He forced Starice to help him, which made her an accessory, and the horror of it all was that they didn't know for sure if she was alive or dead in there."

I shuddered, remembering the aura of diabolical evil I had sensed in the passageway, and I suddenly knew the identity of the second ghost who had haunted Bonnie Brae.

Gavan continued. "They were both driven mad by it. For months afterward they heard knocking in the walls, and my father finally had the whole west wing sealed off."

No wonder Starice became hysterical when she heard me knocking from the passageway, I thought.

"My childhood," he said, "was a nightmare that I don't care to go into, but I vowed that when I grew up, my life would be different. The old beast that I thought to be my grandfather finally drank himself to death, and my so-called father grew more demented every day. When he died, he was a raving maniac, and hardly even human."

He stood up and paced the floor. "What a legacy they left me! But I still had hopes of escaping the family curse."

He looked at me with a strange expression on his face. "And then I met you, Elly, and you were everything Hugh said you would be—courageous and beautiful, and with a proud family history behind you."

He shook his head. "Ah, how I envied Hugh Kincaid in those days. I'd have given my right arm for his background, his family, and a gracious home to inherit like Glengarra."

His eyes softened. "I hadn't counted on falling in love with you, Elly." He smiled and shrugged. "What did I know of love, I'd never been exposed to it? But

I knew I wanted you for my wife and the mother of my children."

If only he had opened his heart to me then, I thought. But would I have understood, spoiled, sheltered little girl that I was?

"I was so happy when you agreed to marry me. I thought at long last heaven is smiling on a Mitchell." I saw his jaw tighten and his expression harden. "Then, when I found out about the Fenian, it was like the devil's fist had punched my heart out.

"All the Mitchell traits that I despised rose to the surface. I had murder in my heart when I left Hugh and rode to Dublin. I would have strangled Avery James with my bare hands if I could have gotten to him, but it was Brendan who talked sense into me."

I was astonished to hear this. "Brendan Kelly?" I asked.

"Aye. We go back a long way, Brendan and me." He colored slightly. "I use to frequent a certain street in one of the more sordid sections of Dublin, and late one night when I was very drunk, I was ambushed by three thugs. One of them was Brendan Kelly."

He smiled in remembrance. "The other two wanted to finish me off and dump me in the river, but I objected. So did Brendan, and between the two of us we fought our way out.

"I offered him a job at Bonnie Brae, and he took it. He's been with me ever since, and no truer friend do I have."

I nodded my head. I, too, considered Brendan a friend.

"Anyway, he said with a deep sigh. "It was Brendan who convinced me that if the Fenian died, he would become a martyr, not only to his cause, but to you, also, Elly. It was then that I decided to help him escape. . . ."

I gasped. "You helped Avery escape?"

He put up a hand to silence me. "Don't. Please don't attribute this to any benevolence on my part. I hated him as I had never hated any man."

He stared pointedly at the dregs of amber liquid in his glass. "Since there's to be naught but truth between us, I'll add that I still do hate him."

Never would I have guessed that it was Gavan who had helped Avery escape. "But how did you . . . ?"

"Brendan still had connections in Dublin." He shook his head. "That bunch of blackguards and thieves could break into hell if they had a mind to. Anyway, I supplied the money, and they got the Fenians out."

"Oh, Gavan, I—"

He interrupted me. "Ironic, isn't it?" His lip curled in a contemptuous smile. "Because the plan exploded in my face. You went right on thinking about him, day in and day out."

He turned his head away then, and spoke softly. "Even in our most intimate moments I could never be sure that you weren't thinking of him instead of me."

I shook my head. "That's not true." But he ignored me.

"When you inherited Glengarra, I knew our marriage was over, but I wasn't going to make it easy for you. I wasn't going to let you have our son."

"Gavan, if only you had talked to me then," I said.

"Let me finish, Elly, and then we can have the post-mortems," he said impatiently.

For some reason his sharp retort made me feel better. He hasn't changed completely, I thought.

He poured himself another drink and stared into it. "The fire turned all my dreams to ashes. The past reached out to touch our son through Lauren and then, when my mother's body was found, I knew there was no chance for us."

He looked at me and his eyes were full of pain. "I couldn't live with the thought that I might lose my mind and harm you or Emmet, and so I decided to let you both go."

Suddenly I understood the full extent of his torment. "History has a way of repeating itself," he had said.

My heart cried out to him then. "You would never have harmed us, Gavan."

"How could I be sure?"

"I was."

"Well, I don't have to worry about that anymore," he said. "I'm just a normal man with a bad temper, I suppose. Incidentally, my father was a French army officer, so perhaps I inherited it from him."

"How do you know about your father?" I asked.

"Do you remember the letters you found in my mother's desk?"

"Of course. They disappeared."

Starice took them. She was afraid of you, Elly, afraid you might discover too much. She's a Gypsy, you know, and even today the law deals harshly with them. She had nightmares of being hanged for murder, she told me."

He seemed calmer, and he sipped his drink slowly. "Starice gave me the letters. There was a return address on the envelopes, and I went to Paris, hoping to locate my grandfather."

He leaned back in the chair, and for the first time he smiled. "I found him, still living at the same address. He's a tall, handsome old gentleman of seventy-five with snow-white hair and eyes as black as my own.

"After the initial shock he welcomed me with open arms. He showed me a letter from my mother's husband advising him that his daughter and grandson had died in a smallpox epidemic.

"He wept bitterly when I told him the truth, and he blamed himself for my mother's marriage to Mitchell. She had been secretly meeting a young army officer, he told me, and he had disapproved of the match. The

308

young man had been sent to an outpost in one of the French colonies, and my mother had evidently married Mitchell to avoid disgrace.

"She was his only child, he said, and his life has been very lonely. I felt sorry for him, but God, it made me proud to know that he was my grandfather, and that all I carry of the Mitchells is their tainted name."

He reached into his pocket and brought out a small miniature. Handing it to me, he said, "This is my mother at sixteen. My grandfather gave it to me."

The dark-haired young woman was smiling, but I recognized her immediately as my beautiful, sad apparition. Perhaps now, at long last, she is at peace, I thought.

I handed the miniature back to him. "She's lovely, Gavan," I said.

It was a long story, and an involved one. I was glad he had told me, but it mattered little to me. I loved Gavan for himself, not because of his ancestors, but I didn't know if I could convince him of that now.

He stood up. "I've decided not to rebuild Bonnie Brae." The pained expression returned to his face. "I could never live there, not after all this. I may go back to France, spend some time with my grandfather." He shrugged his shoulders. "Maybe I'll stay on. I've not one drop of Irish blood in my veins, so what's to hold me here?"

I avoided his eyes because I couldn't bear to look at them if the love wasn't there, but I swallowed every ounce of pride and said, "What's to hold you here? Only a wife and son who love you. That's all, Gavan."

The silence drove me mad, and then he said slowly, "What did you say, Elly?"

"I said I love you. I didn't realize it until I'd lost you, but that's my misfortune." Still avoiding his eyes,

I poured a little of the brandy into the glass and drank it myself.

The hot liquid gave me courage. "You wanted truth between us; well, this is the truth, Gavan. I love you more than I ever loved Avery James. That was a childish fantasy, and I held on to it far too long. So long, in fact, that it blinded me to what I really felt for you.

"What you told me today has nothing to do with it," I added. "I don't care about your ancestors, or whether you are or are not a Mitchell, and if you want to go to France, I'll be waiting, and maybe someday—"

He smothered my words with a kiss, and his arms crushed me to him. "We'll go to France together. It'll be the honeymoon we never had." He whispered in my ear. "We'll start all over, and this time we'll be happy. I love you so much, Elly."

"And I love you," I whispered back, "Please believe me, Gavan. You're the only man I've ever loved."

His strong arms tightened around me. I could hardly breathe, but I didn't care. This was where I belonged.

"If you only knew how I longed to hear you say those words," he murmured.

It's true, I thought. I loved a little boy, and still do, but I'm a woman now, and this is the only man I'll ever love.

I felt myself being lifted in his arms, and he said, "Would it shock your staff if we went to bed?"

"Probably, but I think if Mrs. Stewart were here, she'd applaud."

I let him carry me upstairs. What did I care if the servants knew. The master was home, and the mistress was ready to welcome him back.

He deposited me on the bed, and we ripped off our clothes with frantic hands.

I had forgotten how beautiful his body was, with its broad shoulders and narrow waist, and I loved the muscles that rippled in his arms and the black hair that

310

curled on his chest. Our bodies ached for each other, and we came together quickly with a sudden, white-hot passion.

I drew him deep within me, wanting to possess and to be possessed. Taking leave of all my inhibitions, I made love to my husband without any reservations for the very first time.

Locked in each other's arms, we lay spent, our bodies still pressed closely together as we talked.

"God, but I've missed you, Elly. I dreamed about nights like this."

"Me too."

He leaned up and looked me in the eye. "Lady Mitchell, are you saying that you enjoy this sort of thing? You're not just doing your wifely duty?"

"Doing me wifely duty, and enjoying every minute of it, I am."

"You're a brazen little hussy, and I've a good mind to—"

He never finished, because this time I smothered his words with a kiss!

Epilogue

The wind whistles eerily through blackened trees lining the driveway. Like tall, dark sentinels, they stand guard over the corpse of Bonnie Brae.

Vines and decaying branches litter the ground, and the carriage horses pick their way slowly over the debris. No one comes here. Nay, not even adventurous lads dare wander too close, for this is Bonnie Brae, legendary house of evil, a dwelling place for banshees and ghosts.

The carriage rounds the bend, and suddenly my heart stops. Before my eyes stretch the ruins of what was once a tall, forbidding castle with candle-snuffer roofs and a tower that rose to pierce the sky. Even in death it has the power to disturb me, and I hesitate before calling my driver to halt the carriage.

"You may wait," I tell him. "I'll be just a minute."

He looks uneasy. A newcomer to Antrim he is; nevertheless, no newcomer to tales of Bonnie Brae.

Parts of the castle lay twisted and charred, and I walk through the rubble, catching sight here and there of some relic that managed to escape the ravages of the fire.

I pick up part of a broken candlestick, and pieces of a heavy metal chain, and think of the tormented souls who were bound by this chain, tethered like animals to the walls of the tower.

Something shiny catches my eye, and I stoop down and pull from the ashes a crystal prism; a piece, no doubt, from the magnificent chandelier that had hung

313

over the dining room table. It glitters through its coating of soot, and I toss it back onto the heap.

Tomorrow all of this will be gone, cleared and carted away, and not one trace will remain of Bonnie Brae. None shall mourn its passing, least of all I, who hated this dark and evil old house since first I saw it.

But good quite often comes from evil, and so it shall be with Bonnie Brae, for from these ashes will rise a new monument, one that I hope will abrogate the greed and oppression of the past, and replace them with a new dedication to mercy and love.

This land, which once encompassed the castle and its surrounding grounds, has been deeded over to young Dr. Eoin McTavish to establish in his father's name a medical center for Bonnie Brae's tenants and their families.

It has been five years since the fire destroyed Bonnie Brae, laying bare its final secret. And in that time changes have taken place for both the living and the dead who figured so significantly in our own lives.

Lady Gabrielle Rousseau Mitchell rests now in France in her family vault outside Paris. Her restless spirit walks no more, for she is at peace. She lies beside her father, Claude Rousseau, whom Gavan and I and our children came to know and love as *Grandpère*.

We have spent these last five years with Gavan's grandfather in his chateau outside of Paris. A distinguished and wonderful man, he did much to heal the wounds in Gavan's heart.

We returned only last month to Ireland and my beloved Glengarra. We shall make our home there, for Gavan loves it as much as I. It is a happy home once again, filled with love and the laughter of children, for we have three.

Emmet is a dark-haired little replica of his father. At six, he is a rather serious little boy with a warm and loving nature.

Three-year-old John Claude is just the opposite, blond and blue-eyed with his father's quick temper and my stubbornness—a combination that tries my patience sometimes, but he is such a lovable little lad that I forgive him much.

Gabrielle, a sprightly two-year-old, is a beautiful child with black hair and the cornflower-blue eyes of all the Kincaids. She has the delicate beauty of her namesake, though, and I like to think that her tragic *grandmère* will keep her always in her prayers, as I am sure she keeps us all.

I owe her much, this sad and beautiful lady whom I would have been proud to know as a mother-in-law. I am certain now that her appearances to me were in the nature of an appeal. She tried to use me to disclose her secret, and mutely she pleaded with me to give love and understanding to her son.

I think she would be pleased to know that all her prayers for him have been answered. We are happy, and our love for each other grows stronger every day.

Gavan is all that I in my romantic dreams could ever have hoped for in a husband, and I have left my love for Avery behind, in The Paradise, where childhood fantasies belong.

My brother's child is often on my mind. The monthly checks from the trust fund are regularly cashed, but I have neither seen nor heard from Molly.

Hugh's son would be as old as Emmet, and I wonder what he looks like and if he is a happy lad. I hope so.

Lady Fitzgerald has at long last acquired, not one, but two daughters-in-law. Alex and Clyde married sisters, lovely, quiet girls who smile shyly at the antics of their outrageous husbands. They visited us in France while they were on their honeymoons and we all had a wonderful time sightseeing in Paris.

"I love them both, Elly," Lady Fitzgerald wrote me. "But no one will ever take your place in my heart."

It's good to be home again and once more in the company of dear friends.

Brendan managed the affairs of both Glengarra and Bonnie Brae in our absence, and his stewardship was as always, exemplary. It was his suggestion that a hospital be built on the ruins of Bonnie Brae, and Gavan has embraced the idea with enthusiasm.

Bridget, who had been with us in France, was called back to Ireland six months ago to nurse her sick mother. Since we were soon to follow, she remained here after her mother's health had improved, and much to my delight, upon our return, she confided, "Brendan and me, we've been keepin' company, yere ladyship." And giggling, she added, "I'm thinkin' the priest'll be calling out our banns come summer."

I still hear from Mrs. Stewart in Glasgow. She says she misses all of us, but I know she is happy to be home in the land of her birth, as I am also.

She gave me good advice once, and I've never forgotten it.

Yesterday is gone. Dinna lose tomorrow by looking back.